Neetika Modi is a dental surgeon by profession, also a spiritual seeker and a lifelong student of Vedanta. She has immersed herself into the ancient wisdom of India, unravelling the secrets of Vedanta for the modern world. She believes that a practical philosophy can empower one to live a life of excellence, happiness, and peace. *Antim: The Last Avatar* is Neetika's first book. She is also an accomplished speaker, who shares her insights and perspectives on various forums and platforms. She lives in Mumbai with her husband and two sons.

AF516656

ANTIM

The Last Avatar

Neetika Modi

Om Books International

First published in 2023 by

Om Books International

Corporate & Editorial Office
A-12, Sector 64, Noida 201 301
Uttar Pradesh, India
Phone: +91 120 477 4100
Email: editorial@ombooks.com
Website: www.ombooksinternational.com

Sales Office
107, Ansari Road, Darya Ganj,
New Delhi 110 002, India
Phone: +91 11 4000 9000
Email: sales@ombooks.com
Website: www.ombooks.com

Copyright © Neetika Modi 2023

ALL RIGHTS RESERVED. This is a work of fiction. Names, characters, business, events and incidents are the products of the author's imagination. Any resemblance to actual persons, living or dead, or actual events is purely coincidental.

ISBN: 978-93-5376-842-3

Printed in India

10 9 8 7 6 5 4 3 2 1

What feels like the end, is often the beginning.

Aavartano nivrittatma samvritas sampramardanah
Aha samvartako vanhir anilo dharaneedharah

Bhagavan is *Avartanah* as He is forever engaged in keeping the wheels of life in motion

— *Vishnu Sahasranamam*

Om Narayanaye Vidmahe, Vasudevaya Dheemahi
Tanno Vishnu Prachodayat

Om, As I meditate on you O Narayana,
O Vasudeva, bless me
with a higher intellect and ignite my mind so that
The Fire of Knowledge burns all karmas to ashes

— *Shri Krishna, Bhagavad Gita*

The Relationships

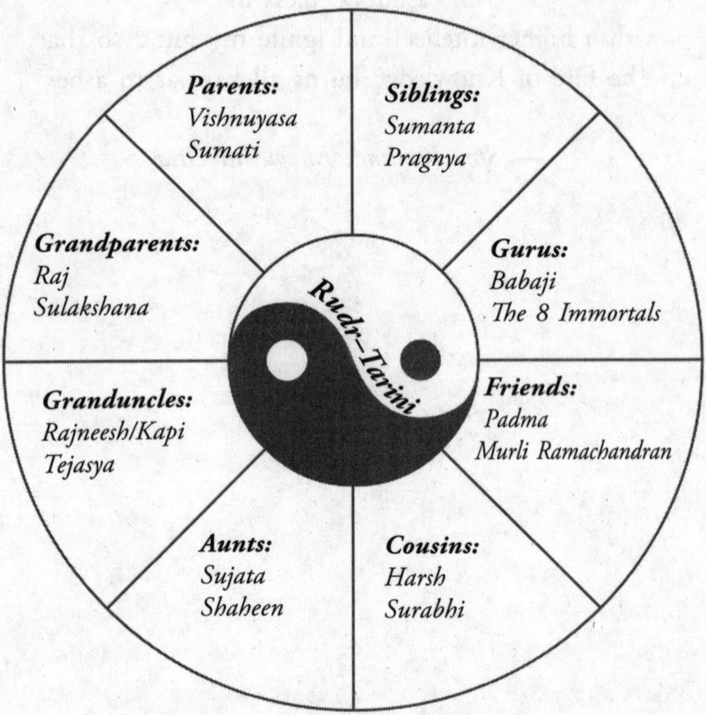

Cast of Characters

Kalki: Saviour of the World, whose identity must remain a secret till the opportune time
Rudr, Tarini: The Nanda twins
Pragnya: Older brother of the twins
Sumanta: Oldest brother of the twins
Sumati: Mother of the twins
Vishnuyasa: Father of the twins
Raj: Grandfather of the twins
Sulakshana: Raj's wife and grandmother of the twins
Sujata: Adopted daughter of Raj; sister of Vishnuyasa
Anil Anand: Sujata's husband; London-based steel tycoon
Harsh: Sujata's son, paternal cousin of the twins; evil and manipulative
Surabhi: Sujata's daughter; cousin of the twins
Ramneesh: Father of Raj, Rajneesh (Kapi) and Tejasya
Rajneesh aka Kapi: Evil uncle of the twins; Raj's older brother; dark soul in rebirth; Shukra's protégé; *Kali Yuga* role: Perpetrator of evil
Tejasya: Raj and Kapi's younger brother; traitor

Shaheen: Tejasya's wife; evil aunt of the twins
Ashwatthama: Immortal; invincible warrior from the Mahabharata era, friend of Duryodhana and Karna; cursed with immortality by Krishna; *Kali Yuga* role: Custodian of celestial weapons and protector of Kalki
Mahabali: Immortal; *Asura* King, Lord of the Netherworld, of generous and benevolent disposition; disciple of Shukracharya but devotee of Vishnu; blessed with immortality by Vishnu; *Kali Yuga* role: Custodian of the wealth in the universe
Ved Vyas: Immortal; legendary sage and astrologer, composer of the *Vedas, Puranas, Brahmasutras* and the *Mahabharata* epic; blessed to remain on earth for all time; *Kali Yuga* role: Guru to Nanda twins Rudr and Tarini
Hanuman: Immortal; world's foremost devotee of the Rama Avatar; blessed with immortality by Sita; *Kali Yuga* role: Protector of Kalki
Vibhishan: Immortal; younger brother of Ravana, King of Lanka, from the Ramayana era; demon by birth, but devoted to the Rama Avatar; blessed with immortality by Lord Rama; *Kali Yuga* role: geneticist; engineers birth of the twins
Kripacharya: Immortal; Guru to the Kauravas and Pandavas; the unborn who can never die; *Kali Yuga* role: Mentor to the twins; military strategist
Parashuram: Immortal; the sixth Vishnu Avatar, prophesied to appear at the end of *Kali Yuga*; *Kali Yuga* role: Guru to Kalki; imparts training in use of celestial weapons
Markandeya: Immortal; youthful sage from the clan of Rishi Bhrigu; blessed by Shiva with immortality; *Kali Yuga* role: Mentor to Tarini
Babaji: Brilliant physicist and Guru to Raj Nanda's family
Shukracharya: Guru of the Asuras; sworn enemy of Vishnu; *Kali Yuga* role: Masterminds the downfall of humanity

Kali: Lord of *Kali Yuga*; Shukra's protégé; *Kali Yuga* role: Satanic magician, biowarfare specialist; Kalki's nemesis
Jabari: Drug and mafia don; head of criminal syndicate Sphinx
Bibi Maya: Threshold goddess who rules the doorway between life and death; *Kali Yuga* role: Mother of Kali
Indrajit: Son of Ravana, mighty warrior from the Ramayana era; sorcerer, uses celestial weapons
Eklavya: Gifted archer from the Mahabharata era, fights for Shukra
Revati: Warrior pandit; General of the Shambhala monk infantry
Shafique Khan: Underworld kingpin
Saroj Rastogi: Delhi Police Commissioner
Prasad Shinde: Union Home Minister
Rehana: Shafique Khan's disloyal wife
Manoj Dubey: Rehana's lover, Sulakshana Nanda's brother
Sushant: Babaji's follower at Gangotri
Padma: Rudr's collegemate, and perhaps more
Glenn: Roommate of Rudr at Oxford
Jabari: Head of Sphinx, the international crime syndicate
Ama: Jabari's mother
Dr Stephens: Tarini's HOD at the New York hospital
Jenny: Rudr's romantic interest
Murli Ramchandran: Sri Lankan politician, father of Padma
Ruh: Harsh's mysterious bodyguard
Dr Reddy: Chief interventionist and Raj's friend
Moti Singh: Nanda family retainer/old timer/driver
Abhay Sawant: Vishnuyasa's partner at their law firm VAS
Mlecchas: Genetically engineered hybrids of pigs and humans, sired in a lab
MZ-1: Commander-in-chief of the *mleccha* army
AZ-5: *Mleccha* soldier
Sneh: Child monk from Shambala with unusual powers

Forces of Darkness

Kali
Shukracharya
Kapi
Jabari
Bibi Maya
Ruh
Indrajit
Eklavya
Mlecchas

Forces of Light

Kalki
The Eight Immortals
Ashwatthama
Mahabali
Ved Vyas
Hanuman
Vibhishan
Kripacharya
Parashuram
Markandeya
Babaji
Shambhala Monks

Author's Note

My journey with *Antim* started a decade back. It's been an exhilarating and transformative experience. When I started writing this book, it was because I had a story to tell and a compelling need to pen it. As I progressed, I realised that *Antim* was gradually driving the changes in my life I always desired. Waking up at *brahmamuhurata* to write with a fresh mind, meditating early in the morning to get clarity of thought, enrolling in Vedanta courses to understand our scriptures, and much more.

I am blessed to be born in India, and to have access to spiritual gurus and books. To my surprise, they started appearing in my life as the saga and time progressed. My inner circle changed, so did my inner being. My writing style changed and ever so often as I would sit with pen and paper, the thoughts would flow ceaselessly, me being a mere instrument.

Antim is a labour of love. It reflects my humble and absolute dedication to Lord Vishnu and Lord Shiva—the mighty Preserver and Destroyer of the world, as we know it. It is an attempt to explore the wondrous mysteries of unseen forces in the universe, forces that could reveal themselves to those who have the courage to keep an open mind.

This is a book of fiction, based on deep research and wild forays of the imagination into a world of possibilities for us all. No part of this book, the characters, or the plot is intended to hurt anyone's sentiments or beliefs.

I hope the book enriches and ignites your world as much as it did mine.

Antim (The End) is the beginning of my journey as an author.

Prologue

Astride a white horse, a blazing sword drawn, Kalki surveyed the scene of destruction. The barbarians and mlecchas lay dead and the smell of blood and rotting flesh filled the air…

As the sun retreated back into the sea, Kalki's brilliance lit up the sky. The broad forehead glistened with sweat beads; the piercing, teal-grey eyes surveyed the city of Keekatpur as it lay abandoned, wasted.

An army of Brahmin sages sounded the victory conch to the rhythmic chants of "Om Keshavaya Namaha!"

Kalki gently joined the palms together in a namaste. Devdutta, the magnificent white steed, also raised his forelimbs in salutation to the holy personages. Then, together, the divine force and the mystic horse darted into the sky with a bolt of lightning as the sages exulted unanimously in joy: "Our Saviour has arrived!"

Dharma

What is the purpose of life, one's duty?
Can one find the courage to embrace duty,
to walk the path of righteousness that heals the world?

1

The Cave

Sometime in the middle of the Twenty-first Century.

It was as predicted. In fact, precisely as predicted.

The large bathtub that Sumati lay immersed in was remarkably comfortable. The soft lighting and Vedic hymns playing in the background had a calming effect—just what a lady in labour needed. The room was large, partitioned by sliding doors. Next to the tub hung a peach-coloured bathrobe. The adjoining section had the birthing bed with a remote control; a table with a vacuum suction machine, prongs and napkins, gauze and steel implements of all shapes and sizes.

Beyond this section was the O.T. complex, fitted with state-of-the-art equipment, ready to use in case of complications. A team of doctors wearing scrubs waited patiently, in position, in the room.

The senior lady doctor checked Sumati. "The first stage of labour is complete, let's proceed and move you to the birthing bed," she said, as she helped her out of the warm bathtub, and led her to the birthing bed. A sense of urgency filled the room. One of the doctors left the room to come back accompanied by the father-to-be, Vishnuyasa, now dressed in scrubs. He stood by Sumati's side, holding her hand as she lay there, a pregnant woman about to be divested of her creation and weight. Camphor powder in a tiny vaporiser sat on a table top, while a larger one, diagonally placed, let off whiffs of eucalyptus oil. Comforting light from the electric fireplace played on the walls of the room inside the large subterranean chamber. A deep moan escaped Sumati's lips every now and then.

"It's almost time," whispered the senior doctor to her team.

At the far right of Sumati's room was the main living room. Here was a gathering of the aeons. Never before had 'Time' witnessed the coming together of the eight Immortals, the *Chiranjeevis*, who graced the planet with their presence. Some cursed; others blessed. Some denied death; some burdened with unending life.

Ashwatthama, tall and lithe, handsome and muscular, stood near the electric fireplace, his head lowered, staring into the fire. His hair fell loosely around his face and shoulders. If it were not for his pus-oozing forehead; he could have been the man, women find irresistible.

Mahabali, the portly one, sat on a red floor cushion, immersed in his book. His jowls were pronounced, thick eyebrows framing large eyes dominated his face and his knobby fingers held the book clumsily. His forehead was smeared with the mark of Shiva—three white horizontal lines and a red dot at the centre.

Ved Vyas sat in *vajrasana* near Mahabali, hands resting on his lap. He chanted inaudibly, constantly.

Hanuman's appearance was deceptive, he could have been mistaken for a burly construction worker. He sat on his haunches beside the imposing Ashwatthama, clothed in a loose white tee and an even wider white *pyjamas*. Strikingly fair, his cheeks shone red in the light of the fire. He rested his elbows on his knees and blew softly into the hollow of his hands while his eyes glowed as they took in the suppressed excitement in the cave.

Vibhishan was sitting on a cushion, his legs folded comfortably. His proud forehead was shining and his jet-black, thick eyebrows cut a mesmerising picture of subtle self-confidence and strength.

Kripacharya could have been mistaken for a business tycoon straight from the Wall Street. He wore a light blue Chinese-collar jacket embellished with black and gold trim on the sleeves and button clasps. His patrician features were calm and he exuded an air of absolute control.

Parashuram sat flagpole-erect, smack in the middle of the cave. The large hand that lay on the short stick was weather-beaten and rough. His other hand lay on his lap. His face was chiselled and creased, the beard trimmed roughly. The long, sleek, oiled hair was tied in a top knot. A white *dhoti* set off by a blood-red border and a white woollen shawl made him look like an idol straight out of a temple. The short stick by his side was ornately carved, tipped at one end by a gold cap.

Markandeya, the baby-faced monk with an endearing smile, seemed most at peace. Sitting in lotus posture, he was busy jotting down planetary positions. The pink silk of his *angavastram* (upper body garment) added a radiant glow to his skin.

A disquieting silence hung in the air. If it were not for the sound of the waterfall, it would have been unsettling to say the least.

Hanuman looked at the pacing Kripa. "Time?" he asked softly. Kripacharya shook his head. Hanuman went back to blowing on his hands.

Ashwatthama silently walked up to Kripacharya and asked, "Have we failed?"

Ved Vyas interjected, "How can you say that? You are fully aware what is at stake…"

Hanuman stared coldly at Ashwatthama and whispered, "Rama."

Without missing a heartbeat Markandeya added, "Shiva."

Suddenly a series of loud moans and grunts was heard from Sumati's room. There was a flurry of activities, all could hear the shuffling of feet, pouring of water, the clang of steel and subdued conversation.

Parashuram brought the attention of the seven back to him, addressing them. "The negativity on planet earth seems to have affected us. When we should be rejoicing, we are doubting? And you Hanuman and Markandeya, are only your gods at stake?"

Taking a deep breath he continued, "Life is a balance between what we can control and what we cannot. In spite of having respected this balance for centuries together, each one of us today is finding it difficult to maintain the same. A shift has occurred; the tilt towards the darker forces has warranted this arrival."

Then, more cries, moans, some talk, chatter, and finally, a lusty cry!

Ved Vyas looked up, "The child is born!" Everyone stood up. Ashwatthama moved from his standing position and came to the centre of the room, a step behind Parashuram. Just as the cry had suddenly shattered the silence, there came another one! Everyone looked at each other, puzzled. Hanuman stepped forward, closer to Sumati's room. "Two?" he whispered, almost to himself. "There are two!" He turned around and looked at Parashuram straight in the eye. Kripacharya put his hand up, calming Hanuman. Unconsciously, everyone stood in an arch facing the cave.

Moments later, the senior doctor came out, flanked by her two assistants. She held two infants. "A girl and a boy," she smiled. Ved Vyas smiled back. Kripacharya raised his hand in benediction. Mahabali looked up and mumbled. Vibhishan chanted, "Om!" Hanuman grinned, his incisors prominently sinking into his lower lip. Parashuram closed his eyes and smiled, saying, "Nothing is a coincidence." Ashwatthama announced aloud, "... and Kalki is born!" A tear rolled down his cheek. Maybe he could expect redemption now. Maybe.

2

Twin Blessings

The underground control centre beeped, announcing the arrival of the family Guru. Babaji walked in through the secret corridor, wearing a turquoise robe with *rudraksh* beads adorning his neck and arms. He wore his hair long, and the most enigmatic smile could be seen on his face. He looked fondly at the Immortals and prostrated before them.

"Finally!" he said.

"Yes finally!" the Immortals declared triumphantly.

Babaji, a young, new-age sage, was also a brilliant physicist. He was the spiritual mentor to the Nanda family.

Having greeted the Immortals respectfully, Babaji made his way towards Sumati's room, where the family was eagerly awaiting his presence. He walked up to his friend Raj, the patriarch of the Nanda family and proud grandfather of the twins. The two hugged each other warmly. An elated Sulakshana, Raj's wife, picked up the twins and placed them in Babaji's strong arms. Looking deeply into their eyes, Babaji whispered, "You are the Beginning and you are the End."

Not wanting to be left out, the two young boys in the room, Sumanta and Pragnya, tugged at Babaji's robe. He enveloped them in an avalanche of hugs and kisses and then gave them a gift each. "You both will make the most amazing older brothers to the twins."

Babaji then walked up to Vishnuyasa who stood lonesome, staring intently into the fireplace, the flames reflecting in his eyes. "Congratulations to the father," he said with warmth as he held Vishnuyasa's hand. "Congratulations, your Kalki has arrived! Your miracle baby."

"Which one?" asked Vishnuyasa dryly, as he released his hand from Babaji's, looking away at the blazing fire. The tension between the two was clearly palpable. "Those eight Immortals have been waiting inside the cave for the last 10 hours," Vishnuyasa scoffed, "or centuries, as you say. Why don't you bring them in to meet their God?" He looked piercingly into Babaji's eyes and stormed out of the family chamber.

The Immortals stood transfixed, a flurry of emotions reflecting on their faces. Hanuman was standing by the infant boy's cot, head bent low, eyes admiring the beauty of the new incarnation. He had stayed around as promised, keeping the Rama *naam* alive. It had been tough in the last few centuries, but now, his Lord had arrived, as promised, to vanquish the earth of its evil. He picked up the infant and blessed him with courage and strength, as he softly kissed the young one's feet, placing him gently back in the cot. He blessed the girl with beauty and compassion.

Together, Kripacharya and Ved Vyas stepped forward and lifted one infant each, blessing them with intellect and wisdom. Both would have a prominent role to play in the twins' formative years.

Vibhishan and Mahabali stood close to the cradle and blessed the young ones with righteousness, fortitude and generosity.

Markandeya, the baby-faced monk, blessed them with the knowledge of scriptures. "At the right time, I will disclose the secret of Shiva *bhakti* to you, dear Kalki," he said as he gently marked their foreheads with holy ash.

Ashwatthama had to be nudged by his uncle Kripacharya to move ahead and bless the twins. Lost in deep thought, the fearsome warrior stood afar and promised: "Kalki—I, Ashwatthama, pledge to teach you the use of celestial weapons." With tears flowing from his still-red eyes, he completely overlooked the girl twin and walked away.

Parashuram held up the twins to his chest in a suffocating hug, making them wail out aloud. Relaxing his embrace, and softening his otherwise penetrating gaze, Parashuram, the sixth Vishnu incarnation and Guru to Bheeshma, the Pandavas and Kauravas, pronounced, "I bless you with my presence in your life."

3

Attack of the Mlecchas

A thousand kilometres away from the village of Shambhala, the lone gunman stood near the imposing gates of the Dashavatara complex at Deogarh. He was getting impatient. He could feel the tension in his taut sinews, hours into his deadly vigil.

Deogarh had seen better days. Once the seat of power and religion, it was called 'Fort of the Gods' as it housed the oldest Vishnu temple. Today both the town and the temple were in ruins. The main idol in the sanctum sanctorum was missing. Yet the temple, located inside the fort, still had a compelling presence. In a spate of recent terror attacks, most of the inhabitants of Deogarh had been killed or chased away. The gunman had lost his wife, children and family elders. Yet he waited at the temple. The *mlecchas*, he knew, would return soon to stake claim to Deogarh. This time, he would be ready.

It was early evening and yet a sudden darkness enveloped the abandoned town. The eerie silence was palpable. The single sound, one that only he could hear, was his throbbing temples. A slow but constant drum beat. The ominous silence was suddenly shattered by the piercing cry of a woman. Jolted out of his vigil, he watched as a heavily pregnant young woman, making her way stealthily through the mossy ruins, stumbled over a gnarled banyan root sticking out of the ground like a still python. She sank to the ground, her back coming to rest against the trunk. Her legs were splayed apart, one hand on the ground, the other holding her stomach. Her face was ashen, smeared with soot, her clothes torn, hair falling all over her face and bulging breasts. She looked beseechingly into his eyes. "Please," she pleaded, "please can you help? I think I am about to have my baby..." She broke into sobs, losing her voice for a minute. "The *mlecchas* invaded our town and killed all … including my husband. My father, the temple priest, was hung in the town square. Somehow, I managed to escape," she lamented.

"Follow me, quick," he said, helping the woman rush into the sanctum sanctorum, as she babbled on.

"Stay here. This is the safest place in the temple. I'll be outside."

He rushed out, aiming his gun at the iron gates of the fort. As he double-checked the locks, he heard the telltale buzzing of swarms of insects overhead—a portentous sign of the *mlecchas* barging in. The sound was coming from the west gate. Never before had the fort been approached from the west, where the Betwa flowed. But that was a long time ago when the river was known for its treacherous, icy currents and rocky bed. Now the river was merely a deep but dry bed that ran alongside the fort. Time was running out. He had not even considered securing that gate! As he edged towards the gate, he stumbled and fell flat on his face. Not losing a moment, he stood up using his rifle as a crutch. As he stood on the rocky wall that was flush with the escarpment, the sight he saw chilled his very bones. A steady stream of blood was flowing through the riverbed. He knew instantly that the city on the other side of the river had been taken over. Keekatpur had fallen. From his vantage point, he saw the *mleccha* army scaling the wall of the riverbed with the help of ropes. His hands trembled as he made the call.

"Babaji they are here, the *mlecchas*! Hundreds of them, send help!" he muttered, barely able to speak out of fear.

"Right away Manu, hold on till then," assured Babaji. "The Dashavatara Temple must be protected at any cost."

"Keekatpur has been taken!"

"How do you know?"

"The daughter of the priest of Keekatpur escaped and is here in the temple complex."

"Revati! She is a warrior pandit. Ask for her help."

"Can't."

"Why?"

"She is about to deliver her child any time now."

"Heavens protect her then. The *mlecchas* are killing every newborn child this year."

Manu disconnected the phone and rushed back to the sanctum sanctorum.

"Please can you get me a few banyan roots and a sharp bark," whispered Revati, lying in a pool of blood, her baby on her abdomen. Manu's stomach churned at the sight. He rushed out and threw up. He closed his eyes for a second, and regaining his composure, hurriedly made his way inside and handed the roots and bark to Revati, looking away.

She propped herself up on an elbow, held the wailing infant, and in a swift motion using the bark separated herself from her son. Her momentary happiness was cut short by the snorts and grunts of the *mlecchas*. Three of them had broken into the temple and surrounded the sanctum sanctorum. Uttering excited grunts and reeking of filth, they presented a terrifying sight; each had the face of a pig and the body of a human. This was no natural evolution; this brute force was sired in a laboratory, the direct result of gene mutation.

Manu hid himself behind a pillar and opened fire, killing the three. The sound of the rifle shots immediately attracted the remaining *mlecchas* into the temple. Revati, incredibly agile for her condition, crawled to hide herself and her baby behind the large column near the entrance door while Manu engaged some of the *mlecchas* in combat. She had latched the baby onto her breast in a bid to silence his cries. But a hard fall dislodged the infant and even as she held on to him fiercely, his wails betrayed her location.

It was an impossible situation thought Manu as the bullets in his rifle ran out. It was only a matter of time before they all perished. Why hadn't help arrived yet? He checked his watch and realised that only twenty minutes had passed since his phone call. The longest twenty minutes of his life! "Oh God please, please let not the dark forces penetrate your home," he prayed fervently.

The inner temple was swarming with *mlecchas* by now. Revati lay pinned to the floor, but she was not ready to give up yet. She was trying hard to overpower the huge pig-men who held her down while the others passed her wailing infant around, each one licking him, enjoying the taste of the amniotic fluid still fresh on the baby's tender skin.

A furious and fearsome Revati rose up in a last bid at defence. Her helplessness was heart-breaking as she pushed and pulled trying to put up a vain fight. Suddenly, the frenzied dance of death that the *mlecchas* had started came to an abrupt halt as a man and child walked in.

"Horrible animals! What are you doing? Hand over the infant to me now!"

Manu watched from behind the pillar as all the *mlecchas* went down on their knees and folded their hands, like well-trained dogs before their master.

The short man had a large forehead and a disproportionate body frame with short hands and legs. He moved with an awkward, monkey-like gait. His gaze was cruel and voice gruff, indicating a breathing disorder. The child, in contrast, was handsome with neatly slicked-back hair, and deep green eyes.

The man emptied the contents of a bag into the sanctum sanctorum with one hand whilst he held the hapless newborn in the other.

"It's time to mould ... come play with clay Kali," he said in a hypnotic voice, guiding the child.

"Let's see if the infant is doing all right," he said, turning the newborn upside down and slapping him hard on his buttocks. The baby let out a loud wail amid the cheers of the *mlecchas*.

Kali mixed the clay with a red liquid that looked like blood and started giving it a shape.

"I am ready, Kapi *Dada*."

"Good, let's install a new idol for the new era."

In a sudden, swift motion the man placed the infant upside down onto the clay slab created by Kali, the wet plaster entered the infant's mouth, nose and ears as the baby gasped for breath.

Quietly, with complete focus, the four-year-old continued adding clay onto the now-dead infant's body, carefully shaping it.

Revati shut her eyes to the unfolding horror, screaming, "You will have to pay for this!"

The man and the child continued undisturbed; they had now placed a sign near the dead infant's statue that read: "Kalki—Welcome to *Kali Yuga*."

Crouched low, Ashwatthama watched from above the temple dome through the broken ceiling. He had just arrived, at Babaji's behest, aborting his mission of protecting another sacred temple complex from rampaging *mlecchas*. Not losing a minute, he jumped from the dome into the sanctum sanctorum—a blue baseball cap protecting his bandaged wound.

"Kapi!" he thundered, landing a few feet from the short man. He tensed, ready for the offensive he knew was coming. The ground shuddered as the grunting *mlecchas* charged towards him.

"Halt!" ordered the man. "Don't attack!" Confused, the charging pig-men stopped dead on their tracks. "It's time to leave Ashwatthama alone." The mutant army retreated behind the short man.

"Cowards, come on attack me!" Ashwatthama taunted the *mlecchas*—but in vain. He looked around in frustration as only Revati, Manu and he were left inside the temple.

"Why did you let them go? Didn't Babaji send you to protect us?" demanded Manu in anger.

Ashwatthama folded his hands in apology. Tears rolled down his eyes. This life was indeed a curse.

The Immortal

Ashwatthama

"Don't pretend you are delighted to see me. This tall, firm, ageless body, this perpetual youth, these sinewy limbs and perfect musculature, these dark piercing eyes and the thunderous voice that has not yet lost its timbre. These jet-black thick locks that dripped with sweat in the wrestling pits of Hastinapur, these adamantine knuckles that glistened with the blood of fallen adversaries, this heaving chest that I thumped when I tamed wild elephants… Still, don't pretend as if you are delighted to see me.

"Don't I know what lurks in your mind when you hear my name? Don't I know what you think of me? The slayer of Upapandavas. The most heinous murderer history has ever produced. The detested one. Despite my fame and reputation as a warrior of warriors, I am not anyone's role model. I am just a despicable murderer. There are murderers who kill adults, women, their own gurus and parents … but whoever heard of one who kills children? I know how you look at me … I see that look in your eyes—turn your gaze away from me, you judgemental readers of history, you ordinary, blinkered masses!

"There were rathis, atirathis, maharathis … Bheeshma, my own father Drona, Arjun, Karna, Drupad, Alambush, Bhagadatta, Vrishasena, Bheem—all were maharathis. I was one too—but greater. I was manifested by Lord Shiva himself. Dare anyone club me with all these? I was near invincible. Yes, anger was my bane. My father Drona used to tell me to fear my own anger—that it would change me in an instant from Shiva to Rudr! I would be the wrath of all the gods put together. But I never did get angry. My dear friend Karna encouraged me to spend time in nature every time he feared I would flare up; that always had a calming effect. But he was wrong. The Great War did not anger me. Nor did Krishna's machinations. Nor the arrogant Bheem. I saw war as just another facet of life and

especially the life of Kshatriyas like me. I fought like any other warrior—fiercely but not enough to wipe out the Pandavas completely, decisively.

"Even my father's death by deception did not anger me enough to strike down my foes like lightning. I raged, but not enough. Krishna, the master manipulator, Yuddhishthir, the model of righteousness-turned-liar, Bheem, the collaborator, and Dhrishtadyumna, the passive slayer—were they any match for me? I could have struck their heads off in a blink. But I let that pass too. I fought on. A warrior whose heart is laden with grief and mind clouded by confusion and revenge is not an ideal warrior. And then the war ended—with the fall of our venerable Lord, Bheeshma, my friend Karna, all the Kauravas and then, finally, Duryodhana. That was the last straw. There were only three that I truly loved—my father, Karna and Duryodhana. With the fall of Duryodhana, everything else ceased to matter.

"Yes, I crept into the tents of the sleeping enemy and slaughtered all I could. The manipulative Krishna already knew of my plans; perhaps but even he could not save a whole generation of the Pandavas. I killed them all—but in ignorance. Why would I murder children in cold blood? Why would I? Me? I confess wrath and revenge had blinded me but first and foremost, I am a warrior. I fight my match. I sought stealth against Krishna who sought deception. My fault was not stealth. My fault was ignorance. How was I to know I had smeared my hands and destiny with young blood?

"If all is fair in love and war, then the same should apply to me as well. You saw how they killed the mighty Karna? Jaydrath? Our Grandsire Bheeshma? And that is pardonable? But just because we are not on that clever Yadav's side we do not qualify? Did Arjun possess the ability to slay my friend, the warrior of all warriors, Karna? Could anyone thwart the havoc wreaked by

my father? And me? Had I been in a blind rage, could anyone, anyone, have stood the ground against me? Even Krishna?

"Many centuries have passed by since that time. Krishna's curse stays with me. I—mighty Ashwatthama—will roam the earth as a destitute commoner. The wound in my forehead perpetually bleeds, a reminder of the state of my mind. Death does not approach me. Cannot approach me. I stay immortal.

"And here is the difference: while the rest of the Immortals are blessed, I am the only one who carries this as a curse. And yet I have obligations to fulfil. And hope.

"Kalki is not just an avatar but perhaps, also my redemption. Perhaps. As tutor to the avatar of this age, I might ask for absolution—finally. That might be my gurudakshina, the fee for my services. Imagine, a teacher begging for his fee! But this is my destiny, unfulfilled, unending, undesired..."

4

Escape

"Impossible!" murmured Raj to himself as he rushed to Kripacharya's bunker in Shambhala. As he entered, he saw the aristocratic old man pacing the floor, head down, hands clasped behind his back.

"How did they know the divine secret?" blurted Raj, shocked at the tone of his own voice.

"They have penetrated the Fort of the Gods and left a message."

"Yes, yes, I know. The sages are very worried. I have called for an urgent meeting tonight to reassure them."

"How do you explain last night's ghastly act at Deogarh? I think it was a direct warning to us."

"It seems to be the work of Shukracharya," said Kripa, swiftly double checking the bunker's security systems.

Outside, as the sun set on the Himalayan crags, north winds began to rush in hungrily to claim their space. The deodars shook in an orchestrated symphony of the demonic.

The gushing river flowing nearby sent up a tall spray as an offering to the gods of the night. In moments the wind would be howling through the tight crevasses and slim passes of the mighty mountain range. Not a soul ventured out. It was a noisy calm; a forbidden one.

Near the strip of the road parallel to the river that led from the sparsely populated village, ten miles far south, lay the thickly wooded region of Ādi. That was its name, Ādi—meaning primal. Most would pass by without having a look because there was nothing to look at here except a wild, dense growth, lush green and impenetrable. It was a mystery why did it even have a name. It seemed everything grew here, nothing died. Yet the villagers collected not even dry wood from here, simply because it was prohibited. No folklore whispered it, no book announced it, no priest ordered it; it just was so. The daunting forest seemed to stretch infinitely, menacingly claiming its piece on the surface of the earth.

Where the road blind-curved left and the river dipped suddenly into an innocuous freshet, stood a massive clump of banyan trees. It was an uncommon sight, almost inexplicable. The rare villager who came by never forgot to bow and place an offering in one of its innumerable crevices. A few steps down, the path sharply turned right and continued hazily into the mountains. Unknown to most, a hundred yards left into Ādi from there, the faintest outline of a flight of steps was visible through the overgrowth. Only a select few in the world knew where they led.

It was the entrance to another world; a world that was not this, but of it.

The steps worked as pressure pads for a concealed entrance. As you stepped forward and down, each step opened a dovetailed combination lock in the mountain face running left.

The steep, mossy, and perpetually wet flank was eminently avoidable. Only those who knew, knew it was a remarkable feat. At the end of the last step, a small part of the mountain swung in with a barely audible rumble. An immaculate, laser-cut square opened into a dark passage. Stepping in, you would barely notice that the dislodged rock had moved back into place. As your eyes adjusted to the darkness, you would notice an ambient light filling the passage and the comforting sound of a small waterfall. If you had a sensitive nose, you would inhale whiffs of camphor, sulphur, frankincense, sandalwood, saffron and wet earth wafting in the air. The short walk would end in a series of sophisticated hi-tech bunkers done up like a cruise ship.

The bunkers were serviced by climate and ventilation systems. Self-contained water and power generation systems ensured survival without support from the outside world. In addition, there was a water treatment plant with deep water wells, a power plant, an organic farm, meeting rooms, a biotechnology laboratory and a private zone.

Past the kitchen on the right was a ledge overlooking a waterfall. Slightly to its right, a series of steps led to the splash stone of the waterfall. This was the entrance to the highly guarded private chambers of overlord Raj Nanda and his family.

The underground bunkers stretched deep into the jungle, and opened up into the mystical village of Shambhala on the other side. The brainchild of Kripacharya, it was established to protect 'the men of god' from the *mlecchas*, 'the men of evil'.

Shambhala, a numinous abode of purity and peace, was a hidden land inhabited by a secret mystic brotherhood of 108 sages, whose members laboured for the good of humanity. It was said that the blood that flowed in the sages of Shambhala had traces of gold, making them the rarest and the purest of the human race.

Situated amidst the Himalayas, Shambhala was off the grid. It had never been photographed or discovered. The thick umbrella of the conifers prevented the sighting of the village even by the aerial satellites. There was only one way to leave or enter Shambhala—through the heavily guarded and patrolled bunkers with state-of-the-art security and communication systems; and that way was through the dense forests of Ādi.

Here it was in Shambhala, amidst the gathering of venerable sages, that Babaji had blessed the divine twins.

"Rudr, the Destroyer, God Shiva!" The name was met with cheers. The infant seemed to smile, with a twinkle in his eyes.

The younger of the twins, the girl child, was gently lifted from the cot as she slept peacefully. Babaji had whispered her name into her ears: "Tarini, the Saviour, Goddess Durga."

Much later, Babaji had pronounced the prophecies before the family.

"It is with blessings and grace of the Almighty that I have been chosen to make the most auspicious horoscopes of my lifetime. The children were born on Tuesday, the 23rd of April, when the moon was inclined in the *Dhanishta Nakshatra* and sun in the *Swati Nakshatra*. This most opportune birth will give the children beauty, compassion, intelligence, wealth and leadership.

"Rudr—the missions that he takes up as a man having divine energies flowing within him will create a complex web. He will respect and be respected on the basis of moral grounds and intellect; yet if cheated he will take brutal revenge. The Age of Darkness will come to an end with the realisation of his *siddhis*.

"Tarini is a new young sapling under the influence of a blowing wind. Born a minute later than her brother, she will easily adapt to all that life bestows on her. She will be highly ethical, intelligent and fiercely independent, and will enjoy a high social position.

"The twins have come to teach us balance and, together, they will change the course of history."

He then looked at Raj and added softly, "However, there is always a price to pay." What he said next drained the colour off the faces of all present in the room.

***

The outrage at Deogarh that followed indicated that events portended had already been set in motion.

Raj addressed Shambhala's sages. "The barbarity at the Dashavatara Temple has left us shocked. The time has come for me to return with my family back to the plains of Hindustan."

Kripacharya rose from his seat. "Yes. For now, we must all scatter ourselves in different directions to survive. We will gather our forces against this evil. They have taken over Keekatpur and will be here soon. The brutality of last night is hard to stomach."

"I agree, Kripacharyaji," said Raj. "The evil forces have reigned far too long. Mother Nature has turned against us in anger—the earth is barren, the rivers are drying up, the oceans are acidifying and turning poisonous."

The stately old man's forehead wrinkled up in deep thought as he looked up at the clear sky. "The gods have finally heard our prayers. Kalki has arrived and will lead the world into a new era. All of us should abandon this bunker and village and merge back into society. We will spread ourselves around the world." He then addressed Raj, "Go back to our country's capital and use your power in the judiciary circles, keep Rudr and Tarini protected and away from the public eye."

5

Shukra

Somewhere in the universe Shukracharya sat in deep meditation. He, the preceptor of *asuras*, occupied the dark space, a mysterious invisible plane that repelled light and gravity. Few had the power to enter this bizarre and forbidding plane. Dark energy flourished here. It was, in fact, mysteriously expanding in the universe.

The quintessential Guru from the beginning of 'Time', mentor to both the *devas* and *asuras*, Shukracharya had an overpowering persona and a magnetic presence. He had deep-set eyes with long lashes and an abundance of body hair on his short frame. The death of his mother at the hands of the *devas* had turned him against them forever. He had vowed to destroy them. He undertook deep penance and severe austerities and was blessed by Lord Shiva himself with the *Mrityasanjeevani mantra*—that brought the dead back to life.

The time had come for him to use his blessings. To use darkness to initiate, incubate and generate a new world order. In this turbulent age, he would not unleash external darkness but rather, attack the internal world of the mind and intellect causing a shift, a corruption of thought processes. "This is the essence of *Kali Yuga*," reflected Shukracharya, lost in meditation. "Most humans have been trapped by dark forces beyond their comprehension or control."

Yet a few light sources continued to exist, thinking of which agitated the mighty Shukra always, even in deep meditation. He hadn't been able to break the eight Immortals—yet. Were it not for them—these gatekeepers of the world—the balance of the Universe would have tilted towards the dark side long ago.

To counteract the brilliance and formidable power of the Immortals, Shukracharya had visited countless graves and resting places of the dead and spent nights at burial grounds to appease the threshold goddess between the three worlds.

Bibi Maya, the force of death and destruction, manifested at last, eyes red with absolute rage, hair dishevelled, wearing a garland of human skulls, offsetting her pendulous breasts and full, rounded belly.

Her voice was loud, almost screechy: "Shukra, this better be important!"

"Bibi, it is time for you to procreate," said Shukracharya matter-of-factly.

She cackled loudly exposing her decaying, broken teeth. "Are you proposing a fuck, you dirty old man?"

"No time for your wicked humour Bibi … it is in darkness that the roots of our being can be found. You inhabit the world of primordial instincts and our deepest wisdom. A child born of you will rule the universe…

"Close your eyes as I show you a vision," continued Shukra.

Images of the distant past started flashing before her eyes:

The earth trembled and wept with the birth of Jalandhara, the result of the powerful union between the ocean and the seed of Lord Shiva's uncontrollable anger. Jalandhara could fly on the winds, float over the oceans, tame the most savage of beasts and even raise the dead. Lord Brahma had perceived the power of the child and given him his name. But even Lord Brahma couldn't predict that this child would grow up to be their worst nemesis. This powerful evil, an almost indestructible being, waged a war with heaven, a war so brutal that it took all the gods' combined strength to defeat him.

The war had threatened to destroy heaven thousands of years ago; a war in which the gods believed that they had destroyed Jalandhara once and for all. But it was not so. A drop of Jalandhara's blood had escaped. It fell onto a field, making it instantly barren. In its epicentre grew a magical plant, the fruit of which contained the poison of Jalandhara.

Bibi Maya opened her eyes and extended her left hand—aware that the time ordained by Shiva had arrived. Shukracharya placed the bright red fruit into her palms, and she quickly gobbled up Shiva's seed. He smiled.

"The blood that had been dormant for generations will now resurrect in the veins of my protégé Kali," he declared triumphantly.

Shukracharya tended to Bibi Maya during her pregnancy. He fed her wine, fruits, tobacco, and narrated ancient stories to her womb. The day Kali was born, a devastating typhoon ripped through the Indian Ocean destroying lives in thousands, and dark grey clouds enveloped the planet for days together.

Shukracharya was a sage in a hurry. He introduced the deeper sciences of physics and chemistry to Kali right from birth.

Sitting in sub-zero temperatures in a state-of-the-art laboratory in Antarctica, Shukracharya fumed despite his perfect yoga *mudra*. Wherefrom came the brilliant, blinding light and whiff of sandalwood? Who dared disturb him? That pesky Hanuman? Or perhaps the arrogant Parashuram? True, the Immortals could travel through space and time, and hinder his dark thoughts with their brilliant light. Only these two alone had the power to disturb him. With his eyes still shut he scanned his surroundings. He was right—they were both here.

"Stop this insanity Shukra," said Parashuram agitatedly. "What more do you want to destroy?"

"What I destroy, you no longer need," replied Shukracharya, as he blessed the prostrating Hanuman.

"When will your revenge saga end? For all your knowledge, your ego has not left you. You have made this world your personal battleground!" admonished Parashuram.

"Amazing, these words coming from someone who single-handedly destroyed twenty-one generations of Kshatriyas," retorted Shukra. "Soon the world as we know it, will end. And then my revenge will be complete," he said in a chilling tone. "It's time for war!"

"You have used the same cosmic forces as me to perpetuate a seed. We are interconnected in a perpetual relationship, one that started from the beginning of 'Time'. Together you and I create opposing forces that interact to form a dynamic system—evil versus good—over and over again."

The majestic and broad-chested Hanuman interrupted, disrupting the cold vibrations. "Shadows cannot exist without light. The presence of just the two of us lights up your dark world—you will never be a match for us, Shukracharyaji."

"Anjaney, you are known for your humility and yet you speak in arrogance. Go prepare. It's time for you to do more than just survive," taunted Shukracharya. "Kali is proving to be my best student. His powers are phenomenal, his intellect unmatched. The Lord of *Kali Yuga*, Kali is ready to take on the world."

"Not as long as I exist!" retorted Hanuman, moving his gaze towards Parashuram. "Guruji permit me to annihilate Kali and his mentor. Let's finish this once and for all."

"It's not for us to do so mighty Hanuman. Why do you think I look on helplessly? The strong alone protect. It's the weak who need to take recourse to attack. We are cursed to be in the system and yet not of it. To live, yet not actively participate. To teach, but not engage. We, the *Chiranjeevis*, have together seen the collapse of the world. The dominance of evil. The suppression of good. Our *siddhis* remain only as long as we use them to protect ourselves and others; they will disappear if we use them to attack anyone. It's destined, Sankatmochan, that *Kali Yuga* will meet its end at the hands of the tenth Vishnu Avatar, Kalki."

"My eyes are on him," warned Shukracharya, "your Vishnu Avatar."

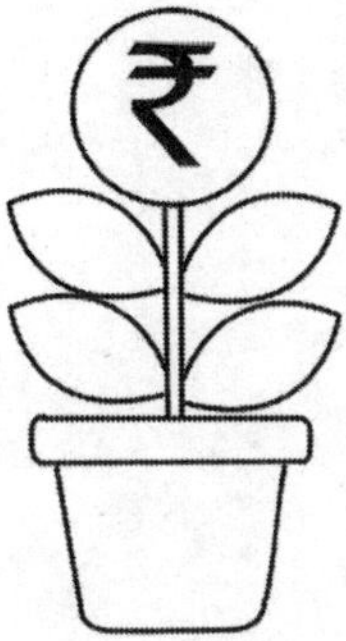

Artha

What is the pursuit of happiness? By what means will you prosper?
Tread nobly on earth—she bears the weight of your existence.

6

Raj

New Delhi. Before the Birth.

Rajkumar Nanda was furious. The hotline in his private court chambers had just confirmed his worst fears—there was no way his sharpest advocate, Cyrus, would make a court appearance today. He was missing without warning again. This was the third time Cyrus was absconding when they had a hearing. Hardly matters, thought Raj grimly, taking a deep breath and putting on his game face. He had yet to plead a case he couldn't win.

Rajkumar Nanda was a charismatic man—the kind who easily attracted power by sheer force of personality. An eminent public figure, his days were busier than ever. Nanda & Sons, his brainchild, was the go-to firm for the country's top business houses and politicians. Raj's artful efforts at nurturing the 'Who's Who' of business, politics, and celebrities had paid off richly. The firm attracted the best talent from premium law schools and Raj enjoyed mentoring them into astute lawyers and courtroom wizards. As a result, his court appearances reduced considerably while his reputation grew larger than life.

It was only high-profile cases with the potential to stir up a hornet's nest that prompted a court appearance by Raj. He was known to be a great storyteller. It was said he used this skill to score impossible wins. Detractors believed he was simply gifted at obscuring the truth. His latest case—a popular cricketer accused of the murder of his glamorous actress wife—had received wide media coverage. All evidence pointed towards the cricketer, yet the Mumbai High Court pronounced him 'not guilty' thanks to the brilliant manoeuvring of Raj Nanda.

"Raj, I am amazed! Who is this key witness Suresh, who vouched for the presence of a third person at the scene of crime?" enquired Rajat Singh, relieved his innings in the game would not be cut short by a foolish mistake. "How did you find him?"

"Oh, Suresh? He was easy to persuade. He has terminal Stage IV cancer and the doctors have given him no more than three months to live. He has a family of five children, all under eleven, and a handicapped wife. I told him that his children's education would be taken care of at an English boarding school and an additional thirty lakh would come his way.

"Another ten lakh was spent on managing circumstantial evidence to create a watertight case. Rajat, I hope it wasn't too much?"

"Brilliant Raj! You're a miracle-man!"

"Not at all—I am just an old horse, thoroughly familiar with the judiciary system of our times. I know the loose ends and work them to my advantage… And hey, if you have to overdose—switch to coffee next time! At least you will remember what you have been doing!" he said with a broad wink, as his mobile buzzed.

"Now, if you will excuse me, I have a flight to catch," he said, buttoning his coat.

Raj Nanda hopped into his six-seater private jet and went straight to the cockpit.

"All checks done?" he inquired of the pilot seated at right.

"Yes sir. Back home to Delhi?"

"Yes Pete, an important arrest today. It is going to change things forever."

Captain Pete Hagge nodded, smiling, and continued with the pre-departure clearance checks.

Raj's phone buzzed incessantly. "Yes, Sulakshana. Is it urgent?"

"Yes."

"What could…"

"Manoj has eloped with Rehana!"

"So?" Raj snapped, a bit irritated. "There's never a dull moment in your brother's life!"

"She is the wife of Shafique Khan," said Sulakshana, her voice breaking nervously.

Captain Pete was alarmed to see the colour drain away from Raj's face.

***

Shafique Khan stood tall, his triceps and chest almost bursting out of his fine silk shirt. The French windows of his office on the 99th floor of the impressive building he had built gave him a bird's eye view of the city he practically owned. From his office in Connaught Place he could see what a maze the city was—its chaos, its magnetic charm, its raw power. Up here he was the king of the world; untouchable. And yet…

Despite the air-conditioning, beads of sweat dotted his forehead and nose, and dampened his shirt at the armpits. He picked up the remote, set it on maximum and threw it across the room. It bounced off the large conference table, driving fear into the bunch of people huddled there—men of power and repute; men in charge of running the country.

Police Commissioner Saroj Rastogi whispered to the man next to him, "He has gone insane, talk him out of this madness."

"Shh, quiet. I don't want a bullet in any head," warned Home Minister Prasad Shinde, a wily old hand.

Staring sharply at Rastogi, Shafique roared, "I will burn the city down!"

His animosity was like acid—burning, slicing, potent. "I did everything you wanted, everything! Wasn't this your brief Shinde? An entire city and its periphery reduced to mental rubble so your political ambitions were met? So why the impotence when I want something? All you had to do was locate one person. One!"

He pulled Rastogi to the window by his collar. "Look down," he raged. "A generation of wasted minds—sacrificed for your ambition." Below swarmed a sea of young men and women, ostensibly going about their work. Heat mercilessly beat down at their sunburned faces and coiled around their limbs like a great slithering serpent. The ground sent up a disorienting haze. Even the birds were silent; and the leaves were still as if too hot or shocked to move.

In truth, for all his raw fury, Shafique Khan, kingmaker and drug lord, felt utterly helpless. He had but one obsession, one weakness—his doe-eyed wife Rehana. And Rehana had eloped with one Manoj Dubey, scion of a wealthy family from Banaras.

"You and your city are finished now. I will destroy it!" spat Shafique at the hallowed assembly.

"If you had concentrated more on your home instead of the city, Rehana would probably be around," confronted Shinde.

The others in the room shrank with fear wondering which of these two was crazier. Some of them quietly started moving towards the exit.

"Shut up Shinde or I will blow your brains off," screamed Shafique, pointing his gun towards him, and then at those trying to exit. "Come back! Nobody leaves till my wife is found. Rastogi—get your police department to move their butts. I want Rehana home before midnight. Shinde—declare a state of emergency and shut down the country!"

Suddenly, the door burst open and Black Cat commandos stormed in. Four clamped down on Shafique, snatching his gun away. Behind them came the country's most influential lawyer, Raj Nanda, architect of the coup.

As the others quickly exited, a visibly relieved Shinde shook hands with Raj. "Great timing, Mr Nanda—I was losing hope!"

Turning to Shafique, Shinde said, "I made you, you gutter rat! But you got too big for your boots. You want me, the home minister, to shut down the country, because your wife eloped with her lover?"

Shafique strained against the men holding him down. "You son of a bitch Shinde … I will take you down!" he roared.

With quick footwork the hefty Rastogi pushed back a raging Shafique. "Mr Nanda, you and your squad can leave Shafique to Shinde and me," he said, waving away the commandos.

Surprised, Raj asked, "Are you sure? I have an arrest warrant for Shafique, and it's best you talk once he is under arrest."

"Raj, leave us alone," commanded Shinde. "Your job is done for now. You can wait outside—give us 15 minutes."

Raj Nanda shook his head and reluctantly walked out, as the door of the soundproof chamber glided shut.

The dry, wasted riverbed of the once-flowing Yamuna flashed before Raj's eyes.

It was symptomatic of the state of the nation, or at least of Delhi, its capital. The decline had started a decade earlier, the day the national election results were declared. The two leading political parties had fallen short of a clear mandate and were scavenging for allies. So it came to pass that an entirely unexpected coalition came together to govern the largest democracy in the world. The simple truth was that a once-efficient system that managed to balance and neutralise the inevitable unsavoury elements in its fold, was now dominated by rabid fundamentalists and even mafia elements.

Above all, the seed for the destruction of Delhi could be traced to one man: Shafique Khan. Under his influence, the city, once the power centre of *Bharatvarsh*, had succumbed to vice and corruption. Shafique Khan's drug cartel had slowly infiltrated the capital's streets as much as its high-rises and elite farmhouses. It was now silently advancing to the suburbs and villages beyond, beckoning the youth with its magic promise: Get rich quick!

Its prime product, RIZE, offered the promise of better performance and higher productivity despite odds. RIZE came as a slim pack of gel sheets fashioned after thin, melt-in-your-mouth mints. All you had to do was pop one on your tongue. Within seconds you felt alert, focused, with a never-before-seen clarity. The drug was a favourite with undergraduate students and those pursuing higher education. Its cheaper version was a rage on the streets with everyone from small vendors and labourers to school students. It helped everyone do whatever they had to do, better and faster—initially, that is. Over a year the drug worked its way into physiology to become highly addictive. But its true power as a weapon of destruction was to cloud judgement and weaken the mind over time, where once it bestowed unbelievable and instant mental clarity and strength.

Delhi's soaring temperatures, stoked higher still by global warming, only worsened the situation. There was little to soothe the vast majority of troubled and confused minds. They fell easy prey then, to the false promises, propaganda and lies dished out by the so-called leaders and politicians.

Raj Nanda had lost a couple of his brightest minds to RIZE. Cyrus Minawala, a gifted young criminal advocate, was the latest one to succumb. Having experimented with RIZE at a Chattarpur rave party, Cyrus found he could easily think of unheard-of workarounds for loopholes in two of his long-pending cases the next morning. Ironically the deep satisfaction of seeing justice delivered for his clients had sent him right back to RIZE for more clarity and inspiration, more justice—and more RIZE. One year down the line, the decline started. Cyrus could not stay away from the drug. Then came the absences … like clockwork, Cyrus would now become dysfunctional, confused and incapable of thinking clearly—like the others before him.

Stung where it hurt him most, Raj had vowed to fight Shafique Khan and his drug cartel. Undercover investigations indicated that there were murkier aspects to Shafique's operations. Circumstantial evidence pointed to the fact that drug money was being channelled into legit enterprises, and even to fund a secret society that dabbled in black magic, with ambitions of world dominance. However, proof was hard to come by.

Some of the team members investigating this had suffered horrific deaths. Raj took this personally and swore vengeance against Shafique.

In Raj's eyes, Shafique was pure evil—and only now he was beginning to understand the deadly reach of his power.

Raj stared dully at the paper in his hands. Shafique's arrest warrant—extracted after months of patient and persistent persuasion of political and legal bigwigs.

Fifteen minutes had flown by. Raj strode into the conference room.

It was empty. The floor and walls were splattered with blood and the gory trail stopped just short of the French windows, still shut. It was as if the trio had just vanished into thin air.

It didn't end there.

The next morning Rehana and Manoj were killed in Paris in broad daylight, in a freak firing incident. The entire Dubey clan—Manoj's family—was gunned down in Banaras, including infants and children, in the week that followed. There was, finally, a violent attack at the Nanda residence—mysteriously sabotaged, the media said, by two commandos in masks.

Raj hugged Babaji tight. "I had the bastard under arrest. All this bloodshed could have been avoided. Sulakshana has lost her entire family. All because the police commissioner and home minister were trying to save their ass. Now all our lives are in grave danger."

"The universe is very intelligent and uses us to fulfil its purpose. Let me introduce you to someone very special—*Chiranjeevi* Markandeya," offered Babaji by way of explanation. The second commando slowly discarded his uniform to reveal his true self: a young monk with glowing, baby-pink skin.

Raj froze in amazement, as a completely different plane of existence unfolded before his eyes. He had just made contact with one of the eight fabled Immortals! He prayed to at least one he realised with a start, recalling the marble figurine of Hanuman in the shrine at home. He had read about some; and some he recollected from the stories his grandmother had told him.

But seeing one in flesh and blood was surreal. He could not withhold the flow of tears as the space around him crackled with powerful energies, sweeping through his entire being. The air-conditioning stopped; the tungsten in the lights burst; and all the doors and windows in the large Nanda living room flew open inviting a noisy gust of wind. Though it was well past midnight, the room was bathed in dazzling white light emanating from this other-worldly entity. Its brilliance was blinding. As Raj instinctively shut his eyes, a reassuring calmness suffused his mind. His tense body relaxed and he let go of all the past-life conditioning, giving in to the compelling feeling of love that permeated his very being.

Gathering himself, he prostrated before the Immortal.

Markandeya, the Baby Monk, gently helped him up and spoke.

"It's time to fulfil your purpose on earth. You need to leave everything and move with your family."

Raj managed to stammer, "Move where—when?"

"No questions. In time, you will find your answers."

"Trust us and allow us to take the decisions," commanded Babaji. As Babaji turned to leave with Markandeya, he added, almost as an afterthought, "Shafique has vanished, but the coast isn't clear yet. Tread carefully, my friend! Beware of your inner circle."

It was an encounter that changed the course of Raj's life forever. It brought him to Shambhala.

***

New Delhi. After the Birth.

The Nanda household was full of laughter and chatter of four growing children. Pragnya was showing Rudr how to hold a bat. "Bend just a bit and spread your legs just enough to balance your weight. Keep the bat at an angle to the ground. Focus on the ball and hit it with all your strength," said the confident seven-year-old to his younger brother.

"Good. You've got it right. Now I'm going to run up and throw the ball at you. Try to hit it."

"Yes *Bhaiya*," said the cherubic Rudr. He looked intently at the ball coming towards him and slammed it out of sight.

An astonished Pragnya gasped. "How did you manage that, Rudr? Even I can't hit that far."

"*Bhaiya*, you asked me to use all my strength," said the proud five-year-old.

Pragnya rushed into his eldest brother's room. "I told you Rudr is very strong." Sumanta, who was immersed in a book on space, offered a bored glance.

"Now what? What did Rudr do?"

"He hit the ball beyond the ground's wall, the very first time he held the bat!"

"So, what's the big deal? I'll believe he is strong only if he can defeat me at the obstacle course. Let's compete against Rudr and Tarini."

"Yes, that will be exciting. It'll be such fun," said Pragnya.

"We will compete on Sunday. Now go play and let me concentrate on my studies," said Sumanta, as he got back to his books.

Tarini was playing by herself on the lawns chasing butterflies when she saw her grandfather come home. She rushed into his arms saying, "*Bade Papa* everybody is very busy. Nobody wants to play with me!" She accompanied her granddad into the house and was soon sitting on his lap drinking chocolate milkshake. She was his favourite grandchild.

He smiled as he gently stroked her hair. "You're going to be busy too. Your school starts tomorrow. Now tell me—what did you do today?"

"I made up names for all my brothers because *Badi Mumma* doesn't want me to take their real names. Calling all of them 'bhaiya' is very confusing for them and me."

"That's good. So what have you named them?"

"Sumanta is *Bhaiya Bade* since he is the oldest. Pragnya is *Bhaiyaji* and Rudr, *Bhaiya*."

"That's very good Tarini. What are your *Bhaiya Bade* and *Bhaiyaji* doing now? And where is Rudr… err *Bhaiya*?"

"*Bhaiya Bade* is studying. Today he told me about space and aircraft. Do you know that he has started making his own aircraft? *Bhaiyaji* is playing cricket with Rudr *bhaiya*."

Raj put Tarini down on the floor gently and gazed at her light eyes and dimpled cheeks. He loved the fact that Tarini waited for him every evening and spent time talking to him. Of late Tarini had become very expressive and he enjoyed their lively conversations.

"*Bade Papa*, on Sunday we have a competition. We will do the obstacle course to see who is the strongest of us all."

"You can't do the obstacle course! You are too small for it."

"Yes, I can! I have been practising with *Bhaiyaji*. Mother saw us today and said I could win," said Tarini excitedly as she made her way towards the lawns.

Raj waited for Tarini to move out of earshot before he called for Sumati. "What nonsense is this child talking about? Are you aware?"

"Yes Papa, Sumanta has challenged Rudr and Tarini and the children are really excited."

"That's so unfair. Sumanta and Pragnya are nine and seven and they are competing against Rudr and Tarini, aged five?"

"Yes Papa, but the older boys don't stand a chance of winning against the twins," smiled Sumati.

"We know why. But we can't let the children know. They have to grow up normally. Their true identity has to be kept hidden from all, including themselves. Remember, Rudr has to be treated like his other siblings. Not like an avatar. Am I clear Sumati? His strength has to be kept under wraps. I will tell the older children to compete after receiving a month of training from a warfare expert."

Raj had recently set up the obstacle course on the grounds with ropes, nets, bars, ditches and rappelling walls. This was to familiarise the older boys with tactical movement and improve their physical training and problem-solving skills. The Nanda siblings were being trained on the obstacle course by Kripacharya himself.

On the day of the competition Rudr announced to all present: "I will only participate on one condition."

"And what condition is that?" asked an amused Kripacharya.

"I will make the rules." Everybody agreed.

Later that night when they were alone in their room Tarini asked Rudr, "Why did you make the rules?"

Rudr smiled and said, "I made the rules and we won. Whoever makes the rules wins. This I have understood."

Tarini continued, "…and if you can't make the rules, change the game!" They both laughed out loud.

7

Conflict

"Your worst enemy will be born as your son."

Raj remembered Babaji's ominous words decades ago while he was still a bachelor.

"Impossible … how can a part of you, your flesh and blood, be your enemy?" Raj had argued.

"It's the Law of Karma, to teach you lessons. The person you have inflicted the most pain upon in a previous life is born as your child and when he puts you through pain, you can't do anything but still love him."

At the time Raj had scoffed at the statement and the ways of his maverick friend who, as a successful Wall Street investment banker, had given up an eight-figure income with perks to wander the Himalayas in search of a higher truth.

The loud ringing of the telephone distracted Raj from his papers. It was his secretary.

"Sir, Vishnuyasa wants to see you urgently. May I send him in?"

"Yes, of course."

The anxiety of yet another argument with his only son made Raj slump deeper into his chair.

"Papa, we have been fooled! There is no integrity left in the firm—and it's all happening right under your watchful eye. What's making you look away?" declared an angry Vishnuyasa striding in.

Angry at the slight, Raj retorted, "Come to the point."

"Your brother Tejasya is dealing with the underworld in your name."

"Vishnu, you are mistaken. The company has grown under his leadership. I trust him completely."

"Well—then it's either me or him. Who do you want Papa?"

Raj was quiet, unwilling to make a choice.

"That's it. Your silence spells it out—I quit!" said Vishnuyasa as he stormed out of the room.

Raj had anticipated this eventuality. Vishnuyasa had been a brilliant student, but a rebel at heart. His tendency to question everything, especially who Nanda & Sons chose to defend, had only sharpened in his adulthood. Their mutual animosity had been palpable at Shambhala. As time passed, their arguments had increased, creating a deep rift in their relationship.

Raj walked out of his cabin and excused himself for the day. He headed straight for home. He needed the comforting presence of his wife Sulakshana to be able to deal with the latest volley by his son.

He found Sulakshana on the lawn. One look at her and he knew. She was aware of what had happened.

"You heard?"

"Yes. How did you guess?"

"Don't you deal with stress by talking to your plants, pouring your heart out to them?"

"Hmm … yes, Vishnu spoke to me about it. Let's go inside and talk over a cup of tea. RK don't worry. I have spoken to him."

"He's stubborn and foolish. He will not change his mind."

"Maybe Sumati will be able to talk sense into him."

"Maybe," said Raj, as he followed his wife indoors.

Rudr and Tarini were playing inside. Happy to see her granddad home early, Tarini rushed into his arms and kissed him.

"*Bade Papa*, is your office closed today? Papa has also come home."

Raj hugged his granddaughter tightly.

"It's your afternoon naptime, kids. Go and rest for a while. In the evening I will take you to the park."

"Yippee! Okay, *Bade Papa*!" rejoiced Rudr as he raced with Tarini to their room.

Alone at last with his wife in their room, Raj expressed his concern about Vishnuyasa.

"He wants Tejasya ousted and policies changed. He feels that the firm has become corrupt, with links to the underworld," said Raj, loosening his silk tie and undoing the collar button. He eased himself into his favourite Chesterfield and lit a cigar. Stirring a cup of freshly brewed Assam tea, Sulakshana nodded.

"He has always rebelled against me. I don't understand the aggression and anger," said a dejected Raj.

"RK, let's face it. You have always admonished him. Ridiculed all his interests, stopped him from playing cricket and the guitar."

"Both traits he inherited from your brother Manoj; a sheer waste of time. Look at what happened to him thanks to a life devoted to music—and passion," quipped Raj, his sarcasm cutting Sulakshana to the core.

Raj fell silent, aware he had opened an old wound. However wayward, Sulakshana had been fond of Manoj. It pleased her to see that Vishnu had taken after his uncle in some aspects.

"Vishnu completely distanced himself from you in his teens. Even after marriage, you forced him to stay in Shambhala. The relationship has not healed since then."

"You know why we had to leave for Shambhala. Delhi was too volatile. Your entire Dubey clan was wiped out—and our family would have been next in the Shafique Khan bloodbath."

"Yes, I understand that you had our best interests at heart. Even Vishnu's children were born there. That bothered him a lot. You and your friends were experimenting with genes and modifying them. He did not have much of a role to play."

"Quiet!" roared Raj. "Not one more word." Raj glowered in anger. He was astounded that the generally quiet and docile Sulakshana had dared to speak out today.

A floor above, the younger Nanda couple were also arguing.

"Please reconsider your decision," begged Sumati.

"I haven't rushed into it. I've been thinking about it for years. Finally, I have gathered the courage to stand up to my father," said Vishnuyasa.

"Why? Vishnu, why are you putting all of us through this?"

"My father and I believe in different things. We want different things from life," he said, pacing the room with nervous energy. "My college friend Abhay Sawant and I are starting our own law firm in Mumbai, which will go by the name VAS—Vishnu & Abhay Solicitors," said Vishnuyasa, unable to hide his elation. "I will join next month. So that gives us enough time to pack, move and settle into our new home and surroundings." The excitement in his eyes was infectious.

But Sumati looked away and muttered, "The children and I are not going anywhere!"

"What? What do you mean?" shouted Vishnuyasa.

"We are very happy here. Can't you see the amazing relationship your dad and the children share? The comforts they have here? No, I will not uproot them again. They still miss Shambhala and they have just started getting comfortable here."

Sumati hoped her refusal would make him rethink his plan. But Vishnu was adamant.

"Our relationship and being together is not important to you? I am amazed that you choose to stay with your in-laws and not with your husband!"

"That's not true. I accompanied you to Shambhala—had our four children inside a bunker in the small village!"

"Yes, then too, you agreed to his decision. Your children, not mine!" he said accusingly.

"What options did I have?" she shot back, tears welling up in her eyes.

"Oh, quit the lost woman act Sumati," he spat out. "Nobody forced you into it. You willingly lent your womb not once but thrice to be mother to superheroes. You got completely taken in by my father, Babaji and his strange friends—the so-called Immortals. Can't believe you were so blinded ... you don't even know who impregnated you!"

"Shut up Vishnu," she choked, tears rolling down. "The only reason I want to be here is for the protection of our children. Remember what Babaji had prophesied at the birth of the twins?"

"Unbelievable—you'd rather believe them than me! Is there something I am missing here? An affair perhaps?" He accused, took a deep breath and shouted, "Is Papa the father of your children?"

She slapped him hard on his face and locked herself in the bathroom.

In ten years of their marriage, Sumati hadn't ever seen this side of Vishnuyasa. He had treated her with love and affection. In Shambhala, though, they had had many arguments and cracks had developed in their relationship over the birth of the children. She looked at her reflection in the mirror. Red, puffy eyes with kohl smudged all over, stared back at her. Babaji's words echoed in her ears. "You are the chosen one. It's predestined. I bless you with the strength to endure the life that is going to unfold. As the mother of the avatar your path is going to be the most difficult. You must ensure the children are always with Raj, under his protection."

Agitated and desperate to be heard, Vishnuyasa walked up to the one anchor in his life who would understand his decision. His mother Sulakshana was sitting on the steps of the mandir on the lawns, gazing blankly into space. Her eyes moist with tears, she didn't even notice him approaching her. So, when he put his hands on her shoulders, she was startled.

"Oh, *baccha* … you!"

"Yes Ma, what are you doing here? There is still time for the sunset *arati*."

"Nothing … just sitting by myself looking at the lawn."

"Ma, I've finally got the opportunity to prove myself."

"Prove what? And to whom?"

"To myself. I want to stand up for the things I believe in. Use my law degree to serve the needy and the nation. Not fill my own coffers. At Nanda & Sons, we represent only the elite and upwardly mobile, many of them criminals, and ensure they win."

"*Beta*, your father has worked very hard to reach this position in society; the innocent don't need lawyers. Only criminals do," she said naively, bringing on an inadvertent, fond smile from Vishnu.

"With Uncle Tejasya managing affairs, we are the criminals now," he said quietly. "Things have changed since we left for Shambhala. Papa doesn't believe me. My repeated attempts to warn him have resulted in him doubting me and my intentions.

"VAS, our law firm, will work for the underprivileged and innocent who get framed by the likes of father and uncle."

"This doesn't sound good. How can you stand against your father in court?"

"I am looking forward to getting away from the scrutiny of dad's eyes. But I will miss you Ma."

"You are not shifting to Mumbai!"

"Don't worry Ma—and I promise to see you every month," said Vishnuyasa as he lovingly placed his head on his mother's lap.

Tears flowed from Sulakshana's eyes and ran down his cheeks. Wiping them with his hands he said, "Sumati and the kids will be here with you; only I will relocate. Like you, she too has chosen him over me," he mumbled softly as he closed his tired eyes, comforted by the gentle hands stroking his head.

8

Vishnuyasa

Vishnuyasa looked preoccupied and disturbed as he interacted with his older sons, barely making eye contact as he exchanged pleasantries. His visits to his home in Delhi had reduced considerably. He was meeting the family after six months. There was a visible dullness in his eyes, a droop in his shoulders as if he was tired of everything in life.

"What's the matter?" enquired Sumati. "You've lost a lot of weight!"

"It's nothing. How are the boys doing at school?" questioned Vishnuyasa.

"Is there stress at work in Mumbai?" Sumati tried asking again.

"Yes, but what do you care? You chose to live in the comfort of the Nanda household with your children."

"That's not true Vishnu … you know that," she pleaded. "We belong here. Ma and Papa will be alone here without us."

"What about me? Am I not alone there?" he snapped. "I have lived alone for one year in Mumbai."

"Come back then. Why are you severing your ties with your roots?"

"Never. I'd rather struggle in an unfamiliar city, and work earnestly than succumb to a lifestyle of luxury based on ill-gotten wealth and blood money."

"That's no way to speak about your dad. You've been too harsh on him."

"Ever since our return from Shambhala I noticed that the values our law firm stood for have changed. I've unearthed disturbing facts, brought them to Papa's notice. Nanda & Sons has been taken over and become Tejasya & Sons!"

"Talk to your mother. Tell her. I'm sure she can help," Sumati tried to comfort her husband.

Post dinner, whilst Raj and the children were reading, Sulakshana walked up to her son's room. He was on the phone talking in an agitated manner. Seeing his mother, he hung up and hugged her as he had held himself for the past two decades. And cried his heart out.

"Ma, I am tired. I am tired of fighting alone. The rot is endless and has percolated deep into our lives. It seems everything can be bought … even love."

"What happened, son? Why are you so dejected?"

"Ma … I have unearthed facts that would shake the ground under your feet, so they are best left unsaid."

"No, tell me what is troubling you," she insisted.

"There is a secret society that is trying to control the world. The reason we had to run away and hide in Shambhala."

"What? I don't understand! This sounds crazy. We left for Shambhala due to personal reasons and the violence. Once peace was restored, we came back."

"It's a sham. There is no peace. The entire electoral system is rigged around the world. In reality the secret society and global elite that control them select leaders they want in any given era, in any given country. This secret society's ultimate goal is complete domination of the world. And to achieve that they will stop at nothing."

"I don't understand."

"They have their representatives at all the highest levels in society—in judicial, financial, and even military systems. I have come across evidence that shows they had a hand in the spate of viruses that ravaged mankind in the last decade. All so that they could rake in vaccine profits to fund their hidden agenda ... and our family is mixed up in this sordid business."

"I am not sure what you are trying to say Vishnu." She looked at him with empathy. She noticed his hands were trembling as he spoke. He reeked of a mix of alcohol and weed, his eyes were bloodshot and speech a little slurred. Could she really trust what he was ranting about?

"What has come over you, Vishnu? Why are you bent upon destroying yourself? I can see that you have been drinking."

"No … no … Ma! Just once in a while," he lied. "To handle my depression."

"What depression?" she asked, now alarmed, moving closer to her son. "Forget the world. Just focus on your home—four amazing children, a lovely wife … involve yourself with them."

"Whose home? Whose children? Aren't they genetically modified uterine conceptions? I had no role to play in their births. There too I fell short! They were conceived in a laboratory in Shambhala and who knows about their paternal DNA…" He screamed in frustration, "Is it your husband's? He and his friend Babaji's plan to rid the world of evil by giving it four superheroes? Your husband has grandly taken it upon himself to right the wrong but isn't he part of the wrong himself?" Vishnuyasa held his head, muttering, "This is so confusing."

"Shhh … shut up Vishnu, the kids are awake. Stop your drunken rant," commanded Raj as he strode into the room.

"Oh welcome, Mr Nanda, your controlling authoritative attitude makes me sick."

"Cut the crap Vishnu—you've had a bit too much today."

"Yes Papa, I have." He fell on the floor crying. "It's my antidote to being under your control."

His speech was becoming more and more slurred. He continued, "You didn't even ask me before using my wife for your experiments."

"Shut up before I lose my cool!" shouted an alarmed Raj. Then, looking at Sulakshana with anger he said, "Call the doctor; your son is bordering on drug-induced paranoia. He needs a psychiatrist."

Vishnuyasa stood up and laughed. "Always deciding what to do and with whom. Please tell Ma what you did with your older brother Rajneesh. As for your younger stepbrother Tejasya—do you know he has underworld connections?"

"No, he doesn't! Don't you dare talk about Tejasya like that!" yelled Raj.

Vishnuyasa laughed and fell on the floor.

"Okay, keep believing the lies your brother has been feeding you."

Sulakshana helped her son up with great difficulty and seated him on the couch. She looked up at Raj with questioning eyes, but before he could say a word, Vishnu spoke again. He fumbled with his posture and speech, "We are living in a web of lies … pride … anger … envy. Tejasya Uncle has taken over our firm and is gradually leading us into destruction—and our deaths. I believe he is being guided in this by someone. Soon, I will know who."

Holding back with great restraint, Raj walked away from the room, disturbed at his son's behaviour and ranting. He wondered if the demon he was fighting outside had made inroads into his own home. Sulakshana held on to her son and tried to pacify him. He leaned on her for a few seconds then turned and left the room.

As Vishnuyasa hurriedly made his way out of the house, he heard the twins calling out to him from behind. "Papa!"

He turned around in anger at being stopped. He never spoke to the twins, disregarding their presence always. Rudr and Tarini ran up to him and looked at him with love.

"We hear your cries Papa!" said Rudr.

"We see your truth Papa!" said Tarini.

"Do you see us Papa?" they said together with their arms stretched out towards their father, eyes closed expecting a hug.

Vishnuyasa looked at them blankly … and walked away.

***

"You've failed me, Tejasya," complained an angry Shaheen, moving her hand nervously over her husband's bald pate.

"I had hoped that with your connect to the darker forces, you would have been able to keep Raj and his family in the hole they had retreated to a decade back. But you fell short there too. It's been a year since Vishnuyasa left home and we haven't got anything out of him yet. He is back in Delhi now and it's a matter of time before his mother convinces him to take over the reins of Nanda & Sons."

Banging the table hard with her right hand she screamed, "I want him dead now!"

"Shh… stop screaming," said Tejasya calmly. Fixing Shaheen with a sharp gaze he spoke in a soft, menacing undertone, "Don't talk to me like that! Don't tell me what to do. You're a short-sighted fool. My brother's long absence was bothering me. I knew he had something up his sleeve. A lion doesn't disappear with his brood into a cave forever. There is more to this than meets the eye.

"Thankfully he has emerged from wherever he was hiding. We are safer with him back in Delhi. Trust me. As for his son, don't you worry he will meet his end soon. That bastard has been tolerated by me for so long only to get answers regarding their disappearance.

"At least we have been successful in converting an upright, idealistic, stubborn man into a RIZE addict. The bastard is really messed up in his head now—and is doubting his own father. Watch how I tear apart the family.

"As for my connect with the darker forces, they are now stronger than ever before. In fact, I have requested them to invite you to be a member of the most influential organisation in the world today—Sphinx. Are you ready for more power dear wife?"

Tejasya laughed, blowing rings of smoke from his cigar into Shaheen's stunned face.

9

Kali

He stepped off a wooden boat onto the banks of the burning *ghat* and nonchalantly weaved through a maze of funeral pyres hissing, crackling and spitting orange embers into the night sky.

Sweat streamed down his face from the blazing heat. Smoke and ash were strewn everywhere. Little boys his age were crouched over a bed of glowing charcoal, sifting through the ashes, sinking their fingers into hot embers looking for something, anything that could buy them their next meal.

Kali reached into his pockets and threw some gold rings discreetly into the pile of ashes. He picked up a few broken, half-burnt bones and threw them to the dogs scavenging outside. Partially decomposed bodies floated downstream leaving behind a rancid smell. The silhouette of an abandoned mandir steeped in darkness with fire randomly emanating from within its tiny crevices was mesmerising. It was this temple that he had visited twice a year since his birth. His education had taken him all across the world but on his birthday and on the festival of Mahashivratri he would invariably be in the oldest city of the world: Banaras. Earlier, his Guru Shukracharya would accompany him; but since the past year, since he turned ten, Guruji had said, "Kali you're now old enough to travel alone."

His earliest memories were linked to this place. His eyes welled up as he recalled the nights he had spent alone in the crematorium at the tender age of three. His Guru had left him alone for two nights in the biting cold of December.

"Befriend the dead. Make peace with death. Understand, it's the only place we all are headed to."

Scared and cold, he had wrapped his hands around his knees and dug his face between them, petrified even to look up. The eerie silence was broken by a rough voice that spoke gently to him. "Don't be afraid, son." He looked up curiously and met her eyes. They were blood-red and her presence startled him. Yet when she held open her arms, he quickly let her envelop him. For the remaining two days he slept peacefully on her bosom, as she stroked his black hair, whispering into his ears words that remained buried deep inside him.

"My son, you're born to rule the world. This world and the others await your coronation. Be true to your breeding and Guru Shukracharya, and soon the three worlds will be yours to own."

When Shukracharya came back, he found the child drinking milk from a skull. Kali ran to him saying, "Guruji! Guruji! I met my mother. She is not an angel. She is a demon."

Shukracharya smiled. Bibi Maya had appeared as promised. Now the transformation of the child would be complete. "Looks can be deceiving my son. Your mother is no demon, but the threshold goddess of the three worlds and your father is Lord Shiva himself. That makes you invincible."

Kali was an alarmingly normal kid on the surface but his blind obedience to Shukracharya had profoundly horrific consequences. Having conquered fear, he experimented with life, often living on the edge. Mutation of genes and virology were his favourite subjects, and his Guru had set up a high-tech laboratory for him in the mountains of Antarctica. He had recently achieved success in infecting a local child with a deadly new virus, one that he named Kā.

"Guruji I've had a breakthrough," he beamed, as he explained his success to a visibly pleased Shukracharya.

"The virus causes a breakdown in a combination of molecular, neural and psychological patterns of the brain leading to a corrupt neural pathway that ensures that each following generation would be more evil than the previous one."

Shukracharya was ecstatic as he asked, "Have you infected anyone yet?"

"Tomorrow the world will be infected as I reach Banaras for my birthday. Mother will be so pleased with me!" Kali's green eyes shone in anticipation.

The Immortal
Mahabali

"Pookalams. Payasam. Sadya. Kaikottikali. Bliss unadulterated. It's my favourite time of the year, when my sleepy village in Kerala wakes up to festivities celebrating my annual visit to earth.

"Ah! The fragrant aroma of pulissery, that amazing concoction of pumpkin, yogurt and cucumber cooked tenderly over a slow flame … I salivate at the sheer memory. Today I am going to feast on Onam sadya, the traditional banquet with twenty-four vegetarian delicacies served on a banana leaf. All my favourite dishes are lovingly prepared in every kitchen today, and I make it a point to visit each household remembering me with love. See—now you know the reason for my pot belly!

"The bright flowers arranged in pookalams, the village damsels dressed up in golden mundu and neriyathu with jasmine garlands adorning their long tresses, their hips swaying gently as they dance the kaikottikali … it makes me nostalgic each time.

"Nothing has changed, the vibrant colours, the grandeur, the returning of families home for Onam … you see the joy around?"

"No, I don't see anything you're describing. All I see is darkness."

"No, no. Rub your eyes, look again," Mahabali urged the trembling man before him.

The hugely obese King of the Netherworld was once again daydreaming at night. Attired in the finest silk of the South, his exuberant personality was reflected in his gold jewellery and red veshti tossed casually over his broad shoulders. Mahabali cursed under his breath and wiped the corners of his betel leaf-stained mouth with his hand.

"Everything has changed, hasn't it?" he asked again in a gruff tone, staring deep into the man's eyes—and then broke into a hearty laugh. "Ha ha! You're looking down my ass, chances are you are going down to hell!"

Scared and confused, the young man looked around the large room for help. He deserved no mercy; he had masterminded a terrorist attack at a school in Antwerp. Kripacharya had left him with this eccentric man who told stories from the past.

The Immortals dispensed their own form of justice, presided over by Mahabali. Offenders that escaped the failing law and order machinery of the world were caught by their divine noose and brought to Mahabali. He then decided their fate in hell, but only after they transferred all their wealth into a secret account. Mahabali was the undisputed king of the shadow world—with unwavering faith in Vishnu. He always held the rosary on one hand, whilst executing criminals with the other.

Mahabali wrapped his strong arm around the murderer's neck, almost choking him, and continued with his storytelling.

"Lord Vishnu himself visited me in his dwarf reincarnation, the Vaman Avatar, when I was the ruler of the three worlds. It was the first time that an asura commanded such respect. The demigods and gods were running helter skelter after being dethroned by me. They sought Vishnu's help and he obliged, taking birth as a dwarf saint in a poor Brahmin family to recover all that the demigods had lost.

"I was aware it was Vishnu himself in the guise of a poor beggar who had come to ask for alms. I freely gave away all that I owned. He could have just asked and I would have obliged—but he preferred to hide in disguise. I played along with his act. I generously gave up ownership of the three worlds he asked for and fell at his feet. That's when he blessed me with immortality. All this while my Guru Shukracharya was trying to save me from my fate."

The story finished, Mahabali tightened his grip, snapping the neck and killing the man in seconds. He clapped his hands loudly, and four well-built men arrived. "Throw him into the raging fires," he instructed.

Mahabali rushed into the adjacent room, and poured the holy water of the Ganga, stored in a copper pot, over his head.

He was to meet Kripacharya at a board meeting in Geneva, Switzerland, in the next few minutes. He stood before the mirror and looked intently into it. His body proportions began to change; he was now fair, thin and tall, totally unrecognisable as the portly King of the Asuras. He donned a crisp white shirt and a grey suit, but retained the flamboyance of a red tie. He swirled thrice with his hands outstretched and arrived on the 22nd floor of the appointed building in Geneva.

Kripacharya smiled at Mahabali's current get up. Adept at disguise, he looked the part—an angel investor. The MOU signed with the Swiss gentlemen, the two walked towards a coffee shop.

"Vishnuyasa's life is in danger," said Kripa grimly.

"I cannot intervene. Kapi has Shukra's blessings and I am forever indebted to my Guru."

"Mahabali, we are never going to be able to defeat the dark forces as long as you let Shukra's protégés roam freely. Kapi is the very fount of all evil."

Gulping down a large cappuccino, Mahabali looked at Kripa fondly, and spoke his mind.

"You know this better than me—when the time is right, the dark forces will be defeated."

"But Vishnuyasa's life is at stake now! Can't you help him like you helped his father Raj?"

"Oh, that was a long time ago. Shafique, the Chief of Police and the Home Minister, were in it together and were conspiring against Raj. They would have killed him, had I not picked them up and flung them into the raging fires."

10

Release

Vishnuyasa drifted in and out of consciousness. The pain was unbearable and he kept fainting, only to be woken up with a harsh jet of water. He finally managed to open his eyes to complete darkness, and as his head cleared, he realised he was hanging upside down, his hands and legs completely immobilised. He could hear something breathing in the room; the acrid stench made him want to throw up. As his eyes slowly adjusted to the darkness, he was startled by the creature with pale blue eyes, slithering from one place to another. The pig head bobbed erratically as if it was too heavy for the thin long neck with the protruding Adam's apple. Unnaturally long, thin fingers, each like the tendrils of a parasitic plant, took his dangling face into the palms. He could now hear the pig-man wheezing as he whimpered gibberish into his ear.

The pig-man grunted and swiped his bulbous tongue along Vishnuyasa's face, making him throw up. In a while, the darkness in the room was dispelled with the dim glow of a candle. Vishnuyasa could see the hazy silhouette of a short figure at the far end of the huge chamber surrounded by more pig-men—the *mlecchas*.

All of a sudden, men dressed in full black attire with masks entered the room, each holding a candle. They surrounded a short disfigured man. Tejasya stood to one side of the *mlecchas*. One of them punched him hard on his face just above the nose on the left eye, whilst the others fell on their knees swaying in some bizarre ritual. The pig-man beside Vishnuyasa whined and grunted.

"Yet another befriends pain in the quest to become more powerful; yet another initiated into the cult," rang out a fearsome voice. The room darkened again as the candles were snuffed out. A long, haunting silence descended, inducing Vishnuyasa into a fitful sleep.

Vishnu awoke to a stinging slap—and a familiar voice.

"You son of a bitch, speak up! Come on—tell your uncle—where did you all disappear for ten years?" shouted Tejasya, as he split Vishnu's upper eyelids, one at a time. He himself sported a black left eye.

The torture had been unending. On his arrival from Delhi, Vishnu was picked up by Abhay Sawant and was driven from the airport straight to this hell. He had literally walked into this death trap. In pain, yet relieved that he hadn't spoken, Vishnuyasa turned his face away, more determined than ever. As his vision blurred, all he could see was blood. He called upon his inner strength to remain quiet. Soon the body would perish but his soul would remain untainted.

"Tell us—who all did your wife sleep with? Why do your sons look so different from each other?" mocked a female voice.

Unable to reply or react, Vishnuyasa cried tears of blood as Tejasya poured acid over his eyes, making him faint in pain.

The torture continued. At some point, he passed out.

Vishnuyasa stirred into consciousness feeling as if he were drowning. He soon realised that he was now chained to a bed. Drops of hot oil were hitting his forehead in between the eyebrows, aggravating the burning sensation in his eyes. Blinded and in excruciating pain, he cried out for merciful death.

There was a sudden silence in the dark, windowless, shabby room. A bright white light filled the space, the magnificence of which made Vishnuyasa see the truth clearly for the first time. He was now free of all physical and emotional pain. He saw himself standing in front of Rudr and Tarini as they spoke to him.

Rudr said: "We hear your cries Papa!"

Tarini said: "We see your truth Papa!"

"Do you see us Papa?" they asked together with their arms outstretched and eyes closed, expecting a hug.

He hugged them tightly. "Yes, I see you now."

He fell on his knees, hands folded and head bowed. He wept with joy and called out lovingly, "Kalki!"

Yada yada hi dharmasya glanir bhavati bharata
Abhyutthanam adharmasya tadatmanam srijanyaham
Paritranaya sadhunama vinashaya cha dushkritam
Dharmasansthapanathaya sambhavami yuge yuge

Whenever virtue subsides and wickedness prevails, I manifest Myself.
To establish virtue, to destroy evil, to save the good
I manifest from age (yuga) to age.

11

Angkor Wat

The aristocratic Kripacharya kept pacing around in a frenzy. He looked at his smartwatch set according to the Vedic calendar yet again to make sure he had calibrated it to local time. He was awaiting the arrival of seven other Immortals at Angkor Wat, a magnificent temple complex in Siem Reap Cambodia—the largest Hindu monument in the world.

Angkor Wat (Temple City) was built around the 12th century AD. It was originally a Hindu temple dedicated to Lord Vishnu, its central tower representing Mount Meru, the Abode of the Gods, considered the centre of the universe. Lore had it that since Vishnu is the supreme deity, before whom all other deities sit, facing east, Vishnu faces west. Hence Angkor Wat, dedicated to Vishnu, faces west.

Ancient Hindus believed in the sanctity of funerals done at this vast, serene temple complex.

Kripacharya had called for this clandestine meeting rather urgently and the other seven were arriving from different corners of the world. Now, finally, they were all here.

The tallest of them all, Ashwatthama, spoke first.

"*Pranam* Guruji. It's surreal that the last time we met was at this very location."

"Yes, this time too I have got the mortal remains of yet another departed brother. His ashes should be blessed and buried facing the west beside his ancestors. Vedji, it is only befitting that you chant the holy verses and invoke the mercy of God."

An angry voice interjected. "This savagery has to be stopped now. Vishnuyasa was tortured in the most inhuman way. I am getting impatient. We have lost many to this depravity. *Pralay* has arrived. Guruji, give me permission to get back at this evil," said the broad-chested Hanuman with folded hands.

"Not yet! We have to be patient and prepare ourselves for war, Anjaney!!" said the soft-spoken scholar, Ved Vyas.

Irritated and anxious, Hanuman enquired, "What are we waiting for? This long and arduous wait doesn't seem to end."

With an endearing smile, the baby-faced monk Markandeya spoke: "Good things come to those who wait, dear brother. Our time will soon come."

"Yes … if anybody should be complaining it should be me," said the man with the pus-oozing forehead. "The agony that I have lived with … each day seems like a century. Yet, I know we are closer to our goal than ever before."

Incessant rain fell at Angkor Wat accompanied with lightning and thunder, raising the water level of the rivers, as the eight men chanted.

"Om Houm Jum Sah
Om Bhur Bhuvah Svah

Om Tryambakam Yajamahe
Sugandhim Pushti Vardhanam
Urvarukamiva Bandhanan
Mrityor Mukshiya Maamritat
Om Suva Bhuva Bhu
Om Saa Juun Houn Om."

Facing the west, the eight Immortals formed a circle, each holding the silver urn covered in red cloth. The water level at the temple complex was rising and by the time they completed the 108 chants most of the temple was submerged in knee-deep water. Yet the eight remained dry as if standing a few feet above the ground. They entered the central foyer of the temple complex, and with a flick of his fingers, the baby-faced monk moved the lattice formation of the tiles to disclose an iron-walled chest beneath. Inside was a gold box with an inscription of Vishnu's pledge:

//Dharmasansthapanathaya sambhvami yuge yuge//
(I will manifest age after age to establish virtue)

They opened the sacred box filled with urns and placed a single silver urn inside with the vow: "Today we leave you here dear Vishnuyasa. We will come back with our Saviour, your child, in due course to immerse you in the holy Ganga. Till then rest here in peace dear brother; your death shall be avenged."

12

Betrayal

Nattily dressed in a royal blue wool and silk blended suit, with diamond cufflinks, Raj Nanda puffed away at his Bolivar, an uncharacteristic frown marring his handsome face. He could barely trust his eyes as the details scrolled up on the 42-inch touch screen monitor at his desk. A few flicks of the finger and there was no escaping the truth: Nanda & Sons was embroiled in scams of great magnitude. In disbelief, he removed his glasses, cleaned them and placed them back on his aquiline nose. With enhanced clarity he could now see through the maze of deceit and lies that had been built over the decade he had been away at Shambhala. The flash drive that had arrived mysteriously at his home, and was handed over to him by Tarini, shook him to the very core of his being. It detailed reports of all the transactions at the law firm including some unmentionable businesses that were being run under his name. Also detailed were the firm's stakes in the pharma business that had made blood money by vaccinating the world against various viruses.

He was furious as he stepped out of his private jet a while later and ordered his secretary to leave him alone. He walked towards his Range Rover deep in thought. Vishnuyasa had been right all along!

Raj sat in stunned silence as the car sped ahead. It was the ultimate betrayal. He felt his throat explode as a piercing cry escaped his mouth, scaring his driver, Moti Singh, who brought the car to a screeching halt.

"*Saheb* are you okay?" he enquired, turning around.

Raj didn't reply, only nodded his head. His ashen face however revealed the pain of deceit. Moti Singh drove his master silently and swiftly to the law firm. This was the first time he had seen a distressed Raj.

"What the hell has been going on here?" shouted Raj as he strode into his brother's cabin.

"Plenty. I am glad you finally asked. We have been accumulating wealth. Our turnover quadrupled since the time you were away," said Tejasya, beaming.

"Vishnuyasa was right. I didn't believe him when he warned me against you and the evil that perpetuated in the firm."

"What nonsense. Vishnuyasa was a junkie, a RIZEr who needed a fix every day! Admit it—he was a thorn in your side doing you more damage than I ever could. It's just as well you got rid of him."

"Shut up Tejasya," roared Raj. "Are you accusing me of the murder of my own son?"

"I have proof that you're the legal representative to the dark group Sphinx that murdered your son. So, yes!"

Raj stared at his brother in anger and disbelief. The reputation that Raj had painstakingly built over a lifetime as the subcontinent's best counsel was about to be destroyed. There were loud whispers that Nanda & Sons was amongst the most corrupt law firms, having vested interests in money laundering and high-end land and mining deals. Everything that Raj valued—honesty, integrity, family—was at stake. The final blow was being accused of having a hand in his son's death. He drew a shaky breath as his shoulders slumped in defeat.

"Look away as you did in the last year and you can still get a share," offered Tejasya nastily.

"Or what?" screamed Raj, as he reached out and caught Tejasya by the scruff of his neck. Raj was practically choking his younger brother in rage, the brother he had loved and trusted.

"Who is breaking us, tell me Tejas, who?"

Tejasya managed to press a hidden button and two burly security guards stormed in and separated the two at the nick of time.

Tejasya fixed his shirt and moved a trembling hand over his head. Still a little shaken by the sudden turn of events, he gulped down a glass of water and lashed out at a furious Raj, now in the grip of his guards.

"It's quite simple—I switched sides to feel powerful; something I could never feel with you around. I am now addicted to all it gives me … and what you call 'evil' I see merely as a brand new way of living, of doing things. I have already kept the documents ready. Sign them and walk free."

"Or what?" spat Raj.

"Or else Mr Raj Nanda, I'll tell your wife the truth about our brother Rajneesh. Better still, I could send your precious grandchildren to join their dad. The one you got killed."

"No!" screamed Raj, the colour draining from his face.

Rajneesh was the family's dirty dark secret, a secret Raj had buried in the past. He would do anything to keep it that way—for it would only bring his family shame and dishonour.

Raj had lost his son to a terrible death because of his blind faith in Tejas. No more. It mattered not what he possessed. He needed to protect what he still had. It was now the time to choose between good and evil.

Raj quickly signed the papers and walked out on the empire he had built from scratch four decades ago. He turned back to look at Tejasya one last time, with contempt, anger and finally, pity. "You don't know what you have done, who you are up against. Kalki will destroy you!" he spat out.

13

Naked Truth

"Wake up and smell the coffee," said Babaji as he walked into the house he so loved. The Nanda mansion wore a desolate look as the playful chatter of the children was nowhere to be heard.

"What have you done Raj? Your arrogance and anger have done you in once again!"

Sulakshana prostrated before Babaji. Her face betrayed her loss. Raj was slumped in a chair, sunk in an abyss of despair.

"Raj get up and move, your words to your brother have put the entire family at risk. No one is safe here anymore," said Babaji sharply.

"We have Kalki. Why can't he protect us and avenge us? What is the point of his being in my house if he can't even protect his own family?" mumbled a disconsolate Raj.

"You are not the centre of the universe. Stop making it all about you and your family. It's your resistance to what is happening that is causing your suffering. It's time again to make a change in your lifestyle, in your thinking."

At that moment Sumati walked into the room.

"You had blessed us!! What happened?" she cried accusingly, hurt and confused.

"Every man's journey towards his death begins the day he is born. Vishnuyasa was a good soul; he had fulfilled his purpose on earth and is on a forward journey. As for you, my precious, it's time to say goodbye to your children."

"What do you mean? No, please don't make it any more difficult for me," sobbed Sumati. She looked pleadingly at Sulakshana. "I am just beginning to get a hold of myself. I won't be able to go through any more changes."

"The only thing constant in life is change my dear," reassured Babaji calmly.

"This isn't about you or me or us … it's about the children and their future and, in turn, the future of the world."

"I am not ready for this."

"Look beyond yourself Sumati—go back to their births. Didn't we all know that the path we had chosen was going to be difficult?" Babaji continued, "Your children are not your property; they are just born through you. They have come to fulfil their karmic journeys."

"They are so small, how will they manage to live on their own?" she pleaded.

"Brilliantly. They will bloom in their independence. The blight of attachment that is destroying this house and its people has to be lifted."

Sulakshana intervened, "Can we get some more time with the children? I am afraid all this will be too sudden for them. Rudr and Tarini are still in preschool."

Kripacharya walked into the house and joined the discussion, unannounced.

"It's time for the children to leave the comforts of home to follow their own destinies. It's paramount that everyone in the family goes their separate way. It is essential to keep the family safe.

"Guru Shukracharya has raised a formidable dark force, it's spreading everywhere and penetrating all aspects of life. He has eyes and ears everywhere.

"Sumanta, the oldest, will accompany me to Germany. He will be homeschooled at a fellow brother's home in astrophysics. Pragnya will study numbers and finance in the UK. He will join a boarding school at Leeds."

As all eyes in the room questioned his decision, Kripacharya clarified, "These are choices made by Sumanta and Pragnya themselves.

"Sumanta is a loner. He is an idealist, who loves to work alone, and physics is his favourite subject. He prefers homeschooling. Pragnya thrives on competition and wants to go to boarding school. They are ready and excited with the opportunity."

It was Babaji's turn to speak.

"Raj, while this house has been in mourning, I have been regularly meeting the boys through teleportation."

"Babaji, teleportation! How?"

"Quantum physics is about the bizarre and impossible. About objects disappearing and reappearing elsewhere and being in two places at the same time. It's a highly evolved yogic science practised by a handful of *yogis*."

He further explained, "There are trillions of atoms in the human body, which can be broken down, reconfigured, digitalised and teleported—only to be reconstructed again at the new location."

"That's incredible!"

"Yes, it is. The scientific world is yet to get a breakthrough in what we *yogis* have been doing for millennia."

"And Rudr-Tarini? Where do they go?" asked Sumati, breaking into the conversation. She was feeling more lost than ever with the sudden change of circumstances in her life.

"The twins need a *gurukul* for a few years. Our learned and trusted brother Ved Vyas will set up an *ashram* at his home in Uttaranchal," informed Kripacharya.

"*Gurukul?* But that's outdated, Babaji. Will that prepare the children for this world?"

"It's the need of the hour. The *ashram* is the safest place. It's impenetrable as long as Ved Vyas resides there. First and foremost the twins will receive spiritual education as recommended by our ancient scholars. They will study grammar, logic and ancient scriptures. This foundation will prepare them for their formal education, empowering them with confidence and empathy, enabling them to be of service to the society.

"Sumanta and Pragnya also learnt the Vedic scriptures at Shambhala. I taught them myself. Did they go to a formal school at Shambhala? No. Yet on commencement of their formal education in a Delhi school, they outdid all the students. Didn't they, Sumati?" Kripacharya pointed out attempting to drive home his point.

14

Sumati

Sumati sat lost in the huge house, reminiscing the good times gone by. She was staring out at the beautiful Nanda lawns but her mind was anchored in the past, when she was a newlywed bride…

The coming together of two different musical notes can either create music, or cacophony. Vishnuyasa and Sumati created music. He, with his restrained, upright outlook, and she with her happy, childlike disposition. They completed each other's voids and rounded off each other's personalities. Sumati warmed up to the Nanda household instantly; they made her feel so loved and Vishnuyasa was always gentle and caring.

As she packed her bags for a holiday, she hummed a tune softly, looking forward to Paris and Venice. Then she heard her husband's agitated voice in the adjacent room. "But, this wasn't planned."

"Yes, I know. Babaji couldn't make it to the wedding hence the need to go to Gangotri to seek his blessings."

"We leave in two days for Europe."

"So what! We can come back in a day from Rishikesh."

"No, I am not going now, we can go later."

"Let me ask Sumati if she's not too exhausted to travel."

Sulakshana intervened in the father-son duel, as usual.

"Vishnu, it's beautiful up in Gangotri now. The snow is beginning to melt. Start your new life with the cherished blessings of Babaji," she cajoled.

"Who is Babaji, Papa?" enquired Sumati, walking into the room.

"Babaji is my friend and spiritual guide."

"I would love to meet him."

"Great, we leave early tomorrow morning."

On their way in the car from Rishikesh to Gangotri, Raj spoke to Sumati about Babaji and the important place he occupied in their lives.

"I've heard that if a friendship lasts longer than seven years, then it will last a lifetime. It's been so true about Babaji and me. I can't remember our first meeting, since I have known him all my life. We were one other's shadows from our earliest days. But I do remember our first fight. I was angry with him for cycling on my brand new Atlas. I pulled him down and kicked him hard in the stomach. He suffered in pain for a week, missing both school and play. Yet when I went to apologise, at my mother's insistence, he smiled gently and held my hand.

"Aditya, or Babaji as he is now known, had always been saint-like in his disposition. He was a genius in mathematics. While I topped the class in history and language, he topped in science and math. We were inseparable, often dining in each other's houses. After that day, we shared everything. Adolescence and teenage years were fun because together we were a brat pack! He loved nature and would accompany me and my parents to our summer home in Dehradun. While I'd play soccer, he would be gazing at the mountains for hours, as if in deep conversation with them. It was during one such summer break that a monk showed up at our door, asking for Aditya. They hugged each other like long-lost brothers and to our amazement, Aditya left to accompany him to the Himalayas.

'My Guru has called for me. I need to go.'

'What Guru, you don't even know these people!'

'Don't be impulsive, come back, your parents will be mad at me for letting you go,' admonished my father.

'Tell them. They will understand,' he said, as he hugged me and walked out.

"Surprisingly, his parents did not react when we called to inform them. They said their son would be fine. They were sure.

"For the longest time my parents and I worried about him, till I received a letter from him. He was well and undergoing rigorous training. My teenage mind declared Aditya mad and I got busy with studies and other friends.

"He returned unannounced, a few years later, leaner and fitter.

"We spent endless nights looking into the skies, while he told me stories he had heard and things he had experienced up in the Himalayas. I was enthralled and promised him that one day I would accompany him to his mystical land. He had finished his schooling through distance education, in the meantime I completed mine in Delhi. Both of us applied to Oxford for further studies. Our applications were accepted and together we set off to explore the world.

"I studied law and he, astrophysics. We were roommates but as my debating and social nature blossomed, his reclusiveness increased. Till one day he decided to move out of our room to a single room. I was shocked initially, but he gently explained his need for quiet introspection and deep meditation. Imagine—our friendship suffered its first blow due to quantum physics!

"After he moved out, I barely saw him since our courses and lectures were in different university blocks. I went to meet him the day his thesis on quantum physics was given a gold medal and he earned a scholarship to study further in the University of California, Berkeley. Yet again, he surprised us all by declining the scholarship.

'Why? What's wrong with you Aditya?'

'Nothing. Physics is not my life path.'

'You've realised pretty soon brother!'

'No, I always knew it. I wanted to do research on the cosmology of *tantra* vis-à-vis the cosmology of quantum mechanics. Having done that, my mind is satiated.'

'And?'

'And, I now know how the astonishing coexistence of incoherent and contradictory ideas creates turbulence and chaos in our lives, just like in the universe.'

'Aditya, my friend, don't you see you are brilliant in physics? Pursue it further, rethink before declining the scholarship.'

'I have applied to universities in the US to study management in finance.'

'What? Where did that come from?'

'Numbers entice me,' he said with an enigmatic smile, leaving me totally perplexed as I walked back that cold December morning from his dormitory to mine."

"Papa, did he pursue finance then? When did he become a monk?" enquired an eager Sumati.

Vishnuyasa slept peacefully in the comfortable bucket seat of his newly acquired Range Rover. The drive from Rishikesh to Gangotri was a long one, but the conversation had kept them preoccupied and soon, they were at their destination.

"Yes, he always achieved what he wanted to. Investment banking was booming two decades ago, and he was at the forefront of the industry, leading the mergers of state and public banks in the US."

"Awesome, then!"

Raj continued. "He called me one day to meet him at a pub near Heathrow Airport. We had a great time, laughed and drank together and then he startled me yet again.

'Raj ergodic averages for almost all initial conditions from the evolution of time are always perturbed by some noise, being replaced by a stochastic process.'

'Umm!! What Aditya?'

'I mean, I'm done with the world and its noise. I now seek silence and solitude in the Himalayas. My master is no more. I have to go back.'

"I nearly fell off my chair. I was a few drinks down, but this revelation got me cold sober. All I could mumble was a meek, 'Are you sure?' At which he laughed yet again."

"That's crazy," said Sumati.

"No, it's not," retorted Raj. "My friend understood the meaning of life long before I did. He has been my guide ever since, my spiritual Guru, my connect to the divine. He has stood by me and supported me through, specially tough times."

The swanky car arrived near the sparse hut in Gangotri. The two friends embraced. One living a Spartan life, the other, caught up in the web of luxuries he had created. They hugged and shared tea from the same tumbler, as they had done in the old days when there wasn't enough money.

Babaji met Sumati warmly and blessed the newlyweds.

"Your coming together is preordained by the universe, my children. May you live in love, peace and abundance. May the Goddess bless your womb and fill it with divine energy." Vishnuyasa and Sumati blushed, touched Babaji's feet and thanked him for the blessings.

A gentle knock on the door got Sumati back to the present. It was her father-in-law. "You cannot spend your life in the past. Come, let's find you a new home," he said gently.

"I am at my home," she cried, tears welling up in her eyes.

"This will always be your home Sumati. But you need to think of your future. We will not be around forever and you will need companionship."

"I am not leaving you two. Never!" She closed the door on him and flung herself on her bed and cried bitterly.

Raj had kept quiet all this while. He had expected this reaction, but he knew he would eventually be able to talk sense into her. Meanwhile he had to find the perfect match for his sensitive daughter-in-law.

"Aren't you being too picky, RK?" chided Sulakshana.

"Yes, I am. But I have to make sure that Sumati is happier in her new home than she was here. That the man she marries gives her more happiness than our son ever could. She has been an exceptional daughter to us, and we must gift her a life of love and happiness."

"RK her apprehensions are justified. As a woman you don't just marry the man, you marry the family. Not too many people are receptive to a second marriage, especially where the woman has children."

"Who said anything about the children?"

"What do you mean?"

"They are my responsibility, my grandchildren. I am never going to abandon them. She will have a new life; a new beginning. She is lonely with all the four kids gone. It is not going to be easy for her."

"Excellent. You seem to have it all worked out. Please let me know too what I should do after she leaves as the loneliness in this huge house weighs on me."

"You and I will be fine Sush. And, like you said, the house is too large for us; once they all go we both can move into something smaller," he said, looking away.

"RK look at me, what's wrong? You are hiding something from me," she demanded.

He held her hand and led her to the sofa. "I have been swindled by Tejas, my own brother … we have nothing left except this house."

Sulakshana stared in disbelief. "The firm Nanda & Sons. It's yours."

"Written off."

"How could this happen? My son was right—but you never listened to him. You kept quiet when he suddenly died," she said accusingly, sitting down suddenly, in exhaustion. "Was my son killed by your brother? I need an answer!"

"No, Sush. It's more complicated than that. I am beginning to believe…"

Her face turned ashen, as time froze for her.

"I will chase that at a later time. For now, I have pressing tasks to finish," was Raj's brusque response.

Sulakshana watched in disbelief as he stood up and poured himself a drink.

"A few sacrifices, for the greater good. Long ago, even before our marriage, Babaji had declared that my family would be the cradle of the impending avatar. That the weaklings in the family would either have to be hidden or destroyed. Each generation would require the sacrifice of its weakest."

"Who is the weakling Raj, are you referring to our son?"

"No, no, Sush … well maybe," he said as an afterthought, not wanting to say more.

Sulakshana sat stunned, unable to comprehend the man she had spent so many years with.

"I need an answer Raj, who is the weakling?" she demanded.

"Rajneesh, my oldest brother," he whispered under his breath.

"Did he not die very young in a car accident along with your parents? What about him?"

"Let's forget the past, we have a lot to plan for in the present."

"Now I understand the urgency in wanting to send everyone away," said Sulakshana sadly.

"I have put our house up for sale. Have found a buyer already; he has given us three months to vacate. With the money received, the kids' education will be secure.

"The Immortals have taken over the responsibility of the children. To shape their future, to protect and guide them to fulfil the destiny they were born for. The least I can do is pay for their education."

Wiping tears from Sulakshana's eyes gently he said, "No one else should know of our tribulations."

"Where will we live?" she cried.

"Moti Singh has found us an accommodation near his home. I'm sorry, but that's all the money we will have left for."

"Why can't we go to Shambhala?"

"Evil is tracking us, we will need to tread carefully. Shambhala was created by the Immortals specifically for the birth of the avatar and our other grandchildren. Access to it is only at the will of Babaji and the Immortals."

Shocked and confused at the sudden turn of events in her life, the demure and ever-giving Sulakshana started mumbling to herself. "Sacrifice ... each generation. Oh God! My son. Avatar. Immortals..." Her head was spinning with the revelations. She pressed her temples in distress.

Wanting to reassure himself as much as his wife, Raj spoke.

"Don't worry. Babaji is bringing together his banker friends to help me set up a new venture. We will be fine. We have so much to be grateful about..." he stopped mid-sentence as his eyes fell on Sumati, standing quietly in a corner.

The look on her face said everything.

Her eyes were red with anger, her long hair a mess around her face. She spoke in outrage: "Was my Vishnu murdered? Did you keep it from us? Told us he died of drug overdose?

"Today I can see through your lies. I never believed my husband when he said you wanted to control our lives for your selfish gains. Our relationship suffered because of you. You are a megalomaniac Mr Nanda!"

Sulakshana stood up and walked towards Sumati, asking her to keep quiet with a gesture of her hand.

"No Ma! Let me speak today." She helped the distraught Sulakshana to a sofa.

"What's going on here Mr Nanda? The shit has hit the roof! What sacrifices are you talking about? Are you talking about the death of my husband as a sacrifice? I believed you and your Immortals and lent my womb not once but three times for the greater good, much against my husband's wishes; stayed with you, while he walked away towards isolation, addiction and finally death."

"Sumati, have patience, it will all be okay." Raj tried to sound convincing.

"What will be okay? Your son is dead. Your brother has taken over your law firm. Ma has lost her house and my children have been taken away from me!

"And if that wasn't enough, you are planning to get me married off again. I say no to you and your plans. I am not going to be a part of this circus anymore!"

Without looking back, Sumati turned and walked up to her room, feeling a surge of independence for the first time since her marriage. A few hours later she left the Nanda home.

The Immortal
Ved Vyas

"If you live in this realm, chances are you have heard of me, Ved Vyas Krishna Dwaipayana (the twice born). I, of course, know you, just like I did your grandfather and his grandfather. Stupefied? Don't be.

"As the world's astrologer and foremost author, I ought to know, don't I?

"Now don't ask me about the future of your world. That question is outdated—I had answered it all five thousand years ago.

"I, Krishna Dwaipayana, have watched my predictions come true—the degeneration of the human intellect and along with it, the fall of the human race. I had laid it down for you, simplified our ancient scriptures and divided them into four. Taught you about the one reality—that one goal we are seeking.

"I insisted time and again through the Puranas, Upanishads and Bhagwatam that the goal of life is to seek one's true self. And yet look what you have done—gone to the moon and back and yet never spoken to yourself! I had taken pains, spent decades condensing our sacred texts to make them easy for you to grasp—and what did you do with all that knowledge? The only thing that interested you was the tragic tale of fratricide amongst my descendants, 'The Mahabharata'.

"I was born to a mixed parentage. My father was a Brahmin sage, an astute astrologer, Sage Parashar. My mother, a fisherwoman, Satyavati. I inherited my mother's dark colour and medium frame and my father's brilliant intellect and fierce demeanour.

"As a young child, I chose to be with my illustrious father after promising my unwed mother that I would be there for her, whenever called upon. As a disciple, I eagerly learnt scriptures from my father. I was an outstanding student and in my teens had begun documenting our scriptures in the written form. Till then, they were only passed on orally.

"Meanwhile my mother married the Kuru King Shantanu, thus making me and his son Bheeshma stepbrothers.

"Bheeshma came searching for me at my mother's behest after the Kuru clan abruptly ended with the death of our stepbrother Vichitraveerya. Bheeshma had vowed celibacy and hence my mother called upon me to perpetuate the Kuru clan. Thus were born my children Dhritarashtra, Pandu and Vidur. I also fathered Shuka, my spiritual heir from my wife Pinjala.

"The war that ensued between my sons' children was the fault of the older generation. Their opposition to evil was ineffectual. While they postured advocacy of dharma (righteousness), they actively propagated its exact opposite, adharma.

"And though I knew, I could do nothing but stand by helplessly. To foresee destruction yet being helpless is no boon!

"The immortality I was blessed with is a dual-edged sword, just like my birth between two islands … neither here nor there.

"Having lived in the deep chasm between the yugas, in quiet introspection, my last notes were authored five thousand years ago. I live in cosmic consciousness with the ability to be where I want when I want, at the speed of thought.

"Puzzled? Yes, of course you are. How would you understand?

"You would probably call me a paranormal phenomenon. The difference between you and me is death. Death separates us. You live a lifetime, die and forget, suffer rebirth with no knowledge of your past, live again, die again, forget again—on and on. I live, and continue to live through the yugas in higher consciousness, totally aware of myself and my being.

"Yet your atman is eternal just like me.

"Wondering what I do with my time and do I have a family in this, your time on earth? I teach courses on history and philosophy at universities as visiting faculty. I change my place of work every few years—it would hardly do for my colleagues to

realise that I am not ageing! I come back to my ashram in my original avatar when generations change.

"The entire world is my family—Vasudhaiva kutumbakam.

"It is time for me to be a Guru to the Vishnu Avatar yet again, and while I trust him, I don't trust the times! Will his sanskaras be tarnished by the effect of Kali Yuga? I wonder … my efforts, therefore, will be to keep him protected from the scheming Shukra.

"We are all seekers, each one wanting a different slice of life. I seek to end the story I had scripted.

"I seek mortality…"

15

Kamadhenu

At the *gurukul*, Ved Vyas initiated the lotus-eyed Rudr, who was sober, solemn and smart enough to understand the significance of wearing the sacred thread called '*Brahma Sanskara*'.

"Guruji why does Rudr wear the sacred white thread and not me?" demanded Tarini.

"Be grateful girl you are getting an education in a *gurukul*, which was out of bounds for girls earlier."

"Yes, I am grateful Vedji; but that does not answer my question."

"The thread ceremony is only performed for Brahmin boys."

"Says who?"

"Our scriptures."

"You wrote them. Can't you correct your mistakes now?"

"What do you mean Tarini?"

"Tarini means that boys and girls are equal," intervened Rudr.

"True that. Thanks, Rudr," said the pleased sister.

Ved Vyas smiled at being questioned by the twins. They were quite a handful! But that night he lay awake wondering if he was responsible for the patriarchal world of today.

Rudr and Tarini soon commenced their study of the Vedas.

"Vedji please tell me another story," pleaded Tarini, as the twins sat with folded hands on the mat. Ved Vyas, of medium build, with dark skin, long beard and shoulder-length hair tied into a knot with a string of *rudraksh* beads, sat on a small rectangular plank across his two students.

Every day the Guru would teach his wards through stories from the Vedas and Indian scriptures. With this knowledge called '*stuti*' (that which is heard), they learnt the right pronunciation of words. The twins would then have to comprehend, assimilate and interpret the meaning of the lessons imparted by their Guru. The knowledge thus received had to be meditated upon till there was complete internalisation of its essence.

"Guruji, have you seen cows?" asked a bright-eyed Tarini after listening to a story about the divine cow Kamadhenu.

"Yes. At one time my *ashram* was full of cows. Each student had to look after three to four cows. Their milk nourished the growth of the student," said Vedji, with a faraway look in his eyes.

"What happened to all the cows then?"

"They perished in a pandemic last decade. The world has changed much, dear children, in the last 30 years. The coronavirus lasted half a decade, killing millions and bringing the world to a halt. And just when some semblance to normalcy returned, the deadly cow virus struck, killing cattle globally. The culture of mindless consumption and increased urbanisation and industrialisation led to depletion of natural resources, including grazing grounds for the cattle." He rolled his eyes. "I haven't had pure cow's milk in a while. My stomach doesn't take too well to processed milk, so I became vegan."

"Let's start creating the right habitat for cattle to grow," said an angry Tarini to Rudr.

"Yes, Tarini. I think Guruji really misses the cows."

The next morning Ved Vyas was pleasantly surprised to see the Kamadhenu cow herself at the *ashram*, and Rudr and Tarini playing with her calf. He immediately knew that Rudr had used his *siddhis* (supernatural powers) to manifest the divine cow. Pleased, he instructed the twins to drink as much of her milk as they could to help with their mental and physical development. A few days later, the two students along with their Guru went for a walk towards the sea.

"Guruji, you look tired. Allow me to carry you." So saying, Rudr, all of eight years, effortlessly swooped up the lean sage into his arms and leapt up to fly to the shore, with Tarini running far behind.

"Here Guruji," he said to a startled Ved Vyas, as he placed him by the waves, smiling indulgently.

Ved Vyas looked around uncomfortably to make sure no one had seen them flying. He could not believe what he saw next! As the twins ran towards the sea, the waves retreated. The further their feet ventured, the further the sea retreated. Rudr and Tarini were laughing their hearts out at the playfulness of the sea as they kept jumping ahead and the sea kept retreating. Vedji realised that Rudr had complete control over the elements now and was enjoying displaying his *siddhis*. It worried him.

"Enough Rudr. The sea can't go any further. Stop the game—now!"

"Yes Guruji," smiled the lotus-eyed boy.

The twins were inseparable. They loved each other's company and encouraged one another constantly.

"Rudr, I'm missing *Bhaiya Bade* and *Bhaiyaji*," said Tarini one day.

"Let's go and meet them then!"

"What? How?"

"Remember how Babaji used to meet us through teleportation? I can do that too."

Astonished, Tarini exclaimed, "What!"

"I wanted to meet *Badi Mumma* the other day so I closed my eyes and meditated on her. I was in her room the next minute, eating my favourite pudding from her hands."

"What did she say?"

"She smiled as if she was expecting me and said to keep meeting her."

"Weird, these grandmothers," said Tarini.

"Yeah," said Rudr.

"So is it that simple? Will I be able to teleport? No! No! It's too scary. What if I can't come back? I am not doing this Rudr!" exclaimed Tarini.

"Of course you can. Remember who we are," reminded Rudr as he flew up and down in his room. He was enjoying his superpowers.

"When did you get these superpowers?"

"Don't know, I guess from the beginning, but I realised it only when I saw the look in Vedji's eyes while talking about Kamadhenu. I wanted to gift her to him. So I concentrated and meditated on her and she appeared. I was shocked myself. Then I started experimenting and realised I could fly if I wanted to. Could become small or big, could control nature, could manifest what I wanted, from chocolates … to a plane!"

"Cool! My superhero!" said Tarini as she hugged Rudr. "So much fun! Hey … did you say plane? Can we take one to go to meet our elder brothers?"

"Yes! Of course. But what do we tell Guruji? It will take a few hours.

"But he is away meeting Guru Kripacharya—so let's not say anything. We will come back soon. He won't know."

"Great! Call for your plane then. Let's go, Rudr, I am so excited!"

A supersonic aircraft soon appeared at the *ashram* and the twins took off on their journey to Europe. They arrived shortly outside Pragnya's school at Leeds. They had wisely chosen a forested area near the school to land so as to not being seen. As soon as they landed, Rudr commanded the vehicle to disappear. They walked to Pragnya's room where he was studying.

"Oh my God! How are you two here!" exclaimed Pragnya, hugging his younger siblings in delight. "Where are mom and *Bade Papa*?"

"Shhh … we have come alone."

"No way! How?"

They explained, and convinced him to accompany them to meet Sumanta in Germany.

In a short while, they were narrating their adventure to Sumanta, who sat listening bemused. But the next minute he was admonishing them. "You both will be in major trouble. Vedji and Guru Kripacharyaji will be worried and looking out for you."

"Don't worry *Bhaiya Bade*, we will reach back in an hour. You have to see the supersonic plane. It's the most brilliant piece of technology ever made. It travels above the earth's atmosphere in space at supersonic speed," exclaimed Tarini unfazed. She had so much to say to her older brothers about her twin's magical superpowers.

"Rudr stop being a show-off. You know that these superpowers cannot be misused. They are there to achieve more significant things other than a sweetmeat or a joyride," Sumanta chided Rudr. "And you, Tarini, need to keep this a secret and not tell the world. Remember Babaji told us that we each have superpowers. At the right time, we will need to use them. Till then we have to be normal, blend in society, hone our skills and build on our strengths—not dissipate them."

Sumanta then looked at Pragnya. "And you should have known better. You are more aware of the world scenario today..."

"As for you two, now rush back, apologise to Vedji and never do this again," concluded Sumanta as he accompanied his siblings to the supersonic plane and, secretly excited, made his way to the cockpit.

"Wow!" he gasped, admiring the stealth technology and zero emission engine. This was no ordinary pair of wings—it was a highly evolved futuristic machine, the likes of which was still being researched. He looked at Rudr with a new sense of pride, and a slight hint of envy.

Once Sumanta left, the siblings spoke. Tarini was scared as she inquired, "Why was *Bhaiya Bade* so upset? He wasn't happy seeing us at all."

Rudr too looked puzzled.

Pragnya whispered, "I am not sure, but I have heard the seniors in the dormitory talk about Kā, a terrible virus that has spread across the world which corrupts the minds of people and makes them demon-like. There are only a few of us protected from the virus by an inbuilt mechanism, something to do with eugenics. Our revered sages like Kripacharyaji are keeping us safe in hidden bunkers like in Shambhala, in highly guarded sanctuaries, or helping us blend into the populace unobtrusively such as here at Leeds. We have lived all our lives cocooned from the reality of the world."

"What is the reality of the world *Bhaiyaji*?" enquired Tarini, wide-eyed and eager to know.

"What is Kā?" asked Rudr.

"The virus that is making humans into mindless, savage demons. They are a cross between human and pig—as terrifying as they are filthy. We call them *mlecchas*."

"I don't understand, if we are protected, why do we have to hide?" questioned Tarini.

"We hide to be alive, or we could be dead meat for the demons."

As he disembarked from the plane, near Leeds, he warned the twins, "Be safe!"

16

Kali Yuga

Ved Vyas turned the pages of the *Bhagwat Purana*, a literary text he had written thousands of years ago.

"What do you want me to read?" he questioned Kripa.

"*Kali Yuga*," came the reply.

"In *Kali Yuga*, deception, dishonesty, sloth, somnolence, cruelty of every kind, grief, delusion, terror, and wretchedness rule. This is the Age of *Tamas.*

"Depleted by dreadful taxes, tormented by disease and drought, starved, owning no bare necessities, men will seem more like *bhuta* and *pishacha*. As the age turns to evil, every virtue decays and vanishes; honesty, forbearance, cleanliness, kindness, longevity, memory, and strength."

Vyas' old eyes looked up at Kripa, who was staring out into the dark sky.

"Oh Vyas!" he sighed, "Didn't we start with *Sat Yuga*? How did we get from there to here?"

The two wise men stood on the horizon, looking down at the world in decline.

Yet another city was plunged into darkness and despair due to floods—but not of water; floods of disease and corruption, death and devastation.

The earth, as if conspiring along with its inhabitants to destroy itself, was relentless in bringing on natural calamities. The magnetic field of the earth was shifting at a speed never seen before, causing the molten iron in the earth's core to erupt. Volcanoes, earthquakes and tsunamis had become frequent. As the poles shifted, the hot and cold air drifts collided to create steam and clouds so dense they enveloped the earth in darkness. The sun was shut out from the earth's atmosphere for months at a time. Without its healing rays, bacteria and viruses flourished, unleashing disease and death.

But those who hold power, hold hope. They shoulder the responsibility to save creation. So the two sages did what they had to let the sun shine on the planet they protected.

Just as the world was waking up to sunlight after months of darkness, and the sages were ready to take a breather, Hanuman appeared with a look of concern.

"The twins are travelling," he announced with agitation.

"Travelling? Where?" inquired a shocked Vyas.

"To meet their siblings, Vedji."

Kripa shook his head in disbelief. "But how is that even possible? Be clear, dear Vayuputra!"

"Rudr and Tarini are travelling in a supersonic aircraft."

There was a long silence.

Kripa closed his eyes and a tear rolled down. Finally, he spoke.

"Thousands of children were massacred by Shukra and his allies the year the twins were born. My heart goes out to each mother that lost her infant to Shukra's insane purge of newborns in an attempt to kill the Avatar at birth. Especially the woman whose infant was sacrificed at the Dashavatara Temple.

"Shukra and his allies have already got earth on life support. They have burnt the canopy, polluted the skies and the oceans, and flooded the world with waves of disease. He has fanned famine, hunger, strife, and brought the world again and again to the brink of war. He is hoping to flush out Kalki—to create such chaos and destruction that the Saviour will be forced to reveal himself...

"We have literally moved heaven and earth and everything in our control to keep the twins protected. But look at them—so carefree and unconcerned with consequences, like ordinary kids. They are well aware they are special!"

"I always believed that we are investing too much of ourselves in saving this planet, its self-centred people and their gods," said Parashuram curtly, as he appeared beside the trio.

"Dear Anjaney, leave right away and protect the twins at any cost. Shukra has been waiting for moments like this. We cannot let him have his evil way. Vedji—set up another *ashram*; I am afraid this has been exposed.

"Kripa, your plans for the children's education will have to change. Let them study remotely as far as possible. I have heard of universities that have no fixed location; where the campus periodically moves overnight to any city in the world—nothing is predictable because they believe in training their wards to survive and thrive in a world of uncertainty and chaos. This might be a good alternative for the twins' higher education. Let them not remain at any place for too long. It's going to be a continuous effort to keep them from being exposed."

Hanumanji bowed before the three venerable sages and faded into thin air. Soon, he was a raging tornado moving towards Ved Vyas' *ashram*.

17

Trial by Fire

"Oh no—something is wrong Tarini," screamed Rudr as they were tossed up violently inside the aircraft. "I am losing control."

"Look there Rudr," pointed Tarini as they looked down at their *ashram* which was ablaze. The aircraft had been hit. Rudr pressed the emergency door open as Tarini hugged him tightly. The twins leapt out of the blazing plane embraced in a tight hug. On their way down Tarini saw an army of *mlecchas* and Rudr could see the destruction around.

"Don't be afraid Tarini—remember who we are," assured Rudr.

"It's all our doing Rudr!" she blurted, terrified.

They landed with a thud on the ground and were immediately surrounded by the pig-men. They made a formation of '8' whereby each twin was separated by a circle of *mlecchas*. Wasting no time Rudr started tackling *mleccha* after *mleccha* in a burst of physical agility. Tarini too sprang into action striking the martial arts capoeira pose which she had mastered at the *ashram*.

The skies now started raining bullets and were overcast by fighter planes. The children huddled together, cornered.

"We are dead meat," announced Tarini to Rudr.

The irritating buzz of the flies was replaced by the distant whistle of a ferocious wind, which gradually grew louder, and was finally accompanied by a blinding dust storm. Minutes later as the haze lifted, the bodies of *mlecchas* and some monks were seen. The *ashram* had been reduced to a pile of ashes.

Tarini felt herself sucked into a huge gust of wind like a tornado, swirling high, round and round. She was nauseous and about to throw up when they landed on the floor of their bunker at Shambhala. Hanuman materialised briefly, hands folded, with concern in his eyes. Having accomplished his task, leaving the twins in the secure presence of the great sages, he made quick eye contact with the Immortals present and vanished yet again to rush to the rescue of a devotee calling out his name.

Kripacharya, Ved Vyas, Babaji and Raj looked at the twins in anger.

"You have exposed us all! Wide-ranging attacks have been launched on all our hideouts. Sumanta and Pragnya have suffered grave injuries, but thankfully timely help arrived and they are recovering under medical care," hollered a furious Raj. "We have lost a lot of lives today, to ensure your protection. If it were not for Hanumanji's timely intervention, you both would be dead today."

"I am so sorry *Bade Papa*," Rudr apologised, his eyes full of tears, his head bowed, hands folded.

"*Bacche* … your ways fascinate me," scolded Kripacharya. "Let me explain. Natural disasters have made water and food scarce; the Kā virus has corrupted the human DNA. We in India are at the centre of it all."

"How is that Guruji?" asked Raj.

"We have the Himalayas and our rivers are still flowing, though barely. The land is thus fertile and cultivable and we are one of the few countries that are the source of food and water for the planet. However, the *mlecchas* have already taken over most of the once-great *Bharatvarsh*," said Kripacharya grimly.

"Let's kill all the *mlecchas* Guruji. I am ready," Rudr spoke calmly.

"No, it's not time yet. We have to equip ourselves better to fight this powerful evil. You have to be in hiding till the masters teach you all that they know."

Ved Vyas looked sombre. "I should have stopped the children when I first saw the manifestations of their superpowers. But I enjoyed their trysts with nature. I had no idea that Rudr had called for a supersonic plane. The fact that it has been brought down despite its stealth technology speaks volumes for the preparedness of the enemy.

"I faltered, I will correct my mistake." He looked sharply at Tarini and said, "You will leave now to live in America and not return for the next 20 years."

"And you Rudr, as *gurudakshina*, I take away all your superpowers. For the next 20 years, you will live like a normal human being, get educated and gain profound knowledge. The memory of any superpowers will also vanish now!"

Raj stood speechless with his head down. The decision had been taken by the Ancient Ones. He revered them and he knew that he and the children were blessed to have their guidance in their life. But 20 years? He thought that was too far away; would he even be around by then?

Kama

To satiate or sublimate desire? Be in bondage or soar free towards a higher bliss?

18

Narkanda

Rudr awoke to the chirping of birds. His head was heavy with confusion. He last remembered being in Shambhala. How did he reach the boarding school at Narkanda? He was beginning to feel like a puzzle that had the central piece missing. It took him a while to get into the rhythm of his new life.

The death of his father Vishnuyasa, the hushing up of events that followed, siblings being sent away—it was altogether a lot to deal with for a ten-year-old. His way of dealing with the inner chaos was to immerse himself in nature. Narkanda, perched at more than 2000 metres above sea level and dotted with conifers, was a haven. Ever since he could remember, on the rare occasions he was confused or upset, he had always found it healing to listen to the twitter of birds, the gurgle of a rushing stream, or the gentle breeze amidst the rustling leaves and swaying trees. He especially loved it when birds and little creatures of the forest flocked to him fearlessly, happy to be petted.

Rudr spent hours on his own exploring this richly scented forest, part of which was enclosed within the school's premises. It was during one of these solo trips that Rudr sensed an eerie and spooky presence. Ghost stories were always doing the rounds at tuck at the boarding school, with friends outdoing each other to narrate the most horrific ones. He stood rooted to the spot. It was just past sunset—6.15 p.m. to be precise. The chill had set in; the breeze had dropped; there was no birdsong or chirp of crickets; just a quiet, eerie silence. Scared, he turned around slowly, despite himself—and saw a tall apparition right before him. He froze. The apparition started floating away and soon disappeared. Rudr thought of the time he had visited the local crematorium with one of the gardeners. Of that eerie sense of peace and comfort he had felt. He felt that same connection with something beyond his ken now. He decided against telling anyone about the incident, lest they think him crazy. Who would believe him?

The next day, sound asleep, he had a sudden feeling of being deeply uncomfortable as if he was being watched. His eyes flew open—and standing at the window was the same apparition, looking at him intently. There was something sad and familiar about the presence, he thought. Why, it even had a ragged bandage on the forehead! But his heart raced with fear. The spectre melted away.

Back into a fitful sleep, Rudr's stomach churned and tears flowed as he saw an unusual looking plane careening out of control—with him in it. He escaped somehow, hurtling headlong towards some strange, menacing creatures. They were clustering around, ready to attack. He felt trapped, helpless—he could almost smell their terrifying stench. He cried aloud and awoke in a deep sweat. But there was no one—only a peaceful darkness broken by the snores of Sumer, his roommate. Days became weeks and then months, till one day Rudr broke out of his cocoon of terror. The nightmares stopped and he was comfortable in his skin.

***

The girls' dormitory was at war. "What were you doing with my boyfriend at tuck?"

"Yours? Really? You stupid girl, see your face. A hunk like Rudr deserves a beauty like me."

"Let's go and ask him because just yesterday he looked into my eyes and said he loved me," claimed yet another girl.

Together they marched off to the football ground where Rudr was practising with the team. Seeing them approach, Sumer mocked, "All your girlfriends together! All the best, buddy."

"No sweat, Sumer. I have it under control, just excuse me for a few minutes from the game."

He ran across to them, smiling. "Hey! What's up?"

"Tell us now—with whom are you in love with? Preeti, Neha or me?" demanded Anu.

"Love … you all!"

"Really! Then why did you tell me yesterday that you love me?"

"I love all of you. I see the 'Devi' in all of you."

"Had enough of your wisecracks. Come clear," sobbed Neha.

"No … really!"

"If I knew what love is I would break my heart into three and give one to each one of you. Till I find out, give me time to perfect my game and ace my grades!"

Rudr was the captain of the football team and also the Head Boy. The surging hormones of adolescence reflected in Rudr's newfound love for girls. He was a charming conversationalist with a personality to match; and his haunting guitar drew fangirls like a magnet.

Rudr's smooth talk saved the day yet again—his girlfriends walked away exasperated, yet each secretly appeased. He grinned as he headed back to the game—there was nothing he loved more than masterminding the moves.

"Anger and aggression are part of football, Coach," protested Rudr a while later, as he was pulled up for yet another foul.

"You broke his front teeth."

"No, I didn't. He hit me and in reflex I kicked him in the face. His luck that his teeth broke … I didn't intend to."

"Get me back in, Coach—the team needs me to score."

"Not until mid-time."

"Thanks! That gives me enough time to look up the kid who got hurt on the opposing team."

"Why would you want to do that? First you hurt him and then go asking about his condition. That's crazy!"

"No, it isn't … on the field it's war. Off the field we are part of the same human race."

"I don't understand you," said the confused Coach.

"Neither do I!" laughed Rudr, as he made his way towards the rival team.

Life is good, reflected Rudr. Graduation Day was approaching and he had an unconditional offer from the Tertön University Consortium to study at their global campuses. The first one, Oxford University, had offered him the PPE (Politics, Philosophy, Economics) programme. The most gorgeous girl from school was dating him and he felt like the king of the world! He was strumming his guitar when he was informed that he had a visitor.

"That's unusual," he thought; no one visited him ever. The rare times Babaji had visited him was clandestine and the meeting was planned months ahead. For his annual holidays too, he never went home like the other children. Instead, he went home with Sumer. Initially it hurt that no one missed him. What had he done, he had often questioned himself. Why did his entire family disappear from his life? Even his mother and twin sister, whom he so loved and missed…

"You will never tell anyone about your family," *Bade Papa* had warned.

"But why? What are we hiding?" He had questioned relentlessly. "My head hurts … I am confused *Bade Papa*."

"When the time is right, everything will be clear. Till then consider us all dead," *Bade Papa* had said as he walked away from his life. Rudr had done just that. Forgotten his past and family and immersed himself into his present. His past life became a complete blur.

Walking towards the visitors' room, he saw a familiar, chilling silhouette. As the figure turned, he noticed the bandaged forehead. Suddenly the sky turned dark, clouds gathered and lightning struck. It seemed as if thunderbolts were going to fall right on top of his head. And then, just as suddenly, the storm clouds passed to bathe the entire region in splendid sunlight as Babaji emerged with hands outstretched and a warm smile. Rudr rushed into his open arms and hugged him tight for a few moments.

"Babaji!" he cried in joy, "Where were you for so long?"

"I am here now son and that is important," Babaji smiled.

"Why are you dressed like a banker, what happened to your robes?" Rudr enquired.

"Need of the moment son," Babaji laughed, adjusting the collar of his shirt.

"Joining me for a ride, Rudr?"

Rudr jumped at the chance to be alone and away with the only family he was left with. The two held hands and walked towards a pristine white Jeep Cherokee, Babaji's favourite wheels.

As the sleek machine zoomed past the school gate, it was put on cruise control, and Babaji began to speak.

"Did you know that when a mother tortoise buries her eggs in sand on a beach, she moves a distance away and then gazes at her eggs with such love and affection that her warm gaze causes the eggs to hatch? In the same way a Karma Guru pulls the strings of his disciple's life, whatever the physical distance."

Babaji parked the car at the top of a hill near a corn-on-the-cob vendor. He jumped out of the car and soon, like a hungry child, started biting into the juicy corn slathered with lemon and spices. Wiping his mouth with his forearms he offered his half-eaten corn to Rudr. "Here enjoy!" he said. Taken aback, Rudr politely declined.

"Let's get to the point Babaji," said Rudr bluntly. Being in boarding had made him independent and outspoken, willing to stand up for what he believed in.

"You feel you have acquired knowledge my son, but there is a whole different world outside academia waiting to be explored."

"Yeah—so?"

"So, I'd like to invite you to my world, up in Gangotri; but it's not for the faint-hearted," he said, baiting the bravado of youth in Rudr.

"Let's go, Babaji. I need to be back soon for my IB graduation and then I leave for the UK."

"No, no son! Has knowledge become so cheap that it can be acquired in days? Finish your graduation. Take a gap year and come to the Himalayas."

19

Gangotri

The water of the Ganga sanctifies all the three worlds…

Rudr landed at Jolly Grant Airport at Doiwala outside Dehradun. As he got into the waiting cab that would take him to Rishikesh, an hour's drive away, he wondered at his bold decision. He had been enthralled as a child with Babaji's stories about the Himalayas. Now here he was, at Babaji's behest, curious and eager to spend a year at Gangotri.

The holy town of Rishikesh is populated with godmen, spiritual gurus, pundits and astrologers, and attracts hordes of believers and divine seekers. To say that every second person in Rishikesh was linked to a godman would not be an exaggeration. The place looked ethereal in the evenings, especially the magnificent Ganga *maha arati* held at sunset by the riverbanks.

Babaji was waiting to receive him at the Haveli Hari Ganga, a quaint palace hotel in town—this time in a simple saffron robe. Babaji generally stayed at one of the *ashrams* but gladly consented to his friend and Rudr's grandfather Raj Nanda's suggestion this once; he knew that from the following day onwards the year would be full of hardships for Rudr.

"Trust *Bade Papa* to make the best arrangements!" exclaimed Rudr, delighted with the place; and more so to see Babaji. They quickly made their way to the riverbank for the *arati*. Almost all the priests knew Babaji and bowed in reverence seeing him, seeking his blessings. It was dusk and almost time. A sonorous crescendo of bells accompanied the ritual chanting of hymns dedicated to the river goddess. The blazing multi-wick brass lamps and simultaneous dispersal of thousands of *diyas* and flowers into the river offered by devotees made the Ganga glow radiantly like a bride. The air crackled with powerful energy and Rudr was, inexplicably, moved to tears. He was captivated by the spiritually uplifting spectacle, and the other-worldly aura of the place.

***

They rose early at 4 a.m. the next day and started for Gangotri, a distance of 248 km from Rishikesh, by car. The picturesque journey was dotted with small towns and villages. Three-and-a-half hours later they reached Gangotri *taluka*. The air was crisp and fresh. Rudr was famished and requested a break before the 17 km trek towards Gaumukh, their final destination.

Piping hot *puris* and *aloo* gulped down with a large glass of *lassi* re-energised Rudr, now all set for the trek.

"Gangotri town is at a height of 3,100 m in the Himalayas. It is located in Uttarkashi district in Uttarakhand, on the banks of the river Bhagirathi," said Babaji.

"The holy river originates 19 km from here, at Gaumukh, in the Gangotri glacier, where it goes by the name Bhagirathi. It becomes the holy 'Ganga' from Devprayag onwards where it meets the Alaknanda." It was fascinating to see the two rivers merge at Devprayag—the fast-flowing, refreshing green Bhagirathi playfully rushing down the mountains literally bumping into the calm, unhurried blue Alaknanda. From Devprayag the mingling waters coursed ahead as the mighty Ganga, emerald-hued, expansive and serene.

The Gangotri glacier was a tough place to live in but Babaji had made his abode in a natural cave amidst dense jungles and high mountains. The steep climb made even the taut and athletic Rudr breathless.

"Rudr, by the time you leave Gangotri in a year, you will be physically, mentally and spiritually transformed," pronounced Babaji, patting him fondly on his back.

They spent that night in a tented accommodation at Chirbasa, midway towards Gaumukh. Seventeen-year-old Rudr could not sleep the whole night as he was cold and was disturbed by the sounds of the jungle. The thin mattress spread over the cold grass was a far cry from the luxuries of life he was used to. He realised that the coming year was going to be full of new challenges; this was only the beginning. Babaji was up at 4 a.m. and soon they proceeded towards Gaumukh.

The most dangerous part of the trek was the Geela Pahar, a notorious rockfall zone. It was known as much for its dangerous landslides as for its mountain goats called *bharals*. But with Babaji guiding Rudr, they soon made it to Bhojbasa. Here they were received by a group of Babaji's followers or *chelas*. The entourage slowly moved up the treacherous path towards the majestic Mount Shivling, crossing the boulder zone on the way. By late evening they reached the *kutir*, the simple hut that Babaji called home.

Rudr was both tired and hungry, but was embarrassed to admit his exhaustion to group members who were at least two to three decades older than him, but looked entirely unfazed. The thin mountain air was making Rudr extremely uncomfortable, and when he saw the hut he was to spend a year in, he felt dizzy with anxiety. One of the younger *chelas*, Sushant, noticed Rudr's state and immediately arranged for hot tea. He covered Rudr with blankets and made him lie down. The warmth of the blankets and the hot tea lulled a fatigued Rudr into deep sleep.

"What time is it, where is Babaji?" mumbled Rudr, awake after 20 hours. A relieved Sushant explained, "You have slept for almost an entire day and night. I was worried you wouldn't get up. But Babaji assured me that you were fine and would wake up once the body acclimatised to the high-altitude terrain. Babaji has gone into his cave to be in solitude and has asked not to be disturbed till he decides to come out. He has asked me to explain to you the duties you need to take up and leave you here alone till he joins you."

"My duties? Leave me alone? Why is Babaji doing this to me?" an agitated Rudr asked Sushant.

"You will gradually understand the reason for all that Babaji does, but for now please do abide by his orders.

"For the next three weeks, your routine shall be as follows..."

The next morning Rudr woke up at 4 a.m., piled on all his warm clothes and started his walk towards the Ganga.

His morning duties were to fetch two pitchers of water from the icy Ganga. It was dark and cold as he tried to find his way to the river. The monkeys and the birds were yet to wake up. Freezing and alone in the dark, he abandoned the trip, found his way back to the *kutir* and slept till noon. On waking up, he reached for the water pitcher, it was empty; not a drop of water in it. He looked around the small room—there was no water or food. Just then Sushant walked in.

"Hello Rudr, how was the walk to the Ganga?"

"Cold and crappy. I came back less than midway."

"Why?"

"Because it was uncomfortable, scary and too early."

"So now, you will have to live without water or food … till you fill the pitchers."

"Can I not buy bottled water from somewhere?"

"Sure, you can but you will have to walk to the nearest village, about twenty kilometres away."

"Where do you get your water from?"

"Babaji said that from today you would be looking after my needs for water too."

"What? How does he expect me to go back and forth so many times with filled pitchers?"

Sushant answered with a shrug of his shoulders.

"Okay, let's go, the sun is out, won't be as difficult now."

"Sorry Rudr, I can't accompany you."

"Why?"

"Babaji has told me not to." So saying, he walked away.

Shaking his head in disbelief, Rudr picked up the empty pitchers and started for the Ganga again. He raced down the narrow trails 75 metres below, but slipped and slid grazing his elbows and knees, the copper pitchers rolling away merrily. He dusted off the mud, grabbed the pitchers and started yet again. Thirsty and irritated, he finally made it to the river.

The icy cold water, flowing at a frantic pace, soothed his nerves as he bent down to quench his thirst. Sated at last, he looked around and was spellbound by the beauty of his surroundings. The majestic snow-clad Himalayas, endless green mountain slopes, and the sparkling azure water darting across the gleaming river stones were all in complete sync with each other. A sudden sense of peace descended, stilling his troubled mind. He quickly filled the 20-litre pitchers and started back. The long walk carrying 20 litres in each hand turned out to be an intense cardiovascular workout. A merciless sun made it all the more difficult to go up and down carrying weights six times. He reflected, sheepishly, that early mornings were a far superior idea!

The next morning, he started for the Ganga at 4 a.m. sharp and experienced the joy of seeing the breaking of dawn in the Himalayas. As the sun rose, the mountains draped in dawn acquired a beautiful golden hue … the birds chirped and bees buzzed, the *langurs* playfully jumped tree-to-tree in search of food, and from high up the slopes the *bharals* came down towards the water. He inhaled the crisp dew-laden mountain air and once again felt a tranquil peace within him. The breeze whispered in his ears as if chanting "Om … Om … Om…" He felt an amazing burst of energy within every cell in his body. As he observed the gentle swirling foam of the glacier, he picked up the silt and rubbed it on his wounds. Sushant had spoken about the wonders of Himalayan silt on the skin the previous night. Being rich in minerals it worked as a moisturising disinfectant.

Soon, his first challenge in Gangotri—carrying the water-filled pitchers—no longer felt so exhausting, as the lungs were functioning optimally, renewed by the cold mountain air. Where once he had dreaded the drudgery of this trip, he now looked forward to going to and fro because each journey was unique.

The first few weeks were a time of building awareness and minimising needs. The branded clothes were replaced by a white *langoti* and *phatua* (cotton loincloth and shirt). He gathered *pangdi, kanda* and *mool* (edible roots and tubers) from wherever they grew and cooked them on a wood fire he built. He seasoned the dishes with *lado* (mountain spice). Sushant had given him a bit of ghee to cook with. "All monks carry *ghee* up to Gangotri from the plains. Food prepared in *ghee* keeps the joints lubricated in the cold air up in the mountains," Sushant said.

The early evenings were meant for gaining knowledge that had been passed down the centuries. An old monk, Gyan Vatsal Swami, guided Rudr through various *stotras* every day: *Panchadhsodhyaya*, 15th chapter of the *Gita* called *Purushottam Yoga; Shivmahima stotra; Adityahriday stotra; Sahasranam stotra; Shiv Stuti; Upanishad Shantipath;* and more. He would study late into the night, by the light of a kerosene lamp made out of a used *ghee* box and wick. The light emanating from this rustic lamp was filled with earnest and spiritual intensity that enriched each cell in his brain and body. He pursued the study of scriptures relentlessly, drinking to his heart's content the nectar of wise words. Treatises written a couple of thousands of years ago were still relevant for today's day and age.

One day as Rudr emerged from deep meditation, he felt a powerful blow on his head. Caught unawares, he held up his hands protectively, only to be beaten blue on his feet. He pushed his perpetrator—a gaunt, fierce man with exceptionally bright eyes—and put up a brave fight, bleeding profusely till the sages in the nearby *ashram* came to his rescue. On seeing the attacker, they all bowed in reverence—it was Tyaga Baba himself.

"Salutations, Respected Guru, blessed are we to get your *darshan*," said the sages in chorus. "What auspicious event brings you to us—what could have made you give up your meditation, high up on Mount Kailash?" enquired a senior sage.

"This boy here is special and I have been drawn to him," said the ascetic. Holding Rudr, he lovingly ran his rough hands on the wounds on his legs. The bleeding stopped and the pain ceased. Rudr was wonderstruck to see his wounds heal in a matter of seconds.

"Miraculous! I have never seen anything like this before!" he exclaimed.

"You haven't seen me before either," smiled the sage. "I hereby accept you as my student. From today I will train you in the art of self-defence and *Kriya Yoga*.

"Mind you, in our lineage, the Guru always chooses his disciples, and I have chosen you, so live up to my expectations."

"W-why me?" was all Rudr could stammer.

"You ignorant fool, are you questioning my judgement?" roared Tyaga Baba as his eyes turned red.

The two elder sages hurried up to Tyaga Baba and got him busy in conversation while a few *brahmacharis* quickly took Rudr to one side and whispered in his ears.

"Just bow down, touch his feet and accept him as your Guru."

"Who is he and why are you all scared of him?"

"We will explain everything later. For now, fall at his feet."

Rudr prostrated before Tyaga Baba. "We start your mental and physical strength building from tomorrow."

"What time and where sir?" enquired Rudr.

"Learn to let life flow, Rudr. Don't compartmentalise and pre-plan everything. And please stop calling me Sir. Call me Guruji."

The *sadhus* of the *ashram* lovingly prepared a feast for the sage who rarely descended from the elusive Mount Kailash.

Not one of them, or anybody else they knew, had ever been able to scale this sacred mountain. Tyaga Baba ate to his heart's content and walked away into thin air, just as he had arrived.

"Gosh, did you see that Sushant? He just melted away in front of our eyes."

"Unbelievable … almost like a mirage. Who is this great soul?" questioned Sushant.

"Sushant, you should know!. You're writing on the Himalayan saints," chided an old sage.

"No, I don't. Who is he?"

"He is one of the *Chiranjeevis*—a Saptarishi … a direct disciple of Shiva."

"What—oh my God!" gasped Sushant.

"Can someone please tell me what's going on?"

"He is a *mahapurush*, the male ancestral founder of the Tyaga, Anavati and Nambudiri Brahmin communities," said another sage.

"The Guru to Bheeshma, Drona and Karna, the mighty *maharathi* and Immortal—Parashuram!"

The sages were talking animatedly amongst themselves; a lot of them were there only to touch the hallowed ground Parashuram had walked on.

"But why is he called Tyaga Baba then and not Guru Parashuram?"

"Because he sacrificed the bliss of the heavens to remain amongst mankind. He was there during Rama Avatar in *Sat Yuga* and the Krishna Avatar in *Dwapar Yuga*, and they say he will be the Guru to *Treta* Avatar Kalki too."

All eyes were on Rudr suddenly. "What? Why are you looking at me like that?"

"They think you are the last Vishnu Avatar Kalki," said an awed Sushant.

"Why, just because a thought-to-be Parashuram decides to be my Guru, I become Kalki? Outrageous! How do you even know that Tyaga Baba is Parashuram … hearsay I'm guessing."

"Because I told them so," intercepted Babaji, as he joined the company.

"Will you take my word for it or do your lawyer genes need more proof?"

"No—I trust you completely Babaji! I'm just a bit overwhelmed by all the attention I'm getting."

Babaji laughed and said, "Enjoy it, son, while it lasts. Now that Tyaga Baba has taken it upon himself to mentor you, I am relaxed and can go back to my cave."

"But, I don't know him. It is absurd that he appears out of thin air, gives me a beating, heals my wounds and then embraces me as his student."

"I knew you were special the day you were born … when I was called upon to make your natal chart. Son, our life is the result of many past births and karma accumulated through them. The universe is very intelligent. Each one of us is exactly where we are supposed to be. You will not find a coconut tree up here in the Himalayas, just as you will not find a pine tree by the sea.

"The great masters can look beyond the normal.

"To my Guru Parashuram you are an open book. And let me tell you that to reach here and be blessed to not only have *darshan* of one of the living spiritual Gurus, but also be accepted as his disciple, speaks volumes about your soul and karmic journeys.

"I can understand all this is very overwhelming. But look at the Ganga … she has only one goal and that is to unite with the sea. For that she sometimes becomes a narrow rivulet, at times gushes with full force, at times is quiet and slow, and flows over boulders and stones with just one focus—to reach the sea. You too should just have one goal: to merge back into the divinity you have come from. For that, go with the flow. Don't judge. Don't intercept. Float and flow in this beautiful journey called life," explained Babaji.

"Guru Parashuram is one of the seven living masters, the hallowed Saptrishi, who have walked the earth in every age from the beginning of 'Time' and will be here long after you and I are gone. He is also known as one of the Vishnu avatars, so understand the magnitude of him choosing you as his disciple."

"How can anybody live for thousands of years? Scientifically it doesn't make sense," said Rudr.

"*Parkaya pravesh* is an ancient yogic technique perfected by the masters. It has to do with physics and bringing the body down to the molecular level. It is a great science and takes a lifetime to understand."

"I'm curious, please explain."

"When the body becomes too old to be of any use, then the yogi searches for an abandoned dead body of a young man. On finding one, he gives up his old body, and enters the body of the young man to continue living."

"What! That's crazy. Unbelievable. How can this even be possible?" asked Rudr.

"Through penance, yoga and discipline. You can will anything. You are gifted by the universe. It's almost the same as astral travel ... works on the same principles."

Astonished at the knowledge he had just received, Rudr fell at Babaji's feet with tears of joy streaming down his eyes.

"Son, let me warn you that the terrain from here on will be daunting and will break you many times, but hold on with determination and follow Parashuramji's instructions. He tends to lose his temper frequently and doesn't forgive easily."

Smiling, he continued, "In the last few months son, you have learnt self-reliance, to pare your needs to the bare minimum, be self-sufficient and bare-bodied. It takes 21 days to form a new habit and you have done exceptionally well my son. The walk to and from the Ganga was to teach you the importance of waking up early and exercising. It is cold, hard work to carry pitchers of water uphill, but you did it with determination; and cooking for yourself taught you self-reliance. You had a lot of unanswered questions and hence the evening hours of introspection.

"Tell me son, how do you feel … are you ready for more challenges? Because the journey is only going to get tougher from here. Life is about challenges—and those of us who can hold our heads high in the face of adversity, succeed. The teachings of this old sage are not to be studied, learnt and forgotten. They are life lessons that need to be incorporated into our daily routine; and most importantly they are simple and beneficial.

"Now son I will be going back to my cave and you will have to leave the *kutir* to go to *Tapovan*. You will fend for yourself in the depths of the jungle for three months. This will teach you to hunt and be fearless. Remember Rudr, you are out there alone and you have to survive. Also remember, to keep life going, everything is allowed," he ended enigmatically. Rudr couldn't believe his ears.

"Guru Parashuram will join you any time as per his wish."

It was the thought of leaving the little hut that made Rudr realise how comfortable he had become in a sparse hut with a coal stove and a blanket. It was time to leave Gaumukh. The few things he carried included a sleeping bag, a hunter's knife, a diary and a pointed staff to check the terrain that he would be walking on.

The trek from Gaumukh to *Tapovan* was far more difficult than any he had undertaken before, but the beauty of the mystical Mount Shivling kept him going. On the way he met a few trekkers headed for the peak, who had set up a base camp. He shared their lunch and started at a brisk pace towards his destination. He was acclimated to the cold, thin air by now and his fitness levels were the best he ever had.

Tapovan was picturesque. The extreme cold and dense forests, however, kept tourists away. Only true spiritual seekers and monks made *Tapovan* their abode. He met one such lady monk fondly called 'Mataji', who lived with her followers in an *ashram*. He politely declined her offer to stay at the *ashram*.

Babaji was clear. The *Tapovan* trimester had to be experienced alone. It was with this determination that Rudr found a secluded rock by a stream, and decided to start his inward journey there. The peace and tranquillity of the landscape and its serene silence helped him achieve calmness at will. For the first few days, he wept like a child mourning for the loss of his dad, for his mom's going away, and for a hundred other hurts. He wept till he had made peace with all that life had bestowed and taken away from him. Finally, like the stream he was sitting next to, he was cleansed and ready to move on. He felt as if the dead weight of a boulder had been lifted from his head.

'*Tapovan*' means 'forest of austerities'—and he was forced to practice aplenty here.

He learnt many lessons. Hunger taught him to eat anything and everything and also digest it. His tolerance for all kinds of food grew, so did his ability to bear pain. He learnt the primitive ways of life as he hunted fish and deer. The semi-cooked meat with no spices and oil was the only way to survive in this harsh and hostile environment. His instincts of sight and smell sharpened to perceive threats from wild animals. His muscles hardened, as did his spirits in the cold, harsh conditions. To protect himself from the freezing nights, he learnt to sleep between the crevices of huge rocks.

Life had become a meditation—living in the moment in unison with the universe.

He had learnt to survive. But each day unveiled a new danger. The soles of his feet were cut and burnt as he walked in *Tapovan*. He learned to coexist with animals and spirits. As he moved deeper into the forest, the parallel existence of different planes astonished him. Often while he tried to meditate, he would be disturbed by the slight brush of a cold, chill wind accompanied by the howling spirits.

***

It was the darkest night of all; the night of *Amavasya* or 'no moon'. Few stars twinkled in the sky. As the shrill, terrifying howl of the jungle wolf rent the air, Rudr tried to stay alert and keep calm. By now his eyes had adapted to facilitate some night vision; he could see in the dark far better than before. He turned instinctively and there, in direct line of sight, was the tall apparition from Narkanda. It had no eyes yet there was a sadness about it; no mouth, yet it seemed to be saying something. There was a familiarity to the presence. As the apparition came closer, Rudr sensed another presence. He turned around and looked straight into the red, blazing eyes of a hungry snow leopard. The animal was so close, he could feel its warm breath on his face. Rudr let out a loud scream that made the leopard retract a few steps as the apparition moved away noiselessly. The beast uttered a low growl with its mouth closed, unable to fathom its opponent. Rudr looked deep into the eyes of the leopard and the predator retreated further and finally disappeared into the night. Aware that the leopard would be back, Rudr sprinted to his rock and lay between its slim crevices through the night, wide awake.

Early next morning, just as he had dozed off, Rudr felt a sticky warm liquid run down from his forehead towards his ear. He opened his eyes in a flash and saw the leopard standing above the rock salivating. The large cat could not reach into the slim crevice in which Rudr hid. Rudr marvelled at his opponent who stood tall at 7 feet. He himself seemed small at 6 feet. The leopard was looking down at Rudr with its limbs spread out on the two rocks. Rudr could see the underbelly of the large male leopard; food was sparse in this part of the mountain and the animal had definitely returned to hunt its prey.

Rudr remained in the same position for hours, while the snow leopard stretched and extended his limbs playfully as if to invite Rudr to a bout, never once leaving its place. It was going to be a battle of wits. Who would make the first move?

Up close, Rudr studied each detail of the leopard. The muscular body had large and powerful forelimbs; the teeth in its handsome jaw were long and sharp. He guessed the canines would be at least 3.5 cm long. The cat had a long tail, thickly covered with fur. He tried his best to scare it away by making different sounds from growls to grunts and hisses and snarls but the animal didn't budge. Rather, the leopard returned each sound with a chuff. He opened his mouth so wide that Rudr could see the hyoid apparatus and the razor-sharp teeth. The chuff was uttered three to four times in succession and being so near, had a deafening effect on Rudr. Hours of lying squeezed in one position made him stiff and now his legs were hurting too. But his mind was sharp and ticking.

'I have to think of something quick else I will get fossilised in the rock,' he thought grimly. He looked around. The sky was dotted with tiny cumulus clouds floating languorously in the sky; the snow-clad peaks all around in 360 degrees, and the majestic Mount Shivling loomed large above him. He prayed to the rain and wind gods for intervention.

Mid-afternoon, the leopard took a stroll up to the river to drink water. Seeing his chance, Rudr leapt out and stretched his limbs. Seeing movement, the leopard raced back to the rock but Rudr slipped back in, just out of reach! It was a battle of nerves, and the snow leopard was beginning to get impatient. He stared hard at Rudr, pupils enlarged, ears flattened while he bared his teeth. Just then the wind howled like a banshee slinging snowflakes as sharp as needles. The leopard moaned a subdued mew with its mouth closed as if bowing to nature, looked sharply yet again at Rudr, turned around, leapt down from the rock and ran into the forest. Rudr waited for a few minutes before emerging from the two boulders that had protected him for so long. The wind was hissing and he could see a blizzard coming. He had to quickly find shelter for himself—or die of hypothermia.

Late evening, and wind speeds of almost 99 mph, had made visibility poor. Freezing, exhausted and blinded by the snow, Rudr had minutes to make a choice … get into his sleeping bag and get back into the boulders or sprint up to the cave he had seen on his way, a couple of miles away. He chose the latter. He grabbed his belongings and ran towards the river, panting with thirst.

The last time he had had water was a day-and-a-half ago just before the leopard had decided to keep him company. He quickly drank up from the gushing Ramganga. The water was icy and had a ferocious velocity; he sensed the blizzard would be followed by an avalanche and hurried towards the cave, eastward from the river. He picked up fallen branches of trees as he moved adroitly. He hadn't eaten for a week, so was surprised by his energy levels. On reaching the cave, he threw his belongings in as he quickly lined up the branches against the opening of the cave and started a fire. Out of breath, and with a heightened pulse rate, he looked inside the cave—and froze. He saw the reflection of the flames in the leopard's eyes, his companion in the cave!

The leopard didn't move; just watched him unwaveringly. The cave was barely able to accommodate the two of them. Rudr reached for the knife in his pocket, ready for the leopard's first move. The dimension of the cave, 7 ft × 8 ft, and 5 ft in height, packed them so close together that yet again Rudr could hear the beast's breathing.

It was snowing heavily outside by now and the wind howled louder than ever. Rudr was still shivering, more out of fear than the cold, since the cave was comfortably warm thanks to the fire. The forest of austerity was truly testing his nerves as he felt helplessly stuck between the beast and the storm. Yet for some uncanny reason the cave with the leopard seemed a better option than nature in her fury. He inhaled deeply, mustered all his courage, and once again looked the leopard in the eye and calmly said, "Buddy, you and I have to keep each other warm here tonight. Tomorrow morning once the blizzard stops we can fight. Until then rest and stay still."

In response the leopard just turned its back on Rudr facing the inside of the cave, stretched its body and slept, leaving just enough space for Rudr to fit in snugly. Exhausted and thankful that the leopard was in no mood for combat he slipped into his sleeping bag and rested his aching body, but sleep eluded him. Proximity to the ferocious beast kept him in constant vigil. The leopard, however, slept peacefully.

Rudr was unable to understand the predator, who till a few hours ago had waited endlessly to attack him, but now that he had the opportunity, was uninterested. The fire died down a few hours later and the cave was dark. Rudr could barely see a thing, and unable to keep his eyes open anymore, dozed off. A few hours later as the first rays of the sun hit the cave, Rudr opened his eyes to a magical sight: the predator had just given birth to a cub, and was licking off the sticky amniotic fluid! She then lay down on one side again and Rudr watched in awe the birth of the second and third cubs. The magic of the moment made him bow down his head in reverence. The cubs looked perfect, even though their eyes were closed. Having licked all her cubs clean, the leopardess looked up at Rudr with a gentle gaze as they practically stumbled over him trying to find a teat to suck. He froze, not making any movement or action. He knew he was a breath away from death and though he felt a connection with the cubs, he could be seen as a threat. In a while, the cubs were safely suckling, lying in the warm crook of their exhausted mother's forearm. He folded his sleeping bag very, very slowly, and crawled out of the cave. Once out and safe, he smiled at the snow leopard, thanked her for sharing her space with him and stepped out into the sheer whiteness all around.

The blizzard had died down and calm reigned once again in the mountains. He was drawn to a cascading icefall. He walked towards it and stood underneath the icefall. He saw a brilliant sight: the emergence of the Bhagirathi with gushing fury. He continued walking and came to a hillock that formed one of the high banks of the glacier, dropping into the glacier floor. He walked into a natural balcony with breathtaking views of

Gaumukh (the source of the Bhagirathi river) and the Gangotri glacier and bowed, palms in supplication, overwhelmed by the pristine beauty of the surroundings. He stood transfixed, marvelling at the vastness of the universe and minuteness of his place in it, as the 'I' in him crumbled to dust.

There was so much to learn from nature! Poor visibility and the conditioning of his mind had made him mistake the female leopard for the male beast who had tormented him for two days. He said a quick prayer for the leopardess who had gracefully shared her cave with him through her most intimate ordeal.

It was a beautiful, clear day with the sun shining brightly. Rudr was famished. He decided to try his hand at fishing, and walked towards the riverbank. After a few hours spent with feet submerged in icy cold water, he was yet to spot a single fish. It seemed they had all migrated downstream due to the cold. Dejected and numb, he sat down on the blanket of white and closed his eyes. For an 18-year-old, the journey had been life-changing. He felt overwhelmed by the exhaustion and struggle for survival. "What was Babaji thinking when he decided to put me through this?" he raged within.

There was a sudden movement, as the white snow beside him seemed to rise. Seconds later, a stocky body with dark florets charged at him. He leapt back, his mind racing as he took in the advancing form of his latest threat—his old foe, the male leopard! The beast took a 5-foot-high leap and landed on Rudr, using his massive 50-kg body weight and strength to knock him down. Rudr lay dazed and badly injured in the snow, his thigh torn and bleeding. But he was ready for this final face-off—he would win, or go down fighting, he decided. Mustering strength he did not know he had, he kicked the leopard's belly hard, making him yowl and take a step back in pain. Two species—two alpha males, armed and dangerous, ready for a fight to the finish. The leopard with his teeth and claws; the man with his knife; biting, slashing at each other, drawing blood. An unequal yet unpredictable battle. The snow leopard is a fearsome beast; a natural predator driven by instinct. Could the man, so puny by comparison, pit his intellect, his imagination, against the beast's massive size and primal instincts?

The leopard's ability to dominate space in three dimensions had him simultaneously leap, knock and grab at Rudr's throat with his powerful jaws. With a quick feint and sleight of hand, Rudr managed to slash at the beast's throat with his knife even as he felt immense, searing pain at his own throat.

Bleeding and fatally wounded, both fell on opposite sides. Mental resolve made Rudr stagger up on his feet once again, despite the agonising pain. The cold, white blanket now had big red blotches of blood from man and beast.

The leopard snarled in pain, struggling to get to his feet. Rudr made his final, bold move: he fell on the cat and stabbed its mighty jugular with his knife. As blood squirted, the leopard rose ferociously one more time bringing Rudr down with his enormous paw.

There was complete silence. Both victim and predator lay side by side; one was taking his last breath. As his eyelids drooped, Rudr thought he saw Guru Parashuram.

***

"Okay Rudr, you are fine now and can start your training with me." Rudr had been nursed back to health at Mataji's *ashram* after that fateful encounter. With Parashuram himself dressing his wounds every day Rudr had recovered fully, left with only a large scar running from the inner thigh to the back of the knee.

"But Guruji..."

"No buts! Struggles and disappointment, injuries and hardships are part of life; they should not deter you from your final goal. I was impressed with the way you fought the young male snow leopard. However, you were grievously injured too. Had help not arrived at the opportune time, you wouldn't have lived to see this day."

"Yes, thank you Guruji for saving my life."

"It's all preordained son."

Rudr suddenly recalled something that had been puzzling him through his recovery.

"Guruji, snow leopards never attack human beings ... they are fearsome predators but pose no danger to us. How come this leopard changed his spots?"

An enigmatic smile was all he got in response.

***

"Martial art is the art of self-defence. Pay heed so that your next encounter with a wild beast doesn't hurt you," said Parashuram, as he went into a classic shallow standing squat, an ideal starting point for attack and defence.

Through the next eight weeks, Rudr mastered all that his Guru taught him about peak performance and physical injuries. "Rudr, a *Siddha* is born when he has finished his karmic bondage in previous births. He is born into a wealthy family with an exceptional intellect and an extremely powerful body. Having complete knowledge of the universe, he's not an active participant in the race of life as he is already a Master.

"I am like a gardener that can only give the sapling care so that your subtle powers are evoked. I'll test you to hone your skills, will prepare and protect you since it is easy to lose subtle powers in the ravages of time. As your Guru, I can't give you any more than that. You're a born *Siddha* and I am just unveiling your true identity to you: a ruthless warrior equal to none."

Parashuram then decided to teach Rudr *Raj Yoga*. The inward journey was more difficult than the physical one; but gradually with guidance Rudr learnt to go into deeper and deeper states of meditation, till one day he found himself on his own. His Guru had left, having completed his training.

With renewed confidence and a quest for deeper knowledge of the self, Rudr went into deep meditation and remained in a state of *samadhi* for weeks.

The first thing he noticed was that his facial hair had grown till his navel, and hair till his shoulders—and realised with a start that he had come out of the state of *samadhi*. He laughed at his reflection in the flowing stream, for a minute not recognising himself. The world around had changed too. The trees were orange and brown and the chirping of the birds was barely heard. Winter had set in.

"Thank God you are back! Tell me buddy, have you graduated in deep sleep lessons from somewhere?" asked Sushant.

"What … what are you doing here?" enquired a pleased Rudr, hugging Sushant.

"Dear friend, the winter months are not easy here and all the *yogis* migrate towards the plains—Mataji and her followers too. It was she who informed us that you were in deep *samadhi*; and that repeated attempts by her followers to wake you up were fruitless. I was worried since you had been gone for three months and all at Gangotri were expecting you back."

"Have I been here for three months? Impossible! I thought it was a fortnight."

"No, it's been four months since July 15, the day you left Gaumukh. It is November—freezing November, and Diwali is approaching.

"Can we talk once we reach the plains? The roads will soon close due to blizzards."

Two days later they reached Rishikesh. The *ashram* had shifted there for the winter.

"Rudr, my beloved son, how glad I am to see you," rejoiced Babaji, hugging him tightly. He smiled back at Babaji with gratitude. The joy and radiance that he felt reflected in his persona. Like an eager child he talked about his experiences through the night. Babaji reflected that Rudr was made of tougher stuff than he had expected. Besides himself, he knew of only Rudr who had survived the cold *Tapovan* with its blizzards and chill winds through October–November. Rudr spoke to Babaji about the ghosts of *Tapovan*; about his father; about the strange encounter with the leopards; and finally his inward journey into previous lifetimes.

In his knowledge he was complete and happy, undeterred by life's calamities. When Babaji questioned that, Rudr said, "The universe is fair; and everything in our lives is there to teach us a lesson, to make us grow into stronger individuals. One lifetime is too short a time to pass judgement on sorrow and happiness but when you look at the picture as a whole, everything fits in and falls into place. It's like a jigsaw puzzle—all unattractive and broken as pieces but a perfect square when put together."

"Son, you have truly gained spiritual depth, and as you know by now, it's because of previous lifetimes of hard and rigorous penance. The yoga system as recommended in the *Gita* helps concentrate mental activities internally and thus enables you to 'see the feet of the Lord within oneself'—and you have attained that. But your destiny, my child, is not to be a monk or Babaji like me ... so allow me to erase the visions and experiences; the lessons and aura will stay."

The months that followed were spent blissfully, absorbing knowledge from the different masters in the Himalayas, knowledge that was profound, deep, practical and simple. The great souls of the Himalayas would gather together under one roof at Rishikesh during the winter months. Rudr took to the venerable old sages like long-lost friends. Their presence, though enlightened, seemed familiar and for all their simplicity, most of the sages were very well read and abreast with events happening around the world.

"So Rudr, are you as enthralled by these Himalayan monks as me?" asked Sushant. He was writing a book on Babaji, and hence spending time with him.

"Hmmm ... they are unbelievably gentle and quiet souls, far removed from the arrogant ones that roam the plains. Supremely intelligent and yet unbelievably detached.

"Attired in white or orange robes when they walk, it almost looks like they are gliding in air, above the ground. And Sushant have you inhaled the sweet sandalwood fragrance that accompanies most of them?"

"Yeah for the longest time I thought they used the same brand of perfume, till I was corrected. These simple monks never use any products, I am told."

"Sushant, I feel I belong here and don't ever want to leave this magical world."

"Come on Rudr, you know you have to go back in a couple of months."

"But I feel at peace here. I could easily renounce the world and adopt the life of a monk."

Babaji had just walked in and joined the conversation. "Of course, my son, you will renounce the world and will be a much sought after saint; but not yet."

"Dear Rudr and Sushant you both are very special young boys and the universe has big plans for you. It's your karma that exposed you to the essence and meaning of life so early. I want you to apply everything you have learnt here in every decision you make."

The year passed by quickly and it was time to say goodbye. Babaji was very proud of Rudr's achievements. "Go, my son. You are equipped with everything that you will need to succeed in life. Yours, my son, is no ordinary life."

20

Kali & Shukra

"Ordinary people, that's who they are, living purposeless lives, addicted to substances, wealth or flesh," said Shukracharya.

"Yet, is it right Guruji for us to kill them in such large numbers?" enquired Kali, now a handsome even if slightly effeminate young man. He was the very picture of gentleness with his beguiling green eyes.

"We kill only those whose souls we can't enslave or corrupt."

"And the Brahmins of Shambhala?"

"Yes, the extraordinary race—righteous and dedicated to a higher cause."

"What cause Guruji?"

"Our complete termination," smiled Shukracharya.

"I don't understand. If they are a threat to us, should we not kill them first?"

"Wherever there is light, there is shadow. The stronger the light source, the darker the shadow cast from it. Kali is strong—only because Kalki is stronger.

"Mind you son, Brahmin, to me, is not a caste. 'Brah' means expansion and 'mana' means mind. The amalgamation of Brah + mana is Brahmana or Brahmin, one with an infinitely expanded mind.

"Ravana was a Brahmin and so was Dronacharya. Both Vishnu avatars Rama and Krishna were guilty of *Brahmahatya*, being Kshatriyas. In his sixth avatar Vishnu was the Brahmin Parashuram, who adopted the Kshatriya way of life and killed thousands of Kshatriyas.

"Now we finally have a Vishnu avatar that is of Brahmin origin pitted against you. The die has been cast … and finally it will be a battle of equals. Everything else in the universe is incidental and must go," said Shukracharya with a tone of finality.

The skies were dark and the stench of death seeped through the very air. The Guru and *shishya* recited a few *shlokas* and dissolved into thin air to re-materialise in Antarctica, inside their humongous biowarfare laboratory. It was Kali's favourite playground.

"I set up this lab before you were conceived. In fact a part of you was assimilated here. DNA scripting is the story of today," said Shukracharya stroking his long beard. "You didn't just become a child prodigy. Every effort was made to ensure a powerful intellect and charisma. Your eugenics were crafted with great care. You are the fearsome Jalandhara's direct descendant. Jalandhara himself was born out of Shiva's anger." Kali stood enthralled, all ears. "I didn't leave it to eugenics alone. From the day you were conceived I have been talking to you on astrology, science and the occult. You were born with the knowledge of the Vedas and Puranas. I homeschooled you in biogenetics and you were a pro at age eight when you created your own virus prototype. But because you are a part of this world and its many illusions, I encouraged you to study medicine at a university. You surprised the medical faculty with your research and they were quick to confer on you the master of medicine and surgery titles."

Kali smiled gently. "Of all my titles, I am most proud to be your disciple Guruji!"

"Kali, beware—your path is treacherous. This time, the Kalki Avatar is to be assisted by the eight Immortals, all masters of illusion. Because of our finite existence we feel what we see and hear is the truth. However, ours is a nine-dimensional existence. Every 40,000 years, the entire crust of earth shifts, resulting in the relocation of its continents into new positions. Where we stand today used to be Atlantis in another aeon of existence."

"I wouldn't believe it, if anybody else had said that to me!"

"Today Kali, I want you to listen to the sound of silence. You will be able to hear the primal sound 'Om', the vibration of the pineal gland at 963 megahertz."

The Guru and *shishya* sat cross-legged on a red mat. Kali shut his eyes and started the deep breaths of *pranayam*. An adept *yogi*, he was quickly in a meditative state. Time became meaningless. There was a deafening silence and soon Kali's whole being began to resonate with the 'Om' syllable, flooding each cell with powerful energy. He remained in this meditative bliss for hours. It took the gentle touch of his Guru's hand on the head to draw him back to the present world.

The two walked together towards a peculiar staircase that looked frozen in time, in ice.

"There is a strange energy grid here, Guruji. The vibrational energies are extremely pure."

Kali gasped as a huge pyramid materialised before his eyes.

Shukracharya answered the questioning eyes. "A treasure lies there, buried deep within the ice, waiting to be discovered."

"What is it Guruji?"

"The Akashic Records. The supercomputer of the universe. The Akashic Records refer to the matrix of consciousness grids that create our reality. They carry the imprints of every thought and deed of every soul that ever existed. The Akashic Records are timeless and will be of great help to us," said Shukracharya approaching a large touchscreen monitor.

"Guruji, can I see where Kalki is and his origin?" asked an eager Kali.

"Yes of course. It is the reason I have got you here—for you to see your place in the scheme of things, to understand that your life and Kalki's are intertwined since the beginning of 'Time'. He represents Day and you my son, Night." Shukra trailed off, looking agitated. "It isn't working—never happened before!" He continued to fiddle with the screen, mumbling under his breath. "I swore revenge against the Lord of Gods Vishnu when he killed my innocent mother. My father, the great Sage Bhrigu, cursed him with human birth time and again and I decided to make his every birth on planet earth difficult..."

"And Guruji, me? What is my role in all of this?" enquired Kali wide-eyed.

"Your role, son, is well defined. You are to rule *Kali Yuga*. Never has the time been more opportune for the complete annihilation of the human race! You will pollute their minds, destroy their bodies, make earth a land of *mlecchas* and hybrids—all this while the Vishnu Avatar is himself present on earth!" Shukra's fair skin turned red in rage, as the supercomputer hung in no-response mode.

The skies reacted to Shukracharya's anger with loud thunder and showers.

"Someone has recently blocked out the entire supercomputer."

"Oh, who could that be Guruji?"

"I have always been wary of the Immortals. It has to be one of them," said Shukracharya. "They are known spoilers," he fumed, bringing on a typhoon in the Indian Ocean.

21

Oxford

Oxford, the 'city of dreaming spires', had recently been in the news for terror attacks. The attacks had targeted Cowley Road, east of the Magdalen Bridge, a colourful shopping district by day and a busy leisure hangout by evening. A miscalculation by the terrorists however had meant zero casualties in East Oxford's busiest street, although some iconic shop fronts were permanently scarred.

West Oxford, thankfully, was not under threat—at least for the time being. Rudr had chosen this quiet suburb, away from the hustle and bustle of city life. It was perfect to slowly slip back into the groove of civilised life. After Gangotri, Rudr realised that he needed solitude and silence as much as camaraderie. Rad Cam (Radcliffe Camera) the historic Oxford library was just a few blocks away. Upper Camera was where Rudr spent most of his time. The yearlong break he had taken from academics had fuelled his hunger for the written word. He read voraciously on world politics and history and found a keen interest in debating at the prestigious Oxford Debating Club. Football was a passion that Rudr continued to pursue and though he effortlessly played his way into the A team at the Oxford University Association's Football Club, he politely declined a permanent position in the team. Babaji had been clear about remaining obscure. He had to blend in, not attract attention of any kind.

No one could quite match Rudr's inherent good looks with a 6-foot frame and taut athletic body. The confidence and energy Rudr exuded was palpable. And blending in wasn't easy; he attracted girls in plenty, who drooled over his physique and were mystified by his brilliant mind.

Padma and Glenn were Rudr's closest friends. Padma was his senior and Glenn his roommate. Padma was the cultural secretary of the roving campus at Oxford. She hailed from an affluent political family in Sri Lanka and was pursuing political science. Oxford was the last campus in her final year at the global education programme.

Rudr had met her at a debate on the topic, 'Eastern Values in a Western World'. Her wit, knowledge and compassion impressed him and soon they had become close friends. It was only Padma with whom Rudr had shared his adventurous year at Gangotri. She understood him completely and instinctively knew when to engage with him and when to let him be by himself. Rudr looked up to her. Padma always had answers to his questions and reminded him of his roots. She loved teasing him about his huge fan following of girls just to see him smile coyly, for once at a loss for words.

Rudr loved the company of his women friends and admirers and flitted easily from one relationship to another.

"Hey, Padma … you're probably the only gorgeous woman at the campus that I haven't dated."

"Mr Nanda, I know you too well to get taken in by your charming looks, and no thanks I want a one-woman man, not a social butterfly," she quipped.

"Ha ha … monogamy, Ms Padma, doesn't exist—oh my God, don't tell me you haven't had a boyfriend?" teased Rudr.

"Of course not. I am precious, I will give my heart, body and soul to only one man—my husband," stated Padma firmly. The look in her eyes was dreamy.

"Damn, I can't believe I'm hearing this from you, a highly educated well-travelled girl..."

"What does education have to do with values? From where I come we are taught to love ourselves enough and think deeply before committing to a person or relationship," said Padma.

"Yes … yes … but Padma, I am not debating East vs West. All I am saying is that at our age, we shouldn't take ourselves so seriously and definitely not our relationships!" smiled Rudr.

"Yes, Mr Nanda, how could I forget you're an immature hot-blooded teenager with surging hormones?" teased Padma as Rudr chased her down the stairway. He caught up with her and held her hand tight. He looked deep into her eyes and said softly, "Padma, I love you."

"No, you don't Rudr … let go of my hand!" said Padma, embarrassed by their proximity. She could smell his minty breath and was this close to getting intoxicated by his charm. But she knew he was pulling a fast one on her to prove his point and she was not the one to be giddy-headed.

"Rudr Nanda," she said sternly, "leave my hand. Your attempts to charm me won't work."

Rudr let go and roared in laughter. "I almost had you there!"

"Stop being so vain Rudr! You're not going to get every girl you set your eyes on, and definitely not this one," said Padma.

With a twinkle in his eye he proclaimed: "Rudr will move heaven and earth to get what he wants and will not rest till he gets what he believes is righteously his."

"Great attitude Rudr, hope you apply it to more meaningful stuff than jumping into bed with every girl!"

"Point noted Ms Monogamy."

"Good, Mr Have-It-All."

They worked hard on their submissions and participated and won accolades for their debating skills as a team.

"Where did you get that Shiv Shakti bit from Rudr? That was brilliant. I knew we had won, with the applause you got."

"From the Himalayan sages."

"Why didn't you share that point with me before the debate?"

"To impress you unexpectedly," retorted Rudr.

"Gosh, you are incorrigible Rudr."

"And you, Padma, are gorgeous!"

At the 'Missing Bean' café Glenn and the boys were teasing Rudr. "The Perennial Virgin Padma too falls prey to the charms of a certain Mr Nanda!" announced Glenn wickedly evoking an unexpectedly volatile reaction from Rudr. "Don't you dare malign her name," he snapped, as he caught Glenn's neck. Seeing the anger in his eyes the remaining boys backed off. Just as Rudr released his hold, Padma entered the cafe with her friends, much to Rudr's relief. But she had been privy to the entire scene. She smiled, secretly happy to see the aggression in the otherwise unruffled Rudr.

It was an unusual relationship—she was his closest confidant; and he, an endless source of knowledge and inspiration for her. Padma had fallen in love with Rudr the day she saw him at the first of many debates to come. But Rudr was too occupied with other women to notice this. Padma found it difficult to cope with his never-ending flings but kept her peace and had the upper hand teasing him mercilessly about it. Having earned her political science degree she was headed back to Sri Lanka. She wanted the distance to refine their feelings for each other. Friends for life—or something more perhaps?

Padma looked ravishingly beautiful. Her long straight hair was flying around her face and her traditional white lace sari made her look ethereal. Her large kohl-rimmed eyes were brimming with tears, and her porcelain skin had turned pink, adding to her radiance. Rudr captured her on his Nikon camera and commented:

"Why is it that we begin to appreciate something only when we are about to lose it? Gosh, I never realised you're so beautiful Padma. What am I going to do here without you?"

"Get yourself an education ... if I may say!"

***

As Rudr manoeuvred his Blue Mustang at the airport kerb, his eyes fell on the man standing in the middle of the expressway, unaffected by the teaming traffic. The next second, a blast blew up multiple cars and fires spread rapidly. In a terrible flash, the freeway was torn from the city, amidst debris of glass and broken limbs. Next to him lay the lifeless bodies of a mother and child, thrown out of their car still strapped on to their seats. Horrified, he undid their seatbelts and lay them together, closed his eyes in prayer and touched their foreheads gently. He then sprinted towards the moaning sound on his right. An elderly man was bleeding, his legs locked under the steering wheel, his car doors jammed.

With heroic effort, he held the wheel with one hand and lifted the old man out with the other. He placed him on the road and gently touched the broken leg. The excruciating pain that the man was in disappeared instantly, and he smiled gratefully at Rudr, amazed at the strength he possessed.

Right then, out of nowhere, appeared a man with a bleeding forehead … the one Rudr had been haunted by all his life. The one Rudr had just seen, moments before the blast. But this was no apparition. The man looked Rudr in the eye for a brief second, in approval, before vanishing into the chaos.

22

Sphinx

Cobbled streets that once thronged with life stood empty; the sidewalks were cracked, and spent cartridges dotted the roads. Up until a few years earlier this picturesque town with winding canals and pastel-coloured houses was a chic shopper's paradise. It was a favourite of fashion connoisseurs with its riot of colour and the revelry of art and artists. Annecy was home to haute couture, to designer jewellery, bags and shoes. The Michelin-starred restaurants dotting its bay required bookings months in advance.

Gone was the buzz of that vibrant town; in its place were monuments in disrepair and corpses strewn on the streets awaiting mass burials.

It had all started with water—or rather, the lack of it. Severe drought had hit France and the country had received 85% less rainfall for five consecutive years. Global warming made temperatures soar above 104°F. After a while, the rivers ran dry, affecting the hydroelectric power supply; soon, the canals became sewage reservoirs.

Tejasya and Shaheen had made Annecy their base, seeing opportunity in this devastation. Having eliminated their nosy nephew Vishnuyasa, the duo had made away with the Nanda wealth enjoying their life in the Alps. News of the natural disaster in France prompted their move to this alpine town in south-eastern France.

Tejasya was now head of the Sphinx in Europe. He called for an urgent meeting of members. "It's time we introduce RIZE to France. It's what they desperately need. Their taps are dry and soil infertile; the cattle and livestock have perished and hunger is killing the nation."

"You're so kind sir," spoke up a masked member of the organisation. "RIZE reduces thirst and appetite."

"It also weakens immunity," continued Tejasya. "All the better for the Kā virus to work. We can destroy their lives, tear them down from every side," he finished.

"We already know how the triad of global warming, RIZE and the Kā virus created mayhem in the African continent. Our members, under the able guidance of Jabari, have been able to make inroads into the political and national fabric and fuel strife in Chad and northern Africa. Yemen, Jordan, Libya and Western Sahara have no access to clean tap water anymore. Children are dying of water-borne diseases. Jabari has ingeniously brought to halt the aid and resources being provided by diverting them to our organisation.

"Today, Sphinx controls Africa, the Middle East, and a large part of Asia. All eyes are on me as we take over Europe."

The masked members bent down together in the low customary bow, making a loud clicking noise with their tongues. New affluent members were inducted next, with a hard blow on their left eye. The party began soon after. Shaheen, forever the seductress, walked into the gathering with excitement written all over her face.

"Kali Sir has invited us all to the Satanic Black Magic Conference he is organising in Canada."

***

Jabari walked with a quiet, slow gait, behind the veil. It was very difficult for the gathering to gauge the various moods of their leader. The last two days had been particularly difficult. Jabari never spoke, or showed emotion; gestures of the forearm were the only method of communication, besides the formidable handwritten instructions. Ama sat at the extreme left of the courtyard. She saw him move intently. It made her uncomfortable. The lanky movement was perceived as a threat and she knew that Jabari retreated only before a bloody carnage. Having witnessed many violent deaths, she was tired and her old shoulders were bent. Soon, she felt, the weight of all her sins would make her walk on all fours like him...

Her husband had asked her to abandon the child or leave. She chose the deformed child. She wouldn't give up a part of herself at any cost.

The doctors at the hospital said that the child with short legs would not live too long and probably be mentally retarded. They were wrong. She had left the poor country of Chad in the horn of Africa and travelled to the Central Republic by train, keeping her child wrapped from head to toe. She kept him close as she did her housework and laboured through the day to feed him. As the child grew she kept him draped lest the world see his ugly truth. But to her relief, the child was responsive and a quick learner. She taught the child everything she knew about the world—the big, bad dirty world—and the child reciprocated in anger. Today, at 40, Jabari was the most dreaded criminal in Africa, equally feared and respected for his formidable intellect. He used his deformity to create an aura of menace around him. His speech was minimal and disjointed; he preferred to write instead or use periods of silence to communicate.

Ama looked at him again and a chill went down her spine. She had truly created a monster. She missed her younger days, when there was no money, no home, no food. Yet, poverty had been better! Today there was untold wealth and all its luxuries. But all the Hermes and diamonds couldn't buy her peaceful sleep. There were too many demons that kept her up. Her gnawing guilt was killing her appetite and she was on antidepressants. The time had come to put a stop to this insanity. The spiritual master she had been meeting the last few days had promised to cleanse her soul—if she surrendered herself along with Jabari at his feet.

Aware of the potential aggravation her suggestion would cause, she nevertheless decided to approach Jabari to surrender. But first she wanted to know what was disturbing him. Why was he so quiet?

As she walked up to him, she asked, "Who is bothering you now?" Next moment, a bullet pierced her brain and she fell on her side. "You!" croaked Jabari, as he cradled her head on his fours.

His men sprang into action. Within minutes the entire den was evacuated.

Ama's body was laid to rest in a graveyard. The gang and its leader relocated to a new address.

Sphinx had been informed two days earlier about Ama's meeting with the spiritual master. It didn't take Jabari long to guess that the police had laid a trap. Unfortunately, Ama had already given away relevant information by then. Jabari executed both the disciple and the Guru at the same time at different locations. Hardened and desensitised, he felt no remorse about having killed his own mother. Yet, there was that initial hesitation. Having buried Ama dutifully, his mind was now free, working on the next target on his hit list.

A call from the Indian wing of the organisation had provoked interest. He himself was mentored in occult and black magic by an Indian scientist, Kapi; the same short bony man now had Kali as his protégé and together the duo had created a DNA operating system that could hack into genes to create personalised bioweapons.

Jabari roared loudly. How he loved the idea of technology disruption! Having had no formal education, yet well versed in artillery and warfare, Jabari was constantly in search of new scientific breakthroughs. He was fascinated by the devastation caused by the Kā virus, named after its inventors Kali and Kapi. The virus attached itself to the spinal cord and travelled to the brain, degenerating it before causing eventual death. It was what Kā did to a person before killing him that Jabari loved most, having used it to maximum effect in Africa and parts of Asia.

Jabari remembered clearly how, as a deeply malnourished child, he was taken in by Kapi who promised him a bright future and freedom from hunger. In Africa, like other underdeveloped pockets of the world, it was easy to buy the loyalty of the poorest of the poor with food and water rations. In exchange Jabari had to swear absolute allegiance to the cult of Sphinx and internalise its ideologies. Then, he was to mentor young minds and send them to various countries and institutions of power to mingle and spread. It had taken him three decades to corrupt and break the youth and achieve his position of power. But Kā had achieved all this in less than a year of its emergence. At the basic level, it corrupted the minds of those affected, making them acquiescent and thus capable of amoral, demonic acts before they succumbed to sudden death. The pig-men or hybrids—the next level of Kā experiments—were built for endurance and could go without food and water for weeks. A mind corrupted by the Kā virus and a body manipulated for extreme endurance was a winning combination.

He roared yet again.

The head of Sphinx in Europe, Tejasya, would meet him shortly. Together they would travel to Canada to meet Kali, the young man he so admired.

23

Eight Monks

Ashwatthama was furiously firing darts at the dartboard waiting for the arrival of the other Immortals. His uncle, Kripacharya, walked in first.

"What happened? Why this sudden need to meet?"

They were in the arena of the Colosseum in Rome, Italy.

"Unbelievable … you still carry your dartboard around," laughed Markandeya as he materialised.

The steps of the Colosseum began to shake as Mahabali and Anjaney walked in together. A gust of wind settled into the middle of sand announcing the arrival of Parashuram and Ved Vyas. And finally, the loud clanging of bells and the sweet aroma of incense gave away the presence of Vibhishan. The eight *Chiranjeevis* together chanted 'Om' thrice, the sound reverberating solemnly within the Colosseum.

Ashwatthama spoke up in anger. "We have waited 5,000 years for the arrival of Kalki—to support him in his mission of cleansing the planet and restoring world peace. Yet today, when the human race is on the verge of destruction our Saviour is busy enjoying the trappings and distractions of a human life—in spite of his *siddhis*!" His forehead began oozing blood, matching the savagery of his mood. "Can someone explain what is going on?"

Parashuram spoke. "It's all Ved Vyas and Kripacharya's doing. Annoyed at Rudr's show of superpowers at the *gurukul*, Vyas took away all his superpowers as *gurudakshina*."

"What?" cried Mahabali. "For how long?"

"Twenty years," said Parashuram, rolling his eyes.

"He was eight then. Today he is twenty-three. That leaves five more years," reflected Markandeya.

Vibhishan spoke gently. "Vedji, can you not revoke your *gurudakshina* and reduce the time?"

Ved Vyas, astrologer, mathematician, author of the Vedas and grandfather of the Pandavas and Kauravas, materialised a board and pen and drew celestial bodies, and stars around the earth and the sun. He began to narrate a story.

"Thousands of years ago, in another *kalpa,* the heavens bled with a war so fierce that it threatened to vanquish all of civilisation. It was a war that saw evil like no other. A war where all the gods united to fight an enemy as powerful as them—an enemy created by their own hands.

"The earth trembled and wept with the birth of Jalandhara, the result of a powerful union between the ocean and the seed of Lord Shiva's uncontrollable anger. Jalandhara could fly on the wind, float over the oceans, tame the most savage of lions and even raise the dead. Lord Brahma had foreseen the power of the child and given him his name. But even Lord Brahma couldn't predict that this child would grow up to be their nemesis. This evil and almost indestructible being waged a war with heaven—a war so brutal it took the gods' combined strength to defeat him.

"Let's come to the present—a time of *ghor Kali Yuga*. When evil is prophesied to take over the universe and corrupt all mortals. Lord Shiva awakes from his meditative state with flashes of an imminent war. A war greater than any ever seen. A war in which evil will cast its long shadow on all the three worlds—Heaven, Earth, and the Netherworld. Lord Shiva holds an emergency meeting with Lord Brahma and Lord Vishnu and urges them to send the tenth impending Vishnu avatar—Kalki—down to earth earlier than his destined time in the hope of preventing this terrible war. But what is prophesied cannot be changed so easily, even on a divine hunch. Lord Brahma resolves not to allow such an act, which could spell doom for the entire human race.

"A massive argument then ensues between the Holy Trinity. Finally, Lord Vishnu proposes a solution that respects both Lord Shiva's strong hunch as well as Lord Brahma's apprehensions: he suggests they send Kalki down to earth but restrict his powers till such time that evil raises its head and Lord Shiva's inkling becomes a reality.

"When the twins came to my *ashram*, their prayers and meditation opened Kalki's *mooladhara chakra* allowing the superpowers to manifest. I was then ordered by the Holy Trinity to immediately close the *mooladhara*. The Kalki Avatar would thus live like a normal human till his third decade." He lapsed into a pensive silence. "While I cannot revoke the orders of the Trinity, I can prepone the opening of the *mooladhara* by a few years, given the urgent need."

"Meantime, the evil blood that had been dormant for aeons is now finding resurrection in the veins of Kali—a talented young magician and a gifted doctor with powers beyond his understanding," finished Vyas.

The arena was quiet. The hallowed company gathered there was still processing the information just disclosed to them.

Parashuram was the first to speak up. "Kalki can tackle evil even without superpowers. I have trained Kalki to be a mighty warrior. Meantime, we, the Immortals, will continue to be the guardians of earth—its immune system, so to say. We have been cleansing it of toxic elements for centuries. We will hold fort till Kalki manifests with all the *siddhis*," he said confidently. And then added, as an afterthought, "Even the avatar is not free of karma."

"Yes Guruji," bowed Anjaney. "Enough of working under cover. It's time we let the world know of our presence."

They huddled together, the Immortals, finalising next steps. Minutes later they disintegrated into nothingness.

24

Tarini

The emergency room was abuzz with the low hum of life support equipment. Patients lay inert, hooked up to all manner of tubes, with machines doing the breathing, providing the heartbeat, and cleansing the blood of toxins. The occasional cough, wheeze and grunt kept the nurses assured that life, strapped to the machines, still hung on.

This morning was like any other at the ER at the New York Hospital on Staten Island. The aroma of coffee mingled with disinfectant pervaded the air. The sirens went on suddenly as the metallic double doors of the ER opened to a continuous stream of stretchers being brought in—yet another neighbourhood infected with the Kā virus. Doctors and nurses got to work at a frantic pace, trying CPR to revive as many teenagers before the virus passed the blood-brain barrier forever altering their neurophysiology and body composition.

"Tarini!" barked the senior doctor, as a tall, striking young intern in scrubs rushed to pick the right instrument from the surgical tray. Their eyes met under the protective headgear, as she reached out for the artery forceps and clamped the internal jugular vein on the right side of the patient's neck.

"Well done. Now let's see how many more we can save! I must say you work fast," Dr Stephens commented approvingly as he handed her a blood-soaked gauze. Having clamped the vein, the doctor would now infuse antiviral drugs and special plasma-infused blood to save the patient. This hospital was the only place where Kā patients had a chance of recovery.

At the end of a gruelling day, Tarini entered the ladies' locker and emerged a few minutes later, looking radiant in blue jeans and a pink knitted sweater, hair left loose, cascading down her back. But it was her mile-long smile that captivated everyone she met. She radiated happiness, warmth and a gentle reassurance that made her a favourite with her patients and colleagues alike.

Dr Stephens was waiting in his car, as she emerged through the hospital lobby. Autumn had set in and the orange leaves gave the campus a soft glow, far removed from the grim reality of the hospital indoors. She walked towards his car and got into the passenger seat.

"Yes, sir? It must be urgent for you to wait for me," she spoke to her mentor with affection.

"Tarini, I have received several calls today from the Heads of Department across hospitals in our country and beyond wanting to know the source of our plasma-infused blood. They too are staring at an outbreak of the Kā virus."

She smiled. "How many vials do you need?"

"Tarini, tell me girl where do you get them from? You cannot keep this hidden from me or the world anymore."

"Give me till tomorrow, sir," she smiled.

A few minutes later, she boarded the bus to Hoboken. Having made herself comfortable at a window seat, she opened her laptop and got to work on it. Some stops later, a large man in faded overalls, probably a construction worker, took the seat next to hers. She tried to make space for him but soon realised that he was comfortable and oddly didn't look as large anymore. He had a twinkle in his eye as he smiled, exuding a feel-good positivity. Charmed, she smiled back at him.

Tarini got back to her laptop. The bank transfer had gone through. The hedge fund that she had created years earlier with angel investors was soaring in value and *Bade Papa*'s company was now one of the most sought after litigation firms in the world. She smiled as she saw the bullish predictions for the firm.

"Does he know?" The rough voice was startling; she almost jumped out of her skin.

"Who, what?" she mumbled, looking at the smiling stranger beside her.

"Does Raj, your grandfather, know that you are the source behind his wealth?"

Her large eyes grew wide with astonishment and she could scarcely believe what she saw: he was becoming huge again, pushing her towards the corner.

"Gosh, you're a shape-shifter!" she exclaimed.

He laughed aloud as he now became smaller than her. "Anjaney," he said, offering his hand.

Looking straight into his eyes, she folded her palms in greeting and said, "*Pranam* Hanumanji."

"Vijayi bhavah bitiya," he blessed her.

"What good fortune brings you to me sir?" she smiled.

"Sir?" his eyebrows wiggled comically. "Ah! Well okay. I have been told that you are a whiz with computer programming."

"Can goof around with the gadgets, yes. How can I help?"

"I need help on a supercomputer I have managed to shut access to. But won't be too long before he tampers with it again."

"He—who?" quipped Tarini.

"That's a story for another day *bitiya*. For now, just do what I say."

The Immortal

Hanuman

"I'll tell you a secret. I am not what you perceive me to be," said Hanuman to the crowd of photographers and journalists. Then vanished into thin air.

He had just rescued a group of children from the jaws of death. The children were travelling back home from their boarding school in Shimla when the bus driver lost control at a hairpin bend in the mountains and the bus plunged down the sheer cliff face. The youngest child, aged 6, started chanting the 'Hanuman Chalisa'. In a jiffy, Hanuman materialised, in the guise of a construction worker, lifted the bus from its deathly plunge, and placed it back on the road, amid tears and claps from the children. He would have left immediately, but the love and devotion in the tiny eyes had made him stay a couple of minutes more. The news had travelled fast and photographers and reporters had already landed at the accident site, witnesses to this feat. He smiled his mischievous grin, as he held the crowd in thrall, distracting them from the fact that he had disabled all cameras and mobiles. Nobody had ever been able to capture him on their devices—though many had enshrined him in their hearts.

Hanuman entered his cosy cottage in the Pocono Mountains of Pennsylvania. It was snowing outside but he never felt cold—or hot. He was blessed to stay unaffected by the weather. Yet, to create an ambience, he lit the fireplace, made a hot cup of ginger lemon tea and got down to typing his autobiography on his iMac Pro.

"I don't believe I need to be written about. After all, who am I, but a servant to my Lord Rama … yet Guru Ved Vyas has insisted; so, I write.

"I had written once before—it was the entire Ramayana as I had seen it. I wrote with my nails on banana leaves. Only Sage Valmiki read it, but I saw the look in his eyes and swallowed my manuscript. Valmiki needed his Ramayana to make him

what he became. I had my Siyaram in my heart and soul. My every breath is dedicated to them. My Ramayana stayed with me.

"That was ages ago. Times have changed; the world has changed; people have changed. But I remain in absolute consciousness; my every cell reverberates with Rama naam.

"Ved Vyas has declared that the Kalki Avatar's story will be written by me, and Lord Rama as Kalki will want that too, but only after a detailed introduction to me, by me.

"So here, I humbly pen a few details of my life and times.

"My mother Anjani was a celestial nymph who was cursed to live on earth as a monkey. She was a devout Shiva bhakt and spent her days in prayer. My birth itself was a miracle. In the town of Ayodhya, King Dashrath held a yagna to pray to the gods for a male heir. The sweet offering, kheer prasadam, was fed to his three queens. A bird flying by dipped its feet into the offering and flew to where my mother was praying. The prasadam fell into her upturned palms. The Wind God Vayu had willed this, and thus I, Anjaney was born—at the same time as Lord Rama, Laxman, and their twin brothers. My mother told me that I am an ansh of Lord Shiva and my foster father is Vayu, the God of Wind.

"Endowed with unlimited physical prowess by my father, Vayu, I had the ability to shape-shift and fly across the planet and solar system.

"As a naughty child I once sought the sun. Its yellow brilliance reminded me of a juicy mango. I wanted to eat it, so I flew towards it, increasing my size as I got closer. Fearing that the world would perish without the sun, Indra, King of the Gods, shot me down with a thunderbolt and I landed hard on the ground fracturing my jaw and breathing my last.

"My father Vayu was enraged with Indra and refused to move, thus rendering the universe devoid of air, wind and movement.

To save the world, Brahma had to intervene and revive me to appease Vayu. In addition, all the devas granted me boons. Shiva blessed me with physical and mental strength; Indra, immunity from his weapons, and Vayu, my father, blessed me with the ability to move faster than the wind. Agni promised protection from fire; and Varun, who ruled the oceans, from water. Yama, the Lord of Death, granted me eternal life; Kuber, the God of Wealth, blessed me with boundless riches; and Kama, the God of Love, vowed to protect me from the desires of the flesh. On Shiva's recommendation, Ma Saraswati taught me music.

"Everything was given to me. I live in eternal bliss, with no doership—quite like Hari's flute, a hollow bamboo that only resonates the music of its beloved. The same one Krishna as Hari incarnate played for his beloved Radha.

"And then I met my Master, my eternal Lord, Shri Rama, the magnificent, benevolent King of Ayodhya. He was in a yogi's attire, hands folded, asking for help to locate his kidnapped wife Sita Ma. One look at him and the 'I' in me dissolved. Standing before me was the Lord Supreme, humble and egoless. That moment, I immersed myself in his bhav. I felt so small about having an ego and let it go forever. I decided to become his mirror, to reflect all his brilliance unto mankind. No wonder I earned the name 'Middleman'!

"Rama flows in me; courses through my blood, lives in every breath. Thousands of years on I continue to be in his service, in complete devotion. Wherever there is Rama, I will be. Wherever, whenever a devotee calls out my name, I will be. All in the name of my Lord Rama.

"Ma Sita blessed me with immortality. She also blessed me with eight siddhis and nine nidhis—superpowers and boons, you know? With her blessing I can reach anywhere in seconds, earning me the nickname LMG—Last Minute God!

"I am no God of course. But if you call out to me with sincere devotion, I will be there, travelling across oceans, to hold on to you in your time of need. You will never see me though, master of disguise that I am—I could take any physical or subtle, invisible form.

"Being a Karma Yogi, my work is my devotion. I am complete within and seek only Rama naam.

"I am so fortunate to be around all his avatars and am excitedly awaiting the resurgence of the Kalki Avatar. Once again, I can be of service to my Lord. In the meantime, I am looking after the security of the Nanda twins and their siblings. The twins have been a real handful. Rescuing them from the flaming plane during the mleccha attack at the gurukul, needed might. As always, though, I felt overwhelmingly blessed to hold the Avatar close to my heart..."

25

New York

It was a reunion of sorts at the New York Central Park as all four Nanda siblings were meeting after years. A lot had transpired by this time and there was cheerful banter at the Trattoria Coffee Shop.

"The haptic wearables keep intimacy alive in the digital realm, but don't compare to a tight hug in reality," joked Tarini as she hugged each one of her brothers. With her exuberant personality, Tarini stood out amongst her brothers. She made great efforts to be in touch with her entire family. "Welcome dear brothers to my part of the world," she beamed affectionately. "*Bhaiya Bade* and *Bhaiyaji* I am so glad you agreed to this reunion."

"It's been difficult to convince Guru Kripacharya. He has requested all of us to go our separate ways soon," said Sumanta.

"I'm so done with being told what to do at every step," exclaimed Pragnya. "We have sacrificed much in fear of being discovered ... lived apart from each other for so long. And for what?" he finished. The others agreed in unison with a nod of their heads. Rudr merely smiled with a twinkle in his eyes. "All for a good cause."

"No serious talk—we need to practise! We siblings are performing live right here tomorrow to a sold-out show," announced Tarini.

"What?!" chorused the other three. "It's a 'We Love New York' event with various acts. I've signed us up for the Indie Classical Sequence. *Bhaiya Bade* on the sitar, *Bhaiyaji* on the tabla, me on the *tanpura*, and Rudr with his mesmerising flute."

"Why do you want to be a shocking bore to the youngsters? No one listens to our kind of music," said Sumanta.

"The event is put together by students advocating world peace and I wanted us to participate and be a part of it," she said.

"I'm in," smiled Rudr reassuringly.

"Me too," Pragnya pitched in. All eyes were on the tall and reserved Sumanta. "Okay, okay ... don't look at me like that. What are the other acts?" he enquired.

"There is a rock band and an act by a renowned magician. He is a doctor by profession and a part-time magician. And yes—he is of Indian origin too."

"Interesting—do you know him?"

"No. He joined the hospital recently, just around the time the Kā virus found its way into the American continent. So I have all been tied up dealing with trying to curtail its spread."

"Can it be curtailed?" enquired Sumanta.

"How?" asked Pragnya. "The entire Asian, African and Australian continents are affected. Many countries have declared a state of emergency and the media says soon 70% of the world will be affected."

"Plasma-infused blood from the sages of Shambhala is the only antidote," Tarini boasted.

"Shush, quiet!" whispered Sumanta. "Not so loud. These are dangerous times and we are not to trust anyone. We need to disperse soon."

"Right after the show, Pragnya and I will leave for London."

"We will meet again in December to celebrate *Mumma-Bade Papa*'s 50th wedding anniversary."

Tarini looked away dejected. "I won't be able to make it," she said, remembering her promise to Vedji.

"Let's go home and practise. We must make our performance worthwhile," said Rudr, changing Tarini's mood.

They decided to play *Raag Pahadi*, an evening *raag* that combines both playful and pensive aspects in its charming folksy melody. For the uninitiated audience however, it was boring and slow. Their performance was cut short with screams of "We want Kali … we want Kali…" The Nandas barely managed to bow out with a *namaste*. The next performer was already rushing past them on stage, a jocular look on his handsome face hearing the reverberating chants of his name.

In a ringing, magnetic voice Kali the Magician thanked the crowd and plunged into his performance. After a couple of short opening acts, his eyes fell on the young, pretty girl with blue eyes and blonde hair in the front rows. He charmingly invited her on stage saying, "'Beautiful One', do you fear death?" She laughed, confidently replying, "No … go ahead and kill me!" Amused at her answer, he spoke again. "Close your eyes and face death … now. If you live, you can tell us about your journey from here to hell and back."

The audience quietened down and held their breath as Kali lay the girl on the high slab. He then moved his hand about as he levitated the girl above his towering figure. She was soon floating around the stage. Then, just as suddenly, he wedged a sword on the table vertically, with its sharp tip pointing skywards. He now directed the levitating girl towards the sword and placed her perfectly perpendicular on its sharp tip. There was a gush of blood as she fell from the tip to the base of the sword, which ripped her insides. There was a deathly silence. The audience waited with bated breath.

The girl had stopped breathing—the ECG monitor attached to her had begun to show the flatline.

"Do you guys want her back?" Kali screamed.

"Yes!" roared the audience. His assistants then picked up the dead, bleeding girl and placed her on the slab once more. They covered her chest as Kali put on his gloves and mask and got to work. A timer was placed in front of the gasping audience. In less than two minutes he removed the cloth covering her torso, degloved and kissed her forehead as she opened her eyes and put her arms around him. A soft spotlight focusing on the girl showed her tidying her dress at the waist, standing up and breaking into a little dance.

"Explain 'Death' as you saw it 'Beautiful One'," cajoled Kali. "Did you see a white light and hear soft music?" he asked.

"No … it was terrible. I kept dying every second ... could feel the pain of death again and again. Till I went blank and felt nothing."

"Exactly." He accompanied the girl back to the crowd, thanking her as he seated her next to the Nanda siblings, smiling jubilantly. Then he made his way back up, onstage. "So dear friends, death is the end. End of your story. Nothing exists after death. No light. No God. I can free you of death. I can bring you back from death. I am your only answer. I am your only saviour."

The audience went hysterical and clapped. "Now—let's live it up dear friends. My assistants are going to join you with a miracle smoke. Just a couple of puffs and you will feel light and happy." A troop of youths wearing all-black ensembles walked around with trays carrying joints. The lights dimmed and the music became loud as the entire arena was filled with cannabis fumes and the young audience began to loosen up and groove to EDM.

Pragnya got up suddenly. "Let's leave right now," he said nervously. The others quietly got up and moved out, except Rudr. He was busy flirting with the beautiful girl who had just been killed and brought back from dead by Kali.

Hanuman walked into the arena disguised as a stoner, and came and sat next to Rudr. The girl immediately got up and left in a rush. Rudr gave a polite smile to Hanuman and joined his siblings.

On the overhead speakers Kali's deep baritone enquired, "Are you relaxed? Are you having fun?"

"Yes!" the crowd screamed.

"Good! Thank you and bye..." in his mind he laughed, adding, "...world peace!"

***

It all happened so fast—the siblings were thankful to be alive and together.

"I'm not sure who that man was who helped us!" exclaimed a shaken Sumanta.

"Yes, he saved us and disappeared," said Tarini as she recollected the events.

The quartet had stood aside observing, having refused the smoke. "Everyone was dancing in a trance. Next, I heard a huge blast and saw fire engulfing the stage, blazing its way towards the audience. Before I could bat an eyelid or run, I was swooped into someone's strong arms and found myself at home."

"Incredible. Exactly what I felt!" said Pragnya. "The news feed says everyone present there died instantly. Innocent students, all 1,200 of them were there for the cause of world peace. Almost feel guilty for surviving this. Someone up there loves us dearly. There is no other explanation."

"Being privileged and having our Gurus does have its share of advantages," said Rudr wryly, looking at Pragnya.

"Did he wear a bandage on his forehead?" asked Rudr.

"No," said Sumanta. "He was muscular."

"We must be more responsible about following Guru Kripacharya's instructions. And never again should all the four step out together," said Sumanta. "We could have perished in the incident. We must now go our separate ways and only you, Rudr, will attend *Bade Papa*'s 50th wedding anniversary. It's too risky to be together in one place."

"You're right, *Bhaiya Bade*. I'll leave early in the morning for Oxford and you should head to Europe. We will meet again when fate and Kripacharyaji deem fit."

Outside the apartment on the street bench sat Hanuman, looking mighty pleased, munching on bananas.

26

Jenny

Back in the UK Rudr felt the need to expound the Indian philosophy of non-violence to the violence-prone western world. The bombings he had recently witnessed, shook him to the core. The Kā virus too was creating panic and all the countries and states in Europe were on high alert. Citizens were leaving home in fear and Oxford had recently reported a Kā case at the university campus, forcing it to shut down. International students were flying back home to safety—but was any place safe?

Rudr felt an inner turmoil. His sleep was frequently disturbed once again by the visions and nightmares of his boarding school days. The face of the bandaged man continued to haunt him, more so because he was not able to identify him. Yet he also carried a sense of deep serenity from his Gangotri interlude. Most mornings he awoke feeling heavy-headed and lost. Part of him wanted to break free and do more for the world. The solitude of Gangotri had allowed him to release the divine energies whenever they got overpowering, At Oxford, it was difficult with the urban settings; the energies could cause destruction.

Every few days he would drive away from Oxford towards the forest conservation area, park at Coopers Creek, trek towards Ryde Falls—then dive into the falls and disappear. Having unleashed his energies into the water—that flowed towards the thermodynamic dam providing electricity in the Canterbury area—he would emerge relieved. Unbeknownst, Ashwatthama had been observing him.

One night, when Rudr was at the local pub with friends, doing karaoke, a group of girls came up to introduce themselves. Suddenly everything, every sound, ceased to exist for Rudr. All he could see was this gorgeous girl whose eyes left him mesmerised. Large, almond-shaped brown eyes that spoke volumes.

"Hello, I am Jenny," giggled the girl, somewhat uncomfortably. "Hope I'm not disturbing you."

"No, No! I am sorry. Hi, I am Rudr."

"Yes, I know; and I am a big fan of your column. I am studying journalism at Trinity."

Rudr was lost again. He was trying to recollect where he had seen Jenny before.

"Rudr, you never cease to surprise me. I have been following you for the past six months and haven't been able to figure you out yet. I mean you are as comfortable at the pub as you are talking philosophy. Can I please interview you on a convenient day for the *Trinity Times*?"

"Er ... sure. Tomorrow morning, 8 a.m.?" He remembered where he had seen her before.

Jenny didn't sleep the whole night. She was excited and worried that she might oversleep and miss the interview. Jennifer

Rhodes believed in living life to the fullest. Wherever she went, she lit up the room with her presence and joie de vivre; her smile was infectious and warm. Yet she was unruly, chaotic and disorganised. She had been a precocious child who had achieved a lot in life just by her determination and zest. The youngest of five siblings born to American parents of Greek origin, she had questioned their orthodox ways and left home at 15, when her parents expressed their concern about her late night outings and falling grades.

A rebel, she took the first train out from sunny Florida to the green state of New Jersey. She waited tables and did small parts in local plays, making enough to support herself. Soon her striking good looks and angelic baritone won her a role in a Broadway musical, *Applejuice*. She sang captivating toe-tappers, belting high notes in an incredible display of vocal Olympics. Her performance elicited both smiles and tears from the audience. She was an instant success and, in a few months, became the toast of Broadway.

As Jenny's fortunes swelled, so did her dependence on substances. She worked hard and partied harder, and drifted from one relationship to another in search of something deeper.

Ultimately, she ended up at a rehabilitation centre at eighteen. There, the inmates introduced her to RIZE. She emerged from rehab clean, but began using RIZE as a crutch to return to normalcy. Within months, her life slowly started spiralling out of control. The highs were followed by lows. The drug took over her mind, and drove her to use her body to perform acts of depravity to sustain her habit. Soon, she was a walking corpse with no will to live; existing only to get her next fix.

On one occasion, she was flung out of a car by a customer who refused to pay for the sex. Curled up on the kerb, having missed her fix for two days straight, cold turkey set in. A paramedic on her way home happened to notice her and suspecting a panic attack or worse, called the nearest hospital for help. It was at this hospital that Jenny met the charming Asian doctor who changed her life forever. Today, she was at Trinity thanks to this doctor from the East.

Jenny smiled and brought her thoughts back to the present, as she dressed leisurely, dabbing herself with her favourite perfume. Her cosy studio apartment had no mirrors, yet she applied the mascara and gloss perfectly.

She was at the Coffee House at 8 a.m. sharp. Rudr was immersed in a book, sipping his brew.

"Hey Rudr, thank you so much for the time. Truly appreciate it," smiled Jenny, extending her hand for a handshake. Dressed in a pink cotton dress she looked fresh and cheerful. Once again, her beauty overwhelmed Rudr. He smiled.

"Hello, Jennifer."

"Can we start the interview? I have a class at 9:30 a.m."

"Umm ... yeah, sure. Let's do this," he said, putting aside his book.

Jenny didn't make it to the 9:30 class; or the 2 p.m. one. It was easy talking to Rudr. He had a way with words. But most importantly, he was a great listener. Jenny and Rudr talked non-stop till late evening and laughed till their stomachs hurt. So charmed was she with him that she even spoke to him about her de-addiction at the rehab. His comforting words lifted her spirits. None of the counselling sessions had done for her what a day with Rudr Nanda had.

They began to spend all their time with each other, and with each passing day Rudr fell deeply in love with her. There was an enigma about her that was magnetic. All he wanted to do was protect her. Jenny, on her part, was completely besotted by Rudr. The passionate girl that she was, ensured her life revolved around him. They filled each other's voids—his life was no more lonely, Jenny drenched it with music and love and he gently healed her broken soul.

One day however, Jenny didn't show up at the cafe as planned. Later the news that the virus had spread at Trinity made Rudr sprint towards the hospital. On his way he called Tarini, "What was it you said about the antidote to the Kā virus?"

Frail and bone-cold Jenny lay listless with tubes. The entire hospital was in a state of panic. Understaffed for this emergency, there was chaos as there weren't enough beds to accommodate the sick. Young interns were shouting orders at the nursing staff, trying their best to salvage the situation at hand. So, no one noticed when Rudr quietly picked up Jenny in his arms and dashed out. As he made his way towards home, a car followed him. He slowed down to see and froze, staring into the eyes of the bandaged man.

Ashwatthama spoke in a gruff voice, stepping out. "Get in quick. We don't have too much time." Even before Rudr could respond, Ashwatthama had laid Jenny on the back seat of the car, clamped her jugular and started a central line. "I have the antidote that will get her back on her feet," he declared, throwing the car keys towards an amazed Rudr. "Hurry up and drive now while I look after her."

"Where to?" Rudr asked dumbfounded.

"I have a cottage in the woods, it's safe there. Take the first right turn."

When Rudr awoke, Jenny was in the pantry making coffee and singing. Seeing him awake she smiled and ran to him, hugging him tightly. "Thank you for saving my life!"

"Thank the man with the bandage—where is he?"

"There's only you and me here. No one else Rudr," she said coyly. "Let's get out of here," she added, "I don't feel safe."

"Why—did something happen?"

"Nothing I couldn't deal with…" she said with a breezy smile.

He held her close and whispered into her ears, "You're beautiful, talented and…"

"And what?" she teased.

"And dangerous," he smiled.

27

Padma

Padma beamed with pride as she heard her name being called out affectionately by the party president amid thunderous applause.

Strikingly beautiful, she took to the mic and delivered her first political speech. Her poise, and choice of words, spoken softly but firmly, sent a clear, strong message out to the audience.

Padma Ramachandran had dreamt of this moment all her life. Born into a political family in Colombo, Sri Lanka, she was well aware of debates and talks focused on national issues and policy from childhood. Her father, the legendary Murli Ramachandran was one of Sri Lanka's candidates in the New World Order and she had just been announced as the President of the Youth Wing of Sri Lanka's United National Party.

"Sulakshana, you have to meet Padma. Please accompany me to dinner tonight at Mr Murli's home," Raj told his wife that evening.

Having spent 50 years with Raj, she knew immediately that Padma had to be special as her husband rarely ever showed enthusiasm in meeting anyone.

"Mr Murli's daughter? The kid with the runny nose and constant cold? I remember her being a sickly child with two plaits."

"Yes, the sickly child with two plaits has grown into a confident and beautiful young girl with very strong opinions. I heard her introductory speech today at the party headquarters. She is angel-faced and sparkles with intelligence."

"Hmm, RK … what is it? You're being really generous with your compliments. I haven't heard such appreciation from you for a while!" She suddenly understood where her husband's thoughts were headed, but kept quiet.

Murli Ramachandran's home looked resplendent with pre-Diwali decorations. But what impressed Raj and Sulakshana Nanda most was the Krishna shrine located at the northeast corner of the lawns. It was a beautiful white marble replica of the Prem Mandir temple at Vrindavan, India, complete with figurines of Radha-Krishna.

Dinner was an intimate affair; only the top brass of the party was invited along with their families. As the Nandas walked into the house, they were greeted warmly by Ramachandrans. The two families had known each other for decades.

"Padma, come and meet the dynamic Mr and Mrs Nanda," Mrs Ramachandran called out to her daughter.

"Hello, Uncle, Aunty. Wow, I finally get to meet you. I believe you haven't seen Rudr for the longest time."

"Rudr? Do you know him?" enquired the pleasantly surprised Raj.

"Yes, we studied together at Oxford; he was a few years junior to me." She smiled shyly. Her heart was beating so loudly she was afraid the Nandas would hear it.

"That's great. Are you both still in touch?"

"Yes Uncle; I spoke to him this morning." She blushed a deep beetroot red and hurriedly excused herself to join her friend, Aashvi.

"Murli, your daughter is a beautiful young lady. I am very impressed by her."

"Why, thanks Raj," said Murli beaming, handing him a single malt.

"It's great news that Rudr and Padma are friends and that both studied at Oxford."

"Yes, we should meet with the children when Rudr is here. They could have a future together," suggested Raj.

Murli nodded in glee. "You just put in words what I had in mind, Raj!"

Raj was so ecstatic, he softly hummed a song on the drive back home. Sulakshana was overjoyed to see Raj relaxed and happy after ages. She rested her head on his tired shoulders. Life had been rough on them, she reminisced. The storm that had started with the death of their only son Vishnuyasa had left them battered. Soon after Sumati had walked out, they had sold their home in Delhi. She closed her eyes, reliving the harrowing events that followed.

28

Encounter

It was a cold winter evening in Delhi and Sulakshana and Raj had just retired to bed early, when they heard Koko, their golden retriever barking in the room outside. Raj got out of bed and opened the bedroom door. Standing in front of him were his two brothers. One short and bony; the other tall and bald. Near their feet lay Koko, dead, bleeding from the neck.

Raj rushed to his bedside drawer to pull out his gun but was shot in his leg by Tejasya. He fell, bleeding. Rajneesh who looked uncannily like a *langur* with a flat nose and prominent teeth, leapt on the bed, climbed on top of Sulakshana, and slowly stroked her face as she howled in terror.

"Stop!" Raj cried. "You filthy man, she is your sister-in-law!"

"Oh yes how can I forget?" said Rajneesh, as he hopped down and sat next to the bleeding Raj.

His sinister eyes piercing Raj he whimpered, "Strange you bring up family ties.

"You took away my daughter from me..."

"Yes I did, but I should have handed you over to the police, for your dastardly act," retorted Raj, feeling faint as the blood oozed heavily from the wound. "What do you want now?"

"Everything you own and possess, everyone you call yours, is mine from today. It's only natural—it's all in the family," he said. Raj fainted.

"*Naani*, where are you?" Sulakshana heard Harsh walk in and with him was a young, charming boy his age.

Kali spoke softly.

"Kapi *Dada*—here, I have brought your grandson Harsh along."

Rajneesh rushed towards Harsh and held him close. "For family, I will kill family.

Whenever I call for Harsh, you will bring him to us or else I will kill your entire family," he whimpered, looking at Sulakshana.

Kali looked lovingly into Sulakshana's eyes and whispered into her ears. "You will be our link to the family and no one will know."

She stood frozen and shocked as Kapi smothered her face with kisses. "My poor sister-in-law," he smirked. Running his finger down the nape of her neck, he suddenly grabbed a breast, as he held onto Harsh in an unyielding grip with the other hand.

They left as suddenly as they had arrived.

Sulakshana was in a daze. She called the ambulance; she called her driver Moti Singh ... and went and sat on the kitchen stool. As she heard the ambulance siren, confident that Raj would now make it, she picked up the kitchen knife and slashed her wrists.

***

"We choose our joys and sorrows long before we experience them," remarked Babaji.

Raj and Sulakshana lay on adjacent beds in a hospital suite. Sulakshana was crying continuously and felt trapped; her breathing was compromised.

"What are we going to do?" she whispered, looking at Babaji.

Raj spoke up angrily, as he removed the IV from his arms, "I will finish them both. That's what I am going to do."

Babaji walked up to Raj and held him tightly, till his rage subsided. He called for the nurse. Once she left the room he spoke. "Later tonight, you will both travel to Colombo in an air ambulance. Moti Singh will accompany you—I have spoken to him. All arrangements are in place to welcome you to a new life, one of complete obscurity."

"I can't keep disappearing every few years, I have responsibilities and duties to fulfil."

"Your foremost responsibility is to remain alive. Guru Kripacharya has created a protective smokescreen around you three with his *siddhis*, which will keep you hidden.

"Vibhishanji, our Immortal sage, has set up meetings for you in Colombo next week to take your work forward, and an airy comfortable cottage has been designed with a large garden keeping you in mind Sulakshana. Any more questions?"

"Yes. But why Sri Lanka?"

The Immortal

Vibhishan

Deep, intense black eyes peered into the avant-garde microscope; large hands with thin long fingers manipulated the DNA strands that lay exposed on the slide. The hand-eye coordination was precise. The man, the machine and the DNA were in perfect unison as Dr Vibhishan Gunasekera fit in the final genome in the DNA transcript.

All eyes were on him. Dressed in a starched white shirt with dark pleated trousers, his face sparkled with youthful vigour. On his head was a faded golf cap that covered most of his dark hair.

He had finally created his DNA avatar, a digital version of his genetic blueprint that would evolve day-by-day. The avatar would analyse his diet, monitor the interactions between his genes and check thermodynamics within the blood, recommending diet and exercise changes daily.

"Everything okay. No red flags—for now," he said in heavily accented English. Amidst applause and cheers, flashbulbs and cameras popped and clicked as he was swiftly escorted to his limousine by security guards.

A gorgeous young lady in a red chiffon gown greeted him inside the car.

"Dr Vibhishan Gunasekara, the most influential scientist of today, tell us about your journey," she cajoled, gracefully pouring out the champagne.

"Dedication and hard work," he muttered as he sipped from a gold-rimmed flute.

"Dad, you can say more?" she pleaded as photographers surrounded the car. She knew how awkward all this attention was for him. She clinked her champagne glass with his and planted a kiss on his cheek.

For a fleeting moment, his thoughts went back to the centuries gone by, to a life well lived.

"Dad, now have the wounds healed? Those inflicted by our own in Sri Lanka?"

The gentle voice brought him back to his present persona where he led cutting-edge genetic research at the University of Tokyo.

"Yes darling, the President of Sri Lanka is going to be on the panel, felicitating me this evening."

"That brute! He had called you a traitor!"

"Never mind child. He had his reasons; I had mine," he said in a pensive voice. Gently tucking her hair behind her ears, he continued. "I have a story to tell, for your ears only…

"In an era gone by, the world was a more isolated one. There were kings and kingdoms and opulent palaces. I lived in a golden palace in a golden city. No, not I; my older brother Ravana was the king of the land. He was very learned, spiritually accomplished, and had been blessed by the gods. But his knowledge inflated his ego, his wealth made him careless and his arrogance made him unjust. I loved him dearly, so I rebuked him for his wayward ways, tried hard to guide him when ego and arrogance began to lead him astray. The last straw was his coveting another man's wife. No ordinary man at that. But he took deep offence and threw me out of his kingdom. My mother advised me to remain true to my dharma and seek out Lord Vishnu's Avatar, Lord Rama. She reminded me that Lord Brahma himself had blessed me that I would have recourse to the Vishnu Avatar.

"I sought shelter at the feet of Ravana's sworn enemy, my Lord Rama, whose wife he had kidnapped. Lord Rama accepted me as a brother despite suspicion and distrust among his ranks. I helped him to rescue his wife Sita from my brother's palace. Pragmatic and hardworking I stood by what was morally right. To walk the path of truth and righteousness, I even abandoned my family and fought my king, my dearly beloved brother. What pains me the most is my hand in the death of my oldest brother

Kumbhakarna, who chose to follow his dharma of protecting his king and brother even though he was staunchly against Sita Ma's abduction. My dharma was to stand for righteousness, and I did so even in the most challenging circumstances.

"I have consequently been called many names—Traitor; Murderer; Coward. But my mother, wife and daughter stood by me knowing that I had surrendered to the good, to the ethical, to Rama. Later, after Shri Rama's forces annihilated Ravana and his mighty army, in a strategic call for duty, Mandodari, Ravana's pious and righteous wife, married me so that my coronation as king would be acceptable to my praja.

"I ruled Lanka along with Mandodari, she who is revered as one of the panchkanyas (uttering whose name dispels sin) and our reign brought prosperity and dharma into the lives of the asuras too.

"Lord Rama himself ordained me into the life of an Immortal, instructing me to remain on earth and guide people on righteousness and dharma. Dedication to the name of God before self and family has kept me in the illustrious club of Immortals.

"I am blessed that today, my dear Aashvi, I have an even greater role to play in the life of the final Vishnu Avatar, Kalki."

29

Homecoming

As the plane touched down at Bandaranaike International Airport, Colombo, Rudr and Jenny held hands tightly. Rudr was nervous. He hadn't visited home in two decades and wasn't sure what to expect.

But it was *Bade Papa* himself who came to receive them at the airport. Rudr relaxed. As usual, *Bade Papa* had his way with charming words. After a comfortable round of greetings and introductions, he convinced Jenny that she would be more comfortable at a luxury hotel close to the Nanda residence. What he did not mention was that the Nanda guestrooms at the family residence were more luxurious than any hotel by far. Rudr was shocked by the suggestion but knew better than to argue with his granddad at the airport. He decided that once home he would talk to his grandparents into having Jenny stay over.

As the car passed by the main entrance of the Nanda property lined by coconut trees Rudr felt exhilarated. He was finally home. Then he saw *Badi Mumma*, petite and demure, standing with the *puja thali* at the entrance. He ran up to her, touched her feet and then simply lifted her in his arms with a whoop. His childhood anchor, *Mumma* had always showered him with unconditional love. She held him tightly, securing him in the warmth of her love, and instantly they reconnected.

"Rudr, tell me about Jenny. Why has she come here?" asked Raj bluntly a short while later.

"She is a friend and someone I care about deeply. In fact, *Bade Papa*, I would have liked her to stay with us and see our lives and our culture, spend time getting to know you and *Mumma*."

"Rudr, we don't allow strangers home!"

"But she is no stranger."

"To the Nandas she is!"

"All right then ... I will move to the hotel with her!"

The lightning-quick defence and tinge of anger disturbed Raj.

"Rudr, let's not forget that in this part of the world we have a social milieu that is orthodox. You still have to walk your path and play your role in the future of this world—I cannot let you dig your own grave!

"We sacrificed years of separation from you just to keep you safe. A love affair with a runaway American druggie spells political doom for you."

"I see you have been investigating and snooping around my life, granddad! Well, let me correct you. At one point in time Jenny did do drugs but is clean now. She has rebuilt her life. And she never hid her past from me."

"She is bad news Rudr. Trust me when I say you are following in Tejasya's footsteps!"

The conversation at the breakfast table was getting unpleasant. Sulakshana excused herself and rushed to the kitchen, silently remembering her son Vishnuyasa, Rudr's dad, having similar arguments with his father.

"Son … all I'm trying to say is don't expose her to the public. By all means, continue to see her. But for marriage, I have found a lovely young girl who is befitting for our family and a stepping-stone to your political career—the only daughter of a most loved politician."

The suggestion infuriated the otherwise calm Rudr who walked out without saying another word.

In his room, by himself, Rudr picked up his guitar and started strumming. As the chords moved from one note to the other, he reflected on his feelings for *Bade Papa* down the years. They went from feeling secure in his arms, to adulation, to hero worship, and then drift to anger and helplessness. He realised that the only things he had decided for himself were the women in his life. All other decisions were taken by *Bade Papa* and Babaji. Suddenly opposing Raj and standing his own ground were of paramount importance.

Sulakshana gently knocked on the door and entered. Rudr was playing the guitar with a faraway look in his eyes. The look he had as a child when he was denied his favourite toy.

"I will try to reason with your granddad—but you do know that he is very stubborn, Rudr."

With sudden clarity he announced, "*Mumma*, I am getting my friend Jenny home this evening. Please ensure that she receives the hospitality here that a friend of mine deserves." Saying this in a relaxed and soft tone, he left his grandmother to fret and organise.

He headed first to Padma's house where she was anxiously awaiting his arrival. On the way he picked up white tuberoses for her. He knew she loved them and her thoughts had already pacified the anger in his head. As he was escorted into the house by security staff his heart skipped a beat. He had longed for this day for years. Just then she appeared, looking fresh and divine. A lot had changed for both of them in the past few years.

Padma's love for Rudr had grown and his name was always on her lips. For Rudr, she was his alter ego, the one keeping him from committing to Jenny. The hug was hence very restrained. She feared he may recognise her angst; and he was awkward because, suddenly, she was everything that made sense. Her large eyes spoke to him of lonely winters and both knew in their silence that their souls were reconnecting.

Soon they both were talking animatedly about their lives and she jokingly enquired, "So who's the current flame, Rudr? And how many have there been?"

"Padma, you tell me! Have you found your one-woman man?" he asked wickedly in response.

She smiled, her cheeks turning pink, "Yes … my parents have found a man and soon we may be getting engaged."

The happiness and joy in her heart startled, even disturbed, Rudr. So she had found her match—and why not? They had not committed to each other all these years. He had never been insecure about her. How could he have been so wrong to think that Padma would be waiting? After all, he had not put his relationship with Jenny on hold to allow for his innermost feelings for Padma.

But Rudr, being true to his nature, did not show the hurt his heart felt on his face and continued smiling till she asked, "So do you not want to know who he is?"

"Yes, of course … who is the fortunate man?"

"Shall tell you only after you tell me Mr Nanda." She wanted to be sure she wasn't intruding into his life because she was well aware of his Casanova days.

"Oh Padma, I have grown past the Casanova phase! I'm looking for stability."

"Yes, of course..." she said, rolling her eyes.

Rudr continued, "Jenny has accompanied me to India. I love her for her exuberance and joie de vivre, but haven't committed as yet. You must meet her, Padma." Then he went on to tell her all about his grandparents and their disapproval and *Bade Papa*'s ridiculous suggestion of marriage to a politician's daughter.

It was her turn to be shocked and teary-eyed. What he didn't tell her was that he loved her foremost; what she didn't tell him was that she was the politician's daughter.

Looking away from her hastily, Rudr invited her for his grandparents' 50th anniversary and left in an uncharacteristic hurry. Padma stood dazed at the doorway, her eyes moist with tears.

***

"Scores of people were wounded and a few were confirmed dead as a car bomb detonated in the parking lot of the Grand Kandyan Hotel this afternoon, sending a massive plume of smoke over the city, shattering windows and bringing down a part of the west wing of the luxury hotel." Rudr couldn't believe the news flash he had just received. The phone call that followed left him numb.

"I am reaching the hotel, meet you there. Stay strong," was all he could mumble.

He made his way through the firefighters and ambulances, people crying and wounded, and the battered hotel lobby. He saw *Mumma* and Moti Singh at the far end and sprinted towards them. The two he loved more than he knew lay next to each other—one nearing death, one brutally injured.

The next few minutes went by in a daze. Rudr functioned mechanically, as a strange sensation penetrated his being. The trauma and emergency department staff were on their toes, along with the chief interventionist and his team. As soon as the air ambulance reached, Raj was taken to the cardiac ICCU and revival procedures started. After seven to eight minutes of cardiac pumping, a faint heartbeat was detected, egging the team on. Raj was hooked to life support.

Chief Interventionist Dr Ranatunge briefed Sulakshana. They were able to revive the heart and start life support for Raj. But the prognosis was still guarded as the brain had suffered severe hypoxia: Raj was in coma. The next 72 hours would be crucial. The ground shifted from beneath Sulakshana's feet. She looked around for support, and as usual it was only Moti Singh, their driver who stood there quiet and strong.

Rudr was with Jenny. Her breathing was laboured and she hadn't gained consciousness yet. He held her hand and kissed her bruised forehead. He felt responsible—she would have been fine had she not accompanied him to Colombo. Far away from her family, she lay dying for no fault of hers. So young; so beautiful; taking her last few breaths. He never got to tell her that he loved her, he didn't get to hold her close long enough, and yet she never missed a chance to express her love to him. It was as if she knew she had limited time, and she lived each moment in love and happiness. Blinded by the tears in his eyes, engulfed in waves of grief, he placed his hand on her heart.

"Go Beautiful One, go…" he whispered into her ears. Jenny opened her eyes, held Rudr's hand tightly and left this world with a smile on her lips.

30

Harsh

Harsh sat with legs crossed and tapped his Ray-Ban on the cafe table at the airport terminal. His hair was neater than usual and his suit was new. But it was his face that commanded attention. The perfect coming together of different facets had crafted a magnetic, handsome face. His eyes had an intensity, an honesty, a gentleness that made you want to trust him instantly. He spoke softly. "Today's massacre was perfect, yet my grand old man is still breathing. Go Ruh, torment his thoughts and his being, get control of him now at least." Ruh spoke even more softly, "He has protection, two of us have been trying to penetrate his energies, but have given up. Only Kali Sir can help us."

A security dog, a German shepherd patrolling the airport, started barking loudly and circling Harsh. His keeper, the officer said, "Hello sir, something about you is disturbing the canine. Would you mind if I frisk you?"

"Sure," said Harsh, smiling. Ruh meanwhile decided to get even with the ill-tempered dog, and soon the canine was running, barking loudly, across the airport terminal as though possessed. The officer was no longer able to hold on to the leash, and chased the frenzied animal screaming, "Behave Seal! What is it with you?" But Seal sprinted across the terminal towards the exit gate, running straight into a terminal bus. He was breathing his last by the time the officer caught up with him.

Ruh was back with Harsh. The two smiled. They had been together for more than a decade.

Even though Harsh was born into wealth, and nurtured by a loving family, he secretly felt out of place even as a young child. His innate insecurities were further fuelled when, one fine day, he was introduced to his maternal grandfather Kapi. It was strange that his mother Sujata had never mentioned this grandparent to him. For all practical purposes, he grew up believing that Raj and Sulakshana Nanda were his maternal grandparents. Every holiday his mother would visit her parental home in Delhi, along with him and his younger sister Surabhi—these were the faint memories of a toddler. As it happened, these family visits then simply stopped. One day, Kali had turned up at his home saying his grandparents Raj and Sulakshana had called for him. Harsh took an instant liking to Kali and felt he could trust him. It was at his grandparent's home that Harsh first met Kapi. He winced at the distasteful memory of the incident. He realised that far from being revolted by Kapi's actions, he had enjoyed seeing his grandmother wince in pain. Soon after, his grandparents left suddenly and he was sent to a boarding school in Switzerland. It was here that Kapi started meeting him frequently. There was a dark side to Harsh that Kapi tapped into. Harsh had strange urges, which he didn't quite understand. Kapi had understood; he himself had enjoyed the pleasures of what the Germans called *schadenfreude*—diabolical delight in other people's agony or suffering.

Kapi pandered to Harsh's needs and fulfilled those urges. Soon, Harsh decided that he would rather live with Kapi—boarding school and home lacked excitement and he felt smothered by all that family doting and love. For him, a world with Kapi was an enticing, exciting proposition. For his spring break in the eighth grade, he visited Kapi at Keekatpur, while his parents were informed that he was staying at a friend's home in Lausanne.

Kapi was mentor to the brilliant Kali, and together their intellect and experiments inspired Harsh. The experiments on animals and the *mlecchas* at the biogenetics lab in Keekatpur released feel-good hormones in him—the more the suffering, the more he rejoiced.

Kali and he spent a lot of time together. Being Kali's friend came with special perks—he got access to the enigmatic Guru Shukracharya.

It was Guru Shukracharya who instructed him to go back to the boarding school when he rebelled against returning after the spring break. "You can visit here from time to time my boy. You're our ace card Harsh. You have an important role to play in your family affairs. But for that, you need to ensure that nothing breaks their trust, especially your grandfather Raj's trust, in you."

"What's so important about my family?" he had dared to enquire of the sage. Guru Shukra had smiled at the young boy and left the room.

Later that night Kali took Harsh for a walk in the woods around the tech hub at Keekatpur. "There are deep secrets buried within your family, the guardian of which is Raj, your grandfather. He has the support of the Immortals. They also have access to Kalki, the God of today," he explained to the round-eyed fourteen-year-old.

"Kalki? Immortals? What on earth are you talking about?"

"Kalki is the Saviour of the earth, the final Vishnu Avatar, my so-called nemesis—the villain who is supposed to kill me," grinned Kali. "The Immortals, the Forces of Light, are higher beings that have been around the planet forever and are its chief defence. They have the lineage of the gods and are responsible for the birth of Kalki. They have kept him hidden from the world. Guru Shukra has been trying to locate Kalki for years now. We got close many times but Kalki remains elusive. Immortal Kripacharya, a master strategist, has put a smokescreen around Raj and his grandchildren. Raj, your grandpa, is our key to locating Kalki.

"Immortals Hanuman and Parashuram lead the light forces, and we, the dark forces, are led by Guru Shukra. Your grandfather Kapi is the head of the dark forces and a direct disciple of Guru Shukra."

"Sick!" exclaimed Harsh, feeling proud of his lineage, and of the future role he must play in unravelling the mystery of Kalki. Both stunned and elated with what he had heard, Harsh's left eye started twitching. Kali knew it was time to satisfy his friend's urge.

A watchman was patrolling the woods. Kali attacked him from behind with his pocket knife and slowly slashed his neck, bringing on a reaction of glee from Harsh. The twitch vanished.

"It was incredible of you to kill your watchman for me," he beamed at Kali.

Kali moved his hands above the limp corpse, uttering a dark spell. As Harsh watched with horror, the watchman sat up.

"He is alive!" he exclaimed.

"No, he is a dead man walking, a *pishach*, a walker..."

"I don't understand."

"Souls that die suddenly remain in a state of shock for a few years—and stuck in a dimension of existence."

"Explain again."

"Our planet has many different dimensions of existence, some perceivable, some not. All of creation is interdependent, quite like a food chain.

"I tame these traumatised souls to become shapeshifters or even invisible. Different energies require different nourishment, the *pishach* feeds on the blood of humans, draining them, corrupting and influencing their minds."

"Oh my God! That's freaky Kali. How many of them are there in the world?" he asked, shuddering.

"The world is full of spirits. They are forms of energy surrounding us all the time, only that most people are unaware. I rule the World of Spirits, and they listen to my every command," Kali finished, leaving Harsh speechless.

"I will assign Ruh to you; he is a young *pishach*," Kali spoke in a chilling baritone for a sixteen-year-old. "Whenever you want to meet us, close your eyes and think of me, and Ruh will get you to us. It all has to be done secretly. Do you understand?"

Harsh nodded quietly.

Awkward at first with the *pishach*, and a little afraid, Ruh and he nevertheless became inseparable companions. They began to visit Kapi and Kali every week, for a short while. With each visit, he was exposed to more of the dark world that Kapi ruled.

"Why don't we declare war against the light forces?" he once asked Kapi.

"In a world with nuclear weapons, there can be no all-out war. It would be suicide for us all. Instead, we take over the world by undermining its resources—war by another name," Kapi had explained. "We create so much hunger and hatred that people fall easy prey to drinking and drugs, both of which we supply. These high-strung, stressed individuals then will kill each other over petty wants and differences from a loaf of bread to religious slights. We supply the weapons for this war—every shade of dogma—hold back on basic necessities, and we have a society in distress." Kapi had laughed aloud exposing his small, crooked teeth. "Simultaneously, we expose them to acts of violence on the Internet. Repeated viewing of violent acts and words makes people hard-hearted and less empathetic." Kapi came from behind Harsh and whispered into his left ear, "Kill the human in the human, till they are ready to be mutated into *mlecchas*. The candle burns itself down without any help. The light force, too, is dwindling, and a strong exhale from Guru Shukra will wipe them out."

Harsh was the prodigal grandson and Kapi offered him a chance at empire building. "Choose your field of interest," Kapi exhorted the young lad. Harsh, already fascinated by human suffering, favoured the shadowy world of drugs. He was curious about the many ways drugs could destroy a person, unleash suffering and cause mayhem.

Over the years the boy with strange urges became a major player in Kapi's drug trade. Kapi had understood early that Harsh had a sincerity, a charisma, that evoked trust. He cultivated and nurtured these qualities to make him a skilled people manager. Harsh struck an instant rapport with youngsters and could be extremely persuasive. The drug business didn't just do well—it was booming under Harsh.

Through all this though, Harsh maintained a dual life. He remained close to his parents and sister, never once exposing them to his dark side. He branched out from the family business and excelled in whatever he did. Ruh lived in the spooky Epping Forest some distance away from Harsh's home in London. Kapi had ensured Kali warned Ruh to never sully his daughter Sujata's home with his inauspicious presence.

Recently, Kali had been able to locate Rudr at Oxford and had sent for Harsh.

"It's time to up the game, my friend. My sources have located Rudr, and have information that Raj lives in Colombo, Sri Lanka. Leave right away and win the trust of your grandparents."

Harsh turned up at Raj's home, but there was a firewall there that kept Ruh out. His amiable nature soon won the hearts of his grandparents. Yet Raj remained aloof, and didn't disclose much about the family no matter how hard Harsh tried. Sulakshana too spoke little. Frustrated at hitting a wall, he masterminded the bomb attack to kill Raj—hoping to draw out the whole family.

He was now at the airport, waiting for Kali, who had an urgent disclosure to make.

Kali pulled up a chair as Harsh looked up from his phone, smiling in that tense way he did when he had achieved his devious plan to perfection.

"Your old man is still breathing? Tough cookie, eh?" inquired Kali.

"Yes, but he is critical; his story will end soon."

Kali bit into his cigar and chewed on it.

"Harsh, you're my only friend. Guru Shukra never allowed me any time to cultivate friendships. He said friends were a waste of time. Dear friend, take this as a warning: one wrong move, and you could be killed."

"I have it all sorted," reassured Harsh.

"Now, Rudr. He is under the scanner. Beware of him. Guru Shukra is convinced after details from the *pishach* that Rudr is a direct threat."

"Is he Kalki?"

"No way! That incorrigible flirt who dates anyone with two pretty legs, cannot be Kalki."

Kali then whispered a *mantra* into Harsh's ears.

"Whisper this into Rudr's ears. His reaction will reveal his part in the scheme of things. Take care my friend, you have plenty to deal with.

"The stubborn old man hasn't died yet. Rudr is back with his grandparents and his sibling is arriving too. Looks like you shall be having a small family reunion after all," he smirked.

Moti Singh picked up Tarini at the airport, and soon they were on the expressway, headed for home.

"Finally, you're back *bitiya*. Raj *Saheb* will get okay now."

"What happened *Dada*? Any news on the blast?"

"It's so unfortunate. Raj *Saheb* was at work when he got a call from Rudr's American friend Jenny. She wanted to urgently meet him at the hotel. I was out with *Memsaab*, at a charity event. So he drove himself. The blast happened at 4:15 p.m. When we reached the hotel, I saw Harsh *Baba* rushing out laughing, speaking on the phone. He looked happy."

"Who is Harsh?"

"He is Sujata *Didi's* son. He came here around six months ago, and hasn't gone back since. I believe he is responsible for everything that is happening."

"Are you sure *Dada*?"

"I'm an old, uneducated man, but I have served the family long enough to know its friends and enemies. This boy Harsh is up to some mischief; be careful *bitiya*."

31

Karma

Sulakshana had aged in a day. Wrinkles had suddenly appeared overnight along with bags visible under the eyes. She sat praying beside *Bade Papa*'s bed. Today was their 50th wedding anniversary and they were to be celebrating it. Her thoughts sped back to when she was married off to Raj Nanda, 26.

She was an awkward 17-year-old teenager from Lucknow. Her father was a highly respected civil surgeon. Their parents had fixed their match once the family priest had given the nod that their horoscopes matched. She would bring him luck and he would bring her joy.

The first time they saw each other was at their wedding and yet, theirs was a love story that had stood the test of time. She was besotted by Raj's charisma; and he, by her sheer beauty and simplicity.

Sulakshana wiped a tear and took a shuddering breath at the thought of a life without him. He lay helpless in bed, intubated and vulnerable—her invincible Raj. She prayed to Krishna for a miracle.

The twins quietly observed the tenderness with which Sulakshana stroked Raj's forehead. It looked like the two were having a deep conversation and no words were needed. Tarini gently reached out to Sulakshana and held her. Sulakshana looked at her granddaughter and broke down. She looked so fragile, so frail. She hadn't left Raj's bedside for 24 hours and had refused to go home to rest when Rudr insisted.

Outside the ICU in the waiting area, it was freezing. A sinister laughter that only Harsh could hear, was deafening him. "Stop Ruh!" he whispered, leaning against the wall. "Instead of socialising with your fraternity here, you could try switching off the ventilator my granddad is on..."

Rudr walked into the waiting area. Ruh disappeared suddenly as a gust of wind, throwing open the sealed window. Everyone inside was stunned. Rudr walked straight to Harsh and blocked him.

"Who were you whispering to? Have you lost it, or did you never have it?" The anger in his eyes was evident, his athletic frame towering menacingly, dwarfing the small-built Harsh.

"Get out of here! Your true place is behind bars. You have the audacity to stand here after being responsible for *Bade Papa*'s condition?!" roared Harsh as he pushed a surprised Rudr. "We all know *Bade Papa* was with your girlfriend when the blast happened," he continued, punching Rudr in the chest. "You are your father's true son. First, your dad embarrassed *Bade Papa*, and now you..." He was cut off mid-sentence as Rudr scored a clean uppercut on his jaw. Outside, there was lightning and thunder as an angry sky pelted the ground with rain. A large banyan tree outside the hospital gave way and fell on the parked cars. Some branches and leaves came flying into the waiting area through the window that had just broken. Harsh looked around for Ruh, but he was nowhere. Holding the distracted Harsh by his collar, Rudr whispered a *mantra* in Harsh's left ear, which made him freeze. He then landed a crippling blow on Harsh's head, at the fontanelle spot.

"That's it Rudr. Stop now!" commanded Babaji as he walked in. Rudr retreated, prostrating before his Guru. Babaji then reached out to the bleeding Harsh, took out a packet of ash from his pocket and smeared it on his facial wounds. "This will help," he said reassuringly. Harsh was in a daze. Strangely, the constant ringing in his ears that he had lived with since childhood had just stopped.

"Moti Singh please drop Harsh home, he needs rest," Babaji instructed.

Tarini rushed towards Babaji and fell at his feet. He embraced her with love and gently wiped the tears off her face.

"Take care, my children. You have a long journey ahead. Whenever in doubt, close your eyes and meditate and you will get the answers you are seeking. Rudr, remember *Tapovan*—how you savagely fought the beasts in the wild. The world is no different. Everything is allowed when it comes to survival. That is the law of the universe.

"Do not always be upright in your dealings, for you would have seen in the forest that straight trees are cut down, while crooked ones are left standing.

"Your father paid with his life for remaining upright."

Babaji's words jolted the twins into the reality they now faced.

"Now go and seek your answers and make your choices. Your grandfather's blessings shall forever guide you."

"Is someone from the family responsible for *Bade Papa*'s condition?" inquired Tarini promptly.

"The universe is perfect and in balance. It should not be tampered with. Our death is written the day we are born. Circumstances and choices play themselves out and bring us to our rightful place, depending on our karma. Free will further complicates this and we get this mad dance called 'life'.

"Our attractions and repulsions towards people and things are also deep-rooted in our karmic cycle. I have a long karmic history with Raj. And hence I am here during his difficult time to ease things. His offender will be taken care of. This is my word to you."

32

Bitter Truth

The man fired a single bullet, saw his victim fall dead, smiled at a job well done and drove off.

He abandoned the old, red beat-up sedan near Cinnamon Gardens, Colombo. He swiftly walked away and, in a bit, flung his expensive black hoodie over the sleeping beggar on the sidewalk. He walked 200 metres across to his Mercedes B Class and drove homewards.

His modus operandi hadn't changed in decades. He had jackal-like insight into events and could sniff danger from miles away. His method of eliminating his tormentor or adversary was always the same. Alone; just he and his victim; because he depended on no one and trusted no one.

His rise to power and politics was thanks to his chameleon-like nature. A master manipulator with a charming tongue and a suave personality, his ruthless thinking had made him excel in the world of politics. He was so discreet that his left hand didn't know what the right hand was doing, while he knew every move his friends and foes made every day.

***

At Keekatpur, a fuming Kapi was inconsolable.

"How could this happen? Where was Ruh? His one job was to protect Harsh!"

"Ruh was controlled by that wily tantric Babaji. Ruh tried reaching out to the other spirits for Harsh's protection. But the tantric had blocked Harsh's energies by the clever gesture of applying holy ash," said Kali.

"And the *mantra*, did Harsh not use it?"

"No, even before he could utter it, Rudr whispered a verse from the *Hanuman Chalisa* into his ears. Kapi *Da*, our enemies are smarter than we thought. Together they have created a veil of protection around Kalki. I can't wait to know his identity."

Kapi started hopping around the room on one hand, ranting in a high-pitched whine, "I want them all dead now, now! Raj, Rudr, Babaji ... all dead now, dead now, dead now..." He was inconsolable. Kali injected him with an anxiolytic and put him to sleep gently.

***

The loud doorbell at midnight meant trouble. Sulakshana knew there was bad news on the other side of the door as she threw on a Kane shawl heading towards the porch. The house was dark and quiet, just like her life. She opened the door. It was the Director General (DG) of Police, wearing a grave face.

"Deeply sorry to bother you, Ma'am. A body with bullet wounds has been found in the quiet by-lanes of the old town. His identification says 'Harsh Anand'."

She reeled at the news and was about to collapse had it not been for Rudr who had come up right behind her. He seated her gently on the sofa and continued the conversation with the DG. The police wanted to hand over the body to the next of kin after identification. They were still on the lookout for the culprit and needed to question the family.

Tarini was at the hospital with *Bade Papa*.

Rudr quickly accompanied the police in his Benz, with Moti Singh behind the wheels. The rest of the staff rallied around Sulakshana. She cried quietly to herself questioning her fate. She had had an inkling of impending doom a few months ago. She had immediately started chanting her Krishna *naam japa* more fervently. Yet now, in the twilight of her life, she had to face the impending death of her beloved, as well as her grandson.

The room began to spin as she heard Raj's voice. The three realms past, present and future played havoc in her mind as she saw herself now floating, now sinking in some deep sea, all alone. Feeling suffocated as she came up, gasping for breath, she opened her eyes. Raj's large photograph stared back at her, bringing her sharply back to the present.

A single bullet had pierced through the internal jugular vein on the right side of the neck. There were no other injuries or signs of struggle before death. The killer had certainly taken Harsh by surprise. The police informed Rudr that no phone or car was recovered from the area. However, a chip embedded in his wrist was being investigated by the police. The brutal murder of the son of iron and steel tycoon Anil Anand had taken the world by storm.

"Rudr, let Moti Singh spend the night at the hospital today. We both need to speak to *Mumma* about Harsh. I'm leaving the ICU now and reaching home." Since her arrival, Tarini had been spending nights at the hospital ICU. "She could provide definite insights ... she is said to be a keeper of secrets."

They waited patiently as the line of relatives and mourners gradually dispersed. Sujata and Anil Anand, parents of Harsh, quietly, head held low, walked towards their wing in the Nanda home, escorted by Tarini. She saw them to their room and was ensuring they were comfortable when Surabhi Anand walked in. Surabhi was holding up far better than her parents. She persuaded Tarini to go back to Sulakshana assuring that she would look after her parents.

"Come, *Mumma*, let me make you some coffee." They were in the library. Ever since Tarini had taken over the night duty at the hospital, Sulakshana would spend most of her nights here. The room still smelt of a fine blend of Bolivar and Bvlgari. She closed her eyes and inhaled deeply. The aroma of roasted African coffee was taking predominance now.

"How did Harsh land up in Colombo? Your location was hidden from everyone, including all of us," questioned Rudr without much ado.

"And where was he all these years?" asked Tarini. "I heard you hadn't met him for a decade."

"He was with his parents, Sujata and Anil. We cut off from everyone on Babaji's insistence. Except our own blood—you children."

The twins looked puzzled. "Sorry—we don't understand *Mumma*."

Sulakshana's eyes had a steely gaze. "Harsh is Sujata's son; but Sujata is not my daughter."

Shocked, Tarini muttered, "Whose?"

"Your grandfather has an older brother Rajneesh; she was found with him. No one knows who her parents are and how this child reached him."

"What?!" echoed the twins together. Rudr's head was spinning as he spoke.

"Tarini, remember the scuffle that Harsh and I had while *Bade Papa* was in hospital?"

"Yes. Why?"

"Harsh said something in my ear that shocked me."

"What did he say?" enquired Tarini with bated breath.

"He said his granddad was kept hidden by our granddad—*Bade Papa*! I had caught him talking to himself, so I thought he was goofy and didn't pay much attention to him."

"That's weird. What did he mean? This is getting complicated."

Sulakshana remained silent in response to the barrage of questions on Rajneesh, so they decided to steer the conversation back to Harsh.

"Babaji had told us that there was a smokescreen around us to keep us protected, and any third person living with us would deactivate the smokescreen, allowing our enemies and Sphinx to locate us. We lived for two decades here in Colombo without a problem."

"And yet, *Bade Papa* had allowed Harsh entry!"

"Yes, yes. He trusted Harsh. He was family, and even though he was Kapi's grandson, Raj loved him as his own."

"Who is Kapi?"

"Rajneesh, your *Bade Papa*'s older brother, is known by the name Kapi in the dark world he controls. He is the reason we are in hiding," she sobbed.

"This is absurd! You were living with the enemy. And knowingly!" accused Rudr.

"Harsh had convinced Raj of his loyalty. He fell at his feet asking for love and guidance," offered Sulakshana. "Your *Bade Papa* longed for his family ... we had lived alone for so long here. Politics was taking a toll on his time and health and he was working harder than ever before, although behind the scenes. He travelled the length and breadth of the country, helping Murli Ramachandran win the love and trust of people."

"Harsh came in as a breath of fresh air in our dull lives. Not once did he give us any reason to doubt his intentions. He was a loving, caring grandson. We became really fond of him. He so reminded us of your aunt, his mother, Sujata *Bua*."

Tears welled up in her eyes as she continued, "Rudr, your grandfather wanted you all, his grandchildren, to be safe and happy, above all. He sacrificed his law practice back in Delhi, kept himself away from the public eye, moved to Colombo and even gave up his ambitions of a post in the New World Order, for the sake of his family. To him family is power."

Wiping the tears, with a change in tone and hurt writ large on her face, she remarked, "Your growing proximity to Jenny bothered him the most. He had committed to Mr Ramachandran. Padma and you were friends. He believed she was the perfect girl for you … and had proposed marriage for the two of you."

Rudr shifted uncomfortably. His heartbeat slowed down as he said to Tarini. "*Bade Papa* knew that Padma was right for me in one meeting … and it has taken me more than four years to figure that out."

Clearing his throat, he enquired of *Mumma*, "Why was *Bade Papa* so fixated on a political career for me? Why did he never bother to know my likes and dislikes?"

"Son, Rajkumar Nanda never asks. He always advises and his word is the ultimate law. He trusts none but his own decisions."

"Why? What makes him so difficult? Why did he never let us decide and make our own choices and mistakes?" asked Tarini.

"Because your father..." and then, just as quickly she held back, and cried, choking on her emotions. Tarini held her for a long time till her broken sobs subsided.

"Your grandfather changed after your father's death—and your mother's walking away. He blamed himself for it; and decided he would be responsible for your life choices, lest you repeat your father's mistakes." Shuddering with bygone memories and the unhealed scars of Vishnuyasa's tragic loss, she drifted into a quiet, solitary place. Tarini held her hand patiently and waited for her to regain her composure. She knew revisiting the ghosts of the past was traumatic for her *Mumma*; but they were best faced now and conquered forever.

After a while she gently nudged her. "*Mumma*, tell us about our parents."

"Your father was the younger one of my two children and he was born prematurely at seven months, frail and sickly. But he was a fighter and a quick learner. He was always in a hurry, with inexhaustible energy. He had a mind of his own and was stubborn. Your grandfather was very busy during your dad's teenage years and Sujata was already enrolled in a finishing school in Switzerland. Raj travelled a lot and so Vishnu and I were left to ourselves for the most part. He had me wrapped around his little finger and I gave in to all his demands ... always doting on him ... thinking my son could do no wrong. I hid his teenage drinking and nightouts from your granddad. Raj doubted Vishnu and questioned him many times. But that led to further isolation and a breakdown of communication between the two. Yet Vishnuyasa was a sensitive soul seeking love and appreciation.

"He was like me; a seeker of truth. As he grew, he began to question the means and sources of the family wealth and the family law firm's success. He studied law and excelled at it. He joined the firm despite his apprehensions and things were good till a personal tragedy in my paternal family threatened all our lives. At that point Babaji helped us relocate to Shambhala in the forests of Ādi. Stress between your grandfather and father deepened in Shambhala. After your birth, we went back to Delhi, and Raj went back to his firm, which was left in the hands of his younger brother Tejasya. Your father Vishnuyasa smelt a rat, and warned us that things were not as they seemed at the firm. But Raj didn't believe him, so my son walked out on us and you all, his children, to start a small partnership firm in Mumbai. His behaviour hurt your granddad tremendously as he freely gave interviews claiming that Nanda & Sons was built on blood money, that he would expose the politicians and industrialists his father was protecting.

"He rarely visited us. The last time I saw him, he was preoccupied and disturbed as though carrying a huge burden." Taking a sip of water, she continued. "And then one day he was gone—brutally murdered. I cannot bring myself to believe that even today." The three embraced and cried—she for opening of the old wounds, and the twins for the loss of a father whom they were just beginning to know.

"What about our mother? Why did she abandon us?" asked Rudr.

"Sumati, your mother, was the best thing that happened to our family. She brought sunshine and laughter. Then your brothers and you came along … bringing music and light into our lives.

"Sumati would never abandon you! The circumstances at that point were difficult; all four of you had been sent away on Babaji's advice. Only your mother was left with the both of us—and she had just discovered that Vishnu had been murdered."

"Where is she now?"

"No idea. Your grandfather has searched the world for her unsuccessfully."

"Now listen children. Tomorrow at the break of dawn, Sujata, Anil and Surabhi are leaving with Moti Singh for Haridwar to immerse Harsh's ashes in the holy Ganga. You should go too. Ved Vyasji will be there for the final rites. He may have the answers you are looking for."

33

Final Rites

Anil Anand's clout was visible at Haridwar. The low-profile business tycoon from London had his roots in Uttaranchal, India, and special arrangements had been made at Har ki Pauri for the ceremony. A platform had been specially constructed at Brahma Kund to accommodate the multitudes of mourners who had arrived. Most knew the Anand brothers well and the rest knew the Nandas.

The immediate family arrived by helicopter. As Surabhi alighted carrying the urn, she was met by her paternal cousins Akhilesh and Gaurav, who gathered her into their arms. In anger and shock, they vowed not to rest till their brother's culprit was found and punished. Surabhi cried relentlessly while Tarini comforted her. Among the other relatives present were Anil's elder brothers and sisters with their families.

Rudr led Anil and Sujata towards Ved Vyas who was sitting by a pyre ready to perform the final rites. Sujata was crying inconsolably while Anil gazed blankly into the distance. The atmosphere was charged with sorrow but underlying anger was simmering at the brutal murder of a young scion from the illustrious family.

The twins' eyes met their Guru's and they did their *pranams* from a distance. Ved Vyas, along with five of his disciples, started the chanting of the Vedic *mantras*. The *Asthi Visarjan puja* for ritual immersion of the ashes followed. After around 45 minutes Harsh's brothers, wearing white dhotis and small white *angavastrams* over their naked torsos, entered the holy Ganga to consign the ashes to the sacred waters. Akhilesh and Gaurav held the urn as Rudr undid the red cloth covering it. There was a sudden splash as something jumped into the water from an overhanging branch. It was barely human, its naked, bony torso twisted and disfigured, covered in stark white ash. In a swift move, the creature scooped up the dispersing ashes into his palms, made a sign with his fingers and vanished into the strong river current at the *Asthi Pravah Ghat*. Rudr, an accomplished swimmer, dived in to follow him, even as horrified onlookers whispered amongst themselves about this being a bad omen.

Swimming with the river current, Rudr manoeuvred easily to reach and grab the creature. Rudr held him from behind and punched him hard on his face—only to receive a hard blow himself. They didn't let go of each other as the current carried them in a cascading flow. Soon, they reached the other side of the bank, where Ved Vyas was standing with Tarini. "Rudr!" he called, "Come out now!" Distracted for a second, Rudr's grip loosened and the slippery man disappeared into the waters.

Kali watched the entire ceremony from the broken windows of a dilapidated temple. He paid a quiet homage to the only friend he ever had. He vowed revenge and left immediately to find Ruh, who was still missing.

Ved Vyas was grateful to see Rudr back, unhurt. As the last of the relatives left, he invited the family to his *ashram* a few kilometres away. Rudr and Tarini immediately accepted, so did Sujata. But her husband and daughter politely declined the offer. Anil and daughter Surabhi accompanied their relatives to a guesthouse nearby.

Seated in the car, Ved Vyas finally spoke to the twins.

"Rudr why do you always chase trouble? Haven't I warned you to live a normal life?"

Rudr spoke back. "Is it not normal to catch a thief?"

Ved Vyas swiftly turned to Tarini, ignoring Rudr.

"Tarini, my angel … I am so happy to see you!" Tears of joy flowed down Vedji's cheeks as he adoringly kissed his little girl who had been away for so long. "How are you?"

"I'm good. Living my life to the fullest. Waking up each day to a new routine and a new adventure," she said.

"My fiercely independent one, you had everyone worried when you left your Uncle Markandeya's home."

"I spoke to *Bade Papa* and informed him that I wanted to be free and not bound by home, time or place. I wanted to discover the world not through textbooks, but through experience. I have been travelling a lot."

"Wonderful. How is *Bade Papa* now?" Ved Vyas enquired.

"He is still critical."

As their vehicle gently went down the hill, passing Singhthali village, the *ashram*, hidden so far, came into view. Its terraced topography meandered 200 feet, right down to the pebbled banks of the Ganga. All around, the mighty Shivalik mountains played the watchful guardian.

The twins were enchanted by the natural beauty of the *ashram*. Sujata however remained in a trance-like state, entirely oblivious to the beauty around.

Ved Vyas guided them towards his straw and mud hut. The atmosphere was relaxed and steeped in divinity. It instantly calmed their nerves. Sujata too became more aware.

Ved Vyas knew that the time had come to reveal the dark secret he had kept locked inside him. "Sit down. What do you want to know?"

"Everything from the start!" demanded Rudr looking in the eye of his Guru.

Getting to the point, Tarini questioned, "Was our father murdered?"

"Yes. Vishnuyasa was brutally murdered. His body was found without any fingers; his eyes were gouged out."

Surprised and shocked, the twins looked at each other.

"Does *Bade Papa* know?" asked Rudr.

"Of course, he knows."

"Why the silence then?"

"Well, Raj cannot do anything against his family. Your grandfather's older brother Rajneesh was the sacrificial goat for his generation, just like Vishnuyasa in his generation. And Harsh in your generation."

Shocked and confused the twins looked at each other.

"We don't understand. What are you trying to say Guruji?"

Vyas continued in a gentle tone. "The house of the avatar bears the biggest burden. It's both a curse and a boon."

Sujata interrupted the conversation, standing up suddenly, looking broken beyond repair. "I knew a monster, loved him too. But he abused me. Stunted and dwarfed, he knew he was inferior, a curse, a blot on the dynamic Nanda clan. So he bullied and abused me, physically, emotionally till one day he was caught and taken away. And I, a battered child, was adopted by the newly married Raj and Sulakshana Nanda, who gave me love and healed my wounds till I forgot the monster.

"Some days back while cleaning out Harsh's closet, I found letters shared between the monster and my son, and that's when I realised one can't bury the past. My past was influencing my future all along without my knowledge. And today, even more emaciated and ugly, the monster raised his head in the Ganga and took a part of my son along with him."

She broke down, crying. "No one, not even my husband, knows of my horrors. Only my father Raj understands my pain since he saw the monster molest me as a child."

Horrified at what she had just heard, Tarini held her sobbing aunt in a tight embrace.

Angry, Rudr questioned: "What is the house of the avatar? What is the sacrifice and who killed my father and Harsh? And did I just let go of the monster Rajneesh? Guruji you were aware that it was Rajneesh—then why did you command me to leave him, when I had him by his neck?"

"Rudr, you will soon awaken to your true identity. I cannot answer any more questions. What I can tell you though is that your father was killed by one of his own."

"Why and by whom?" asked Tarini angrily.

"It's time to call Sumanta and Pragnya," said Rudr.

"No. We will handle it ourselves," decreed Tarini, with fresh urgency in her voice. "I know where we can get all our answers—the supercomputer!"

It was Ved Vyas now who was shocked. "Do you mean the Akashic Records?"

Tarini nodded.

"Don't go there yet child," warned Ved Vyas. "Who gave you access to them?"

34

Tarini & The Immortals

"It's time we get the old man back. Let's infuse a bit of our energy into him. He can't die just yet," said Ved Vyas to the *Chiranjeevis*.

"Old man? Yes, we ancient souls can sure do some magic to revive our brother Raj," quipped Kripacharya. The *Chiranjeevis* were entering the hospital complex covered in an invisibility cloak. As they breezed their way into the ICU, they saw Tarini whispering into her granddad's ears. She looked in their direction, greeted them with a smile, joined her palms in greeting, and quickly made her way out of the room. It was not easy to startle the Immortals; but Tarini had done just that, leaving behind a flurry of reactions.

"How did she see us?"

"She is the Divine Twin—she will have some superpowers!"

"What a gorgeous girl she is, committed and intelligent. Will always see a task through!"

"Our arguments were always about her deferring and delaying the mess she'd create. She thrives on chaos. She loves getting into people's minds."

"My Tarini is also fiercely independent and her communication skills are as sharp as a sword. Most of the times, like a river, she is a torrent when angry," said Markandeya.

"She is quite an achiever for someone who wasn't supposed to be there at all."

While the others looked puzzled, Vibhishan and Parashuram smiled.

"Vibhishan, please explain my statements to these perplexed folks," said Kripacharya.

"Vishnuyasa and Sumati couldn't conceive as she had polycystic ovarian syndrome. Raj was adamant that he needed his family tree to continue. His childhood friend and Himalayan monk Babaji had prophesied that his family would be the cradle of the impending avatar.

"Babaji introduced us while we were at Gangotri. I started Sumati on hormone therapy, and a few months later, she had ovulated, but her fallopian tubes were blocked. I extracted her ova and froze them for IVF. But to our surprise, Vishnuyasa's sperms couldn't fertilise the ova. We ran tests and discovered he had male factor infertility. We had already lost few ova in the process and just three remained. After much deliberation Raj, Babaji and I, with Sumati's permission, decided to fertilise her ova with Babaji's sperm; our brilliant physicist Sumanta has Babaji's genes in him.

"Seeing him grow healthily, we repeated the IVF, this time with my sperm—and I am proud to be Pragnya's biological father.

"The world situation meanwhile had deteriorated and we felt we could engineer a superhuman who would fight the rot in society. Our dear friend Vedji contacted us at the same time, to inform us that Lord Vishnu was to take birth, and had chosen Raj's family since he had blessed Raj in a previous incarnation. The sixth Vishnu Avatar Parashuram and Sumati were to be the biological parents. We all rejoiced; and thanked the Lord for his *leela*, admiring how he had created conditions leading to his birth.

"However, Vedji was worried. The Kalki Avatar, intent on destroying all evil, is going to be the most fearsome, and the energy emanating from him could itself harm the entire planet, he cautioned.

"We needed to build a room which could withstand that cosmic power.

"Babaji got to work and created a state-of-the-art underground laboratory and bunkers. They needed the lab to be deep underground to contain the highly destructive cosmic rays. The type of rock to excavate was important, as the density and stability of the structure were crucial to provide the low radioactive environment necessary to explore the highest energy scales needed for this extremely rare phenomenon. A large pit filled with cold water to cool the environment and a room with a freezing atmosphere at sub-zero temperatures was created once the underground lab and bunkers were built.

"I entered the freezing room and had the joy of conceiving God with my hands. I implanted the fertilised embryo into Sumati.

"We scanned her every day to check our success. All was well for two weeks. But on the fifteenth day, I was startled to discover a fresh embryo growing inside her. At first, I thought they were twin pregnancies and rechecked older scans. But to my utter disbelief, it was a separate embryo.

"This condition is known as 'superfetation'. It's an incredibly rare biological event, where two separate instances of fertilisation take place in a woman who is already pregnant."

"Thankfully both the pregnancies went well and Tarini was born a minute later after Rudr."

Amazed at what they had just heard, the monks cheered as Parashuram smiled, observing, "Life always finds a way."

"Besides us in the room and Raj and Babaji, nobody—not even Sumati—knows of the paternal genes that her children carry. Babaji had explained to her that it would be best that she didn't know. He didn't want to complicate her life. He wanted her to be happy to be a mother and rejoice in the fact that each one of her children would have their own superpowers."

"*He* Rama! God's *leela* is unique," said Hanuman with folded hands.

35

Awakening

Room No. 105 at Kandy Private Hospital was abuzz with activity. The doctors and nurses were pacing in and out of the room. Raj Nanda was conscious and out of the coma after nearly six weeks. Amazingly, he was coherent. Dr Reddy rushed into the room and was pleasantly surprised to see Raj sitting upright.

"Hello, how have you been? How long have you kept me here? Where is Sulakshana? I can't find my phone … and your staff kept me from calling her."

Dr Reddy smiled said a small prayer of gratefulness. In 40 years of practising medicine he had seen some miraculous recoveries, but this one definitely had the hand of God in it. He swiftly went about checking all the vital signs. The heart function, respiratory rate, C.N.S. functions, all were within normal range. He clasped hands together and then hugged Raj. "My dearest friend! Welcome back!"

"Why? You're almost behaving as though you brought me back from the dead. Now, now … stop hugging me and get me in touch with my wife."

"Mrs Nanda is on her way. You're lucky. She has been by your side all the while, turning you on your side every few hours so that you don't develop bedsores. In the past six weeks whilst you have been in and out of the ICU she hung on determinedly. We all had given up. But she told me last week, 'Dr Reddy, you'll see … he will surprise you one day.' And she was so right."

Raj smiled. "Now can you please send your grooming team in so I can look and smell presentable? Your hospital makes me nauseous. And please ask your accounts department to prepare my final bill as I want to leave as soon as my wife arrives."

"No Raj, it's too premature. I want to keep you under observation for 72 hours at least."

"Reddy, I need to go. I have a lot of work to finish and set right some old scores. Don't worry about me. I am fine and promise to drop in every day so that you can be sure too."

"*Namaste Bade Papa*," Tarini greeted her favourite person in the whole world. She had run into the room on hearing the big news.

"*Arre … bacche* ... you!" said Raj tenderly. "How is my little princess? When did you come?"

"A few days ago, *Bade Papa*."

"You are not supposed to be here."

"Neither are you! Just came to see you recover; once you're back home and well, I shall leave."

"Tell me Tarini that Harsh is well and at work…"

She pondered a moment before answering. Instantly, the colour drained from Raj's face and he slumped back on his hospital bed.

36

Turbulence

The homecoming of Raj Nanda was a quiet, subdued affair. Though everyone was happy and thankful to have him back, the atmosphere at home was sombre since the family had lost a grandson and the culprit was still at large.

Raj couldn't bring himself to look at the large portrait of Harsh, garlanded in sandalwood flowers. He broke down inconsolably. Rudr was a little aloof. He had unearthed several facts about Raj while he lay in a coma and was uncomfortable dealing with him. The image of the ever-so-right Mr Nanda had been shattered and, in its place, standing before him, he saw a selfish, arrogant and conniving old man.

"Rudr, tomorrow morning I want you to accompany me to meet Murli, who is a New World Order candidate. He has managed to spare us an hour of his busy campaigning schedule."

"Sorry, *Bade Papa*, I can't make it. You go ahead."

"Do you realise how important this is? And why on earth can't you make it?" roared Raj, scaring Sulakshana.

"Coz it is not important enough for me. I leave tonight for Mumbai to get some leads on my father's murder."

The mention of his son drained the colour from Raj Nanda's face as he sought Tarini's hand to help him sit down. "Rudr, someone has been filling you with nonsense. Who said Vishnu was murdered?" enquired Raj agitatedly.

"I now know everything, *Bade Papa*. Your lies, your treachery, your dark dealings and my dad's untimely death." Unable to control his anger anymore, Raj slapped Rudr hard on his face. "Are you implying that I killed my son?"

Stunned, yet unabashed, Rudr replied, "Yes, I will gather enough evidence to prove my claim," and barged out of the room. Tarini looked on helplessly, with detached benevolence.

A deep numbness starting from the left toe, spread up her legs, up her torso and finally reached up to her heart made Sulakshana cry out in pain.

"Raj Nanda, I want to know right now—who killed my son?"

That day, for the first time, Tarini saw Raj looking helpless. He sat awkwardly on his lazyboy, tears glazing his eyes, lost in deep contemplation.

"Sush—yes our Vishnu was murdered. But you definitely don't believe that I was involved! Our grandson has opened a can of worms. I need to protect him. I couldn't save our son. But I'll hold on to Rudr forever. Probably the reason I lived through the stroke is to finally end the terrible saga that started two decades ago."

"*Bade Papa*, please don't worry. Give Rudr time to find his own truth; he will come around. As for the can of worms, it's good that it's finally out in the open. I am leaving to meet

Hanumanji in Antarctica. He has called for me. We may find our answers in the Akashic Records that are stored there."

An agitated Raj, lost in his own thoughts, barely listened to Tarini.

He summoned his car and driver. "It's time to face our dark secret, Moti," he announced. The colour drained from Moti Singh's face as the car swerved out of the Nanda Estate.

Moksha

What shackles you? Balance dharma, artha,
kama to begin the inward journey towards liberation…

37

Wages of Sin

Atop the Trikuta mountains overlooking the town of Katra, stood the mythical sage Shukracharya. Beside him stood a young man with a slender physique, with clothes and mannerisms of another time.

"But Guruji, why would you bring me back from dead, to destroy a temple? Isn't this a sin?"

"O Son of Devashrava, all holy temples of Bharatvarsh are already destroyed, barring four. The world isn't how you left it Dhrishtadyumna. You were beheaded by Ashwatthama along with your nephews, the Upapandavas, while still asleep.

"Five thousand years have passed since. I have been a witness to the times and have kept the light flickering by providing for the darkness that engulfs the planet today. And now, we have arrived at a moment in the world's history where the light and dark meet, creating miracles."

The look of confusion on Dhrishtadyumna's face made Shukra grin. "Let's make it simple. Your *sakha* is back in his tenth avatar. Let me tell you a story that originated in the time of the Ramayana and is to end now.

"The Vaishnodevi temple that we are looking down upon, has three rocks inside a cave..."

"Yes Guruji. My sister Draupadi and I visited here to seek the benevolent *Devi's* blessings."

"Vaishnavi was a gorgeous princess in the times of Rama. Her undying love for Rama made her meditate on him day and night. Amazed by her dedication, he promised her the rocks that he would install in the cave would be worshipped as feminine energy and would fulfil all devotees' wishes. The rocks are so heavy that even modern-day machinery cannot move them.

"The tenth avatar will have to visit these four temples to add to his *siddhis* and become invincible.

"The world today is ours to rule. Your resurgence was necessary. Destroy the three rocks, displace them with the power of your arrows," commanded the fearsome Guru.

With unwavering faith and loyalty, the young disciple reached out to his quiver of arrows, and strung one onto the bow, recoiling the thread. The hand was firm and had a sturdy grip, and then he realised—he didn't have a thumb!

The energy unleashed from his arrows easily dislodged the three sacred rocks from their position, sending them spinning into the air. Shukra's eyes gleamed. None but he could have achieved this. "Talent never dies! Well done, Eklavya!"

"Pardon me Guruji, but I am Dhrishtadyumna," said the young man shifting uncomfortably, looking up questioningly at his Guru, palms joined together. At that moment, his right peripheral vision fell on the three rocks that were falling back from the skies with menacing speed. Soon he was zooming towards the skies enveloped in his Guru's arm in a whirlwind, almost brushing past the rocks as they landed on the temple ground throwing up vast amounts of dust and gravel on impact. The entire temple complex and its surrounding village were razed leaving a gaping crater in its place. A single stone however remained intact covered in the pile of gravel, safe from the Guru's eyes. The scale of destruction brought a thin, satisfied smile to Shukra's lips.

"We are not what we seem to be. The truth is we are energy, and energy never ceases to be. It flows from one form to another. So yes, you were Eklavya in one lifetime, and Dhrishtadyumna in another." Shukracharya closed his eyes as they descended together in a quiet corner of the sleepy village of Khadsa in Haryana. He brushed off the dust from his bare chest and lovingly dusted the forehead of his confused disciple. As he led the way in quick steps, the disciple followed close behind. Soon they entered a single-room temple. It was dark and unkempt inside. A granite grey statue of a young man dominated the tiny space.

Dhrishtadyumna inquired, "Who is this? He is dressed like a Bhil..." he stopped short, as his eyes fell on the right hand of the statue. It had a thumb missing.

"Son, this temple is dedicated to Eklavya. Underneath, buried deep within, is a treasure that now seeks its rightful master."

Horizontal lines marked Eklavya's forehead as he was transported back to the painful moment when he had chopped off his thumb as *gurudakshina*, and placed it at his Guru Dronacharya's feet. He suddenly felt that pain cruising through his body and his right hand began to go numb and heavy. He felt a thousand sensations as the blood nerve network gushed out from his palms, protruding into a thumb. Elated, he stood complete, tears flowing down his cheeks.

"You create an enemy by punishing someone who is innocent," said Shukra grimly. "Drona's karma got written the day he unjustly asked for your thumb.

"Anguished and dejected you then joined the forces of Shishupal. And though both you and Shishupal were first cousins of Krishna, he killed you both.

"You took rebirth as Dhrishtadyumna, and emerged as a young man from the *yagna* flames along with your twin Draupadi. But this time you were Krishna's ally. In the Mahabharata war you fought as the chief of the Pandava army, and were killed by Ashwatthama while asleep.

"Your destiny has been woven by unfortunate circumstances. Yet darkness restores what light cannot repair. The murderers of your past births are back, and hence you are too." Shukra looked far away into the dark night and sighed, "Karma has no deadline."

38

Safed Mahal

Safed Mahal, the quaint summer home of the Nandas, was located in the Kumaon Hills in Nainital district, North India. Perched at the edge of a fragrant oak and rhododendron forest, it had an imposing view of the White Himalayas. It was secluded and far away from the nearest village.

Moti Singh knew the curves and bends of the torturous route like the back of his hand. But today, as he drove a just-recovered Raj to Nainital his hands were shaking, and the car was swerving. Raj, lost in thought, ignored the bad driving but screamed aloud when the car screeched to a sudden halt outside the imposing gates of Safed Mahal. "What the hell Moti, you're getting too old to drive!" As he looked out, he saw a white Jeep Cherokee flashing its headlights at them. He rushed out knowing it was Babaji.

"Hop in Raj—quick!" Babaji ordered.

Before speeding away, Babaji rolled his window down and told Moti Singh, "Go to your home in Almora, and wait for us there. Leave now!"

"What do you think you are doing Raj? Hadn't I warned you against entering Safed Mahal?" Babaji spoke angrily. "Look at you. You've just walked out of hospital, and are already walking to your death. For God's sake can't you sit quietly and keep yourself out of trouble? What was the point of sending you off to Colombo?"

Raj's hands were shaking, and his voice quivered like grass in the wind. "What more will I have to see before my old eyes are finally at rest?"

"Harsh was well disposed of by Murli—I made the final call. Harsh was a mole. He was planted by Shukra to get info about you and Kalki. He had a *pishach* beside him all the while, protecting him. I had to do away with the *pishach* too. It was their evil plan—the bombing of the hotel—to get rid of you."

Raj was speechless at this disclosure. They were seated in a cottage at Bhowali that belonged to one of Babaji's followers.

"The children doubt me—they think I killed my son. As for Rajneesh—I haven't yet done so, but today I will forever put an end to my family's dark secret."

"*Uff* Raj, age hasn't slowed down your racing mind and the obsession to control everything. Don't forget that the house of the avatar bears a great curse too."

"How can I forget that? Haven't I seen the untimely deaths of my son, my grandson?"

"That's not the curse—that was their destiny."

"Then what is the curse?" asked a bewildered Raj.

"Rajneesh."

"Of course, I know he is our curse, our dark secret, the reason he has been kept at Safed Mahal."

"No Raj. There is more.

"The day Rajneesh was born to your parents, your grandfather died. There were several other omens. Disturbed, your father Ramneesh called my Guru to make his astrological chart. One look at the infant, and my Guru was so shaken, he left immediately, assuring your father that he would send a *Siddha* to do the needful. When the high soul came, he was shocked—and full of fear—on seeing the infant. He touched the infant's feet and said to your father, 'Keep him locked up forever. Or kill him now.'" Babaji looked out towards the mountains with a deep sigh.

"... that's why my parents kept him in Safed Mahal and moved to Haldwani," continued Raj.

"Yes. Being locked up without much sunlight resulted in the infant's stunted growth. Your parents however made sure that Rajneesh received the best of home education. Persuaded by your parents, Guru Shukracharya landed up at Safed Mahal, and took the child under his wing."

"You mean the Shukracharya, our arch enemy?"

"Yes. Gradually Safed Mahal became darker and darker as the sins of its inmates escalated. And one day the most heinous of acts occurred within its four walls, the result of which is Sujata."

"My parents died shortly after a car crash, on one of their trips back from Safed Mahal."

"No. Your father killed your mother and himself, unable to face the world."

Raj stood up shocked. Babaji walked up to Raj, put a hand on his shoulder and said, "I cleaned up the suicide site with the help of young Moti Singh and made it appear like a car accident. What we all missed completely was the presence of a baby girl at Safed Mahal."

"The monster kept her hidden from all, till one day on his monthly trip, Moti Singh heard a child crying. Shocked he informed me immediately and I landed up at Safed Mahal for the first time in my life, having never met my older brother. Tejasya went with me," Raj recalled.

"Having rescued the girl from the monster's clutches, I decided to hand him over to the police. Tejasya stopped me saying our parents died keeping Rajneesh a secret, and we should keep the family name intact."

"Yes, I know," said Babaji. He was about to say something, but then stopped.

"Sujata told me that she saw the monster at Haridwar and that he took some of Harsh's ashes with him," said a resigned Raj. "I am done with him. Babaji, why can't we do something about Rajneesh and end the curse forever?"

"As we talk, Safed Mahal is burning. My men have done the job."

Raj smiled, relieved. "Thank you Babaji! Finally, the end of the monster!"

"Rajneesh has the protection of Shukracharya. And the boon of Indra. No one but the Vishnu Avatar can kill him," said Babaji quietly. "But we have forever burnt the dark secrets of Safed Mahal."

"Where is Rajneesh now?" asked a rattled Raj.

"Keekatpur."

39

Nagpash

In a parallel, subtle plane of existence, in Badrinath, India.

A slash of radiant light broke through the cauldron grey sky. Hanuman materialised out of the bolt of lightning, his presence lighting up the dreary battlefield. The ground was slippery with entrails and a sickly odour arose from it. The sodden earth was oily with ichor. The *mlecchas*, the pig-men, lay ambushed on the ground, their corpses exuding a nauseating stench.

Hanuman put his hands on his waist, striking his favourite pose. Puckering up his nose in disgust, he roared, "Ashwatthama where are you?" He got no response. To get a bird's view and locate his fellow Immortal, Hanuman began to grow in size till he could see across the city. He found Ashwatthama at the rear entrance of the Badrinath Temple in combat with a man of powerful musculature. His focus soon shifted to his own feet as he felt a nibbling sensation. He was under attack by a group of honey badgers! He immediately began to shrink in size to look at his attackers more closely.

"He Rama!" he mouthed as he picked up one of the nibblers. "What are you?" In response the creature squirted a stinky liquid from the base of its tail stub, while others started climbing up Hanuman's body. The creatures had a thick rubbery epidermis that was slimy. As Hanuman tried to grab them, they easily slipped out of his grasp, and began chewing into his body. He finally held one between his teeth, but soon that too wriggled out of his mouth. Irritated and angry he stomped them all dead, and was surprised to see purple blood oozing out. He quickly moved towards Ashwatthama.

In countless centuries of living, he had seen all kinds of creatures but these were downright ferocious, fearless and mean. Growing up in the jungles, he knew they were honey badgers but what were they doing in civilised habitats? What was the world coming to? It was already fouled up with the *mlecchas* and now these honey badgers, he rued.

A weird sensation started snaking up his spine so, quickly, without losing a moment, Hanuman dived into the Taptkund nearby. He knew the hot sulphur springs had unfathomable medicinal properties and healed all ailments.

Restored in health and feeling energised he raced towards the Badrinath Temple where Ashwatthama was struggling. Never before had Ashwatthama called for support.

The world had changed gradually, but the last five decades had seen a rapid rise of the dark forces and a steady decline of the human race. All holy shrines the world over had been taken over by Shukracharya. Vaishnodevi had also been ambushed recently, and now the Immortals were fighting to save the sacred *shaligram* stone said to be a manifestation of

Lord Vishnu, that had arisen from the Alaknanda river and was worshipped in the Badrinath Temple. For Hanuman though, more important than the stone was the Nandka, the Sword of Vishnu, that needed to be protected.

What he saw next, made Hanuman's head spin. He rubbed his eyes again and again to make sure it wasn't an illusion.

"Indrajit?" he gasped. The world's most powerful warrior of all time; trained to be invincible in battle. Master of sorcery and magic and the only person in the universe having access to the three ultimate divine weapons—Brahmandastra, Pashupatastra and Vaishnavastra. Indrajit, the *atimaharathi,* trained in warfare by Shukracharya himself!

Ashwatthama's entire body was wrapped by a hundred venomous snakes, all coiling around him, biting. The wound in his forehead was bleeding profusely.

Hanuman had to think and act quickly, but before he could blink, Indrajit suddenly appeared before him, laughing loudly—then disappeared. He was enjoying teasing Hanuman with his sorcery.

Indrajit then unleashed the Nagpash *astra* on Hanuman. Hundreds of snakes coiled onto his body binding him in a slithering rope-like chain. Hanuman used his *siddhis* to expand to enormous proportions, splitting the bodies of the snakes, throwing them off. The master shape-shifter then shrank to the size of a bee. The epic war against Ravana in Lanka still fresh in his mind, Hanuman remembered being captured and defeated by Indrajit. He flew down to Indrajit's foot and stung him hard, taking him by surprise. Next, he stung both his upper eyelids. Indrajit, blinded but not defeated, let out an agonised cry. Knowing fully well that Indrajit would soon prevail over his situation by chanting his *kuldevi* (family goddess) *mantra,* Hanuman buzzed inside Indrajit's ears, distracting, irritating and annoying him. Unable to focus or concentrate, Indrajit vanished from the site.

Soon Ashwatthama was released from the snake chain, exhausted and in pain, blood and pus dripping all over. Hanuman covered his nose with a mask he promptly pulled out of his trousers and helped Ashwatthama to enter the Taptkund.

40

First Move

"Hello Rudr … your call was such a surprise and took me back several years," said Abhay Sawant, extending a warm handshake.

The office was large with many people busy at their desks. Rudr had read that Care Enterprises was a large NGO that took up various issues, and was primarily dedicated to empowering villages in the Uttaranchal belt with electricity, roadways and basic infrastructure.

"I would have preferred to host you at home, but completely understand your emergency. Tell me, how can I be of help?"

"I suspect that my father was killed and need more information. I have reopened the investigation into his death fifteen years ago. The inspector in Delhi gave me your number and asked me to meet you."

Abhay Sawant was caught completely off guard and coughed uneasily. The phlegm in his lungs was making his breathing noisy. "When your father and I started VAS—our aim was to represent the underprivileged, stand for the truth and expose the system.

"We began to win our cases and earn a name for ourselves. In a year we had grown phenomenally and made many enemies. After your dad's death, I too received many threats and had to shift to Cape Town in South Africa.

"I have returned to Mumbai after a decade and we are a non-profit organisation now going by the name of 'Care'. That's all that I know son," finished Sawant, wiping the sweat from his brow.

Rudr gave him a deep, penetrating glance, shook hands to thank him and left.

Abhay Sawant cancelled all his appointments for the day and lit yet another cigarette before finally dialling a number in Cape Town. He spoke in Afrikaans, in a hurried, nervous manner, feeling slightly dizzy.

"No … it's not the father. No, not the politician either. But another head has risen against Sphinx—the son this time."

As he put down the phone, he undid his tie. Perspiring, he opened his lunchbox. He quickly devoured the warm food lovingly prepared at home. Feeling satiated and yet very thirsty and confused, he started pacing the room up and down until he felt a burst of energy literally shooting up to his brain—and collapsed. The preliminary tests done by the doctors revealed a blood sugar level of 620. The cause of death mentioned on the death certificate was hypoglycaemic shock, leading to myocardial infarction (MI).

***

Rudr carefully disposed of the thumb-sized insulin pen that Babaji had handed him. The twins had decided to avenge their father's death and Sawant was the first in a line of traitors who had cheated their father.

Rudr sat in meditation at the seaside lounge of a luxury hotel as he contemplated his next move—the difficult one.

The Immortal

Kripacharya

"Every night I visit the battleground at Hastinapur. The smell of blood, death and something worse, much worse, tugs at my memory. I shudder, shiver and shake as the fateful night plays out yet again in my consciousness.

"It was the 18th day of the war. We had been defeated by the Pandavas. Duryodhana was breathing his last, immersed in a lake, waist deep. The night was sinister with ghosts dancing on abandoned bodies, owls hooting menacingly and the irritating buzz of the flies all adding to my throbbing headache.

"There were only three of us left from the Kaurava camp. My nephew Ashwatthama, Kritavarma, and me. We sat defeated under a lone banyan tree, home to a family of crows. We noticed how, taking advantage of the dark, the crows hunted down their prey. Ashwatthama had a sinister idea; I flatly refused to be a part of it. He reminded me then of the scheming Pandavas; how they tricked and cheated my brother-in-law—his father—Drona into his death; how by unfair means they brought the great Bheeshma down. I was forced to agree.

"I, Kripacharya, have always taught my students to be fair and truthful, and in this war the Pandavas had truly let me down. Angry, I accompanied my nephew Ashwatthama, and stood vigil at the door as he ravaged the Pandava camp.

"It was only later that we discovered to our horror that Ashwatthama had beheaded the young Upapandavas! Something deep in my heart tore at that moment—I was abettor to the worst injustice, the worst tragedy of the Mahabharata. I haven't forgiven myself, and my heart hasn't healed thousands of years later. That's why I come to Hastinapur at night, to seek solace amidst the ashes and memories of all those I lost. Yes, I get sleep only here, amidst the noise and stench of the massacre, which plays out like déjà vu in my mind every single night.

"My immortality is unlike the others'. I am neither cursed nor blessed. I am neither a devotee nor an avatar. I am pure consciousness, unbiased and non-judgemental. Only those who take birth die. But I was never 'born'.

"A descendant of Gautam Rishi, my father Shardwan was a great archer. He practised severe penance and was well versed in the art of warfare.

"My twin sister and I manifested when his seed fell on a weed on the ground, splitting it into two. We were found lying on the forest floor by the Kuru King Shantanu. Enchanted by our beauty, he carried us back to his palace. I was named Kripa, and my sister, Kripi.

"On finding out about us, my father came to Hastinapur and took me under his wing and taught me warfare. Once proficient, I became Kulguru to the young Kuru princes.

"I soon became their beloved acharya (teacher), and they called me Kripacharya. I gave them initial grounding in our scriptures and in self-defence. I also advised the blind King Dhritarashtra in matters of governance. Administrative duties took up most of my time and I decided to hand over the young princes to my brother-in-law Dronacharya, a Brahmin and an expert in archery and warfare.

"My life has been one of contradictions. While I taught dharma (righteousness/duty) I supported adharma. I practised impartiality, yet defended the Kauravaṣ. I gave sermons on righteousness yet fought for wrong—but I was indebted to Hastinapur, to King Dhritarashtra, for my sustenance.

"Our lives are destined and shaped according to our karma, our actions, by a very intelligent universe that keeps checks and balances. We are energy, and energy only flows from one medium to another; it never ceases to exist. All universes coexist at the same time. Immortality isn't about living forever in the

universe. Rather it's about the frugality of time and space, and living outside of it. There are so many planes of existence, and I have access to them at will.

"I am the universal balance. To balance I have to be still and upright. I meditate long hours and eat only Himalayan herbs and fruits. This keeps my body replenished, aiding in continuous cell renewal. I am eternal energy and can materialise and dematerialise at will, often taking the form of a bird or butterfly.

"I live in an astral plane called Shambhala situated between Yamunotri in the West, Nanda Devi mountains in the east and Mount Kailash in the North. I run a training institute for yogis where we impart knowledge on the inner realms.

"Shambhala is not accessible to ordinary people. Only yogis who have overcome their senses and mind and resonate pure intellect have the privilege of being my students. We are preparing warriors here, to fight alongside the Kalki Avatar in his war against evil.

"I have lived in relative obscurity for aeons. But now I am readily available to Raj Nanda and his grandchildren as their spiritual mentor—guiding their destiny and thus, the destiny of all humankind.

"In the past, I stood for righteousness. Today I know righteousness is useless unless paired with foresight."

41

Negotiation

"Padma has been missing for 48 hours. I seek your help in finding her. Make sure the information is kept discreet and the media does not get a whiff of it."

"Oh Murli! Why didn't you inform me earlier? Let me see what I can do," said a deeply disturbed Raj. Twenty minutes and a few phone calls later, Raj spoke to Murli.

"She was seen alone at Colombo airport boarding a flight to Mumbai at 11.20 the day before yesterday. Don't worry. She has probably taken off on a break."

"No. It's unlike her to not inform me." Murli thought hard, wondering who could have held her in Mumbai. Then he instructed his PA to arrange a private charter flight to Mumbai immediately.

Meanwhile Raj's heartbeat soared as he got off the call. He was praying fervently that Rudr's being in Mumbai had nothing to do with Padma's disappearance. The morning feed carrying the news of the sudden death of Abhay Sawant had made him uneasy and he too decided to fly down to Mumbai. He dialled Murli again.

Aboard the Falcon 900 with no prying eyes or ears, the two settled down to a no-holds-barred conversation.

"Did you hear about the sudden demise of Abhay Sawant?" enquired Raj.

"Yes, he had a diabetic stroke," finished Murli.

"He was a key person, handling your overseas ventures, right?" Murli nodded.

"Murli, I need your help too. Rudr unearthed certain disturbing facts about my son's death and thinks I am involved. We will have to provide protection to him while he takes the Sphinx head on."

"Not now Raj. The support of Sphinx is fundamental to my win as a New World Order candidate. All the monetary backing is from them," snapped an annoyed Murli.

"Your grandson has spelt trouble from the day he came back. It's time he packed his bags and baggage and left or else he will meet a fate similar to his father … and Harsh."

"Now, now, Murli control your tongue. Nothing will happen to Rudr as long as I am around … and count me out in the search operation of your daughter Padma. Also, the inflow of funds for the party will stop immediately!" roared Raj, knowing very well that he had played a trump card and manipulating Murli would now be easy as putty. The disappearance of Padma had worked to his advantage and had finally made Murli as vulnerable as Raj himself.

He lit his cigar as they exited the Falcon, having made truce. It was decided they would stick by each other for the time being.

42

Victoria

"Everything in the universe is interlinked. Quantum mechanics tells us we are all connected by an invisible web," said Sumanta into his phone as he travelled on an Amtrak from Seattle to Vancouver. "This web also connects the Dark to the Light or Satan to God."

"*Bhaiya Bade* are you on the train?"

"Yes Pragnya. Why?"

"No, it's just unusual. You design supersonic planes and missiles and travel in trains!"

"For research dear brother! I'm working on a classified missile and basing it on the concept of a supersonic train."

"Wow! What about Satan and God?"

"Both have complete mastery over what they do. Satanic black magicians pull the strings—not politicians, corporate bosses, military heads, intelligence chiefs or bankers."

"Really! How are you so sure?" asked Pragnya.

"Energy moves in waves which have frequencies. Satanic rituals are designed to meld the energy bio frequencies of the participants with that of other dark entities, so that there is a vibrational match. Once frequencies lock, exchange can take place. Energy intent or information from one being, place or dimension can be transferred into another."

"Sounds interesting. Will I be able to register for the Conference on Black Magic?"

"No way! Tickets were sold out long ago. But I am attending. I'm curious about the metaphysical aspect of black magic and need answers to Kali's act of bringing the dead girl back to life."

"In that case I'll go and see granddad. Have already taken days off."

"Take care, Pragnya. Tarini and Rudr are already there. Don't step out together you three. Stay out of mischief."

"Yes, *Bhaiya Bade*. See you in India soon!"

"What! What was that about?"

"Oh, you will be in India soon…"

"What?"

"My superpower is clairvoyance. What's yours, dear brother?" asked Pragnya, as he closed his eyes and saw Sumanta bent over a drawing board. He was sketching while sipping a cup of coffee as the train passed by the Canadian mountains.

"Pragnya you're weird. You could see me for real on a video call—rather than in your thoughts!"

"Everything happens twice in this world. Once in your thoughts; and once in real life. I grasp the image while it's still forming in your thoughts."

Having finished the conversation, Sumanta pulled out his bag, got himself a coffee and bent over his drawing board—sketching the missile design as the train passed by the scenic Canadian mountains.

43

Facing Facts

The sharpshooter, Grace Woods, had arrived in Mumbai from South Africa and was waiting for details of his mark to move in for the kill. Meanwhile he was enjoying the club scene in Mumbai. The demand for weed and RIZE from S.A. had risen three-fold and drug peddling in this part of the world paid rich dividends.

Rudr was waiting for Padma at the Taj coffee shop in Colaba. He rose as she walked in, and reached out for an embrace. He took her hand in his, and lovingly kissed it.

"I knew I could always count on you!"

"I left home as soon as I got your call. Did not inform anyone; they wouldn't have let me leave!" And then the tears flowed, making her nose and cheeks turn red. Awkwardly she pulled her hands from his and hid her face in her palms, angry at herself for the emotional outburst. She soon regained composure, and squaring her shoulders, looked straight into Rudr's eyes. "So, tell me, how can I help?"

This time, Rudr blurted out, "By never ever leaving my side again!" As both their defences crumbled, they embraced each other like lost lovers. Time stopped as they connected. Somewhere far away temple bells rang and conch shells were heard, and from nowhere, a white tuberose fell into Padma's hair. Surprised, she released the embrace and looked around. She saw a monk sitting across them in baby pink attire, smiling like a child at her, a laptop by his side.

Rudr and Padma blushed looking at him, and walked towards the ocean view. Finding a quiet corner, Rudr started speaking.

"Listen carefully to everything I have to say—it's about our parents. It turns out that *Bade Papa* has accumulated a lot of wealth unscrupulously. The steel factories that Harsh's father owns in the UK, for example, are one of the channels where he launders all the black money.

"Your father was a youth leader in Colombo University. He had great oratory skills and a politician's demeanour. He was hungry for power and wealth … that's when Sphinx hand-picked him."

"Who or what is Sphinx?" enquired Padma.

"It is an international crime organisation with syndicates in India, Europe, the Maldives and South Africa. 'Sphinx' is a moniker coined by the Mumbai Law Enforcement because its leader Jabari walks on all fours like a lion. It dominates organised crime, drug trafficking, cybercrime, human trafficking and much more.

"Sphinx has its own centres to monitor the Internet, social media, and T.V. in real time. In terror attacks, they decide who shall live and who shall die. Using technology in an increasingly open world they are the kingpins of cybercrime and cyber terrorism.

"South Africa is their HQ now, with branches spread out around the world. Their network spread with the help of politicians and they remained untouched by the World Police because of the able manipulation of their lawyers—such as my grandad.

"Your father's rise to political fame was on the backbone of financial clout provided by Sphinx—in exchange for government compliances for their various businesses."

Initially Padma had resisted listening. But Rudr didn't stop … and soon she was all ears as the name Murli Ramachandran came up again and again.

"Tarini and I carried out a search together at the Nanda law firms after Harsh's death."

"Oh?" she mumbled.

"We were left with a lot of unanswered questions. It was while I was snooping around and investigating my cousin Harsh's cold-blooded murder that I unearthed a shocking fact—your father killed Harsh!"

Padma froze. Tears welled up in her eyes. "Enough Rudr! I've heard enough. My ears are sore; my body is shaking with all that you have told me. I am disillusioned. Aren't you? How can you go on about your granddad without a hint of emotion? Aren't you broken from inside?" She closed her eyes, took a deep breath, and then suddenly looked straight into Rudr's eyes and asked, "Why should I believe you? Do you have any proof to validate all this?"

Rudr simply held her hand and looked into her deep brown eyes, saying, "I would never lie to you." In that moment all doubts vanished confirming once again what Padma always knew. She loved him beyond reason, beyond life.

"Okay, go on."

Rudr continued in a hushed tone. "Fifteen years ago, a young man took up the challenge to clean up the filth and corruption in the country. To do so he even left his family in Delhi and moved to Mumbai. He was an idealist and a loner. He eventually found a partner with similar ideals and together the two started a law firm to uphold the truth and punish the guilty. They soon realised that the Mumbai mafia was controlled by Sphinx. They created a watertight case against them and were also able to break into their narcotics cell. This resulted in several arrests and huge financial losses to the organisation. Never challenged before, Sphinx tried to buy them off. One resisted, and one gave in. He betrayed his partner by giving all information collected thus destroying all evidence. Worse, he also shared the personal details of his partner. The next day, his partner died in a drug overdose and the body of the firm's undercover investigator was recovered by fishermen from the sea."

"Rudr, why are you speaking in riddles? I don't understand the connection," said an anxious Padma.

"The man who died by drug overdose, Vishnuyasa Nanda, was my father."

Shocked at this disclosure, Padma enveloped Rudr in her arms. The embrace was broken by the sounds of a gunshot. Both ducked and went towards the windows to see the cause of commotion. Outside, the security guards lay dead. As Rudr was thinking of the next move, they heard the doorknob open. He quickly pushed Padma behind a couch and sprinted towards the door. As the door opened, he gave a chop on the neck of the intruder, immediately rendering him unconscious as he slipped to the floor. It was a tall man of African origin, armed with a gun. Rudr dragged the African to a side, quickly yanking out curtain cords to tie his hands and feet. Picking up the gun, he comfortably placed it in his pocket.

"Come out Padma, all clear." Rudr's physical agility and sharp reflexes had Padma completely floored.

"Wow! Where did you pick up these moves?" she questioned.

"In Gangotri. I practised the art of self-defence. Now hurry, we need to get out of here before we are attacked again." He escorted her to the Land Rover parked outside. Before leaving he called the Director General of Police (DGP) informing him of the attack.

Once in the car, Padma questioned, "What happened to the man who cheated on his partner?" She was eager to know the rest of the story.

"He relocated to Cape Town in South Africa and started a flourishing business in diamonds. However, he came back to India a few years ago and started an NGO, which I believe was started at the insistence of your father, as a channel to park investments."

"Oh! Shouldn't you inform the police and have him arrested? What was his name?" enquired Padma.

"Abhay Sawant died last Thursday of a diabetic stroke. He met his end suddenly and alone just like my father," explained a straight-faced Rudr.

"If your granddad was the lawyer for Sphinx, why did he not protect his son? This is getting murkier. Which father would want his son eliminated?" questioned Padma.

"That's the answer I am seeking. The final piece to this puzzle."

"So what you are saying is that your granddad and my dad are two faces of the same coin!"

"Yes—one, the political face; and the other, the judicial face of Sphinx."

44

Tumble

Tarini had just flown down to Mumbai from Antarctica. Hanuman hadn't given access to the Akashic supercomputer, but had answered all her queries. Looking out at the choppy Arabian Sea, the twins were exchanging notes over black coffee at a cafe. Soon, they were joined by Padma.

"Hello Padma, no wonder my brother is so besotted with you," said Tarini smiling broadly as she cast an admiring glance in Padma's direction. Padma turned pink as usual, glowing in the Mumbai sun.

"Your father and my grandfather will join us soon. There is a lot of ambiguity in the air, and it's best that it is cleared at the earliest. No point in doubting our own—those who have loved us all their lives," she said, looking pointedly at Rudr.

The tall, broad and intense-looking man walked in unannounced. DGP Suryakant Khare extended his hand to Rudr for a handshake.

"Sir, Sphinx has moved out of the old location and is in hiding. The international police are in constant communication with us. Their leader Jabari, the monster, didn't even spare his mother. He killed her once he suspected that the police could be involved. He is probably in India now.

"I recommend you all leave right away for Sri Lanka along with Mr Murli and his daughter—and thanks Mr Nanda, the African you tied up was a contract killer, hired by Sphinx to eliminate you. We are getting a lot of leads from the information provided by him."

"Have you ever seen Jabari? What does he look like?" enquired Tarini of the DGP.

"No, never. I am told that besides his mother, nobody has seen his face. He has a white mask and cowl on all the time. The story goes that he is so ugly and disfigured that the one time he saw his reflection in the mirror he screamed so loudly the mirror broke! Our police psychologist says this internal rejection has led to his brutal, violent behaviour.

"However, I have dealt with his exceptional intellectual prowess. He has the memory of an elephant and wiles of a jackal. He has hand-picked each criminal in Sphinx to create a formidable network of organised crime. It operates out of a small town, Keekatpur. The entire town is inhabited by *mlecchas*."

So saying, the DGP bid the three goodbye, keen to follow Jabari's slim trail.

"What are *mlecchas*?" enquired Padma, trying to process the new horror.

"*Mleccha* is a Sanskrit work for barbarians," explained Tarini. "In ancient Hindu texts they are described as uncivilised people, impure in habits, having crooked faces and noses. They were said to eat human flesh and were devoid of righteousness and purity of conduct. The *mlecchas* of Keekatpur, though bipeds, are experts on all fours, with the face of a pig and the body of a human."

"Are they mutants?" asked a stunned Padma.

"Not exactly; more like hybrids," said Tarini.

"It is time to act—not explain," burst in Raj, as he hurriedly entered, accompanied by Murli.

"This is much more than a personal vendetta and war. It's about cleansing the system from the inside. This criminal enterprise has spread its tentacles beyond Indian shores, into international terrain. From bribery, extortion, and drug peddling, to human trafficking to money laundering they are leading it all."

Padma was both puzzled and curious about Raj's intentions and thus enquired, "Uncle, are you not the legal representative to Sphinx? Are not your and my father's hands soiled with this heinous corruption? Whose side are you on? The good or the bad?"

Raj sat up straighter on the chair and replied. "Yes, our hands are soiled. In fact, my soul was soiled when I presented as legal counsel for Sphinx the first time, more than a decade ago. Something in my heart snapped. But I had no choice. A lot was at stake."

"What was at stake?" Rudr intervened this time, slightly cynical.

"My son, your father, Vishnuyasa had raised hackles by openly challenging the crime syndicate. He was in a hurry and didn't listen to my advice to go slow and build a watertight case against Sphinx. He ended up, as I feared, being held captive by the organisation. To save my son, I sold my soul to the devil. I agreed on paper to represent them for all their nefarious activities in the courts of law. But instead of releasing Vishnuyasa as promised, Sphinx cheated—and released him from the world.

"Meanwhile, my brother Tejasya turned hostile towards me and as a result I lost everything I had. Cheated, grieving and alone, I was nearly destroyed. Thankfully Babaji and his friends stepped in to look after the four of you. Truce was made with the organisation that as long as I keep quiet, your lives would be safe. It was therefore imperative to send you all away to different countries."

Raj took a deep breath and drank a glass of water. "I have had to bury the horrors of the past to protect the future," he said grimly. Looking at Rudr, he softly mumbled, "I will never let anything happen to you."

Padma gazed at her father with a look that screamed 'I need answers too'! Murli cleared his throat and said that any alliance with Sphinx was purely on business and political grounds. "Whenever I needed funds for the party, I received them and whatever they needed in terms of obligations and permissions, I enabled."

"And Harsh?" she probed. "Did you kill him?"

"Yes," he said, after hesitating for a moment. Nodding towards Raj, he continued, "I followed Babaji's orders. Harsh was a two-faced psychopath."

All eyes were on Raj.

"All to protect you Rudr," said Raj smoothly, inwardly hurting at how easily he had been taken in. "Had Harsh not been killed, he would have killed you. He was responsible for the hotel bombing—his intent was to kill me."

Rudr looked away, moist-eyed, at the mention of the bombing. He had lost Jenny to the attack, and the wound was still raw. Padma reached out to Rudr's hand under the table and held it firmly. She understood his pain. There was a brief silence for a moment.

Tarini looked at her beloved grandfather. "I have information that Tejasya Uncle, your younger brother, is a member of Sphinx, which also breeds the *mlecchas*." Tarini paused, looked deep into her *Bade Papa*'s eyes, then continued softly, "Your brother killed your son, our father."

Raj seemed to sink into his chair. His darkest fears had come true. He had known deep within, but now it was out in the open. Rudr was stunned into silence.

"There is a different world across the room, Rudr, waiting for us to intervene. We must leave now," said Tarini briskly. "Murli Uncle, you can return to Colombo. I will make sure Padma is safe in our company," she smiled, bowing slightly in a formal *namaste*.

Raj, Padma and Rudr followed her quietly into the cafe's adjoining room. It was empty. She walked towards the far corner and placed her hand on the colourful mural. In seconds, a small door neatly camouflaged by the mural swung open and the quartet walked through.

45

Sleight of Hand

"For a spell to work, it must have complete control and domination over a situation. We magicians can play God or Devil, having access to both the good and bad. As your president elect, I will take you to places you haven't seen before.

"Thank you for your faith in me. We are about to see the dawn of a new epoch—our era. Never before has the time been more right for dark forces and satanic magicians to shake hands."

The crowd cheered loudly. Kali put his hand on his left breast, bowed and smiled.

"Please enjoy the conference dear friends, as the masters from around the world enlighten us on black magic."

His eyes scanned the crowd and he couldn't help but smirk. "Unbelievable!" he thought, as his eyes settled on a singular attendee. The tall, broad-chested man wearing a cape was walking into the auditorium as Kali left the stage and headed straight for the closed-door meeting.

It was a full house. Around the conference table were heads of state and military chiefs. With them was the World Bank CEO, and all the office bearers of the New World Order that they were proposing. Shaheen and Jabari sat quietly, intimidated by the power elite that had gathered here to finalise the details of the proposed New World Order.

The President of the People's Republic of China, the world's top superpower, spoke. "It's with great pride that I state that the world of tomorrow will be a single global marketplace, policed by the One World Army and financially regulated by the One World Central Bank, using one global currency," said Yong Ying.

The military head of the One World Army, Lutin, spoke next. "We will manufacture crises to keep the world in a state of perpetual wars."

"Excellent!" said Her Highness, queen of a once powerful but now failing nation. "I'd like to look after the Law portfolio." Each of the others proposed their names for different portfolios.

Bon-Hwa the Korean hedge fund wiz, spoke last. "Money excites me. I will handle the Finance portfolio."

"And sir, what about you? What portfolio do you desire?" Kali smiled, his green eyes crinkling delightedly. "I do not require any portfolio to rule the world! Do I?" he asked rhetorically. "I have created the most dangerous thing on the planet. The Kā virus. All trials around the world across different genetic make-ups have been successful.

"If the corona virus destabilised the world, the Kā virus will completely finish it."

There was a thunderous applause in the room, along with the sound of clicking tongues.

"Now for a live demonstration. Who would like to be infected?" Kali gestured dramatically. Surprisingly, most hands in the room went up. The old queen, not as adventurous as her younger colleagues, pushed her face into her gloved hands, inhaling the heady aroma of Jo Malone. Her face turned beetroot red as her name was chosen unanimously.

Kali walked up to her, and in an instant, she lay unconscious on the floor.

The elite gathering stood shocked, as they saw their favourite grande dame suffer continuous convulsions. Her bodyguards aimed their guns at Kali, but one look from him and they froze.

Kali spoke. "She didn't even feel the prick."

"Is she going to die?" asked a dumbfounded Lutin.

"Genetic engineering of deadly biological pathogens can help their spread. They cannot be treated or contained. Genome editing by the Kā virus will thus destabilise the planet." Kali smiled, scanning for the look of approval from those who mattered.

"The virus travels quickly through the blood-brain barrier, locking itself in the neurons of the frontal lobe. The toxic shock is immediate, making the person faint. As the brain detects a foreign body inside it, a chemical change takes place, causing seizures. Once attached to the neurons of the frontal lobe, Kā releases a second burst of toxins, bathing the cells of the brain in a purple blood bath—or should I say royal blood bath in this case?" he joked, glancing at Her Highness, who lay still.

"What happens next?" enquired the Chinese President eagerly.

"She will wake up soon, to an altered sense of reality. She will have the mind of a honey badger and the body of a woman."

The elite company waited impatiently for Her Highness to recover.

Meanwhile, right outside the secret meeting room, the caped attendee blended into the conference activities. Hanuman wouldn't have dared wear his favourite outfit anywhere else, but here it fit right in. The crowd was swaying to satanic chants with their eyes shut as the aroma of incense filled the air. He shook his head disapprovingly at what the world had come to. There was open sex with bizarre rituals and orgies at one end while other signboards promised mind-blowing sex with animals. Horrified and upset, he quickly walked past towards the garden laden with all kinds of exotic food and drink. His eyes fell on a tall Indian, who looked amused. He walked up to Sumanta.

"Hullo, you look out of place here."

"Yes sir," said Sumanta, as he introduced himself, "I am a physicist—completely enthralled by Kali and his magical powers. I am a fan. And where are you from?"

"The Northern Belt; from a small town called Ayodhya," beamed Hanuman.

"I am hungry. Would you care to join me for a bite?" said Hanuman.

As they saw the spread, they baulked. "Human meat pies?! Disgusting. I'll settle for the fruits," said Hanuman. Partaking of the fruits, Sumanta inquired. "What brings you here?"

"Kali. I'm trailing him. But I'm not a fan."

The closed-door meeting was interrupted by security guards. "Sir, we have a breach in the security. The monitors are signalling the presence of an undesired guest. Should we handle it?"

Kali looked into the monitor and smiled. "No. He is mine."

"May I join you?" inquired Kali as he pulled up the chair next to Sumanta, and looked intently at the imposing man with the long cape. "So, who do we have here? Men of God attending a Satanic Black Magic Conference? Interesting!"

Soon they were surrounded by humanoids wearing smart suits with screens for eyes. Sumanta watched in utter disbelief as the data scrolled up on their screens.

NAME: HANUMAN
SYNONYM: ANJANEY
AGE: IMMORTAL
PROFESSION: SERVANT OF GOD

Kali's glassy gaze was making Hanuman uncomfortable. He stood up and tried to attack—but failed, again and again. He stood rooted to the spot.

"Premier Servant of God, this is my century, not Rama Yuga. Your strength will fail around me," snickered Kali.

Angered and agitated Hanuman tried again—but couldn't move. He couldn't even take his eyes off from Kali's. They were so deep, so intense, so green, so cold; he felt a shiver run down his spine.

"What did your great God reward you with, for your courageous devotion and righteous conduct?" Kali laughed derisively. "Immorality! You've hung around on trees, and roamed the world for centuries waiting for your Saviour, your God … so that you can serve him yet again."

"Stop! Before I pull out your tongue!" spat Hanuman.

Kali laughed out aloud. "You can't even move—and you're threatening me?

"I always knew you were foolish. As a child you mistook the sun to be a ripe mango and went chasing it up in the sky. Do you remember the bolt you received that threw you back on earth, damaging your jaw forever?

"Or when you came in search of Rama's ring to Patal-lok? Do you remember the King of Spirits who told you that the falling of the ring signifies the end of your Ram? I have control of that dark spirit," boasted Kali. "Your God has always been selfish. He blessed you with immortality as long as his name and stories were on people's lips."

Enraged, Hanuman made yet another attempt to move. "You will pay for this, Kali!"

"Ouch … I am scared," mocked the magician. "So where is your God? Where is your final Vishnu Avatar—that Kalki?"

"He has come and he will kill you!" fumed Hanuman.

"It's going to be interesting. In your time, the *Ramayana* era, man fought the demon—Ravana. Later in the *Mahabharata* era, when you were reduced to a prop on a chariot, man fought man.

"But today, in my *yuga*, *Kali Yuga*, God will fight God!" Kali's green eyes blazed with a fierce supernatural energy. "Go tell your Kalki … I AM WAITING!"

He disengaged his stare and walked away confidently. The humanoids followed their master.

Shaken, yet thankful for being ignored, Sumanta snapped Hanuman out of the trance. Relieved at being able to move, Hanuman uttered a chant, making both of them invisible.

"Did you just put an invisibility cloak of metaplex over us?"

"No. It's an invisibility cloak of complete devotion to my Lord."

"I'm feeling weird … what's going on?"

"Teleportation. Keep quiet and concentrate on your inner being. Once we arrive in Shambhala, you will have to rematerialise yourself."

"What! What if I can't? I've never done this before."

"You will have to break out or else remain as matter in space."

The Immortal

Parashuram

It was an impressive sight. Two suns rose behind the Arete mountains in a sea of liquid gold. As the moon set, the few strips of clouds shimmered, enveloping the sky in gold foil. It was breathtaking.

Some worlds have more than one sun in the sky. This one had two. One slightly larger than the other, almost fused together, as if the smaller were emerging from the larger.

There wasn't a speck of dust in the atmosphere. The ground was covered in ammil, its lacquered surface reflecting the brilliance of the suns, twinkling as though a thousand stars had descended on it. There was no breeze, but the place exuded a reassuring calm.

It was the kind of place God would live in.

As he emerged from the orange ocean, tiny drops of water clung to his large torso and ripped muscles. Everything about him from his slicked-back grey hair coiled perfectly at the nape to his wide forehead was imposing.

He bowed down to the suns with an air of authority. Then walked up to a precarious rocky outcrop above a vast chasm. Keeping one hand on a golden staff, he raised the other as if gesturing, commanding the elements.

At the blink of an eye, all that remained in the landscape was an intense white light that was travelling at meteoric speed towards earth.

Parashuram, the warrior sage and sixth Vishnu Avatar, took a deep breath reflecting on the decision, and shook his head. Was it all really worth it? He had been back on earth for thousands of years now, and was quite fed up with its self-seeking inhabitants. He would rather have been in splendid solitude enjoying nature and its elements on the planet he called home.

Unlike his fellow Immortals, Parashuram was least invested in the cause of saving the earth. He had argued with the Holy Trinity too. "Let them kill themselves, they deserve it. Race of selfish idiots. Why waste our time and invest our energies? I would rather bring into existence another planetary system."

"No Parashuram, go back," the Trinity had commanded. "You have to remain on earth as an amshika avatar. Your presence on this planet is vital. You will coexist with the other Vishnu avatars when they take birth, to assist them directly or indirectly."

His thoughts went back to Treta Yuga as he reflected on his life.

"I was born to the Warrior Princess Renuka and Saptrishi Jamadagni. I was their fifth son, blessed by Shiva. A devotee of Shiva, I practised deep penance at a very young age. Lord Shiva, pleased with my devotion, made me his disciple and taught me the scriptures and the art of warfare. Personally trained by Shiva on celestial weapons, I possessed the three ultimate weapons of the Trinity—Brahmandastra, Vishnuastra, Pashupatastra.

"I can create destruction at will—and I did. When the Kshatriya clan began to abuse their power and tyrannise the population, they killed my unarmed father. I waged a war against twenty-one generations of the Kshatriyas, completely destroying them. I became the symbol of Brahmanical resistance against abuse of the powers of a king.

"The mighty Hanuman intervened on their behalf, but I fought him too. Our battle is still remembered as the fiercest ever. Lord Shiva himself had to intervene and stopped us both.

"I realised that my anger and aggression served as a fuel for eradicating my enemies but had also resulted in aimless violence. I decided to use the power of dharma against adharma by adopting Brahmanical ways. Dwapar Yuga arrived and I gifted the entire earth to Prajapati Kashyap and retired to the Mahendra Mountains. Drona was seeking land and wealth for his son Ashwatthama and heard that I was giving away all of mine. But he reached when I had nothing to give except my body and my weapons. He asked for my weapons and I gave them along with their use and

withdrawal. This made Drona the most superior warrior of his times and Guru to the Kaurava princes. Besides Dronacharya, I was Guru to Pitamaha Bheeshma and Karna.

"I live in deep meditation at the Mahendragiri mountains in Orissa and in the Himalayas. Kali Yuga has arrived on the shoulders of Shukracharya and evil is exalting. Shukra's protégé Kali is dynamic and deeply gifted, being the seed of Shiva. But my seed grows in the Kalki Avatar too. Together we will restore dharma. The Kshatriya in me is awakened once again—once again it is personal.

"You attack my family and I will destroy generations of yours…

"Shukra is making my blood boil; aggression is consuming me as I polish my axe, my parshu, ready to be wielded after thousands of years."

46

Shambhala

"Shambhala!" cried Raj, looking around him astonished. He was back in the underground bunkers after two-and-a-half decades. "Unbelievable! How could we walk in from a cafe in Mumbai into Shambhala?" Nonplussed, he looked at Tarini. Padma was trying to figure out the strange place they were in. The cave cluster looked unspoilt by time, the smell of sandalwood was refreshing and each corner of the cave complex shone with a distinct radiance. Tarini guided them towards the huge living space, where once the Immortals had anxiously awaited the birth of their Saviour.

She smiled fondly, as she saw that the room was already occupied by their Gurus Ved Vyas, Kripacharya and Parashuram. They all had beards and were dressed in white. Yet each had a distinct personality. The three sat on mattresses laid out on the floor around a low centre table. Its centrepiece, a copper pot, had floating lotuses.

Parashuram had a chiselled physique and his long, sleek oiled hair was tied in a tight topknot on his head. The ancient furrows on his forehead gave him an air of total control. Seeing the twins, he got up and enveloped them together in his strong arms so tightly that Tarini let out a squeak. Soon both of them were seeking his blessings. "*Vijayi bhavah*," he blessed them, as he patted Rudr on his back and kissed Tarini on her forehead.

Kripacharya, in a white Chinese-collar jacket with diamond studs in his ears, hair and beard clipped short, was businesslike as he blessed the twins. "The world awaits your resurgence," he said authoritatively, looking at Rudr.

Ved Vyas looked darker than ever in his white *angavastram* and *dhoti*, his shoulder length hair left loose. Like a man in a hurry who does away with niceties, he declared, "The time has come."

Completely ignored by the trio, Raj prostrated before them. He felt a sense of déjà vu. Suddenly all the turmoil and curses didn't matter; he could go through all of life again to bask in the radiance and blessings of these divine beings. An unknown weight seemed to lift from his shoulders. Life suddenly didn't feel so hard, knowing these Immortals were on his side.

There was a loud commotion as Hanuman and Sumanta tumbled out of thin air.

Rudr rushed towards Hanuman, feeling at once nervous and joyous. Butterflies in his stomach, he began to bend down and touch his feet, but was stopped by Anjaney. Overwhelmed by a hundred emotions, both embraced halfway, and cried copiously—the long wait of many thousand years had finally ended. It was a magical moment in time. The Divine Keepers of the planet had waited an eternity for this moment. The wait had been frustrating and painful, but the hope that the Kalki Avatar would finally arrive and save the world had kept them going. They were fatigued and individually, they each sought mortality. They hoped that Kalki would bring to an end their story.

There was a peaceful benevolence in the room; no one spoke, words were unnecessary; thoughts flowed and energies connected. Padma stood with her hands folded, completely enthralled and overwhelmed by the events and personages. She had a smile on her lips as her eyes met Tarini's.

Soon, the cave was suffused with the incense of sandalwood and Tarini knew her mentor, Guru Markandeya, was somewhere around; his distinctive fragrance always preceded him. To her surprise, it was Pragnya who materialised—followed by Markandeya. As Raj rushed to embrace his grandson, Padma noticed the love and fondness everyone in the room had for this monk—and realised it was him she saw at the Taj in Mumbai.

Markandeya, *Shiv Sutra* in hand and *rudraksh* beads adorning his neck and wrists, reached out to Rudr without wasting a second and, with a flick of his thumb, anointed his forehead with ash, taking his time to activate the *bhru madhya*, the energy centre between the eyebrows. Instantly the clouds of self-doubt and duality that had haunted Rudr began to lift, ineffable and intangible images, difficult to describe yet bringing clarity began to emerge, taking him away from time-bound consciousness. The 'I' in Rudr got absorbed into superconsciousness revealing his true form to himself. A soft blue radiance akin to moonlight enveloped him. The cave began to resonate with the vibrations of the 'Om' syllable, Vedic chants and the ringing of bells. Everyone in the cave stood transfixed, joining their hands in prayer to Rudr, partaking in this mystical moment.

Parashuram spoke in a booming voice: "The sages of Shambhala anxiously await our arrival. Come it's time to step out from behind the curtain."

The next moment, they were all in the peaceful village of Shambhala, amongst a community of self-realised beings. The sages, all dressed in off-white robes, looked radiant and startlingly young. Raj recognised them all. It was easy—none of them had aged; it was as if these past 25 years hadn't touched them. There was a quiet jubilation in the air, even though there was no outward display of it.

One figure stood out. A woman dressed in battle armour.

"Meet General Revati, the daughter of the head priest of Keekatpur," said Parashuram looking at the twins. "The *mlecchas* brought death to her family and destroyed Keekatpur. Kali, then a child, buried her newborn son alive. She was devastated, alone. At that point Ashwatthama took her under his wing, taught her to fight, to endure, to channelise her pain into aggression, to push the warrior in her to extremes. She has lived in Keekatpur, in proximity to the *mlecchas*, inhaling their toxicity, becoming semi-barbarous herself, only to seek her revenge. She is a decisive, intelligent and ruthless strategist."

Revati squared her shoulders, the pain in her voice evident, yet her tone determined. "I live every moment only to defeat them. I can never forget how my son was buried alive. My innocent baby's heinous murder was to warn you, Kalki, of their presence. I have waited for this moment my entire life."

The Nanda siblings honoured her presence by bowing their heads.

Parashuram roared: "Go Revati, go! Prepare to attack. You will lead us as we take back Keekatpur!"

General Revati bowed gently and left.

Padma stood with the other two Nanda siblings, Sumanta and Pragnya, completely awestruck at the events of the day. "What's going on?" she enquired of them all. "Am I hallucinating or hypnotised?"

"Welcome to the magical kingdom of Shambhala, dear *Devi*," smiled Sage Markandeya. "Here, actions take the speed of thought. Here, consciousness is alive and kicking. This mystical place is off the grid *Devi*. It lies in a different plane of existence. The inhabitants of this place enjoy interplane existence. They can be here and in Mumbai at the same time. In a moment they can reach Alaska, or wherever at their will."

At a loss for words all Padma could do was smile bemused, with her hands folded respectfully.

The baby-faced monk then walked up to Tarini. "Thank these sages for their blood which was available to you every time you needed it. Meet Sage Udipt. It is he who has been organising the blood donation drives. Each pint of blood from these sages is then multiplied manifold in the tech lab that Vibhishan runs here with the assistance of Babaji. Ashwatthama then delivers the blood to me and I hand it over to you."

Tarini was deeply impressed by what she just heard. "Does that mean that the antidote to the Kā virus is sourced from Shambhala alone?"

"Unfortunately, yes. That's because only a few pure Brahmins exist now and all of them live here. And these sages are a rare divine species whose blood is an elixir and cure for any disease. However, it can't be used on everybody, there will be a toxic reaction leading to death if this blood is administered to a *mleccha, asura,* or *pishach*."

Kripacharya looked at his sleek gold watch and enquired. "Where is Ashwatthama? Why hasn't he arrived yet?"

Hanuman answered. "He was injured in a clash with Indrajit protecting the Badrinath shrine."

"Unbelievable! No one can harm Ashwatthama. Who is this Indrajit?" And then he froze. Impossible, he thought as he looked at Hanuman.

"Yes, Guruji it is he! I was taken aback myself when I saw him. The same strength and vigour, the same aggression … the sorcerer Indrajit tied me up too in the nagastra. I have seen Eklavya too recently. He was responsible for the debacle of Vaishnodevi."

Parashuram twirled his moustache. "This is getting interesting. Time truly is an endless entity. And perfection is a manifestation of consciousness—not time."

***

Mahabali was one of the two Immortals missing at Shambhala. He had chosen to meet his Guru Shukracharya instead at this pivotal time. The Ruler of the Worlds Beneath had easy access to his Guru. He knew Shukracharya could be reached only on Fridays.

"*Pranam* Guruji."

"*Pranam shishya.*"

"I come as a messenger of peace. Please Gurudev, stop this insanity! The world is at the brink of a war that will destroy humanity."

Wearing silver and white silk robes, diamond studs in his ears and tony shades, Shukra, the fair-skinned mythical sage with a radiant countenance, smiled. "Who has sent you—that *Ranchod* weakling, Vishnu Avatar?"

"No Gurudev. He is still unaware."

"Why is it taking so long for him to come into his own? This wait is a bane for us." Shukra took off his shades and looked Mahabali in the eye. His glassy gaze terrified the fearsome Immortal. "Look into my eye! Have you forgotten the time Vishnu blinded me disguised as the dwarf Sage Vamana, while I was protecting you?" The scar on his cheeks throbbed prominently as the hot-tempered sage roared, "The earth is tilted towards the South-East, my favoured direction. The time to seek revenge yet again for my mother's death has arrived."

"Guruji, your mother was brought back to life by your father through the *Sanjeevani mantra*. And you have already had your revenge before."

"No. The final retribution is pending—the reason you have immortality has to be executed and finished with!"

"Guruji, why create these baffling layers of contradictions and numerous veils of illusions?"

Shukra laughed out loud. "You haven't seen anything yet. Warn your Vishnu Avatar that this time, while he is aided by you Immortals, my Kali will be supported by titans from the past, as I bring them back to life one by one."

Mahabali shook his head in horror, falling at his Guru's feet, "No Guruji, no!"

Patal Lok trembled as their Lord Mahabali slowly rose, and his loud voice resonated in the worlds beneath: "So be it! Mahabali swears allegiance to the Vishnu Avatar, and along with him will come his forces of *asuras* and demons."

Shukra's face flushed with anger. "Yes, I have cursed the *asuras* in the past that they will never be able to conquer the devas!" He scoffed, "What has the world come to, the *devas* needing the support of the *asuras? Pralay* has truly arrived. But let me bring to your notice, my favourite disciple, that more ferocious demons roam the world today than those locked in Patal Lok. I have corrupted the minds of millions of humans; no virtue remains—hey are worse than the demons now! Tell me O Great Devotee, who has your Lord come to protect? These honey badgers?" He laughed and added, eyes flashing fire, "*Dharma* has succumbed to *adharma*—what is left to save?"

***

Nightfall at Shambhala was a sublime experience. The arches and walls of the cave complex were illuminated in a soft orange glow, with tiny oil lamps lit in each and every corner of the cave. The large living area was adorned with mattresses covered in silk, and thrown around them were cushions in ochre, white and yellow. A brilliantly lit *mandapam* (dais) at the far end of the room set the mood for a musical night.

Hanuman addressed the hallowed company. "We, the Immortals, are elated at being united again with our Source thanks to the cooperation, courage and bravery of the Nandas. And there is no better way to show our gratitude to the Nanda family than music." Then with great generosity of spirit he played the divine Hanumath Veena. The mesmerising tones emerging from this fretless veena bathed the atmosphere in a sweet fragrance. Music is a tangible thing and it touches more than just ears. The playing of the veena by Hanuman himself was yoga, a divine union, as it unified the *anandam* (bliss) of the individual soul with *brahmanandam* (supreme bliss). Everyone in the room relaxed in ultimate bliss and joy. Who could imagine that the strong and powerful Hanuman could also be a soulful musician! The clever arrangement of notes that he played was enchanting because it was brimming with devotion. It was also having the desired effect on Rudr.

He sat in *padmasana* (lotus pose), in deep thought, a gentle smile playing on his lips.

While Hanuman's veena brought bliss and joy, Markandeya's recital of the *Devi Mantra* transformed the mood from light to deep and profound.

Markandeya sang the *Devi Chalisa* in a deep soulful tribute to the Mother Goddess, the Bestower of Love and Prosperity. Padma was moved to tears by the sheer magic of the intimate setting.

Then came a dramatic performance that matched masterful technique with artistry. Parashuram left everyone speechless with his *Perini Sivathandavam*, a dance performed by warriors before leaving for the battlefield. He danced vigorously, in a powerful trance, to the resounding beat of drums, invoking Lord Shiva, the Supreme Dancer. Right then, Ashwatthama walked in and took over the drums like a man possessed, the furious rhythms reflecting the restless storm raging within him. Kripacharya joined them, elevating the energy of the performance. It was a fierce display of pride, strength and unity by the Immortals, setting the mood for war.

Rudr, mesmerised, soon joined the trio in a cosmic dance never seen before, invoking Shiva. Dynamic divine energy began to flow uninterrupted in the room. Everyone present began to feel a strange sensation go up their spine, as their *kundalini*—divine energy coiled at the base of the spine—began to get activated.

Tarini smiled and looked at Markandeya as he got up and brought the performance to an abrupt halt.

When it was over, the company, far too moved by what they had heard and seen to retire to bed, sat in the dark and heard stories from Ved Vyas, including their planned births.

"The theory of God and his siblings being manufactured by you and the Immortals is by far the most enchanting I have heard so far," Sumanta said to Babaji as they had settled into their cave room for the night. The cave complex though large had limited bedrooms, so Babaji and Sumanta were happy when Raj assigned his library to them. Sumanta, the astrophysicist, was used to staying up nights working on his thesis, and this night had been one of deep insight as he and Babaji discussed the physical theory of time and teleportation. Having experienced it himself, Sumanta was even more intrigued by the laws of quantum physics and Babaji was a wellspring of information.

In the room next door, Tarini and Padma were bonding. They had realised within a few hours of being with each other, that they were soul sisters. Padma had a lot of questions and she directed them freely towards Tarini. The ever-effervescent Tarini answered each boldly and truly.

"Is Rudr God?"

"Yes, he is."

"And you?"

Tarini smiled. "I am his twin."

"And me?"

"His life force. The *Devi*."

Padma blushed and pulled the duvet over her face. There was an earthiness to Padma that made Tarini smile. She was so grounded, and exuded an easy sense of camaraderie, and somehow Tarini knew that her aura of tranquillity would be the beacon that would guide the path of her twin brother.

"Padma do you pray?" asked Tarini

"Yes, why?" inquired Padma, surprised.

"Because I see unconditional devotion, pure *bhakti* in you. We need more of your kind of *bhakti* to manifest the true God. Will you please pray for us when we take on Keekatpur tomorrow?"

"With all my heart," said Padma. "I will sit in prayer and meditation till you all return safely back to Shambhala."

The girls smiled at each other, allies in the battle ahead. Tarini dimmed the lights to get some sleep before the long day ahead.

Shambhala had its own rhythm and way of life, quite unlike any other place on earth. The Nanda siblings rose with the rest of the village before sunrise and sat for meditation at *brahmamuhurta* (auspicious early morning period). 'Om' chants and their vibrations filled the air as each cell in each body was bathed in divine reflection.

Suryanamaskars (sun salutations) were performed in a synchronised manner facing the sun as dawn broke across the sky. The entire populace of Shambhala from the youngest to the oldest gathered at the geometric flower garden. Each one held a copper pot filled with water and poured it onto the flowerbeds looking up at the sun, paying obeisance to Him for His grace as they recited the *Surya mantra*.

Breakfast was a cup of green tea and almonds, following which everyone left for their assigned duties. Sage Udipt showed the Nanda family and Padma around. The latest introduction was the underground farm, he informed Raj. "Soil-free hydroponic farms grow produce under high-efficiency LED lights. So far we have grown cabbage and tomatoes with the new technology." Pragnya was hungry and plucked a few tomatoes. The sound of the flowing Ganga and the refreshing fragrance of the blooming burans were everywhere. The Ganga could be heard from anywhere in Shambhala.

A simple lunch of vegetables and sprouts was followed by a glass of buttermilk. Everyone then retired for an hour to their huts and emerged at 4 p.m. for warfare training with Ashwatthama.

Rudr, the first to arrive, thanked Ashwatthama for saving Jenny's life and held out his hand for a handshake.

Rudr did not betray his emotions on his face, and instead chose to smile. Suddenly all he felt for this wounded soldier was empathy and love; gone was the dread and apprehension.

"I believe she is dead yet again. But no thanks needed—one can't save a walker's life. I realised she was a dead woman walking, a *pishach*, when I infused monk blood into her—it curdled. I have been around you often to keep you safe. That day too at the university, I intervened only because I was highly suspicious of Jenny's aura. Monk blood only curdles when injected into the evil dead." Ashwatthama laughed unkindly. "Can't believe you—an avatar—could be attracted to a walker. It indeed is *Kali Yuga*, where God himself can be honey-trapped by a dead woman walking! She was set up by Shukra himself. I would have captured her that day itself, but Kripacharya asked me to let things unfold naturally. We were surprised that you could be so careless to expose her to your grandparents. Babaji had to warn Raj against letting Jenny stay with you at their home in Colombo."

Ashwatthama remained aloof at Shambhala and while he did acknowledge Rudr and Padma, he completely ignored Tarini. The previous night too, Ashwatthama had made a brief appearance, played the drums for his Shiva and disappeared, choosing to overlook the presence of anyone else besides the Immortals. Training was a different matter. While the sages were ready for war under Ashwatthama, the older Nanda siblings could not escape his exacting eye. He put them through a rigorous, gruelling drill and it was perfectly clear why he earned the title of *maharathi* as wrap up was finally declared.

Rudr had watched the entire exercise closely.

"I heard that Guru Parashuram himself has trained you in warfare Rudr. But I have to see it to believe it. When you have the time for some serious stuff, please reach out to me. I have to train you in celestial weaponry," said Ashwatthama to Rudr arrogantly. "But before that you have to prove your worth to me."

"Poor thing. He is so desolate, he comes across as arrogant," observed Tarini, watching him walk away.

"Never mind him Tar, he has proven himself to be our 2 a.m. man! Someone who will always stand by us, in spite of his attitude."

"Correction there. Stand by you, not me! Never before have I been so ignored by a man," Tarini chuckled.

Ashwatthama returned shortly, this time accompanied by General Revati. She spoke without wasting a moment. "I have a 4 × 4 stationed at the forest of Ādi to take us to Deogarh. It can accommodate six. Get the rest of the family and meet us there soon."

47

Deogarh

The 4 × 4 slowed its pace as they drove through a bare landscape all the way uphill. Revati, at the wheel, swerved sharply and stopped in front of a broad paved causeway. The broken pathway led to a solitary temple at a distance, imposing in its ruin. "Welcome to Deogarh," she said grimly. "It means Fortress of Gods—but I just see it as the City of the Dead."

It was a bizarrely picturesque scene, at once a testimony to breathtaking architecture—and cruelty. The company stepped out in silence, soaking in the surroundings. Located at the right bank of the Betwa river, amongst the mountains, Deogarh had been an important centre in the old military and trade corridor between North India and the Deccan. Several temples—Hindu, Buddhist, Jain—stood abandoned and broken, overrun by undergrowth. The small town had been cosmopolitan for its time, its people speaking many tongues. Exquisite stone sculptures and friezes poking out of the ground bore evidence of the heights of art and culture its people enjoyed.

"First they took Keekatpur. Then the sodden *mlecchas*..." Revati choked with fury as images of a babe being buried alive danced in her mind. "The swines came here attacking every home in a mindless rampage. Their bloodbath started right here, looting, killing ... even eating the young."

Revati strode towards Deogarh Fort. Pragnya, keen on knowing more, caught up with her as they approached the dilapidated fortress from the *Hathi Darwaja*, one of the two entrance gates. The enclosure also overlooked three *ghats* whose steps led down to the Betwa river. They walked past *Kashthi Ghat*, west of the fort, where people caught a ferry to Keekatpur in the past.

"There is no water in the riverbed, only red pebbles and stones," observed Pragnya. "When did the river dry up?"

"It dried up while I was still a child," replied Revati. "The *mlecchas* used this very *ghat* to enter Deogarh."

Revati retraced the path she had walked on, heavy with child, over two decades ago. It was a cloudy day but as they set foot in the temple complex, the clouds cleared away and the sun shone in all its magnificence over the Dashavatara Temple. It was the only structure standing proud amid the pillage and ruin.

As they approached its entrance, they were rooted to the spot, absorbed in its compelling presence. Built in red stone, almost square in shape, it could be approached by a flight of seven steps from all sides. The moulded platform of the temple was richly embellished with sculpted panels representing scenes from the lives of the ten Vishnu avatars.

They walked around behind Revati marvelling at all the depictions from the Matsya Avatar to the Krishna Avatar—and were astounded seeing the next panel: five men and a woman.

Surprisingly the woman was the tallest and wore pants, unlike any other female sculptures. Tarini couldn't help but notice the coincidence. She announced with glee, "That's us—Babaji, *Bade Papa*, *Bhaiya Bade*, *Bhaiyaji*, Rudr and me!"

Rudr missed this moment. He had wandered off walking around with a vague sense of familiarity. He walked towards the sanctum sanctorum, deeper inside. At the entrance was a *rudraksh* tree, and several rare *ekmukhis* (one-faced *rudraksh* beads) lay scattered on the broken floor. He bent down, picked each one lovingly and pocketed them.

The sanctum sanctorum looked deserted. A diffused bluish light beaming through the ceiling however cast a shadow where the stone idol of Vishnu once presided. Drawn towards it, he could hear a silent scream of writhing pain. There was just a slab of hardened clay, but he knew instinctively that beneath the cold exterior, was the dwelling place of a very young one. The proximity to the brittle bones made his eyes red in anger, and his breath got faster in visible puffs. In that instant, Rudr knew why he was here.

Rudr was drawn to graveyards as far back as he could remember. He would visit the cemetery at Narkanda and the ones at Oxford. He liked the peace and quiet they offered. He found tranquillity here, a sense of rapport with those who had passed on. But this place made him angry. The horror of the crime aggravated his senses, underlining the urgency for corrective action. A lot of time had passed; and he felt guilty. He felt like a phoenix arising from the ashes. His call was clear and now he was finally ready to execute. He broke the clay slab with a hard blow of his left hand, and out fell a few bones, really tiny and mangled. He picked them up. By now he was joined by the others—Ashwatthama and Revati to his left, Tarini and *Bade Papa* to his right, Babaji and his two older brothers behind. Silently the seven of them followed him as he walked to the banks of the Betwa river carrying the decomposed remains of the infant.

Ashwatthama manifested a sandalwood pyre and Rudr lay the infant on it. Tarini started chanting the *Mahamrityunjaya mantra* and the others joined in. Together they lit the pyre. They watched the flames rise and fall, lost in their own thoughts. Revati had no tears left; she watched the funeral pyre of her only son dry-eyed, her mind on the carnage to come.

The fire had died down and all that remained were ashes. Rudr picked up some in his hands and walked back to the sanctum sanctorum. He placed the ashes here, and scattered some *ekmukhis*. He closed his eyes and prayed to the soul of the infant to move on in its forward journey—and thanked it for awakening his.

Later that evening, Ashwatthama decided to check Rudr's godhood and threw him a gauntlet of one-on-one combat. He was impressed by his actions at the temple but in the past Rudr had disappointed him terribly. The God who lived as a man didn't particularly fascinate him and he wasn't ready to give away any celestial weapon from his arsenal to a half-baked man the other Immortals thought of as God. He took off his long kurta and turned around. The others sucked in a sharp breath as his shirtless torso was exposed. They were mesmerised by his physique. He had a chiselled chest and his abdominals were sculpted to perfection. Tarini let out a sigh of appreciation as Ashwatthama knelt down and brought his palms together in prayer. The biceps almost bursting and the triceps lean and well defined, he did a few squats, preparing himself for hand combat with Rudr.

In the *Mahabharata* epoch, Ashwatthama was amongst the fiercest warriors—one who couldn't be defeated. He had single-handedly destroyed most of the Pandava army; even Krishna feared his fury. That was why he had taken away the *Syron Ratna*, the celestial gem he was born embedded with on his forehead, and cursed him to be a wanderer forever, never finding peace. Ashwatthama had willingly given it away as repentance for the heinous sin of slaying the sleeping Upapandavas, however unknowingly he had committed it. He had accepted his mistake but, in his mind, Krishna continued to be guilty of multiple counts of *adharma* he employed to defeat the Kauravas. It had taken him a lot of living, close to 5,000 years, to understand and come to terms with his curse of immortality. An ardent Shiva devotee and *Devi* follower Ashwatthama was, today, finally ready to forgive the Vishnu Avatar and mentor him in warfare. But his student had to defeat him first.

Remembering his last meeting with Krishna, he said to Rudr, "Perhaps once you stood beyond me and looked back, laughing. Look again. It is I who am now ahead, yet I hold out my hand to help you with sincerity. Though you were the cause of my greatest pain, I remain your greatest hope. But to get my allegiance, come fight me!"

Rudr, ignoring the call to fight, walked straight up to Ashwatthama, and placed his ash-laden hand on his forehead. He kept it there for what seemed like eternity, and when he removed it, Ashwatthama's forehead glowed once again with the *Syron Ratna*, forgotten energies began to circulate within his bloodstream and all his skin infections miraculously disappeared. Humbled and choking with emotion, tears flowed incessantly from this suffering warrior's eyes, blurring his vision. He thought he was hallucinating, but before him he saw the Divine Being in His cosmic form, blinding in His radiant effulgence.

Time stood still for Ashwatthama. Immortality had been worth it, just for this moment.

48

Keekatpur

"Keekatpur was the perfect place. Hunger, grief and isolation had created a cesspool of emotions—anger, resentment and hatred—that routinely spilt over creating distrust and wariness among its residents.

"Like everything else in the country, Keekatpur's roots went back to a forgotten time, across millennia." Ved Vyas eased into a role that came naturally to him: the greatest storyteller of all time.

"It was the Golden Age of ancient India, thousand five hundred years ago, a time when creativity and knowledge, the arts and economy flourished. The kings of north India and the Gupta dynasty were investing in a wonder city they named 'Deogarh'. Elaborate temples and monuments were commissioned, astrologers and astronomers were consulted, and engineers and architects were busy laying the blueprint of the heavens on earth to create Deogarh—literally, the 'Abode of the Gods'. The city's centrepiece, the Dashavatara Temple, was envisioned as the most magnificent Vishnu temple of its time. Artisans and labourers from the Northern Frontier were employed to carve out the most intricate and exquisite friezes and figurines, depicting the ten Vishnu avatars and stories from their lives. The sanctum sanctorum was built facing the west, with a slight tilt to the south to enable the sun's rays to bask the main Vishnu idol in their brilliant light.

"What a magical sight it was! Deogarh represented a world of beauty, of regal spaces and sonorous chants, grand *yagnas*, opulent *havelis*... But it was the blessed sight of hundreds of *diyas* lighting up the sanctum sanctorum of the Dashavatara Temple that stayed with you." Ved Vyas took a deep breath, lost in the splendour of an aeon gone by. His eloquence held the Nanda siblings in thrall. As they listened, they were almost transported to the Golden Era of Samrat Chandragupta II, circa 500 CE.

"The strategic location of Deogarh, en route to the Deccan Plateau made it a trading hub," said Pragnya. "Several business alliances were set up with foreign shores back in the day, is it not Guruji?"

"Yes, my son," smiled Ved Vyas, impressed with Pragnya's knowledge of ancient history.

"The first silver coins and discoveries in science, math, and astronomy happened at the same time, am I right Guruji?" persisted Pragnya.

"Yes," smiled Ved Vyas yet again. "But I have seen the world long enough to know that as human civilisations arose, diseases struck them down."

"What diseases Guruji?" asked Rudr.

"The Justinian Plague that spread from Palestine to the Byzantine Empire and throughout the Mediterranean, came to Deogarh from Istanbul on ships via the trading route," explained Ved Vyas.

"A pandemic, Guruji, so far back in time!" commented Sumanta.

"Yes. It's shocking how an advanced, sophisticated and creative civilisation could be so fragile at the same time. There was chaos as the pneumonic plague spread from person to person, bringing death in multitudes across the classes. Entire households perished. The disease was so contagious that you could die within hours of contracting it.

"The authoritarian regime of that time was in panic. They decided to relocate anyone found with the disease along with their entire household to the land near the swamp, just across the river from Deogarh. Along with them the artisans, labourers and poorer classes were shifted out of Deogarh. The *vaidyas* (doctors) were clueless about the treatment, but they knew that the plague virus was carried by rats and transmitted to humans by the bite of the Indian rat flea.

"The *pandits* believed that the poorer classes and their lifestyles attracted the rodents and the only way to keep the plague away was by keeping the poor away. The nobles agreed. So it was that the first pandemic of *Bharatvarsh*, even before the Mughal era, created a class divide. Affected families from the higher classes were never permitted to return to Deogarh. Thus, many *pandit* and *vaishya* or trader families made Keekatpur their home—but they too kept to themselves, further distancing the lower classes or the untouchables. In time, Keekatpur evolved into two zones, the Inner Circle and Outer Circle," explained Vyas.

Keekatpur existed in the shadows of Deogarh, he continued. Soon, whoever felt victimised or isolated, started moving to Keekatpur. The destitute, the lepers, the sex workers all found favour in Keekatpur. Generations later, nothing much had changed for Keekatpur. Come Independence, and the partition, new states were carved out. Both Uttar Pradesh and Madhya Pradesh abandoned Keekatpur, which lay on their borders, a no man's land no one wanted anything to do with. It was the final straw. The isolation triggered memories buried deep in the past. Stories of atrocity from each house dating generations back resurfaced, and with them resurged bitterness, anger and seething resentment.

Keekatpur was the perfect place for Shukracharya. He made the *Siddh ki Guffa* near Deogarh his home and meditated there for years. When he emerged, he chose to live with the poor of Keekatpur over the merchants of Deogarh, earning the nickname 'Mad Fakir'. Shukracharya strategically hand-picked infants, took them under his wing and taught them his favourite subjects—science and DNA.

"Word about his sagacity spread far and wide. Ramneesh Nanda, your great-grandfather heard about Shukracharya from his Deogarh friends and decided to seek his tutorship for his confined first-born, Kapi," said Vyas looking at Sumanta.

"Your Grand-Uncle Kapi was brilliant to a fault. Yet his physical deformity, and warnings from the *Siddha* forced his parents to lock up the boy in a secluded mansion away from the mainstream society. Despite the best medical treatment money could buy, Kapi's birth defects could not be rectified. Isolated and alone Kapi harboured a simmering anger, and finally a deep interest in biogenetics which Shukra carefully stoked."

From the very first moment Shukra set his eyes on the bony, pale child at Safed Mahal, he was elated—the universe had just handed him the ace of spades!"

"What do you mean Guruji?" asked Sumanta.

"Each soul on the planet keeps taking countless births. And Shukracharya, with his *siddhis*, can look into everyone's past. One look at Kapi, and Shukra knew that the *vanara* king from the time of Rama Avatar was back."

"Who Guruji? Isn't Hanumanji with us, an Immortal?" asked a puzzled Sumanta.

"Hanuman was never the monkey king. In fact, he was a friend of the monkey king's brother."

"Gosh this is so confusing. Who is Kapi really?"

"Your Grand-Uncle Kapi is King Bali incarnate," declared Ved Vyas.

"Sugriv's brother?" exclaimed an astonished Pragnya, and added that the valiant King Bali was killed by Lord Rama.

"Yes. Babaji's Guru visited your great-grandfather's home to bless the newborn. When he entered the room, he was shocked to see the infant and requested the *Siddha* Anjaney to confirm his doubts. Hanuman recognised Bali and bowed to him; he also named the infant Kapi ('monkey' in Kannada). He knew that Bali in the form of a disfigured human had come to create nuisance and warned the parents to keep him locked."

"The arrival of Bali however was a good sign for all of us." Ved Vyas focused his tender gaze on Rudr, and said it reinforced the fact that the Vishnu Avatar would arrive soon. Rudr and his twin smiled at each other.

Tarini spoke up. "What's the connection between the two?"

"Bali has a special boon—in war he will always remain undefeated; whoever fights him will actually transfer half their energy to him, making him the stronger one always," continued Vyas. "Bali-Kapi can only be killed by the Vishnu Avatar. He also has the curse of being the spoiler for each civilisation. His birth marks the beginning of the decay of human values, of *Kali Yuga*, thus setting the milieu for the arrival of the Vishnu Avatar."

Vyas warmed up to the saga. "Kapi was gifted but cruel even as a child—just what Shukra was looking for. He was capable of dispassionate brutality and killed frogs and bats to dissect and study them. He moved on to bigger targets as he grew older, culminating in the small maiden lab to test viruses for interspecies infection at Safed Mahal. Meanwhile, Shukra's coterie of brilliant students farmed out internationally, studying at top research universities. They drew diverse, gifted minds into their web, enhancing both their network and net worth. They directed a steady supply of NRI funds to their hometown, Keekatpur, so that in time, a large sophisticated laboratory for genetic engineering and pathogen studies was set up here, away from prying eyes. It was top secret and so discreet that even the angel investors of this lab couldn't imagine that the brains behind the genome study they were funding were hidden in a small Indian town on the Madhya Pradesh-Uttar Pradesh border.

"Kapi was given complete control of the facility and its research activities and he skilfully kept a tight leash on his team of geniuses. Shukra then concentrated on building a secret cult, having as its members the famous, the influential—and easily corruptible. Today the reach of his organisation, which goes by the name Sphinx, is huge and influences economics and politics at the top echelons across countries of the world."

"Amazing, Guruji," said Sumanta. "No one would know this about Keekatpur!"

"Go on Guruji, what happened then?" cut in Tarini, a bit annoyed with Sumanta's interruption.

"After years of painstaking—and painful—research, Kapi had a breakthrough," continued Ved Vyas. "Years after working on interspecies infection, the Keekatpur lab developed a stable virus that was lethal and killed in multitudes. For Keetkapur's scions, centuries of being isolated was avenged by a microscopic virus that first invaded the body and then the mind, and eventually triggered sudden death. But in the time frame between invasion and death, the virus altered the natural reflexes of hunger, thirst and response to pain to create a shorter-lived tough body capable of ferocious combat in extreme conditions. Kapi, working with Kali, managed to create the blueprint for a formidable army—one that could be generated at will by the mere injection of the Kā virus. He proceeded to mastermind the spread of Kā across the globe. It was easy to lure the poorest of the poor to take a shot with the promise of food and water rations.

"This viral change in human behaviour led to hungry, angry people becoming a shadow of themselves, dark and spiteful. Negative emotions coursed freely, values crumbled further especially among the youth, and many resorted to crime.

"Every city and town had its own story playing out, but here Keekatpur got divided distinctly into two zones, the Inner and Outer circles. The Outer Circle comprised small cottages occupied by the well off with children comfortably settled on foreign shores. The Inner Circle, closer to the swamp, had thatched mud houses of the *mlecchas*, the outcasts. These people had barely progressed over generations and continued to live off the habitat of the swamp. They ate rodents and water snakes and spoke a broken dialect; they did not interact with the people from the Outer Circle or anywhere else. The two zones were separated by a forest of utricularia, drocera, nepenthes and other carnivorous vegetation that grew abundantly in the salt-and sodium-infused swampland. It acted as a natural barrier for the primitive *mlecchas,* who were even known to feed their unwanted children to these parasitic plants.

"Negative energy, creating a dip in the oxygen levels of the environment, thrived. The inner state of the *mlecchas* was quite like their environment—negative. The *mlecchas* were uncouth, uncivilised and barbaric. Their only pastime was incessant mating resulting in their growing population. They were easy subjects for Kapi and Shukra's next-gen genome experiments. The duo used them freely to create hybrids. The pig-men are the outcome of these ruthless experiments. In fact, they—the pig-men—are the most successful species created by the lab, with genetically superior traits than their diverse set of parents.

"Meanwhile, in the outside world, changes were taking place at a rapid pace. Kapi had set the end of *Kali Yuga* into motion, and Shukra had it planned to the last detail."

"How could you and the Immortals allow this to happen Guruji?" demanded Sumanta.

"We wanted the world to know darkness, before it could appreciate the light that is to come. It was an intent sent out to the universe, so that the Vishnu Avatar would take birth as promised," said Vyas, looking at Rudr. "Shukra and we, the Immortals, occupy the penumbra, standing at the two ends of darkness and light. The last straw was the birth of Kali. Shukra spent months in the graveyard to appease Bibi Maya…" Ved Vyas trembled at the memory.

"Kali's eugenics are linked to Shiva himself. He is Shukra's most brilliant pupil. As a child he played in Kapi's labs with genomes. Later, he took the research experiments with the virus to the very edge, focusing on transmissibility and effects, and has altered the Kā virus many times over to be ahead of any vaccines.

"He is an enviable foe, someone I admire for his lineage, knowledge and charisma. And his devotion to his Guru is commendable."

Sumanta nodded. "Yes Guruji, I have seen him paralyse Hanumanji."

"No way," interrupted Tarini, "that's impossible!"

"One would think so, but I am only saying what I saw," said Sumanta drily.

"He is right," said Vyas. "Kali has far more power than all of us put together. Kapi and Shukra have mentored his groundbreaking research on hybrids, and together they have set up the advanced Kā lab in Antarctica. Kapi is also the founder member of Sphinx, a powerful crime syndicate which dabbles in the occult and has offices worldwide. As we speak, Kali is chairing a weeklong conference with world leaders in Canada. I am told he introduced a new mutated strain of the Kā virus at the Satanic Black Magic Conference and his subject this time was the old queen herself." Vyas trailed off shaking his head and closing his eyes.

"Yes. Hanumanji and I were there," confirmed Sumanta. "Humanoids and artificial intelligence dominated the conference."

"I believe this new strain of virus is derived from honey badgers," said Ved Vyas.

Rudr spoke up. "Disgusting isn't it, to play with nature and create destruction?"

He looked intently into Guru Vyas' old eyes and enquired, "So what's your plan for us?"

"Family first. Tackle the darkness in the family—your grandfather's two brothers—avenge your father's death! There is no better time than now. Kapi has stayed back home—he is ageing and his back is giving him trouble again. His younger brother Tejasya is also here giving him company, while his wife Shaheen is in Canada attending the conference," said Ved Vyas.

Ashwatthama walked into the chamber, agitated. "Guru Vyas, can you leave your stories for another day? We attack Keekatpur at daybreak and our warriors need some sleep before that. In this era of unprecedented change, us military planners have to prepare for all possible contingencies!"

***

It was 4.24 a.m. at Shambhala—the auspicious *brahmamahurat*. The Immortals were busy with their daily prayer routine and Shiva chants filled the air.

General Revati walked around tense and anxious, fully geared up. Her hair was braided neatly, her arms jacket fastened tight bearing all manner arms.

She knew she had to rely on seamless interoperability of multi-disciplinary and multi-service forces. Raj's library had been converted into a war room with command, control and communication capabilities. Ashwatthama was briefing the sages on their positions in the infantry, and reiterating that weapons would be more accurate, mobile and lethal through the use of technology. The monks were superior beings who were trained in energy warfare: some used their hands, some their eyes while the others used their fingers, heart or mind to focus balls of energy at the opponent. The greatest purity of thought would create the fiercest energy ball. The child monks were the purest and deadliest. The women were next, followed by the men. And all were prepared to fight the Kalki Avatar's war.

The Nanda siblings were alone with their grandfather in his room.

The weight of a long difficult life had made Raj's shoulders stoop, and today his hunch was prominent. "It's unfair to keep me away from my revenge!" He spoke in frustration. "This saga started with my family and has to end with me."

Tarini reassured him. "We, your children, will avenge your wrongs."

Rudr continued, "At this point, it may seem like a personal vendetta, but it's part of a bigger purge, a deep cleansing of the planet, *Bade Papa*," he smiled, as Tarini's eyes met his.

Sumanta had decided to stay back at the war room in the cave complex. In the last few days, with Hanuman's help, he had seen the workings of the laboratory at Keekatpur and had been able to breach their security systems. He had learnt that non-traditional weapons—lasers, microwaves, sonics, germ warfare, gene therapy, and chemicals—would be utilised in great measure. He was determined to handle communications and direct this tech war to disable the Keekatpur stronghold. Pragnya was to remain with General Revati, guiding her with his power of clairvoyance. He would join the twins if needed. Ashwatthama had approved of Pragnya's ability as a fearsome warrior, trained by Kripacharya himself.

Ved Vyas and Markandeya walked into Raj's library together and started the chanting of the *beej* (seed) *mantra*. Ved Vyas chanted "*Om Kleem Vishnave Namah*" while Markandeya anointed the foreheads of the four siblings with sacred ash.

The Baby Monk spoke gently. "As your Gurus we bless you with victory in all your endeavours, always. The warriors amongst us will support you physically, the Gurus will keep your intellect steady and the materialistic needs will be supported by the Fortune Keepers."

"Sorry we don't understand," said Sumanta.

The Baby Monk explained, "Mahabali and Vibhishan are the Fortune Keepers of the universe. While Mahabali holds the keys to wealth, Vibhishan decides where to invest the wealth."

"Interesting," remarked Sumanta, "that our evil granduncle Kapi, the reborn King Bali, shares a name with Lord Mahabali the Immortal. So will we be meeting the Fortune Keepers?"

"Mahabali and Vibhishan, both *shishyas* of Shukracharya, are at present with him, keeping him preoccupied with their visit to his Antarctica lab. Mahabali has taken investors while Vibhishan has the political clout and policymakers with him.

"With Shukra and Kali both away, it will be easier to attack Keekatpur."

Markandeya added, "The warriors among us *Chiranjeevis* are the defence force of the universe. But for them, mankind wouldn't have survived—from rescuing children to fighting world wars they have done it all. They operate in a clandestine way and always stand up for the truth. They are ferocious and skilled beyond compare. Hanuman and Ashwatthama together can bring down the world, and Parashuram and Kripacharya are master strategists. The four of them are a formidable force."

"And you two?" inquired Pragnya.

"We are the weakest. We occupy the intellect and inculcate values."

"We are the most forgotten in today's time," sighed Ved Vyas. "Yet we are the most needed."

Tarini's eyes widened in concern. "Why do you say that Guruji?"

"But that's the truth, *beta*," said Markandeya. "The world today is in the grip of the lowest vibrations ever. This is not a time to teach or preach, but to pull out all our arsenal and declare all-out war against the evil."

"Go, my children, go! Win your first battle—there are many more to come! Keekatpur will be the curtain call to let the world know that Kalki has arrived."

49

Revati

General Revati didn't leave anything to chance. She had lived closely with the *mlecchas* and pig-men for years, and was aware of their highly developed olfactory senses.

She had washed every monk's uniform herself with soda bicarb the previous day. She had barely slept and revenge was playing on her mind as she bathed herself with a pinch of soda bicarb to neutralise any odour. She had instructed every member of her force, including the Immortals and the Nanda siblings, to do the same.

Ashwatthama had known that the future battlefield would be characterised by short and intense engagement, and precision and high lethal weapon systems in a hybrid warfare environment. He had therefore double-checked the artillery comprising bows and arrows, spears, rifles, guns, self-propelled howitzers and multi-barrel rockets. Yet, Revati tested each weapon for its accuracy and sharpness before handing them out to her forces.

Each monk—man, woman and child—had been trained by her for years under the watchful eye of Ashwatthama.

The warrior monks were suitably vaccinated in the face of an increasing number of new biological agents. They stood, ready to kill—yet a peaceful benevolence shone through their faces.

Sumanta set about disrupting the security systems of the lab complex, leading to a time disruption in the lab automation—quite like pressing the freeze button—to achieve battlefield transparency. The integrated intelligent automation now lapsed behind real time by a couple of hours. He would be monitoring every move of the confrontation via audio visuals (AV), scoping the progress of the battle through a variety of data inputs, having installed mic and cameras in the heads-up display (HUD) helmets that Revati and the Immortals wore. "This is a siege," he announced on the microphone. "Rush, we have to catch the *mlecchas* unawares."

General Revati turned to her infantry of warrior monks at the Outer Circle, and uttered the war cry: "*Akraman!*" It was just before daybreak. Soon the sun would join the moon, and together they would render Venus weak. It was the best time to attack Shukra's forces, Ved Vyas had said.

Revati followed certain classical manoeuvres of warfare. First, they penetrated the centre by pincer movements, creating a gap in the lines of the *mlecchas*, and then by 'double envelopment', exposing both their flanks and then attacking from the rear. By doing so, she used both primary defeat mechanisms—attrition and suppression.

General Revati's forces were met with least resistance in the Outer Circle, barring a couple of *mleccha* guards who they tackled easily. As Revati approached the Inner Circle, the monks covered their noses with their masks to defend against the debilitating stench of the army of *mlecchas*. They swiftly manoeuvred themselves into a *chakravyuh*—the formidable tactical arrangement comprising a multi-tier defensive formation that moves forward like a spinning wheel.

In the centre of the *chakravyuh* were Tarini and Rudr; surrounding and protecting them were the four warrior Immortals marking the *chakravyuh's* innermost circle. Just beyond, was Revati and her strongest foot soldiers, Pragnya and the child monks.

The remaining four concentric circles comprised monk warriors arranged by their level of skill. The women surrounded the children, and were enveloped by the men in the outermost circle.

Sumanta had positioned drones for an aerial view of the battle.

The *chakravyuh* formation cannot be seen from the ground, but seen aerially it resembles the helix of a screw, Ashwatthama had said in the war room. "It is my father Drona's most elaborate war formation—one which confuses the opponent because what you see is not the truth, yet the truth is far from being seen."

Revati's tactical expertise prevailed and she strategically and systematically subjugated the *mlecchas* in the Outer Circle, killing them mercilessly.

As the innermost circle of the *chakravyuh* edged closer to the carnivorous vegetation of the swamp, the stench became overpowering. General Revati sprayed the area with a combination of lavender and melatonin that immediately subdued the carnivorous plants.

The monk infantry stomped over the plants that now lay harmless and inert, quickly making their way towards the *mleccha* stronghold beyond. At this point the remaining concentric wheel broke away from the *chakravyuh*. Now the

Immortals, Rudr and Tarini had to move towards the fortress far beyond. General Revati and the monks were left to finish the *mlecchas*.

***

"Halt," ordered MZ-1, commander of the *mlecchas* force protecting the swampland stronghold.

The *mlecchas* were rushing to their sprawling bunker, exhausted after a night out hunting. Like pack animals, they found comfort and safety in numbers. They were looking forward to the delights of a grubby rubdown in the bunker, rolling in slime and huddling one on top of the other to sleep.

"I sense something," warned MZ-1 as he turned towards the direction of the carnivorous swampland, extending his snout and inhaling deep. "No odour of the plants … something is going on. AZ-5 go do a quick recce," he ordered his fastest soldier.

"We are under attack," boomed AZ-5's voice into the microphone.

MZ-1 was both nervous and excited. He checked the AV screen, reviewing images from the bunker. "Get up, go out and fight, give it your life, you sloths! You have been fed and prepared for this very day." There was chaos amongst the *mlecchas*. The oldest one spoke. "This time is unfavourable for us. We should attack after an hour, or we stand to lose."

"We are ready. Let's go," MZ-1 commanded.

The *mlecchas* were fully equipped with means of surveillance, reconnaissance, target acquisition and directing fire. MZ-1 strategically manoeuvred his army into attack position, using obscurants to hide his tactical movement, relying on dispersal and skirmish order.

The male monks in the Outer Circle of the *chakravyuh* were about to close in after the departure of the twins when AZ-5 attacked. He moved on all fours, trampled and swiftly killed a few monks, taking them by surprise. He then advanced into the *chakravyuh,* gathering intelligence on and location markers for the Shambala monks. He transmitted the data live to MZ-1. He was immediately attacked by energy balls from the monks that had surrounded him. The electrifying currents were crippling and he was dripping blood, but he put up a ferocious resistance, maintaining the breach in the *chakravyuh.* He just had to live long enough to let in a couple of *mlecchas.* The *mleccha* army seized the chance and made their way into the *chakravyuh*, creating chaos.

"The *chakravyuh* has been breached, close in and attack," Sumanta urgently warned Revati.

Instantly the monks came together and went about killing the *mlecchas* in complete coordination. Armed with spears they tore into the thick-skinned *mlecchas* just behind their ear towards the neck, felling them to death instantly. Those who survived and ran, were caught unawares by arrows, and the few that survived the arrows were shot dead by the innermost circle of the *chakravyuh.* The bodies of the dying creatures started emitting a peculiar, malodorous gas, and soon the entire area was filled with smoke that began to asphyxiate the monks.

"Move north," Revati commanded her monks. "And hold your breath!"

The monks, adept at holding their breath for long periods, continued to move forward, even though their eyes were watering. The toxicity of the chemical smoke would have been fatal, but these were Shambhala monks. The gas soon started causing the cornea to tear, causing piercing pain in the eyes.

"Close your eyes, hold your breath, and move forward," Revati instructed, her voice not reflecting her nervousness.

Pragnya's quiet voice came on in Revati's HUD; he was making sure not to distress her. "It was a set-up. They rushed their weakest to attack us, the suicide squad. Their death was to lead to ours."

"I figured. Tell me, what do you foresee?"

"Mayhem," said Pragnya. "They have surrounded us from all sides, the self-exterminating swines want us to die inhaling the poisonous gases released from their body."

Even as he spoke, a drone approached, dropping protective masks into Pragnya's hands. Within seconds the Shambhala sages were masked up with phantom masks. Sumanta smiled to himself, he had prepared well.

MZ-1 spoke to his troops, agitated. "This won't work anymore. Abort the suicide mission. We get into attack mode. Suicide squad, retreat! Await further orders."

Revati ordered her soldiers to keep moving north. Back to breathing under the masks with their eyes, nose and ears protected, the monks took a minute to focus their energies back to their heart centre. And then, they unleashed the mayhem, killing the approaching *mlecchas* with energy balls released from their points of focus.

MZ-1 tried desperately to contact Kapi, but couldn't connect. He realised the enemy was well prepared and had disabled the technology at the Keekatpur fortress. It was now left to him to manoeuvre the *mlecchas* forces.

"Attack the centre, all the children and youth. I want them all dead. Focus only on the part that they are releasing energy beams from. Attack each monk in hundreds—gouge out their eyes, if their energy emits from there, their hands, if it's the palms ... eat into their flesh. You will die as your blood makes contact with theirs, but it will be a delicious death," exhorted MZ-1.

Scores and scores of *mlecchas* appeared, hundreds of them attacking one monk at a time. They, of terrible deeds and nursing great wrath, delighted in battle. Endowed with prowess equal to that of Shukra himself, they proved to be ferocious warriors, difficult to put out like a blazing conflagration. They had been equipped with both 'astra' (bows, arrows, spears, serrated disc or chakram) and 'shastra' (swords, double-handed broadswords, maces, shields). Armed with maces, they rushed against the oncoming enemy, ready to bludgeon the monks to death—or die feasting on their innards.

General Revati's infantry put to good use a melee of weapons, including knives, batons and spears, with brute precision. The *mlecchas* in turn, used the major 'weapons of the body', as well as grappling techniques, jockeying from their positions and then striking—hurting, crippling or killing. They did this with techniques such as 'eye gorge', 'elbow strike', 'long knee', 'up knee' and 'throat punch'.

Right in the midst of this bloodshed was the tiniest monk, sitting in the lotus mudra in meditation. Five-year-old Sneh was the purest. Her aura and vibrations were keeping a protective grid around the light forces.

But the monks, overwhelmed by the *mleccha* waves, soon began to fall. They were outnumbered and though each one of them fought valiantly, the *mleccha* attack was lethal and continuous.

Revati was trying hard to concentrate, but it was devastating for her to see children amongst those killed and eaten. MZ-1 licked his lips, holding on to a bleeding monk. "Revati, is it déjà vu? Do you remember us licking your newborn?" he sneered. "I found him particularly delectable." MZ-1's voice rang out loud in the battlefield, drawing cheers from the ranks of feasting, dying *mlecchas*.

Revati didn't react to his taunts; she continued moving forward till she had guided her remaining forces to the Dashavatara Temple at Deogarh. Time froze for her as the deadly scene from her past played out in her mind.

She looked around, a sense of dejection gnawing deep into her heavy heart. She had lost too many monks. But she had to concentrate and save as many as she could, while killing as many of the *mlecchas* as she could.

Ashwatthama's voice crackled on her HUD. "Go, Revati go! Don't get taken in by the swine's words. You have lived for this. You are a warrior. You are more powerful than all of them. Show them what it is to face the fury of a woman wronged!"

A rush of adrenalin wiped out all thoughts and feelings. Revati was blood-thirsty now. Squaring her shoulders, she turned around, her eyes bloodshot, hair dishevelled, and foul curses on her lips. She may not have had a necklace of skulls, but like the fearsome Goddess Chamundi, she lusted to drink the blood of the enemy. The *mlecchas* didn't stand a chance as her swords slashed, pierced and gutted the slimy creatures.

Pragnya was protecting Sneh from MZ-1 and a large group of *mlecchas*. She thanked God for Pragnya's presence; he had been the most valiant fighter.

"Pragnya, leave them to me. Get the others. Wipe them all out."

Revati reached out to her talisman—the sari strip she had wiped her newborn with, still splotched with his blood. She quickly fashioned a sling for tiny Sneh, fixed it around her waist and shoulder traditional village style. She placed Sneh snugly on her back, and faced the next oncoming, stinky *mleccha*.

It was MZ-1. He laughed as he tried to grab Sneh, bringing his pig face close to Revati's, saying, "Come my lovely, join me in pleasure. Your rightful place is on my bed, not here on the battlefield!" His tongue darted out to lick her—and fell bleeding to the ground. With a swift stroke of her sword, Revati had cut it off. His beastly eyes and salivating tongue had long danced tauntingly in her mind. Today, she unleashed a maniacal dance of death. She grabbed another sword from her arsenal, and plunged both deep into the barbarian's solar plexus, then severed his pig head for good measure. MZ-1 was dead in seconds. Now headless, the *mlecchas* began to run amok.

Sneh smiled, calmly pointing at Revati's HUD that had rolled off in the confrontation. Within seconds the HUD flew back, snugly protecting the hot-headed, unstoppable Revati. Revati and Sneh made a deadly team, chasing and killing the enemy with energy balls and weapons. The *mlecchas* attacked wildly, even if dismembered and bleeding, their cacophony of grunts music to Revati's ears. Although she killed them slow and long till their tongues lolled to one side of the mouth and eyes narrowed in pain, the *mlecchas* fought ferociously, fearless and brutal until the moment of death.

In less than an hour she had seized Deogarh, after killing each and every mleccha and their progeny that came her way. General Revati and her modest army now waited at the east bank of the swamp, ready to move ahead at a signal from Pragnya.

Pragnya looked at the battlefield that lay quiet, a graveyard of the unburied. He shook his head and closed his eyes to the devastation. A large number of Shambhala's divine sages lay dead alongside the evil *mlecchas*. In the end, the king and the pawn go back into the same box, he rued. Death was truly an equaliser. Pragnya said a quick prayer for the holy souls, wishing them Godspeed across the realms.

He had killed mercilessly today, surprised how easily the battlefield had made a savage of him. The years-long gruelling war drill under Guru Kripacharya could not prepare his gentle soul for blood and gore of a real war. It had taken Pragnya all of his mental strength to plunge the dagger into the first evil heart. Anointed by the bloodbath today, he stood tall, a true warrior for the light forces.

Sumanta congratulated Pragnya and Revati for wiping out every *mleccha*. "Now, be on a vigil—not one must escape."

Pragnya was completely in war mode, ready for more action. "I am going to the fortress," he said to Revati.

"No," said Sumanta. "The twins need our support here. Our role is to provide them air cover. Remain right where you are you two, these swines can't be trusted. They may appear again."

Observing developments, Ashwatthama's lips parted in a rare smile as he said, "Sweat more in practice, bleed less in war!"

50

Ground Zero

At the edge of the swamp, Tarini's large eyes opened wide in alarm on seeing the water snakes and reptiles. She hid behind her brother as he smiled and set his foot onto the swampland. Hanuman quickly lifted her up and placed her on his shoulders as he followed Rudr. He would have preferred to fly and not get his legs dirty, but he was the faithful devotee who followed his master without question.

The reptiles of the swamp all started to move towards them. As Ashwatthama mounted his arrow on the bow taking aim, he did the math and smiled: three arrows from his bow would be enough, But suddenly, Rudr turned back and looked at him, shaking his head in discouragement. The venomous snakes raised their body in unison, spread their hoods and hissed loudly—making Ashwatthama draw up his bow string yet again—and then circled around Rudr's feet three times, before disappearing. Three large alligators lined up at Rudr's feet next, and he mounted one, as Tarini swiftly moved from Hanuman's shoulder into his strong arms. She briefly rested her head on his mighty chest, stoking a fire that had remained dormant for centuries. Looking at her adoringly, Hanuman reassured her. "*Bitiya*, don't worry, you're safe in my arms." But in his mind, paradoxically, he felt safe next to her. Amazed and embarrassed at his feelings, he quickly jumped onto the back of the next alligator, balancing his feet on the alligator's scales. Kripa and Ashwatthama followed suit, catching their ride as the next alligator lined up in front of them. The alligators then gently glided ahead underwater taking care to keep their 'riders' dry. They quickly crossed the swamp and made it to the other side of Keekatpur. Rudr got off first, followed by the others. Back on firm ground, Tarini regained her composure and jumped down from Hanuman's arms. The august company turned around to thank the alligators, but were amazed to see all the wild creatures of the swamp lined up with their heads bowed down facing them. The swamp water too suddenly changed colour from murky green to transparent blue.

The Immortals were left tongue-tied by what they had just witnessed. Kripacharya broke the silence when he exclaimed, "You know you're in illustrious company when Nature herself bows before you!"

Rudr smiled and moved ahead.

The fortress of Keekatpur stood high over the swampland, hidden by a dense cluster of tall trees. The imposing structure would have taken roughly 25 million bricks and enormous amounts of steel and glass to build. There was nothing around it, except a swamp infested by mosquitoes and bugs. The glass and steel structure loomed like a solitary menace. Amazed at how something so gigantic could be hidden from the world, Hanuman looked at Ashwatthama.

"What you see is not the truth, yet the truth is far from being seen..."

"I expected this," exclaimed Kripacharya. "He is a master at creating illusions!"

"Who?" inquired Tarini.

"Shukracharya," said Parashuram, as he reunited with them. He had left the *chakravyuh* ahead of the rest to recce the landscape. Having killed everyone on each floor of the 21-storeyed fortress, he stood, calm personified, belying the fact that he was the most ruthless killer ever known, adept at more ways of killing than imaginable. Eschewing the arsenal of celestial weapons he always had at hand, he chose to finish the occupants of this sophisticated laboratory with his bare hands; he could not bear to offend his weapons by using them on these lowly, *tamasic* people.

With great restraint, he had stopped himself from attacking the 22nd floor—Kapi's grand penthouse residence. Ved Vyas' words rang in his ears: "It is essential for Kalki to avenge his father; let this new chapter of Kalki's life, that of a warrior, start with him killing his two uncles."

Having paved a safe route for the entourage, Parashuram instructed Hanuman and Ashwatthama to accompany Rudr to the penthouse. They had reached the 21st floor, where the genetic engineering lab was located. Kripacharya had been asked to stand guard at the entrance of the fortress. Parashuram himself planned to take Tarini to the cutting-edge lab to show her the chilling experiments being carried out on almost all animal species—experiments that had exacerbated the risk of environmental contamination and disease. Sumanta immediately disagreed with the plan. His face appeared on the HUDs as he pleaded, "You have less than 40 minutes to leave Keekatpur—the automated systems will turn on by then and Shukra will know."

"This is our only chance to get into the human hybrid bio lab … we have to see it and understand how genetic engineering is being applied for biological warfare," pressed Parashuram. "The history of warfare and the history of disease are unquestionably interwoven."

Rudr spoke up. "Don't worry *Bhaiya Bade*, I will make sure we are out before Shukra knows. He has been brainwashing a lot of people into believing they can play God by manipulating the human genetic code and using Artificial Intelligence. It's absolutely essential to seek and destroy the source of this falsehood and to ensure that AI is a boon not a bane for humans."

Rudr gestured to Parashuram to continue with his plans as he sprinted up the stairs towards the penthouse. Hanuman and Ashwatthama followed close on his heels, chaste *bhakti* visible in their eyes.

Kapi was pacing the room when Rudr barged in. Tejasya was slouched on a couch, inebriated. Watching Kapi move about the room, Rudr found it hard to believe that they were the same family. Kapi had the same shell all right, the broad forehead and high cheekbones, but there was something almost feral about his eyes. His torso was misshapen, his arms were stunted, and back bent; his legs were crooked and short, and sharp prominent teeth added to an aura of menace.

Kapi cocked his head to one side, looking intently at the three of them. He smirked and fixed his gaze on Rudr. "My dear grandnephew! We meet again!" His voice was a high-pitched whimper. "How is my brother Raj? I was expecting him here too."

Rudr remained silent, giving him a hard stare. His eyes fell on the slim neckpiece that Kapi wore, a black thread with a large capsule pendant.

Kapi caught his stare and whimpered, "Oh this? These are the ashes of my dear Harsh, your grandfather got him killed."

"Grandson for a grandson," he screamed suddenly, as he leapt into the air and pounced on Rudr, pinning him to the floor. Enraged, Ashwatthama lifted Kapi off Rudr and flung him across the room. Kapi recovered instantly and ran surprisingly fast towards him. What ensued was an astounding metaphysical fight between the two. They didn't need to physically hit each other to cause pain. Kapi used movements of his hands to create energy balls that he directed towards Ashwatthama, making him withdraw in pain. In turn, he would be hit by illusory bolts of lightning hurled at him by the mighty Ashwatthama. The frail-looking Kapi was indeed living out the prophecy of Monkey King Bali—every time Ashwatthama attacked, Kapi would absorb half his strength and emerge stronger.

Both possessed great martial prowess, but Ashwatthama brandished his for the victory of good, while Kapi's natural deviousness blossomed and bent towards the dark forces with Shukra.

Rudr looked at Hanuman, who gently and uncharacteristically bowed away. He knew that a fight between Kapi and him would have been everlasting and inconclusive. Rudr nudged Hanuman. "Even though Kapi is very powerful and has the boon of extracting half of his enemy's strength, he is no equal, Hanuman."

Not one to disobey his master or bow out of a fight, Hanuman gently explained. "At one point of time in my past life as a *vanara*, he was my king. As a mark of my respect, I will never fight him. Moreover, my role in this *yuga* is to guide and assist the Vishnu Avatar—this is your war and you must fight it," he finished, with folded hands.

"Time is running out," cried Rudr.

There was a sudden jerky movement at the back of the room. Rudr sprinted towards his Uncle Tejasya, who had suddenly awoken from his slumber and was now pointing an unsteady gun at Ashwatthama.

Memories of his grandfather's anguish on being betrayed by this much-loved younger brother awakened Rudr's latent wrath. He snatched the gun from Tejasya and flung it into the safe hands of Hanuman, and without losing a moment, snapped his uncle's neck with a click. Tejasya met his death quite like his life—uncaring and unaware.

"Perfect," said Hanuman. "Now Kapi. Attack him from behind," he instructed Rudr.

Tarini, who had rushed with Parashuram to the biowarfare lab on the fourth floor, was horrified to see the hybrids and experiments. She realised that genetically engineered pathogens would constitute next-gen biological warfare agents. Her large eyes growing even wider, she said, "Looks like we have the answer to all the pandemics right here." Spread across on operating tables were several species of animals and bugs. Most disturbing of all was an experiment in progress, where a woman was undergoing a painful transformation into a honey badger. Doctors, scientists and technicians in lab coats lay dead on the floor. "I need time," she murmured, looking at Parashuram, who obliged immediately. He shrank the entire lab into a bubble with his *siddhi*, and sent it to General Revati. She personally handed it to Pragnya, who took it to Shambhala and placed it in the deep freezer of the subterranean cave complex.

Tarini and Parashuram reached the penthouse just as Rudr was about to attack Kapi.

But Kapi attacked with the ferocity of a thousand elephants; the more the number in front of him, the more his energy and ferocity. His body was small and disfigured, but his prowess was astounding and mood vengeful.

The Immortals were shocked, and before they could react, Kapi flung open the capsule he wore around his neck, and dispersed its contents into the air.

A sudden capricious, uncontrollable chatter started in the ears of all present, making them cover their ears with their hands, and distracting them for a moment, granting enough time for Kapi to disappear. Soon a hundred forms of Harsh were seen everywhere, laughing. Parashuram picked up his axe, and started killing each, only to have another reappear. He commanded, "Get the monkey, leave the illusions to me. Go—all of you!"

As he swung out of his fortress, Kapi was hit by a high velocity wind, which sent him flying towards a tree. As he fell, another powerful gust of wind flung him towards the opposite tree. He landed with a thud, writhing in pain, clutching his back. Kapi looked around with his sharp eyes, but there was no one. Within minutes, a gigantic draft of air mixed with mud and dust started spiralling upwards, lifting swamp mosquitoes and Kapi up in mid-air right atop the tornado. It gathered wind speeds of 70 mph, uprooting the shrubs and trees of the swampland. Large fissures appeared in the base of the fortress as glass shattered and showered all around. Kapi was trapped in this dust devil swirling darkly towards Keekatpur.

Guru Kripacharya nonchalantly walked past the mayhem he had created. He took one final look at the fortress and, assured that all his people were out, unleashed demonic wind speeds towards the humongous structure.

Eyes covered in dust and grime, atop a swirling tornado, a blinded Kapi felt overwhelmed as he heard his lifelong endeavour and efforts crumble to pieces in the distance. The enormous glass structure came shattering down, ripping poles and other power and tech infrastructure with its impact. With a deafening roar, the swamp waters came gushing out, drowning out the clatter of glass as they engulfed the fallen structure. The grand edifice of Kapi's soaring ambition was wiped out in an instant, without a trace. Mind swirling at the speed of the windstorm and ears hurting with the incessant buzzing of mosquitoes, Kapi let out an anguished, frustrated and agonizing cry.

Kripacharya had lived for thousands of years with virtues like truth, righteousness and impartiality. He hadn't met Sugriv or Kansa, the previous incarnations of Kapi, but was well aware of their gory deeds. Finally, the reason for his immortality made sense to the noblest of all men, as he used his powers to keep the monkey man spinning in mid-air.

Always the perfectionist, he switched on his microphone and gave orders to Sumanta. "Kapi is in my custody; inform the family. Raj would like to meet his brother one last time. We will be at the Keekatpur grounds soon. Warn Revati too of an impending attack."

Kripa lifted himself just a bit off the ground as the waters came gushing, enveloping everything in their fold. His left index finger pointed upwards, controlling the windstorm.

Ashwatthama glanced at Hanuman as the shape-shifter expanded to humongous proportions, and lifted Rudr and Tarini in his arms, taking to the skies. No words were spoken, but Ashwatthama caught the doubt and concern in Hanuman's eyes. They matched his. He had seen the avatar in Rudr—then why and how did Kapi survive? Had the Immortals failed? Had they been fooled into believing Rudr was the Vishnu Avatar? He touched the *Syron Ratna* on his forehead, and looked at his skin, which had miraculously healed. It didn't make sense.

Kapi landed with a thud on the ground, as the storm made a sudden landfall. He looked around and saw the putrefying bodies of the *mlecchas*. The large school ground in Keekatpur was splattered with stinking blood.

And was dead quiet.

Then, rising like a phoenix from thin air, he saw a huge warrior in black approaching him at great speed. He staggered up, holding his injured back, and smiled. He held out his left hand, which was grasped by strong arms as he was lifted off the ground. "Indrajit!" he whimpered, "High time!"

The mighty Indrajit, skilled in the use of mystic missiles, and known for his Brahmastra, Nagpash, sorcery and *tantra*, had unleashed the Nagpash on Kripacaharya. Caught in its serpentine grip, the fearsome Kripa was compelled to release the storm he controlled. As a result, Kapi had come crashing to the ground.

On seeing the shrunken monk regiment led by General Revati, Indrajit had roared in laughter. "Seriously sister! You expect the mighty Indrajit to bother with you—a woman general leading a bunch of monk soldiers? If this isn't *Kali Yuga* what is? Where have all the righteous men disappeared?" he sneered at Revati.

In answer, she unleashed a barrage of arrows towards Indrajit, but he blocked them easily with a celestial shield and thundered before disappearing, "A good fight is always between equals!"

Indrajit gently picked up Kapi, his strong hands supporting the frail man. In a time gone by, this frail man had had the brute strength of 70,000 elephants. He had even defeated Indrajit's father, the Demon King Ravana, tied him to his tail and created havoc in Lanka. Today karma and *Kali Yuga* had together made a mockery of the invincible Monkey King Bali.

Hanuman dropped the twins in the centre of the *chakravyuh's* concentric ring safeguarded by the monks. He downsized to human proportions and rushed to free Kripa from the dreaded Nagpash. A mortal would have swiftly perished in the grip of this poisonous weapon, but the Immortals never perished; they merely suffered. Thousands of poisonous snakes had entwined Kripa's torso completely and were feeding off him. He was bleeding profusely as a result. Hanuman, the only one capable of deactivating every celestial weapon on the planet and beyond, deactivated the Nagpash. He waited till the wounds healed in a couple of minutes and Kripa regained his lost strength.

"Be careful," he warned Kripa and Ashwatthama. "The sorcerer is using his *daivi shaktis*. Celestial weapons haven't been used since the time of the Mahabharata war. It's time we dig into our arsenal too. What's stopping us now?" he asked frustrated, looking at Ashwatthama.

Kripacharya, too, looked questioningly at Ashwatthama. "You are the guardian of the celestial weapons—why are you not unlocking them? Indrajit is undefeatable in war as long as he has access to his *daivi shaktis*. In the past he has captured and defeated Hanuman using the Brahmastra; he defeated Rama and Lakshman using the Nagpash; and more recently all three of us have been attacked by the Nagpash too.

"The dynamics of attack have changed with the entry of Indrajit. Shukracharya has prepared his students well—one a *maharathi* and another full of brute strength despite his frail build. I was able to capture Kapi only because I remained invisible to him," said Kripacharya.

With angst in his voice, Ashwatthama explained, "As the custodian of celestial weapons it is my bounden duty to hand them over to the tenth Vishnu Avatar. If I surrender the weapons to anyone but Vishnu himself, I will bring on the end of the planet ... a burden I could live without."

Kripa was irritated: "What more proof do you want of Rudr's godhood? You've always been bad at judging people!" He further admonished his nephew, "You're doubting the one who released your curse and placed the gem back on your forehead?"

Understanding his plight, Hanuman spoke up. "In all these years of living, I have mastered the deactivation of each celestial weapon, so let me tackle Indrajit. Ashwatthama, you go take on Kapi, and take both the Gurus with you. Use your individual *shaktis* to tackle Kapi."

"And Rudr?" inquired Kripa.

"He will come with us," asserted Parashuram. "I have trained him for this very day."

They were soon joined by Raj, Ved Vyas, Markandeya, Sumanta and Babaji.

"You should take Tarini too," insisted Markandeya. "She is a brilliant warrior."

General Revati quickly guided them to the centre of the war formation, where the twins were in discussion. "The two of you have been called for by the Gurus," she announced.

***

It started with one monk yawning and soon the entire infantry was yawning and collapsing to the ground in a trance. Only the Immortals and the twins remained standing.

Indrajit appeared, looking tall and regal. "The Sanmohan Astra will keep the extras sedated," he announced nastily, "so that we can concentrate on the main players."

What ensued was a never-before-seen battle of the titans. Hanuman faced Indrajit, while the two Gurus, Ashwatthama and the twins fought Kapi.

It was known that this clash between good and evil would be characterised by the deployment of cutting-edge technology. It would feature considerable structural and industrial damage, force dispersion, a smaller tailored-force structure, new personal equipment, data links to the individual soldier, a 360-degree threat, and above all, a non-traditional enemy force structure. With mystical prowess and advanced ballistics, both Indrajit and Hanuman had weapons that were deadly accurate, swift, precise with targets, and technology-driven.

Hanuman, the mighty son of Vayu, was in his element. Indrajit attacked Hanuman with multiple weapons, including torpedoes, Indrastra, machine guns, Agneyastra and flame throwers, vajra and lasers, but without much success. Hanuman easily deflected Indrajit's mystic weapons with his *siddhis* and his other arsenal with multi-purpose munitions, long-range precision fires and air-delivered electronic warfare. In addition, this time he easily destroyed all of the sorcerer's tricks and illusions. He had learnt from past mistakes and constantly chanted the *Vishnu Sahasranama mantra* to further charge his energies.

The battle raged on for hours. This was unexpected in a world where instant gratification ruled, and weapons of mass destruction (WMDs) like germ warfare and nuclear weapons could win wars in a few seconds. Exasperated at the failure of his weapons and in a hurry to end the fight, Indrajit finally resorted to his *daivi shakti* to materialise the weapon of weapons, the ultimate WMD, the Brahmandastra—the weapon with a single projectile charged with all the powers of the universe.

The supernatural weapon manifested with Brahma's fifth head at front was, loaded to destroy not just what was around it but the entire world. Its menacing presence was felt around the world. As it got unlocked from the heavens it made the most deafening sound. Shukra was shell-shocked on hearing the distinct, ominous rumble in Antarctica. Mahabali and Vibhishan, who were with him, froze. The others in the high-level meeting were clueless as to the cause but frightened with the dark lightning and thunderous sounds coming from the skies. The trio excused themselves and vanished into thin air.

"Indrajit, call it back!" roared Shukra, manifesting before the sorcerer. "What have you done?" Looking at the equally shocked Immortals, Shukra pleaded with folded hands, "Is there a way to stop this? Can Kalki finally emerge and at least save the day?" The Guru of the Asuras, having created havoc all around, was today helplessly begging and raging for the continued existence of the universe.

The twins interlocked their hands and together with the other seven Immortals, stood on either side of the mighty Hanuman, ready to take on the ultimate weapon of mass destruction.

The Brahmandastra rushed swirling towards Hanuman. Its incandescent column of smoke and flame as bright as ten thousand suns rose in all its terrifying splendour—and simply dissolved, falling at the feet of the Son of Vayu.

There was complete silence. A huge catastrophe had been averted. Shukra with folded hands bowed before the mighty Anjaney. He then unabashedly rebuked the arrogant Indrajit for irresponsibly calling for a weapon of that magnitude.

Ashwatthama cursed Indrajit, "You will no longer have access to any *daivi shaktis*."

Painfully acknowledging his mistake and conceding to his opponent's strength, Indrajit withdrew and vanished as suddenly as he had appeared. He would be back, better prepared; but for now, he needed to invoke his clan goddess and seek her blessings to fight the strongest being on earth—Hanuman.

As Indrajit withdrew, the Sanmohan Astra's efficacy reduced and Raj and the monks came out of their unnatural slumber.

Shukra shook his head seeing the carnage at Keekatpur where the bodies of the *mlecchas* had stained the ground red. It was time to leave. His time would come—once again.

***

Despite his size, Kapi turned out to be a ferocious opponent. The battle that had started at Kapi's penthouse between him and Ashwatthama continued. The ferociousness of the attacks turned the skies grey, and though this entire war was happening far away from the plane of human existence, its reverberations were felt all over. Most of north India was engulfed in a raging storm. Rudr stepped in to give some relief to Ashwatthama, and fought valiantly but Kapi was behaving like a thousand bull elephants drunk on musth, aggressive and uncontrollable. He unleashed blow after blow on Rudr, who remained unaffected but fully engaged in warding them off.

Meanwhile an agitated Raj appeared on the scene.

"You shouldn't be here, *Bade Papa*," Tarini warned urgently.

Kapi's focus swiftly shifted from Rudr to Raj.

Raj was shocked to see his older brother; he looked like a pile of bones put together in a hurry. Kapi looked intently at his brother and smiled crookedly as he leapt on him, pinning down both Raj and Tarini. Flushed in anger, Rudr's face turned red, the skin between his eyebrows became inflamed and was about to burst. He easily picked up Kapi by the scruff of his neck from above his grandfather and sister and punched him savagely on his face. He lifted him up in the air with one hand, ready to fling him. Tarini meanwhile gently helped her grandfather get up.

"Whose daughter is Sujata, Kapi?" bellowed an incensed and half-crazed Raj thirsting for the answer to a question that had haunted him all his life.

"Our mother's," whimpered Kapi with a sneer.

Shell-shocked, yet doubt-ridden, Raj further asked, "Who is the father?"

"I am!" came Kapi's triumphant whimper. "Our mother loved me intensely—you cannot imagine what..."

"Shut up!" roared Raj as he slapped Kapi hard on his face and suddenly slumped to the floor.

Infuriated, Rudr pinned Kapi to the floor and sat on him. Tarini looked sharply at Guru Parashuram, and at his nod, gestured Rudr to move. As she took his place above Kapi's abdomen, she declared, "This one is mine!"

Ashwatthama looked at Tarini, and then at Parashuram, who nodded. He was ready to risk it. Suddenly more important than the weapon used, was the hand that used it.

Desperate to finish off the Monkey King Bali-Kapi, he said a quick prayer and materialised the Nandka, Sword of Vishnu—and handed it to Tarini.

Holding the Nandka in her hands, within seconds, she turned Kapi on his stomach and plunged the sword into his back with both her hands.

It was a tense moment for all present. Either Kapi would die—or the world would.

Kapi let out a guttural cry—and his head lolled to one side.

Hanuman was the first to move. He walked up to Kapi and checked for his pulse.

Copious tears streaming down his face, he fell at Tarini's feet. "*Prabhu*, you never cease to surprise us!"

The Immortal

Markandeya

The Immortals were as stunned as the Nandas at what had just happened. It was all so quick. Slowly, the magnanimity of the moment began to sink in. Drawing out the blade, Tarini stood in splendour, the Nandka glistening in her strong hands.

Markandeya was the first to move. Eyes filled with tears of joy, the mentor walked up to his pupil and anointing her forehead with chandan (sandalwood paste), uttered, "Om Keshavaya Namah, Om Vishnuaya Namah, Om Kalkiay Namah." He chanted the Kalki Avatar shloka for the first time.

Tarini smiled at her mentor—their secret was now out in the open.

As Ashwatthama shook his head in disbelief, and Hanuman was kneeling on one leg, hands folded in prayer, petals continuously fell on Tarini from the heavens above.

Parashuram chanted the mantra Markandeya had just given for the epoch, closed his eyes and moved his hands in the air. A magnificent white steed appeared, and went straight to Tarini, neighing and sighing. Markandeya handed her the armour he had kept ready for this day. As it moulded itself to her slender form, she looked straight into his eyes, her heart sinking. She knew it was time.

The Baby Monk blessed her, then walked up to Rudr. Markandeya could feel the confused emotions surging in Rudr's heart as he stood apart avoiding eye contact. Godhood had been snatched from him in an instant—and given to his twin sister. The Baby Monk shivered at the thought of things to come. A future that would have a God fight a God and the Immortals choosing sides; a bloody carnage on earth, with Kali dancing on the spoils. The darkest hour had yet to come.

Death is a tragedy in the young, and a rite of passage for the old. For Markandeya it was an oxymoron. The Baby Monk was to live for only 16 years, but Shiva, impressed by his bhakti, had blessed him with immortality. Wise beyond his years, Markandeya had begged for retraction of the boon, pleading, "What will I do for so long?" Shiva had smiled: "Keep innocence alive in the universe. You will be the mentor to the Kalki Avatar, and when your work is done I myself will be there to get you back to your final abode."

Today his Supreme Lord stood before him confused about his place in the scheme of things.

Yet Markandeya had known at the instant of their birth that as twins, Shiva had come along with Vishnu in this era. A reality that all other Immortals completely missed, in spite of their wisdom and foresight.

His heart brimming over with love and devotion, the Baby Monk both sought for and showered blessings on Rudr. As he embraced Markandeya, Rudr's turmoil quietened, and he closed his eyes in deep contemplation.

With an enigmatic smile and a peaceful glow on his face, Markandeya took his leave and levitated eastwards. His hands folded and mind centred, visuals from the last two decades flashed before his eyes. These were the most cherished of his days from the times that he had lived. It had been an absolute joy to be guardian to Tarini; an adventure even. And while she believed he was her mentor, he secretly looked up to her in awe. She was perfect; the heavens had sent the Kalki Avatar prepared.

Markandeya had played crucial roles in the different incarnations of Vishnu, but this role had been the most endearing. Nobody but he had access to Tarini's Kalki avatar. To keep it developing and growing while keeping it hidden had been a task. From channelising her energies for the good of the world without drawing attention to keeping her superpowers in check, he had done it all. And though he was mentoring God, he knew that even God as a girl child had needs only a mother could fulfil.

Everyone needs the love of a mother to nurture them, to make them soar. Kalki wouldn't be complete without her mother. Markandeya had kept the mother and daughter hidden from the world. He knew it is in the absence of noise that creation happens.

Today, the purpose of his life had been achieved. There was nothing left to do. He definitely did not want to choose between Shiva and Vishnu—he loved and revered both equally.

With gratitude, he hovered over his destination: Mother Ganga. Once he was in the middle of the mighty Ganga, he slowly brought himself down, legs crossed, back straight, eyes shut, ready for his jal samadhi.

He smiled in complete surrender as the Trinity, Brahma-Vishnu-Mahesh, blessed him and Mother Ganga engulfed him in her womb.

Epilogue

Astride a white horse, a blazing sword drawn, Kalki surveyed the scene of destruction. The barbarians and *mlecchas* lay dead, as the smell of blood and rotting flesh filled the air…

As the sun retreated back into the sea, Kalki's opulence lit up the sky. The broad forehead glistened with sweat beads; the piercing, teal grey eyes surveyed the city of Keekatpur as it lay abandoned, wasted.

An army of sages sounded the victory conch to the rhythmic chants of "*Om Keshavaya Namaha!*"

Kalki gently joined her palms together in a *namaste*. Devdutta, the magnificent white steed, also raised his forelimbs in salutation to the holy personages. Then, together, the divine force and the mystic horse darted into the sky with a bolt of lightning, as the sages shouted out unanimously in joy: "Our Saviour has arrived!"

Acknowledgements

I have to start by thanking my wonderful grandparents Raj and Sulakshana Sharma—*Bade Papa* and *Mumma*—from whom I learnt the art of storytelling. *Bade Papa* instilled the love of the written word. His library was stocked with literature from around the world, and it was *Mumma*'s *bhakti* for her Krishna that set me off on the path of being a seeker.

My parents Rajendra and Nandini Sharma, for their love and guidance, for always believing in me and inspiring me to achieve everything I set out to do.

Ratin, my brother, my creative go-to. Thank you for all your inputs and suggestions. *Antim* would not be without you.

Major General Praveen Dixit, for invaluable insights on warfare.

Sangita Chandra, Shalini Ahluwalia, Khyati Patel, Richa Gupta Kala, for all your help in the initial days of the book.

Babaji, my spiritual guru, my source of inexhaustible knowledge. His words, his stories, his life will always inspire me. Thank you for pushing me to put this saga to paper.

Swami Swatmananda, from Chinmaya Mission, for his

profound knowledge of the Vedas and *shastras*. His pragmatic teachings of the scriptures keeps me on the path towards self-discovery.

Yogesh Sharma for cheering me enthusiastically through the entire decade and giving crucial advice.

Smarth Bali, my genius advisor, who made sure that I kept the *mahol* alive throughout the entire story. Thank you for being my encyclopaedia at any hour, on any given day.

Mrunalini, thank you so much for the brilliant initial editing, and hanging in there patiently through the many drafts. In you, I have found a dear friend for life.

My gracious thanks to the team at Om Books International—Publisher Ajay Mago for believing and trusting in my story; Editor-in-Chief Shantanu Ray Chaudhuri for steering this project in his able hands; Editor Sheela Roy for polishing the rough edges and bringing it to its present form.

Above all, thank you Hemal, Devansh and Naman, for making *Antim* a part of our everyday existence over the last ten years.

Glossary

Acharya – teacher
Akraman – attack
Amshika – incomplete avatar, one who has not fully realised his powers
Angavastram – upper body garment
Ansh – source
Arati – ritual prayer
Arre – expletive
Asuras – descendants of Brahma; said to be divine, higher beings, possessing great knowledge and supernatural, magical powers equal to that of the *devas* gods; *asuras* were good or evil depending on which side they choose – Light or Darkness; asuras like Ravana and his son Indrajit were powerful, spiritually accomplished, but ego-driven and destructive; asuras like Mahabali, Vibhishan and Mayasura, who architected the magical Mayasabha for the Pandavas, were benevolent and hailed as heroes; *asuras* are not to be confused with lower beings like demons and devils
Atimaharathi – warrior capable of fighting 12 *maharathi* class warriors or 8,640,000 warriors simultaneously

Atman – soul

Avatar – incarnation, usually of a god, especially in Hinduism; popularly associated with Lord Vishnu whose nine Avatars – Matsya, Kurma, Varaha, Narasimha, Vamana, Parashuram, Rama, Balarama, Krishna – are already believed to have appeared; scriptures say His tenth Avatar as Kalki will appear in *Kali Yuga*

Beej – seed/core

Bhaiya – brother

Bhakt – devotee

Bhakti – devotion

Bharatvarsh – ancient name for India

Bhav – expression/emotion

Bhru madhya – spot in the middle of the eyebrows, behind which the pineal gland, associated with altered states of consciousness, is located; in yoga and meditation, one is asked to focus one's internal gaze on the third eye

Bhutas – ghosts

Bitiya – daughter

Brahmahatya – homicide/killing of Brahmins

Brahma Sanskara – rites of passage that mark important stages of transition in life; they served a spiritual, cultural and psychological purpose, ushering an individual into each stage of life, conferring privileges and assigning duties expected of the new role

Brahmachari – bachelor, an unwed youth who practices *brahmacharya* or 'pure conduct'; *brahmacharya* is an Indian cultural concept that literally means one who completely controls his body and mind through ascetic means

Brahmamuhurta – a period of 48 minutes that starts 1 hour 36 minutes before the sunrise and ends 48 minutes before the sunrise; considered the most auspicious time for meditative or spiritual practice, as also to learn or create (Brahma = Creator; muhurta = time)

Bua – aunt (father's sister)

Chakravyuh – 'chakra' means 'spinning wheel' and 'vyuha' means formation; hence, it is the tactical arrangement of soldiers that keeps moving in the form of a spinning wheel; the formation was used in the battle of Kurukshetra by Dronacharya, commander-in-chief of the Kaurava army

Chandan – sandalwood

Chiranjeevis – immortals

Devi – goddess

Dada – elder brother

Daivi shaktis – divine powers; celestial weapons that materialised by the blessings of *devis* in Indian mythology

Darshan – witness the (blessed) sight of, to pay homage to.

Dharma – 'right way of living' and 'path of righteousness'; encompasses ideas such as duty, rights, character, vocation, religion, customs and all behaviour considered appropriate, correct or morally upright

Didi – elder sister

EDM – Electronic dance music

Ghats – flight of steps leading down to a water body/river.

Ghee – clarified butter

Ghor – deep; intense

Gurudakshina – tradition of repaying one's teacher or guru; a form of reciprocity and exchange between student and teacher; the repayment is not exclusively monetary and may be a special task the teacher wants the student to accomplish

Gurukul – traditional residential school in the home of the Guru and his family

Hanuman Chalisa – devotional hymn in praise of Hanuman; it was authored by Tulsidas in the Awadhi language; said to have a powerful protective effect to ward off evil

Hanumath veena – veena (musical instrument) played by Hanuman
Havelis – traditional Indian mansions
Jal samadhi – jal = water; samadhi = highest state of consciousness that one can achieve while still bound to the body which unites them with the ultimate reality
Japa – continuous chanting of the Lord's name or *mantra* for 108 times or multiples thereof
Ji (as in Vedji, Kripcharyaji) – suffix of respect
Kaikottikali – traditional dance performed in Kerala on the auspicious day of Thiruvathira, the birthday of Lord Shiva; performed by women who seek blessings for eternal marital bliss
Kheer prasadam – sweet rice pudding offering
Kshatriyas – warrior caste
Kulguru – clan guru
Kundalini – coiled cosmic energy said to reside, dormant, at the base of the spinal cord
Kutir – simple/humble cottage
Lado – mountain spice
Langoti phatua – Indian innerwear favoured by *sadhus.*
Leela – divine play
Mahaarati – main/grand ritual prayer
Mahapurush – great man
Maharathi – great warrior; said to be capable of killing 7,20,000 soldiers single-handedly
Mahashivratri – Lord Shiva's birth anniversary
Maji – mother
Memsaab – madam
Mlecchas – barbarians in Vedic lore; here, lab-sired hybrids of pigs and humans created for war
Mahol – ambience, background

Mooladhara chakra – subtle energy located at the base of the spine; 'Mooladhara' means root, and is associated with the earth element, linked to the ability to feel firmly rooted in life; when this *chakra* is activated, it provides a calm and steady energy throughout the body

Mrityasanjeevani mantra – a *mantra* that brings the dead back to life; Lord Shiva blessed Shukracharya with this *mantra*, enabling him to bring dead *asuras* back to life; also called *Sanjeevani mantra*; this and the *Gayatri mantra* are said to be the most powerful *mantra*s in all creation

Mudra – movement or pose in yoga

Mundu – garment worn around the waist in Kerala, India

Naam – name

Naani – maternal grandmother

Nagpash – celestial weapon that unfolds as a tendril of smoke and transforms into a cloudburst of venomous reptiles; Indrajit's nagpash is especially deadly for it attacks its victims with reptile venom as well as maggots who eat away the body

Nakshatra – birth star; key element in Vedic astrology; one of the 27 constellations based on the movement of the moon, which travels approximately 27.3 days around its orbit; hence, the birth star of an individual is calculated based on the position of the moon in any of these stars

Neriyathu – traditional attire of women in Kerala, India; the oldest remnant of the ancient form of the sari

Onam – grand annual harvest festival celebrated in Kerala; as per Hindu mythology, Onam commemorates the annual return to earth of (immortal) King Mahabali who rules the Netherworld

Padmasana – lotus pose/cross-legged sitting meditation pose in which each foot is placed on the opposite thigh; widely used for meditation in Hindu, *Tantra*, Jain, and Buddhist traditions

Panchakanya – five (*panch*) iconic women (*kanya*) of the Hindu epics, whose virtues are extolled in a hymn and whose names are believed to dispel sin when recited. They are: Ahalya, Draupadi, Kunti, Tara and Mandodari; while Draupadi and Kunti are mentioned in the Mahabharata, Ahalya, Tara and Mandodari are from the Ramayana

Pangdi, *kanda* and *mool* – edible mountain tubers and root vegetables

Parshu – battle axe used by the sixth Vishnu avatar Parashuram; gifted to him by Lord Shiva

Pishach – flesh-eating demons in Buddhist and Hindu mythology; supposedly possess the paranormal ability to shapeshift and assume any form at will, and may also become invisible; sometimes, they possess human beings and alter their thoughts, and the victims are afflicted with a variety of maladies and abnormalities such as insanity; certain *mantras* are supposed to cure such afflicted persons and drive away the *pishach*

Pooja thali – prayer plate

Pookalam – intricate and colourful flower decoration on the floor

Praja – people who live in or belong to a particular country, usually ruled by a monarch

Pralay – devastating flood that cleanses the earth of all evil; a time of dissolution and destruction of the world, as per various ancient world scriptures

Pranayama – yogic practice of focusing on breath. In Sanskrit, *prana* means 'vital life force', and *yama* means to gain control; in yoga, breath is associated with *prana* and thus, controlling one's breath enables one to control one's life energy

Pranam – a respectful greeting done by putting one's palms together and often touching the feet of the person greeted

Raag – a musical mode in the Indian classical music tradition used in an improvised performance; *raag* means 'colour'. Just as each colour has a unique hue, each *raag* has a unique sound, associated with certain emotions, times of day, Hindu deities, and seasons

Raag Pahadi – an evening *raag* that combines both playful and pensive aspects, and has a charming, folksy flavour

Ramayug – the golden era of the Rama Avatar; after Lord Rama fought and vanquished the King of Lanka, the mighty *Asura* Ravana, he established Rama Rajya or Rama's reign over earth from Ayodhya for 11,000 years, before eventually returning to his original MahaVishnu form

Ranchod – the one who ran away from the battlefield; refers to Krishna who preferred to avoid a battle with the evil Jarasandha and flee Mathura with his people to go to a new city, Dwarka

Rathi – warrior who fights standing in a chariot; capable of contending with 5,000 warriors simultaneously

Rudraksh – a stone fruit, the dried stones of which are used as prayer beads by many religious communities; closely associated with Lord Shiva; they are commonly worn for protection and used for chanting Shiva's *mantra*

Sadhu – saint/sage

Sadya – festive banquet in Kerala, specially during the Onam festival; comprises a variety of traditional vegetarian dishes usually served on a banana leaf

Saheb – sir

Sakha – companion/friend

Samadhi – state of intense concentration achieved through deep meditation

Sankatmochan – trouble-shooter, another name for Hanuman

Sanskaras – rites of passage in a human being's life described in ancient Sanskrit texts

Saptarishi – seven *rishis*, or seers, who appear throughout ancient Vedic and Hindu texts; they are important figures in Hinduism and yoga philosophy; said to possess incredible yogic powers, including the ability to see across time, into the past, present and future

Seva – service

Shaligram – a black stone from the Gandaki River in Nepal; highly revered by devotees of Lord Vishnu; worshipped for bestowing a righteous life, wealth, protection from evil, good health, worldly pleasures and blessings from Lord Vishnu

Shishya – student

Shlokas – verse, proverb, hymn or poem

Siddha – perfect master; one who accomplished perfection through extreme spiritual and physical austerities

Siddhis – supernatural and magical powers (levitation, time travel and more) achieved through rigorous austerities

Stotras – popular devotional literature

Stuti – praise

Surya mantra – recited to seek blessings of the Almighty Sun.

Suryanamaskar – salutation to the Sun; yoga practice

Tabla – small-sized drums

Tamas, tamasic – darkness, dullness, inactivity

Tanpura – large four-stringed lute used in Indian music

Tantra – literally, technique; a comprehensive system for expanding knowledge or consciousness, and realising that the whole world is an interwoven, interconnected entity; from the root meaning 'to weave'

Tulsi – holy basil

Vaidyas – traditional doctors; practitioners of Ayurvedic medicine

Vaishya – merchants and farmers in India's ancient caste system

Vajra – thunderbolt; weapon of the King of Gods, Indra, in the Indian pantheon

Vajrasana – a powerful yoga pose in which you are seated with knees bent, holding your spine erect; strengthens the body and focuses the mind; also called thunderbolt/diamond/admantine pose
Vanara – monkeys; the Ramayana mentions two races that could talk – *vanaras* (half human and half ape, the most famous being Hanuman) and bears/bear-like creatures (Jambavan, the divine King of Bears) – perhaps indicating species that were different from humans and are now extinct; *Vanaras* were not apes; neither were they human; Puranas call these races *kimpurusha* ('what kind of men are these?')
Vasudhaiva kutumbakam – 'the whole world is one family'
Vijayi bhavah – 'may you be victorious'
Veshti – *dhoti*
Yagna – ritual sacrifice with a specific objective
Yogi – person who is proficient in yoga and its mystic powers
Yugas – in Hindu cosmology, an age of humankind; *Each yuga* is progressively shorter than the preceding one, corresponding to a decline in the moral and physical state of humanity; four such *yugas* (called Sat, Treta, Dwapar, and Kali) make up one *mahayuga* (great *yuga*), and 2,000 *mahayugas* make up one cosmic cycle, the *kalpa*
Sat Yuga: The age of truth and perfection; humans are exceptionally tall at 33 ft, powerfully built, virtuous, live 100,000 years, and easily attain *moksha*; the four Vedas are one, undivided Veda; main avatars: Matsya, Kurma, Varaha, Narsimha
Treta Yuga: In the second *yuga* virtue begins to decline by 25%, weather deteriorates and wars are fought for dominance by emperors; humans live for 10,000 years on average, are about 22 ft tall, and practice agriculture and mining; main avatars: Vaman, Parashuram, Rama

Dwapara Yuga: In the third *yuga* virtue and sinfulness are equally prevalent among humans, whose lives are shorter at 1,000 years, and who suffer disease and discontent; Vedas are divided into four parts; main avatars: Krishna, Buddha

Kali Yuga: The last and most degenerate *yuga*; virtue declines to 25% in this age of darkness and conflict; people abandon *dharma*; knowledge and discernment are lost and scriptures are unimportant; humans eat forbidden food; earth is polluted, and there is scarcity of food and water; families disintegrate, crime and disease are rampant, lifespan shrinks to 100 years, and height to 5 ft-6 ft; main avatars: Kalki, at the end of *Kali Yuga*